TWIN CROWNS

PRAISE FOR TWIN CROWNS

*'TWIN CROWNS has all the charm of THE PRINCESS BRIDE
and all the stakes of GAME OF THRONES – but Wren and
Rose are in a league of their own. Addictive, swoony,
tender and vivid – I loved it with all my heart.'*
Kiran Millwood Hargrave, bestselling author of
The Mercies and *The Girl of Ink and Stars*

*'Riotously funny, fast-paced and dripping with romance, TWIN
CROWNS manages to deliver a tale as familiar and nostalgic in
the way of childhood blankets and fireflies in jars, while at the
same time wholly refreshing with its levity, charm and quirky
tale of sisterhood rediscovered. TWIN CROWNS is so
joyous that days after reading, I'm still grinning.'*
Roshani Chokshi, *New York Times* bestselling author of
The Gilded Wolves and the Aru Shah series

*'An absolute delight from start to finish. TWIN CROWNS is a
dazzling gem of a book. Magical, clever, surprising, and pure fun
from its captivating start to its spectacular finish. If you
love wicked kings, sexy bandits, and sister stories that are
full of heart, this is a must read.'*
Stephanie Garber, *New York Times* and *Sunday Times*
bestselling author of *Caraval*

'TWIN CROWNS cast a spell on me from the very first pages with its glittering blend of harrowing adventure, charming wit, and intricate world-building. Add in delightful romance and two unforgettable narrators, and I was thoroughly bewitched by this marvelous book! Don't miss it!'
Sarah J Maas, #1 *New York Times* bestselling author of *A Court of Thorn and Roses* series

'Doyle and Webber give readers twin plots of daring deception, spectacular settings and two very appealing love interests . . . you'll root for both twins in this dangerous web of intrigue.'
Kendare Blake, #1 *New York Times* bestselling author of the *Three Dark Crowns* series

'Reading TWIN CROWNS left me giddy. Adventure, romance, TWO incredible protagonists, magic, sisterhood . . . I loved it.'
Laura Wood, author of *A Sky Painted Gold*

'Fresh, funny and exciting.'
Louise O'Neill, bestselling author of *The Surface Breaks*

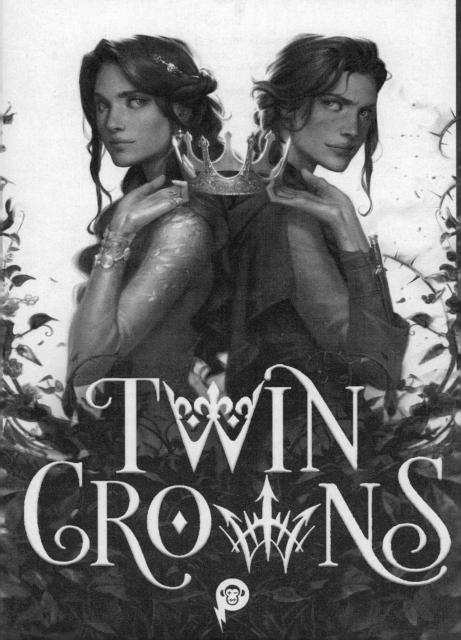

CATHERINE
DOYLE

&

KATHERINE
WEBBER

TWIN
CROWNS

First published in Great Britain in 2022 by Electric Monkey, part of Farshore
An imprint of HarperCollins*Publishers*
1 London Bridge Street, London SE1 9GF

farshore.co.uk

HarperCollins*Publishers*
1st Floor, Watermarque Building, Ringsend Road
Dublin 4, Ireland

ISBN 978 0 7555 0364 3
978 0 0085 4307 5 (Wren)
978 0 0085 4519 2 (Rose)

Printed and bound in the UK using 100% renewable electricity at CPI Group
(UK) Ltd

1

Typeset by Avon DataSet Ltd, Alcester, Warwickshire

MIX
Paper from
responsible sources
FSC™ C007454

For Jane,
The best sister in every way

Fly away safe, little Wren.
Rose, grow strong and true.

Wren
CHAPTER 1

The golden gates of Anadawn Palace glittered in the setting sun, each spike as sharp as a dagger. The sight made Wren Greenrock's stomach churn. Even from a distance, they were taller than she had imagined, their heavy chains clanging faintly in the wind.

She sank into a crouch at the edge of the forest that surrounded the palace grounds. It was too bright to leave the safety of the trees; she would have to wait for the cover of nightfall to venture any closer. A branch snapped underfoot. Wren winced.

'Careful,' hissed a voice from behind her. Shen Lo appeared at her side. Dressed all in black, and with his face partially covered, he moved as swiftly and soundlessly as an adder. 'Eyes on your feet, Greenrock. Remember what I taught you.'

'If I keep my eyes on my feet, how will I count all the scary-looking palace guards who will kill us on sight, Shen?'

Shen's dark eyes moved back and forth, tracking the guards. There were twelve in the lower courtyard alone, and six more guarding the gates, all of them dressed in pristine green uniforms, their swords fastened at their hips. 'I could take them.'

Wren blew out a breath. 'Since we're trying to *avoid* suspicion on our way in, I'd rather not leave eighteen dead bodies behind us.'

'A diversion, then? We could catch an elk and set it loose in the courtyard.'

Wren glanced sidelong at him. 'Remind me why I decided to bring you with me?'

'Because your grandmother told you to,' said Shen, smugly. 'And without me, you would never have made it through the desert.'

Absentmindedly, Wren brushed the sand from her tunic. She was glad to be out of the blistering desert sun, even if her task still lay ahead of her. She inhaled a lungful of crisp air, trying to settle the nerves swilling in her stomach.

In her mind's eye, she pictured her grandmother, Banba, standing stout and sure back on the west coast of Eana, her strong hands squeezing Wren's shoulders.

'*When you break open the stone heart of Anadawn Palace and seize your rightful place on its throne, all the winds of Eana will sing your name. May the courage of the witches go with you, my little bird.*'

Wren set her eyes on the topmost window of the east tower of Anadawn, and tried to summon a morsel of that courage now. But there was only her heart, fluttering like a hummingbird in her chest.

'Does it look like home yet?' said Shen.

She shook her head, grimly. 'It looks like a fortress.'

'Well, you've always loved a challenge.'

'I'm beginning to think I might be getting in over my head with this one,' said Wren, uneasily. But it was Banba who had devised this plan, and they both knew Wren had to follow it.

Shen sank to the ground and propped himself against a tree. 'When night falls, we'll go south to the river and make our way up through the reeds. The walls are older there; the footholds should be easier. We can slip in between patrols.'

Wren's hand came to the drawstring pouch at her waist. It had been given to her by her grandmother on the morning of their departure from Ortha, pressed into Wren's hand like a talisman. *'Keep your magic close at hand, but out of sight. At Anadawn, suspected witches are executed first, and interrogated later.'*

'I can enchant the guards,' said Wren, confidently. 'My sleep spells are lightning-fast now.'

'I know,' said Shen. 'Don't forget who you practised on.'

Wren kicked her legs out and leaned against his shoulder. Above the trill of birdsong, they listened for the distant sounds of palace life, watched servants milling to and fro and the guards standing stiff-backed at their posts, while the last of the sun melted from the sky in coral brushstrokes.

Wren's gaze came to rest on a marble statue protruding from the centre of a beautiful rose garden. She curled her lip. It was the famous Protector of Eana, an obsessive man with ravenous ambition, who had invaded these shores a thousand years ago with the sole intent of stamping out every last vestige of magic. In a brutal war that had left few survivors, the Protector had succeeded in deposing Ortha Starcrest, the last witch queen of Eana, and stealing the kingdom for his own. And even though he had failed to destroy the population of witches entirely – for how can you cut out the beating heart of a kingdom? – the Protector was still worshipped to this day. And his hatred of the witches lived on.

Shen followed her gaze. 'What will you do with that hideous statue when you become Queen?' he asked. 'Smash it into smithereens? Replace it with a statue of me?'

'I'll break it into little pieces,' said Wren. 'And then I'll feed them to whoever commissioned that eyesore in the first place. One spoonful at a time.'

At that moment she spotted someone wandering among the roses. It was a girl about Wren's age. Her dark hair was arranged in loose curls that tumbled all the way to her waist, and she was wearing a fine pink dress with a full skirt. Her dainty chin was tipped to the sky, as though she was lost in thought.

Wren stood up without meaning to.

Shen tugged on the end of her cloak. 'Get down.'

She pointed towards the distant trellises. 'Do you see that girl?'

Shen squinted. 'What about her?'

'That's her. That's my sister.' Wren felt a strange pull in

her heart, like a thread going taut. For a maddening second, she wanted to go barrelling towards those golden gates. 'That's Rose.'

Shen stood up, slowly. 'Princess Rose wandering in her rose garden,' he said, with a low chuckle. 'I'd say that's as sure a sign as any . . . well, that and the fact she appears to have your face.'

Wren was staring so hard she wasn't blinking. She had grown up knowing she had a twin sister half a world away, but seeing her here in the flesh had rendered her speechless for the first time in her life.

Shen turned to her. 'Don't tell me you're having second thoughts about the plan?'

In the back of Wren's mind, her grandmother's face hardened. *'When you get to Anadawn, leave your heart in the forest. A moment of weakness will set us all to ruin.'*

She set her jaw, her gaze still trained on Rose. 'Never.'

Rose
CHAPTER 2

Princess Rose Valhart was used to having eyes on her.

The palace guards were never far away, the gold buttons on their uniforms flashing in the sunlight. The servants watched her just as keenly, often anticipating her needs before she voiced them. Then there was Chapman, the palace steward, who was always flittering around her like a moth. He knew where she was every moment of every day, and made sure Rose was never late, despite her tendency to dawdle and daydream.

Her subjects watched her, too, of course. On the rare occasions she ventured into the capital city of Eshlinn, they would line the streets to catch a glimpse of her. She was their beloved princess, after all, as fair as the flower after which she was named, and as sweet and pure as its scent.

At least Rose *assumed* that was what they thought of her. She wasn't allowed to speak to any of them, only flutter her lashes and waggle her fingers from afar. But that would all change when she became Queen. She was determined to visit the far-flung lands of her kingdom, and to meet the people who lived there. To speak to them and know them . . . to let them know her.

Sometimes Rose swore that even the starcrest birds watched her more closely than they should. But then, she'd always had a fanciful imagination. Chapman blamed Rose's best friend, Celeste, for that. They enjoyed trading silly tales, making each one more outlandish than the last, until they collapsed into laughter. Sometimes, they would write their deepest desires on a piece of parchment and burn it by candlelight, casting the ashes of their wishes out into the night sky.

Rose always wished for love, while Celeste chose adventure. Sometimes, Rose wondered if she could have both. But a life of adventure was not fit for a queen. She would have to make do with the thrill of her daydreams and the wild beauty of her gardens. She smiled as she plucked a pink rose from her flower bed and cut it neatly at its stem. She reached for another . . . and then froze.

She suddenly had the distinctly unsettling feeling that someone was watching her. Someone *new*. She snapped her chin up, straining to see past the guards at the golden gates and into the shadowy woods beyond, where the setting sun had set the canopies ablaze.

An ache bloomed in her chest. She pressed her palm against it. Had she indulged in too many sugar buns this afternoon? Or perhaps it was simply nerves. With her coronation just around the corner, she did have *quite* a lot coming up.

'Rose!' A familiar voice cut through the quiet garden, startling her. 'What are you doing out here all by yourself?'

Of all the people in her life, nobody watched Rose more carefully than the Kingsbreath. Willem Rathborne, the man who had saved her life when she was only minutes old, had been her guardian for almost eighteen years, and he certainly had enough grey hairs to show for it. He scowled as he stalked towards her now, his grimace so deep, it aged him awfully.

Rose dipped into a perfect curtsy on instinct, her pink dress billowing around her. 'I was just collecting some fresh flowers for my bedroom.'

Willem's sigh whistled through his nose. 'That's a servant's job. You shouldn't be out here in the dark.'

Rose laughed lightly, to set him at ease. 'The sun has only just begun to set. And I'm hardly off gallivanting in the streets of Eshlinn. I'm perfectly safe in my gardens.'

Despite Willem being the closest thing she had to a father, there had always been a distance between them. All her life, Rose had craved his approval, and now more than ever, she wanted to show him that she was ready to be Queen. That she could be trusted with the kingdom, the future.

She reached for another flower. 'You worry too much, dear Willem.'

The Kingsbreath regarded her sternly. 'How many times do I have to tell you to pull your head from the clouds, Rose? You *must* be alert at all times. Danger is lurking—'

'Everywhere, and nobody can be trusted,' Rose finished

the sentence for him, with a sigh. Willem had been obsessive about her safety her entire life but now that her coronation was looming, he'd become positively paranoid.

She reminded herself it was only because he cared about her that he worried so much. She rested a gentle hand on his arm. 'Willem, you know no harm can come to Anadawn under the Great Protector's eye.'

They were standing under his statue, after all, the marbled gaze of Rose's noble ancestor silently watching over the palace. Watching over her. Privately, Rose had always found the sculpture a bit overbearing. It blocked the light in her gardens, and the roses in its shadow never grew as tall as the others, but she would rather have it close by than not have it at all. It reminded her that she was blessed, that—

'Come. Now.' Willem curled his fingers around her wrist. 'I'll have flowers sent to your room.'

Rose wilted as she trailed after him, away from the heady evening air and all thoughts of romance and adventure, and into the reaching shadows of the palace.

When I am Queen, everything will be better, she promised herself as she climbed the stairs in her tower, winding round and round and round. *I will dance all night if I want to, and no one will tell me what to do.*

She smiled at the guard in the stairwell as she pushed open the door to her bedroom. It was only when she glimpsed the blood on the doorknob that she realized she had pricked her fingers on the thorns.

Wren
CHAPTER 3

The sky above the white palace was starless, and Wren was ill at ease. It was well past midnight, and the wind was biting. She drew her cloak tighter. 'Something doesn't feel right.'

'Yeah, no kidding,' came Shen's whisper from the dark. 'We're about to break into the palace.'

Wren cast her friend a withering look. 'I mean *generally*, Shen.'

'This is the easy part,' he reminded her. They had already scaled the south wall, and spelled two palace guards into sleep on their patrol. It was only the east tower before them now, rising like a snaggle tooth in the dark. 'It's just hand over hand. Foot over foot.'

'Gravity might not concern you, Shen Lo, but the rest of us have to play by its rules.'

Shen's smirk glinted in the moonlight. 'Go on. I'll be right behind you.'

'Will you catch me if I fall?'

'No, but I'll wave at you on your way down.'

'Ever the gentleman.' Wren pressed her palms against the stone. There were subtle grooves in the paving, just enough that she could dig her calloused fingers into the crannies and drag herself up. She kept her body flush against the tower, her cloak spilling out behind her until the clasp pressed against her throat.

'*Focus now, my little Wren,*' echoed her grandmother's voice in her head. '*Once inside the palace gates, there can be no room for error.*'

Wren's breath made filmy clouds in the air, her drawstring pouch tapping softly against her hip, as if to remind her it was there. Soon, sweat dripped down her face and pooled under the collar of her shirt. Her fingers began to ache, the muscles in her legs screaming as she scrabbled up the tower like a beetle. Hand over hand, foot over foot.

Behind her, Shen moved like a shadow in the dark.

The tower window edged into view. It peered out over the Silvertongue River like a glassy eye. The latch was open, an inch cracked to welcome a slip of cool air, and tonight, the bandits who came with it.

Wren lunged for the clasp. The window swung wide in a keening *creak!* as she hauled herself on to the narrow ledge. She fought the urge to smirk over her shoulder at Shen as she slipped quietly into the room. Gravity, be damned.

Moonlight crept in after her, fracturing across the bedroom in pearly shards.

Wren freed the dagger from her boot and kept one hand on her drawstring pouch, readying herself for the palace guard she suspected was stationed in the stairwell outside. When the silence swelled, she let herself relax. The bedroom was grander than she expected. Fringed tapestries hung on ivory walls and gilded wardrobes loomed like spectres in the dimness. The carpet swallowed her footsteps as she snooped around.

She caught sight of her own ghostly reflection in a mirror and nearly jumped out of her skin. Her braid was coming undone, the runaway strands frizzing around her face, where stubborn smudges of dirt and sand had accumulated over the last two days. She looked as if she had been dragged through the desert backwards, then dipped inside a swamp.

A vase of fresh roses perfumed the room with a sickly sweetness. Wren wrinkled her nose. *Ugh.* The cloying scent was a far cry from the wild heather of Ortha and the familiar tang of seaweed rolling off the ocean. She would have to get used to it.

The sudden rustle of silk drew her to the four-poster bed in the middle of the room. The canopy shifted like mist in the breeze, revealing the crown princess of Eana.

Princess Rose Valhart was as pretty as a painting, and as still and gentle as a cat in slumber.

'*Danger is a faraway thought to Rose,*' said Wren's grandmother's voice in her head. '*She will never see you coming.*'

Wren peered over the sleeping princess, ignoring the furious thudding in her chest. The pull towards her was even stronger now, like a fist closing around her heart. 'Hello, sister,' she whispered. 'At last we meet.'

Rose was smiling in her sleep. Her chestnut-brown hair spilled out around her in a halo. In the moonlight, her pale skin was glowing, the apples of her cheeks absent of freckles. Though their faces were identical, it was clear that Rose had never glimpsed the searing desert sun nor known the icy whip of a sea wind.

Lucky for some.

A shadow fell across the bed.

'You're blocking my light, Shen,' Wren whispered.

'I'm trying not to disturb you.' Shen was crouched on the window ledge. 'In case you wanted to, you know, have –' he cleared his throat – 'an emotion.'

Wren bristled. 'I am *not* having an emotion.'

'Calm down. I won't tell your grandmother.' He swung his legs around and slipped soundlessly into the room. 'You can be yourself with me.'

In the climb, strands of his black hair had escaped from his leather tie and had come to rest along his forehead. Other than that, he looked immaculate.

Wren looked him over. 'Did you even break a sweat?'

'Of course not.'

She kept her voice low. 'Well. What do you think?'

'She's certainly a prettier sleeper than you. You're a hideous drooler.'

Wren punched him in the arm.

He chewed the smile from the inside of his cheek. 'You've got more freckles. And her hair is darker than yours.'

Wren passed a hand over her braid, frowning.

'I bet she's a lot nicer.'

'I will fling you back out of that window, Shen.'

Rose sighed as she turned over. Her eyelids flickered. Now that she was so close, Wren was seized by the sudden desire to look into her sister's eyes. Would Rose know her? Would she scream? Would she—

'*Wren!*' hissed Shen. 'Do the damned spell!'

Rose murmured in her sleep. 'Celeste?'

A bolt of panic coursed through Wren. She whipped a handful of Ortha sand from her drawstring pouch and opened her palm. Enchantment gathered in her fingers. The words spilled out, fast and loose. '*From earth to dust, in dark we creep, please put the princess back to sleep!*'

Rose snapped her eyes open.

Wren's heart stuttered as she blew the sand from her palm. It floated like gold-winged fireflies before disappearing into nothing, taking the princess's gasp with it. Her lids drooped and she flopped against her pillow, unconscious.

Wren tightened the string on her pouch. Her fingers were trembling. She crushed them into her palm. It was foolish really, that moment of hesitation. It wasn't like Wren didn't know what to expect to find in the east tower. She had always known she had a twin sister. She had been raised to steal her life, after all, but seeing Rose here, so close and warm and *alive*, had suddenly filled her with . . . well, an *emotion*.

'Did you see her eyes?' she whispered.

'As green as emeralds.' Shen's gaze shone too brightly in the moonlight. He was watching her in that way of his, as though he were reading the movements of her soul. 'Are you all right?'

'I'm fine.' Wren smiled, thinly. 'We need to hurry. Give me the rope.' She set about unravelling it. 'I'll anchor you.'

'Great,' said Shen, drawing the canopy back. 'I'll go ahead and kidnap your sister.'

Wren tied the rope to the nearest bedpost, then tossed it outside the window. When she turned around, Shen was standing in the middle of the room, the princess slung over his shoulder. With remarkable stealth, he climbed back out on to the window ledge. The rope went taut as he lowered himself down the white tower, Rose's dark hair spilling out like seaweed across his back.

'Wait!' hissed Wren. She unhooked her cloak and tossed it out of the window. 'That nightgown won't do her much good in the desert.'

Shen caught it by the clasp, without so much as wobbling. 'And I thought you'd be the evil twin.'

Wren stuck her tongue out. 'I hope she gives you hell.'

'Good luck, Wren. I'll see you on the throne.' Shen winked as he dropped into darkness, leaving only the echo of his words behind.

Wren jolted into action, then, gathering the rope and burying it under a stack of linens in the bedside table. She slipped out of her climbing clothes, balled up her muddy trousers and loose shirt, and stuffed them under the bed. She stowed her dagger underneath her pillow.

She found a blue nightgown in a chest of drawers and

shrugged it on, revelling in the slip of silk against her skin. It was a little big around her middle and the straps were loose on her narrow shoulders, but it was clean and luxuriously soft.

Wren smirked. By the time the moon was full again in a month's time, she would have her fill of luxury. All she had to do was make it, undetected, to her eighteenth birthday – the day of Rose's long-awaited coronation. And then she would be Queen; the sole ruler of the island nation of Eana. Free to tear it down, and rebuild it exactly as she liked.

Exactly as it once was.

When she became Queen, Wren would finally be able to take revenge on the Kingsbreath, the man whose frenzied devotion to the Protector had led to the murder of her own parents eighteen years ago. Even just the sight of Willem Rathborne in the rose garden earlier had made Wren's fingers itch. But she had learned to be patient. First, she would get the crown and then she would have her revenge.

She settled herself at Rose's dressing table, riffling through endless jars of scented oils and pots of pungent creams. So many perfumes for one princess! Wren unravelled her braid in the mirror, her eyes shining like emeralds in the dark. Her lips were chapped, her skin speckled with desert-borne freckles, and her hair was a bird's nest on top of her head.

'Hmm,' she murmured. 'Not quite a princess.'

She retrieved a pinch of sand from her drawstring pouch, closed her eyes and conjured an image of Rose in the centre of her mind. She raised her arm and offered her spell into the silence, *'From earth to dust, with poise and grace, please help me wear my sister's face.'*

The sand disappeared before it touched the crown of her head. Wren revelled in the feather-light touch of her magic, the gentle prickling underneath her skin. She watched her cheeks glow, her suntanned skin shedding its freckles for a light rosy blush. Her hair thickened, the darkening locks growing long and luscious until they reached her waist.

She smirked at the mirror. 'Hello, Princess.'

Wren turned her hands over, deciding to keep her rough calluses. They reminded her of the wind-battered cliffs of Ortha, and the witches perched along its spine, waiting for a new world.

The world Wren's grandmother had promised them. As if summoned by thoughts of Banba, a rogue gust of wind slipped inside and knocked a perfume bottle over. Wren yelped.

There was a sharp knock at the door, and then the gruff voice of a palace guard. 'Everything all right in there, Princess Rose?'

Wren swore under her breath. 'Perfectly fine, thank you,' she called back, praying her voice sounded like her sister's. 'That pesky wind! I was just getting some fresh air.'

She rushed to slam the window shut, her eyes pinned to the door handle across the room. Silence, then. And with it came the slow trickle of relief. Wren sagged against the glass.

'I can do this,' she reminded herself. 'I was *born* to do this.'

Wren had spent her whole life preparing for the switch.

Under the watchful guidance of her grandmother, she had honed her magic on the beaches of Ortha, until she could fire off quick-tongued enchantments like arrows. She had wiled away long hours with Shen practising stealth and self-defence, sensing when to strike and when to be silent. Thea, Banba's wife, had instructed Wren in royal etiquette. Wren was no princess, but she had learned how to act like one. How to hold her tongue and trap her swear words, smile demurely and skip gaily, as though she hadn't a care in the world.

After all, how hard could it be, to play a girl who has never known life outside these palace walls?

Wren flung herself on to the four-poster bed, landing face down like a starfish. She burrowed between the pillows, sinking into the warmth her sister had left behind. She might have felt strange about it if her blood wasn't buzzing with the success of the switch. She hoped Shen had made it out safely, that the spirit of Ortha Starcrest would guide him safely home to the cliff-side haven the witches had named in her honour.

Wren turned on to her side and slipped her hand underneath her pillow. The dagger was cool to touch; a comfort in this foreign place. With it close at hand, sleep came swiftly. She drifted into darkness, leaving all thoughts of home behind her.

In the morning, she would be Rose Valhart, heir to the throne of Eana.

Sweet and pure and dangerous.

Rose

CHAPTER 4

Rose had never heard the sound of the Restless Sands. She'd never even been outside the capital city of Eshlinn. On the rare occasions she did venture beyond the golden gates of Anadawn Palace, it was always in the company of a chaperone, with a slew of palace guards following close behind.

But the princess often dreamed of places in Eana she'd never been. '*I am Eana; Eana is me,*' she would whisper before bed, her thoughts turning to the far-flung lands in her kingdom. At night, she imagined herself wandering along the white-sand shores of Wishbone Bay, galloping through the verdant plains of the Errinwilde or exploring the bustling marketplaces in the south, where the stalls were brimming with decadently seasoned meat and brightly coloured spices. Rose dreamed of the rolling Ganyeve Desert, too, and the sun floating like a gold coin above it, but the legendary hum of its sands had never been so clear before.

In this dream, it felt as if they were calling out to her, coaxing her awake.

She opened her eyes, expecting to see the white walls of

her bedchamber. Instead, she glimpsed an amber sun rising over the Ganyeve and heard the song of its sands ringing in her ears.

All at once, she was struck by other things. Her lips were dry and her throat was parched. There was sand in her mouth, grains mottled to the sides of her face. She blinked, furiously. She must still be dreaming. How else could she explain waking up in the desert, half slumped on a horse . . . ?

A horse?

Panic pulsed through Rose's body in time with the horse's hoofbeats.

She stiffened, as something else became suddenly and alarmingly clear.

She was not alone.

She was propped against a firm chest that rose and fell with a gentle rhythm. An arm was loosely wrapped around her waist, holding her in place. It took every ounce of her self-control not to react at once. She drew a steadying breath, trying to slow her racing heart.

Stay calm. If she lost control of her senses now, she was done for. She subtly flexed her fingers. Good, her hands were unbound. She glanced down at her lap. No rope there either. Her captor had clearly underestimated her. Well, they were in for a surprise. Her eyes darted, her mind whirring, frantically. The horse was galloping swiftly, but the sand would be soft and she possessed the element of surprise. Best strike now, before the fear spreading inside her took over.

Find your courage. Wield it as a weapon.

With a bellowing cry, Rose shoved her elbow down hard and leaped off the horse.

It was only when her feet hit the sand that she realized she hadn't planned any further than the emergency dismount. Also – and crucially – she had not been expecting the desert sand to be so blisteringly *hot*. Or that she would be *barefoot*. And in her *nightgown*.

'Burning stars!' she cursed, hopping from foot to foot.

'That was surprisingly impressive,' came a voice from above her.

Rose whirled to face her abductor. He made a striking figure, dressed all in black, and sitting atop that magnificent horse. His face was haloed by the rising sun and, although she couldn't make out his features, she could plainly tell he was some sort of bandit.

Stay calm, she reminded herself, even as her heartbeat thundered in her ears. In the past, whenever Rose had let herself imagine the possibility of her own kidnapping, she was always dressed in one of her most ravishing gowns. Not her second-favourite nightgown and someone else's cloak, which was coarse and positively reeking. And she had never pictured there being *quite* so much sand.

Even so, she had to seize control of the situation, and fast. She was the princess, protected by the great and noble Protector. No harm would come to her. Rose told herself that as she rolled her shoulders back, fear still hammering in her chest. 'I don't know who you are but I demand you take me back to my palace this instant.'

The bandit simply stared at her. The horse whinnied a bit. A bead of sweat dripped down Rose's nose. She grimaced. Princesses were *not* supposed to sweat. But then, princesses didn't often hop from foot to foot like this either, caught in some sort of embarrassing peasant dance.

'Right now! Take me back right now!' she said, flinching as she stamped her foot on the hot sand. 'I command you!'

'Oh boy,' muttered the bandit. He dropped off the horse in one smooth motion and took a step towards her.

'Stay back! Stay back, I tell you!' Rose picked up a handful of sand to throw at him.

The bandit sighed as he raked his hair back. Rose saw his face clearly for the first time. He had dark eyes and high cheekbones, and a jaw that looked cut from stone. His skin was a golden tan, and his hair was black, the long strands gathered away from his face with a leather strap. Now that he was closer, she realized he was younger than she'd first thought. Close to her own age.

This gave her a rush of confidence. She could handle him.

She flung the handful of sand at him. 'I'll give you one last chance. Drop to your knees and show me the proper respect. Then give me your horse so I can return home. If you do that, I'll do what I can to ensure a lighter punishment for you.'

The bandit continued to stare at her. The impudence! But she welcomed the wave of anger that coursed through her. Better to be angry than frightened. She would not allow herself to think of what she was going to do if he didn't listen to her.

She cleared her throat. 'And also . . . I'll need you to point me in the right direction.'

The bandit had the audacity to laugh, which made Rose even more furious. She was Princess Rose Valhart, and in one moon's time she would be crowned Queen of Eana. She was *not* someone to laugh at.

And yet, the bandit kept laughing.

She glared at him. 'You must have a death wish.'

'*Princess*,' he said, indulgently. 'I'll kneel if it will make you feel better. But you are not taking my horse. Storm is like me: desert-born and wild.' His smirk revealed a dimple in his right cheek. 'You wouldn't be able to handle her.'

A flush that had nothing to do with the desert heat stole up Rose's cheeks. 'How dare you! You'll find I am an excellent horsewoman.'

'Well, you certainly nailed that dismount.'

Rose contemplated flinging another fistful of sand at him but thought better of it. It didn't seem to be having much effect. Which was a shame, as she had precisely zero other weapons. 'I swear by the Great Protector, every minute you tarry, your punishment grows worse.' She tossed her hair, arcing her voice to hide the tremor in it. 'And I demand to know who you are.'

The bandit stroked his chin, and Rose could tell he was only pretending to consider her order. 'Returning you to the palace would completely defeat the purpose of *taking you* from the palace in the first place, so I'll offer you a compromise. My name.' He dropped into a sweeping bow, so low that his forehead almost kissed the sand. 'I am Shen Lo.'

Rose looked down at him. 'Why have you kidnapped me, Shen Lo? Do you want gold? I can give you gold.' She knew she was worth more than any other person in the land. Much more. She was Eana's future, after all. That was why she was so closely protected, kept under constant watchful guard. Though *clearly* not watchful enough, she thought sourly. Now she was all alone in the desert, with only the Protector to watch over her.

If she had to buy her freedom, then she would do so here, and swiftly. Before they journeyed any further into the blistering Ganyeve.

'Well, kidnapper?' she demanded of the bandit who called himself Shen Lo. 'Name your price.'

He sighed as he straightened. 'I don't want your money, Princess. And I don't like the term *kidnapper*. I'm really more of an accomplice. Shen, the middle man. I'm just in charge of getting you from point A to point B.'

Rose tried not to panic at the stark realization that she could not buy her way home. That she had nothing to trade for her freedom. *Don't let him see your fear.* 'And where, pray tell, is point B?'

'I'll tell you when we get there,' he said, unhelpfully.

'Who are you working for?' pressed Rose.

'We've got a long way to go and we need to cross as much ground as we can before noon,' he went on, as if he hadn't heard her. 'We don't want to be out in the desert when the sun is high. It's too hot even for me, then.' His brow furrowed as he appraised her. 'And you're already wilting.'

'I am *not* wilting,' Rose rasped.

'All the same, we've got to reach the Golden Caves by midday.'

'If you don't take me back, the Kingsbreath will find me,' she threatened. 'I have an entire army dedicated to keeping me safe.'

'Well, they're not doing a very good job,' said Shen, pointedly. 'Honestly, I was hoping for more of a challenge.'

'When they find me – and they *will* find me – they'll kill you on sight,' Rose went on. 'Much better for you if you return me yourself. The Kingsbreath may show you mercy, then.'

Shen spat on the sand. 'That filthy rat can keep his mercy. There will be none for him.'

Rose gasped. 'You watch your dirty mouth! That is your Kingsbreath! If he heard you speak that way, he'd cut out your tongue. And since he is *also* the closest thing I have to a father, he'd cut off your head first, for even daring to kidnap me.'

'He looks more like a captor from where I'm standing. Doesn't he control your every move?' Shen snorted. 'You should thank me for taking you from that tower, Princess.'

Rose's fear burned up in another flare of anger. 'You don't know what you're talking about, *bandit*.' A bead of sweat slid down her temple. It was becoming increasingly difficult to maintain her composure in this forsaken heat. 'And you clearly know nothing of the suffering you will bring upon yourself if you do not return me to the palace right now.'

Shen's eyes flashed. 'I'm surprised you even know that word: *suffering*.' They glared at each other a moment. Then he sighed. 'As entertaining as it is arguing with you out here, I meant what I said about the high-noon sun. Storm is fast, but not that fast. Now get back on the horse.'

Rose took a step away from him. 'No.'

He raised his head to the sky. '*She'll be asleep the whole time*, they said. How *convenient* that when the princess wakes a whole day early, there is nobody but me to deal with her.' He turned back to Rose. 'Don't make me chase you. It won't be fun for either of us.'

'My guards are coming for me,' she said, standing her ground. 'I'm not going one step further.'

'Nobody is coming for you. That, I can guarantee.'

Rose was struck by the sureness in his dark eyes. For the first time since she'd woken up on the horse, true dread slithered into her heart. 'You're lying.'

Shen advanced towards her. 'Get back on the horse, Princess.'

'Look there!' She pointed over his shoulder. 'There's my Captain of the Guard now.' She started to wave.

Shen looked backwards, cursing when he found nothing there. 'I can't believe I fell for that.'

When he turned back, Rose was already scampering down the sand dune in her nightgown. She didn't have a plan, of course. But her guards must be close now. They couldn't be that far into the desert, could they? And no matter what the bandit said, the palace *would* come for her. Her soldiers would scour every inch of Eana with tracking hounds if they had to. All she had to do was distract the bandit long enough for them to arrive.

'Rose! Stop!' Shen was chasing after her on foot, his horse watching bemusedly from atop the dune.

Rose kept running, her feet sinking with every step. She was gaining momentum – much more than she meant to – and as the sands sloped sharply, she lost her balance.

She landed face down in the sand.

An unladylike groan seeped out of her.

'Stand up!' Shen shouted. 'Quick!'

With as much dignity as she could muster, Rose lifted her head and spat a clump of sand from her mouth.

'Get up!' Shen's voice reached a fever pitch as he raced down the dune.

Rose ignored him. She was not going to take orders from some thieving, kidnapping desert bandit. She would move at the pace she wanted. She stood up as slowly and gracefully as she could but her legs were covered in sand, and they were trembling. *Badly.*

As she tried to steady herself, she realized with dawning horror that her knees were not the problem. The dune itself was shaking.

Her heart leaped into her throat. 'The sands are shifting!'

'That isn't the sand! It's a blood beetle!'

Rose screamed as the dune began to churn around her. Sharp ebony pincers pierced through the sand, flinging it everywhere, and then the rest of the creature emerged in a skittering mass of darkness. It was enormous, with a hard leathered shell and a dozen spindly legs dwarfed beneath those terrible shining pinchers.

Rose stumbled away.

Behind her, the bandit moved like a shadow – faster than anyone she had ever seen before. He flew through the air, grabbing a dagger from his boot and angling it skywards as he leaped over her and landed right in front of the insect. 'I told you to get up!' he said, over his shoulder. 'Blood beetles can hear your heartbeat. They smell your sweat and—'

The beetle struck. Shen dodged the pincer with a backflip. Rose gasped as he landed on the creature's head, and in one clean swipe, thrust his dagger into the fleshy part between its eyes. The beetle's screech split the desert air in two. Rose covered her ears as it thrashed in anger, jabbing its pincers at Shen.

'Watch out!' she cried, but it was too late. A pincer sliced across his leg. He winced as blood began to gush out, but he kept his dagger steady, twisting it deeper into the beetle's head until, finally, the wretched beast collapsed in a heap on the sand.

Rose's head swam dangerously, and she thought for a second she might pass out. 'It's dead,' she breathed. 'You killed it.'

Shen slid off the beetle. His golden chain had slipped from his shirt in the fight. Rose noted the ring dangling on the end as he tucked it hastily back into his shirt. He stood for a long moment, breathing heavily, then he wiped the dagger on his shirt and slid it back into his boot. He looked up at Rose. 'Are you all right?'

'I'm f-fine.' Though this time, she failed to keep the tremor from her voice. She had thought blood beetles were myths from storybooks, not terrifyingly real creatures that could kill her. What other abominations were hiding out here in the desert? 'And you . . . are you all right?'

'Fine,' he said, curtly.

Her gaze dropped to the gaping wound in his leg.

'It's *fine*,' he insisted. 'We need to get away from here. Other blood beetles may be coming, and things that like to eat blood beetles will smell this dead one.' He hardened his jaw. 'And trust me, Princess, we do not want to fight anything that eats a blood beetle.'

Rose swallowed. 'That thing would have killed me.'

'Easily.'

'You saved my life.'

A hoarse laugh escaped Shen. 'Don't give me too much credit. I'd be in a lot of trouble if I lost you to a blood beetle. Or anything else for that matter.' He lifted his fingers to his lips and whistled so loudly Rose flinched.

Storm came galloping down the dune.

'Listen, Princess, even if the palace was sending someone for you, no Eshlinn-born horse can go as fast as Storm. They'll never catch up with us. In case you haven't noticed, we're in the middle of the desert.'

Rose looked around, straining for shapes on the horizon.

'That's impossible. Nobody goes *through* the desert.'

The Ganyeve Desert lay like a coiled snake in the middle of the island of Eana, as deadly and dangerous as a viper's bite. The only way to cross it – at least in one piece – was to take the dusty Kerrcal Road that curved around its edges, connecting the small desert towns that led on to the fishing villages by the coast. No sane Eanan would ever dream of cutting a pathway through the heart of the desert. It was the surest road to madness, or death. Often both.

And yet . . . there was *nothing* and no one as far as her eyes could see. Where was the mighty clock tower of Gallanth, the sunrise village to the east? Or the famed red-walled town of Dearg? She couldn't even see the shadow of the Mishnick Mountains from here. All these places she'd never been to but had etched into her memory as she'd studied the maps of her country. Places that belonged to her. Places that she promised herself she'd one day visit. When she was Queen.

Now, there was only sun and sky and sand.

And Shen Lo.

He smirked. 'I was born in this desert and have ridden through it many times, Princess. I know it like the back of my hand.'

Rose appraised the bandit with new eyes. She had always been taught it was impossible to cross the desert, and yet here stood this insufferable boy – barely older than her – claiming he'd done it. *Several times.* And more impossible still – that he was doing it *now*. With her.

Her surprise gave way to wariness. 'What do you want with me, Shen Lo?'

Shen locked eyes with her, staring at her brazenly in a way that nobody had ever dared to before. 'Nothing.'

Rose frowned. 'I don't understand . . .'

'Understand this,' he said. 'I promise I won't hurt you. Can you try to trust me?'

She swallowed thickly, cursing her still-trembling limbs. If she didn't go with him now, she would die in this desert. She had to stay alive until she could escape. 'Very well. But only for now.'

'Now is enough.' Shen knelt in the sand and offered his leg as a step.

She sashayed past him. 'Oh, please. I know how to get on a horse,' she said, as she vaulted herself on to the horse's back. She landed neatly, leaning forward and stroking Storm between the ears.

Shen leaped up behind her. 'Isn't it easier when we get along?'

His breath tickled the back of her neck. Rose's spine stiffened. In that moment, she made a vow to herself. She would survive this kidnapping, and when she was back on her throne, when *she* had the power again, she would make the bandit pay for this.

Shen wrapped an arm around her waist. 'Hold on, Princess,' he said, as they took off across the Restless Sands.

Wren
CHAPTER 5

Long after sunrise, Wren woke to the sound of knocking. She bolted upright in bed and wiped the drool from her chin. Usually, the dawn gulls would be wailing through her creaking walls by now, the children of Ortha knocking on her door, seeking her nose for adventure. But the skies above Anadawn were silent, and somehow she had overslept. *Rotting carp!*

Sunlight flooded the room with syrupy warmth as she leaped out of bed. Wren stole a glance at herself in the mirror to make sure her enchantment from last night had held, just as a round-faced woman with a frizz of grey hair swept inside rump first. She was cradling a large copper jug. 'Morning, Princess Rose,' she said, blue eyes twinkling. 'Not like you to sleep so late. Must have been a pleasant dream?'

Showtime.

Wren tossed her hair back and cleared her throat. 'Oh, the *most* pleasant,' she crowed. 'I dreamed I was galloping on a wild black horse across the Restless Sands!'

The old woman blinked at her, and Wren's heartbeat

slowed in her chest. An age seemed to pass, her fate balancing on the edge of a knife, and then the maidservant threw her head back and released a wheezy laugh.

'Oh, mercy! Sounds like a nightmare to me. That sun would bake me alive!' She chuckled to herself as she bustled across the bedroom and disappeared through a narrow archway, into an adjacent bathing chamber. 'I'll have your bath ready in two ticks, love.'

Triumph flooded Wren, and she giggled like a carefree princess. 'How *wonderful*. Thank you—' She froze mid-speak. Her name. What was her bloody name? She had it parcelled away, but her mind was still foggy from sleep. *Think!* She had learned all of them by heart before coming here – the names and descriptions of Rose's inner circle, the people she would have to fool to get to her coronation – reciting them to her grandmother five times a night. Sometimes more. *Celeste? No. Cam? That's the cook. Oh! It's . . .* 'AGNES!'

Agnes ducked her head around the archway. 'What's happened, Princess? Is it another river spider?' She scanned the floor, frantically. 'A woodroach? I'll call down to Emory.'

Wren cleared her throat. 'I . . . oh, no. No, everything is fine. I was just saying thank you.'

And I hardly need a man to rescue me from a harmless critter.

Agnes's face said differently. She sighed with relief, before returning to drawing Wren's bath. Wren seized the moment to stash her dagger from where it was peeking out from beneath her pillow.

Her grandmother scowled at Wren in her head. *A careless*

witch is a dead witch.

When Wren was a little girl in Ortha, she would swim every day with another young witch called Lia. She was an enchanter, too. Lia loved the sea so much, Wren had to drag her back to shore in time for lunch most days. But one morning, when Wren was still asleep, Lia used a spell to carve gills into her neck and turn herself into a merrow. She swam deep into the belly of the ocean and got so caught up in the thrill of swimming like a fish that she forgot to return to the surface and renew her spell. When her bloated body finally washed up on the shore, Banba left it there to bake for three days and three nights as a warning to the other young witches.

A careless witch is a dead witch.

Wren would never forget that.

'Your bath's a-bubbling, Princess!' Agnes grinned at her around the door frame. 'I'll fetch your breakfast while you bathe. Any special requests this morning?'

'Oh . . . just the usual!'

Wren waited for Agnes to leave before flinging her nightgown off and sinking into the tub. She groaned in pleasure. The water was soft and soapy and deliciously warm – a far cry from the salty bite of the ocean. If this was what it took to be Princess Rose every morning, then Wren could certainly get used to it. After she had popped every bubble and soaked until her fingers crinkled, she donned a silk robe and emerged to find a feast waiting for her in her bedroom. She chuckled to herself.

This was Rose's usual?

Her sister certainly had taste.

Not to mention an appetite.

There were ornate bowls of blueberries and raspberries, grapes still on the vine, and pomegranates bursting with so much flavour Wren devoured them by the fistful. Next, a plate of thickly sliced rye bread, warmed and slathered with butter, and accompanied by fresh marmalade and honey to drizzle. There was freshly squeezed orange juice and a thimble of dark coffee so strong Wren could feel it racing through her bloodstream.

After breakfast, when she was feeling fit to burst, Wren flung the window open, welcoming the morning breeze. It was late spring and the flowers were in full bloom in the capital city of Eshlinn, where the white palace of Anadawn stood. The trees beyond the palace walls swaying lazily in the morning sun. Outside in the courtyard, upon an emerald-green flag, a golden hawk spread its wings in flight. The Eana crest was rippling, valiantly.

Centuries ago, long before Wren was born and the kingdom had been stolen from the witches, there had been a woman riding that hawk. But the crest, like so much else in Eana, had been changed by the Protector. It was a place that still worshipped him, the first in a long line of mortal Valhart rulers, whose mission to rid the land of witches had recently been reinvigorated by the scheming Kingsbreath, Willem Rathborne, Rose's guardian and mentor. A man whose days were numbered.

But first, Wren had bigger things to worry about.

She sat at the vanity to renew her enchantment. Another pinch of Ortha sand and some carefully chosen words would assure Rose's appearance for the rest of the day. Of the five branches of witchcraft, enchanters alone needed earth to trade for their spells. It was a tricky craft, so Wren used rhymes to guide her enchantments. But she knew with enough practise, one day she wouldn't need words any more. Just her thoughts.

Healers, like Thea, used their own energy for their craft. Warriors, like Shen, were born light-footed and charged by the sun. Tempests, like Banba, weaved their storms from a strand of wind, and cast infernos from a single spark of lightning, and Seers turned to the night sky for their visions – an open space to watch the starcrest birds cast patterns of the future among the stars – though that craft was so rare, Wren had never even met a seer in person.

Wren was a gifted enchanter, but she had spent much of her childhood longing to be a tempest like Banba. Over time, she had learned to do the best she could with her craft. To accept it, not just as who she was, but where she had come from.

After all, Wren's mother had been an enchanter. Wren had grown up hearing stories of Lillith Greenrock, a lowly palace gardener, who had wandered into the king's rose garden one day, and soon after that, his heart. And though her mother had died for who she was in this cold and hostile place, Wren was glad to have the same gift inside her. To have any magic at all.

Princess Rose, on the other hand, was no witch. She had inherited nothing from Lillith but her green eyes and her meek temperament. Or at least that was how Wren had always imagined her sister to be. How could she be anything other when she had grown up coddled in her precious tower? With servants to bathe her and footmen to dispose of her spiders! There was certainly nothing meek about Wren. She was a storm brewed by Banba, and when the crown of Eana sat upon her head, she would cast out the memory of the wretched Protector and all those who worshipped him.

Mindful of the time, Wren crossed the room and flung open her sister's wardrobe. Living along the Whisperwind Cliffs made dresses an impracticality at best and a death trap at worst, but now . . . rifling through some of the finest gowns in all of Eana, she was seized by the giddy exhilaration of a child playing dress-up.

She chose a dress of cornflower-blue silk, the bodice delicately embroidered with white flowers – just in time for Agnes's return. The old woman nattered away as she helped Wren get dressed, and though Wren was surprised to find her sister had fostered such friendliness with her maidservant, she couldn't concentrate on a single word of their conversation. Just the desperate wheeze of her breath as the laces cinched her waist tighter and tighter. Did her sister put herself through this fresh hell every *single* day? When she was Queen, Wren would have to introduce the long-suffering noblewomen of Eana to the simple wonder of trousers.

The second Agnes left, Wren tucked her dagger into her corset – just in case – and then set about draping herself in jewellery. Rose had enough bracelets to launch a fleet of ships to the southern continent, and purchase another orchard with the leftovers. It was absurd! If Wren ever dared wear any of it in Ortha, a magpie would come and carry her away.

When she spied a majestic gold crown, Wren let out a gasp of delight. It sat on its own plinth in a glass case at the very top of Rose's armoire and took her four attempts and a stool to lift it down from its perch. It was a beast of a thing, heavy and shining and inlaid, with an intricate row of emeralds. Green and gold – the colours of Eana.

Wren tried the crown on, grinning at herself in the mirror. Every part of her was sparkling, as though she were lit from within by a star. 'I truly am the jewel of my kingdom,' she crooned.

She swished her skirts back and forth.

Swish, swish.

'The beating heart of Eana.'

Swish, swish.

'And I may wear whatever I please.'

Swish, swish.

'For that is what pretty little princesses do.'

'Good grief, Princess Rose! What in the name of the great and noble Protector are you *doing*?'

Wren froze mid swish. Her stomach lurched as Rathborne's face flashed through her mind. But . . . *no*. It wasn't him. In the mirror, she could see a short, scowling man standing behind her. He wore a burgundy frock coat that dwarfed his slight frame, his generous swoop of dark hair perfectly matching his finely groomed moustache. He was clutching a parchment scroll to his chest and staring at her with an expression of such abject horror, he looked like an oil painting.

She knew him at once – Chapman. Willem Rathborne's scurrying assistant; his eyes and ears in the palace.

Wren turned on the heel of her shoe, ignoring the violent flush crawling up her neck. 'Good morning, Chapman,' she said, brightly. 'I was just . . . taking inventory of my many, *many* jewels.'

Chapman waved his hands in a panic. 'Put that away! The royal coronation crown of Eana is *not* a dress-up toy.'

Wren froze. *Oh no.* She was wearing the hissing coronation crown! In front of Rathborne's favourite spy! If Banba could see her now, she'd blast her out to sea in a hurricane.

She ripped the crown off so fast she took a clump of hair with it. 'I was just making sure it fits,' she said, as she set it on the dresser. 'Happily, it does!'

Chapman's moustache twitched in disapproval. 'That's what you said last time.'

Wren was careful not to look surprised. Her stomach twisted at the thought of her sister standing in this very spot doing the very same thing. Somehow, it made Rose feel much more real, and Wren didn't like to think of her sister that way – as a person, rather than an obstacle on her way to the throne.

She pushed the image away before it gave rise to stirrings of guilt, and fixed her hair in the mirror. 'Yes, well, it's just best to be sure, isn't it, Chapman?'

'It's far better to have your priorities in order,' he huffed. 'You're late for your afternoon date!'

Wren blinked. 'My . . . *what?*'

'By the Protector, don't tell me you forgot!' cried Chapman. 'You know very well how important good timekeeping is to the Kingsbreath. It's already past noon!'

'I'm late,' said Wren, slowly. 'For a date. *My* date. Yes. Of course.' She turned from the mirror, keeping her face the perfect picture of calm. A *date* was an unexpected development, certainly, but it was nothing she couldn't handle. 'Goodness. Where *has* the time gone?'

'Perhaps you offended it in another life,' sighed Chapman. 'You do always seem to be two steps behind it. I might add that it was *you* who insisted on courting the prince in the first place.' Chapman removed a feather quill from behind his ear and jabbed it at the piece of parchment. 'It's all here in the schedule!'

Wren could just about read the entry he was pointing at.

Twelve noon – one o'clock: Princess Rose and Prince Ansel have afternoon tea in the lower gardens.

Who on earth is Prince Ansel?

Chapman clucked his tongue. 'I do wonder whether you have a sieve in that head of yours sometimes. We just went over your schedule yesterday.' He ushered her from the room. 'Come along. The Kingsbreath will have my head if you tarry another moment.'

Wren bit her tongue and followed Chapman down one winding stone staircase and then another, past probably the same stern-faced palace guards she and Shen had sneaked around last night.

Wren rifled through all the princes she knew of from surrounding countries, but she couldn't seem to place Prince Ansel.

'Now why are you frowning like that?' said Chapman, anxiously. 'Prince Ansel will want to see you smiling on your date.'

'I'm just nervous,' said Wren, quickly. 'What if Prince Ansel doesn't like me? What if he finds me bland? Or spoilt? Or overdressed? Or underdressed?'

Or, I don't know, A DIFFERENT PERSON ENTIRELY?

Chapman waved his hand in dismissal. 'Nonsense. You are the famed beauty of Eana, with no small fortune to your name. And by all accounts, your first date went rather well, didn't it? Though I do maintain you should have let him win that game of chess. Nobody likes a show-off.'

Wren felt a smattering of respect for her sister. 'Perhaps my brain is not such a sieve after all.'

Before them, the hallway vaulted into a marble archway

that overlooked the sprawling courtyard. Chapman turned from her, murmuring something as he went, but Wren was too dumbstruck to share in his babble. She was adrift now, floating across the pale stones in a cascade of golden sunlight.

And there he was, waiting for her at the edge of the rose garden.

Prince Ansel.

Wren's eyes widened. *Hissing seaweed.*

Ansel was *handsome.*

Being Rose was becoming more enjoyable by the minute.

Rose
CHAPTER 6

The pale gold mountain rose unexpectedly out of the desert. It looked remarkably sturdy amid the shifting sands and sparkled magnificently in the high-noon sun.

It was so bright Rose had to squint at it but the sight was a welcome one. They had been riding for hours. Miles and miles of sand, punctuated by only the undulating dunes. She had never been so exhausted. Her thighs hurt, her back ached and she was drenched in sweat. She had been so focused on not falling off the horse as it raced through the desert, she hadn't let herself think about how frightened she was of what lay before them.

Or how frantic everyone back at Anadawn must be. She could imagine all too well how fiercely Willem would be interrogating the guards and the punishments he would be doling out. Whenever the Kingsbreath was in a fury, all of Anadawn quaked. And someone always paid for it.

And then there was Celeste. She was certainly in a panic! She would chase down Rose herself if given half the chance, and likely do a far better job of finding her, too . . .

But Rose couldn't think about her best friend right now. Or Anadawn. She couldn't afford to let herself fall apart. She had to stay focused and alert.

Storm carried them to the base of the mountain, where four arched openings tunnelled into the rock. Shen hopped off the horse and offered his hand to Rose.

'I'm fine,' she insisted, but as her bare feet hit the blistering sand, her knees buckled.

He caught her before she hit the ground. 'Steady there.'

Rose glared at him. 'Do you always talk to women the way you talk to your horse?'

'You should be flattered. There's no one in this world I respect more than Storm.' Shen's gaze sharpened and his face grew suddenly serious. 'You look as if you've caught sun fever.' Rose froze as he pressed the back of his hand to her brow. 'The forehead goes red first.' He traced his finger along her cheekbone, making her breath catch in her throat. 'And the cheeks go white.'

He dropped his hand, trapping a curse between his teeth. 'I should have made sure your face was covered. I didn't realize how little time you'd spent in the sun.'

Rose took a step away from him. 'I am not as delicate as you seem to think. I spend plenty of time in the sun. I am often in my gardens.'

'All the same, you should drink some water. Come, there's plenty inside.'

It was blessedly cool inside the caves. The light that filtered in from the entranceway cast a glimmering kaleidoscope across the walls, while sparkling clear water pooled in a natural basin at their feet. 'I'd recommend drinking from higher than Storm does,' said Shen, just as the horse ducked her head and drank greedily from the pool.

Rose eyed the basin with disgust. 'You want me to drink alongside your *horse*? Using my *hands*?'

Shen cupped his hands and drank deeply. 'This water is the cleanest in Eana. It trickles all the way down from the Mishnick Mountains, which are just north of—'

'I know where the Mishnick Mountains are,' she snapped. 'They belong to me.'

'Well, so does this desert but you don't seem to know a thing about it . . .' Shen ran his fingers under the water and then raked them through his hair, smoothing the wayward strands from his face. 'It's the only fresh water for miles around, so drink up or expire, Princess. It's up to you.'

Rose reluctantly rolled up the sleeves of her nightgown and rinsed her hands in the water. 'Oh! It's so cold!' And it tasted divine – cool and clean and fresh – though she was mindful not to show it.

Shen watched her carefully. 'Admit it. It's better than the water you drink in that stuffy old palace.'

'You sound as proud of this water as you do of your horse.'

He grinned, crookedly. 'Desert horse, desert water, desert guy . . . all the best you'll find in Eana.'

'Oh, please.'

He ducked for another sip of water and Rose's gaze

slid over his shoulder, to where the walls were covered in strange symbols.

A gasp stuck like a fishbone in her throat. 'Witch markings!'

They were little more than a mismatch of lines and circles grouped together but Rose knew them for what they really were. These same markings had stained the palace walls the night her parents had been murdered. And though they had been long scrubbed from the stone, sometimes when the morning sunlight flooded the palace, she could trace the shadows the ink had left behind.

She tried to yank Shen away from them. 'Get back!'

When he didn't move, she leaped in front of him and raised her arms above her head. Fear guttered inside her as she waved them back and forth, and then in circles, while blowing air out in fierce puffs. 'Gone! Gone! By the will of the Great Protector, be gone!'

From the corner of her eye she could see Shen staring at her in alarm. 'What are you doing?'

Rose briefly halted the ritual to glare at him. 'I suggest you stay behind me if you know what's good for you. Everyone in Eana knows this is how you ward off a witch's curse.'

Shen raised an eyebrow. 'I can't say I've ever heard of this . . . precaution.'

'Well, you are lucky you're with me.' Rose summoned another bout of courage and puffed her cheeks up. She began to swing her hips, her arms spinning wildly above her head. Having never been confronted with such fresh witch markings, she couldn't tell if it was working or not but she was starting to feel dizzy, and she took this to be a good sign. She wished for Celeste with a sharpness that stung her heart. Whenever they chanced upon faint witch markings in the palace, they would do the witch-warding dance together. Twirling and spinning and huffing until their fear faded into laughter. With her best friend, Rose felt brave, as if she could face anything. *Do* anything. But Celeste was far from these cursed desert caves. And worse – she was protecting an insufferable bandit, who hardly deserved it!

Shen tucked his hands behind his back as he moved around her. 'So, you've seen this little dance work, then? Seen it ward off witches?'

'Of course not! The palace guards would never let an actual witch near me.' Rose shuddered at the very thought. 'They'd kill them on sight. As they should.'

Shen's face darkened. 'So, it's true, then. You support the witch killings?'

Rose stopped dancing. She met his gaze, unflinchingly. 'I support the protection of my people.'

Shen's mouth was a hard line. 'Tell me, Princess, how do your *impressively competent* guards sniff out these witches?'

Rose stiffened at the sarcasm in his voice, but she would not let herself be baited by it. 'You should know. Everyone in Eana is taught how to spot them. They are loners, mostly. Often without family and friends. They fear the water, and cannot stand too long in direct sunlight,' she said, reeling off all the things she had learned about witches over the years. 'But the simple truth is, if you watch a witch long enough, they will always reveal their craft. After all, they cannot resist the allure of their own dark magic. Evil always seeps out, sooner or later. That's why at Anadawn, even suspected witches must be severely punished. Willem says it's important to set an example, to warn the rest of them to stay away.'

'Does he now?' said Shen, dryly.

Rose returned her gaze to the witch markings. 'I had a seamstress several years ago, who kept pricking me with her needles when taking my measurements. The first time, I thought it was an accident. The second, I wondered if nerves had made her fingers tremble. And the third, well . . . the third time it happened, I had no choice but to report it to Willem. And he confirmed my fear.'

Beside her, Shen was still as a statue. 'Which was?'

'That she was collecting my blood for some sort of witchcraft!'

The bandit didn't even blink. 'Was she killed?'

Rose faltered. 'No. I . . . I asked that her life be spared. She was so young and frightened, and well, I couldn't be *sure* . . . She refused to admit it. Even when Willem interrogated her.' She scrunched her eyes shut, trying to weather the awful memory, how her complaint had spiralled out of her hands, how quickly Willem had leaped on it, his protectiveness of her consuming him like a terrible inferno. 'Such a punishment . . . it didn't seem right to me.'

'So, it appears you have a heart, after all.'

'Do not mistake mercy for weakness,' Rose warned, at the hint of his smile. 'Willem ordered her hands chopped off so she could never curse anyone again.'

His smile dissolved. 'Nor earn a livelihood.'

'It was necessary to protect my people.' Rose's voice shook as she recalled how she had sobbed to Celeste after it had been done. Even now, her guilt for what had befallen the seamstress still lingered. 'The Protector taught us that magic belongs to the earth. To Eana. When we take it for ourselves, the land suffers. Witches are selfish. They only care for power and they don't care who they hurt to get it. They make the crops fail. They cause the rivers to flood and the bays to freeze over.'

Shen snorted. 'I believe you're thinking of winter.'

Rose went on, undeterred. 'They steal children from their beds. They curse lovers to ruin. They cast plagues in towns and villages. They are evil, every last one of them.' She turned back to the cave wall, staring at the symbols with a renewed hatred. 'My first act as Queen will be to finish what the Great Protector started a thousand years ago, when he first set foot in Eana. Soon, the witches will be nothing but a distant memory in this country and my people will finally be able to sleep soundly, knowing they are safe.' She pointed accusingly at the markings, fear inching up her throat and cracking her voice. 'And I will never have to worry about meeting the same fate as my parents.'

'I'm sorry you lost them at such a young age,' said Shen,

turning back to the basin. He rinsed his hands, taking care to scrub the dirt from his fingernails.

Rose looked down on him. 'Be sorry for what the witches did. One of them sliced my mother's throat when I was only seconds old. She poisoned my father. If it wasn't for Willem, she would have killed me, too. He caught her holding the very knife she'd used on my mother over me.'

Shen's jaw twitched. 'What did he do to the witch? Drown her? Burn her? *Dance* at her?'

'She got away.' Rose soured at the thought, an old fear curdling in her stomach at the idea that this witch might still be out there somewhere, waiting to finish what she'd started. 'And you're old enough to know what happened next. Her cruel-hearted cowardice doomed her people to war.'

'Lillith's War.' Shen looked up at her. A shadow moved behind his eyes. 'Named for your mother. Who was a witch herself. An enchanter, right?'

Rose glared at him, the heat of her anger flaring in her cheeks. 'My mother was a *reformed* witch,' she said, practically hissing the word. 'She gave up her magic to be with my father. But the witches couldn't forgive her. That's why they killed her.'

Shen curled his lip as he straightened. 'And then your soldiers killed thousands of innocent witches.'

'There is no such thing as an innocent witch.'

He folded his arms. 'I would wager there's no such thing as a reformed witch.'

'You have nothing to wager but your arrogance. You may keep it,' snapped Rose.

Shen brushed past her, and had the gall – or perhaps flaming stupidity – to trail his fingers along the symbols. 'The witches won't bother you here,' he said, with such certainty Rose almost believed it. 'The truth is, there used to be a kingdom hidden away in the heart of the Ganyeve. Traders would come and rest inside these caves on their way to find it. These markings aren't a curse. They're just memories, symbols that say "I was here".' He dropped his hand, and his voice became very quiet. 'And now they are not.'

Rose had never heard this story before – which meant it was most likely untrue – but she couldn't help the sudden nearness of her curiosity. And the hushed reverence in Shen's voice had caught her attention, too. 'And what happened to this fanciful kingdom?'

'One day, the desert swallowed it.'

'What a grim fairy tale.'

'It's no fairy tale, Princess.'

Rose let out a short, sharp laugh. 'The country of Eana has only *one* ruler, and she is standing before you. Not to mention, nonsense of this sort has never been written about in Anadawn's long-standing historical records, which I have read many times, by the way.'

Shen shrugged. 'Perhaps the movements of this desert have never been any of your business.'

Rose blinked. '*Excuse* me?'

'You are excused,' said Shen, as he returned to the trickling waterfall.

Rose fumed in silence. She had to remind herself that the ravings of a lowly bandit meant nothing to her. But as she drank, she couldn't shake the uncertainty that his words had sown inside her. This was *her* kingdom, not his. She should know *all* its hidden places and secret tales, no matter how outlandish they were.

'Follow me when you're done seething,' said Shen, as he turned from the water. Rose glowered after him as he wandered deeper into the caves with the lazy confidence of a bandit who knew she had nowhere to run.

Wren

CHAPTER 7

Prince Ansel was built like a soldier, so tall that Wren had to tilt her chin to take him all in. His shoulders were broad, and his arms were thick and corded with muscle. He was pale-skinned with dark tousled hair shot through with strands of copper. He wore a navy frock coat, inlaid with silver brocade, dark trousers and black leather boots. Exquisitely tailored. His face was exquisite, too. His eyes were wide and grey – the exact shade of a sea at storm, and the hard edge of his jaw was softened by the barest hint of a smile. Wren might not have noticed it at all if she hadn't been staring so hard at his lips.

As they stood apart from each other in the courtyard, it occurred to her that she should probably say something. 'Good morn—aftern—hi—hello!' The words came out in a breathless whoosh. She tried again. 'I'm sorry I'm late. I *completely* lost track of—'

'No need to apologize, my flower.' Wren blinked, but Ansel's mouth wasn't moving. He was just . . . staring at her.

A much slighter man stepped out from behind him. He

was a sapling compared to the oak tree towering next to him – with porcelain skin, a dainty nose and a wide, smiling mouth. 'You are, as ever, worth the wait.'

He twirled his hand as he bowed, strands of thick blond hair flopping into his eyes.

Wren's excitement curdled inside her. She dropped her head, masking her disappointment with a curtsy. 'You're too kind.'

The real Prince Ansel offered her his elbow and Wren scurried to take it, ignoring the stormy gaze of his silent companion as she brushed past him.

They wandered into the rose garden, where the bushes were bright and the air was heady. 'You seem a little flustered this afternoon, my flower. I hope my guard's continued presence isn't proving a bother to you.' Ansel tossed his head, flicking his hair away from his face. 'You know I have the *utmost* trust in the Anadawn court. The palace has been nothing but hospitable since the moment we arrived, but I'm afraid my brother *insists* on a personal guard and we've known Captain Tor Iversen so long he is practically family to us. Thankfully, he is a man of few words. He fades right into the background.'

Wren was too embarrassed to look over her shoulder. Ansel might not have noticed her mistake but his soldier had witnessed her salivating in close, agonizing detail. 'It's perfectly fine.' She gestured to the palace guards stationed at the far corners of the courtyard. 'I'm well used to silent company.'

'Well, a treasure as fine as you must have a keeper,'

said Ansel, in what Wren assumed was his attempt at a compliment. 'You know, my brother has long been convinced there are at least ten people looking to kill him at any given time of the day,' he said, with a chuckle. 'Alarik keeps his most trusted guards within arm's reach of him at all times. Even at family dinners! Or perhaps I should say, *especially* at family dinners. My sister does have quite a temper.'

Alarik. A rush of dread coursed through Wren. There was only one royal Alarik known throughout all of Eana, and not for his kindness. Alarik Felsing was the iron-fisted ruler of the icy kingdom of Gevra on the northern continent; a young, feral king who led with brute force and boundless cruelty.

Oh no.

'Sit down, my flower. You don't look quite well.' They had reached a table set in the middle of the garden. There was a platter of miniature cucumber sandwiches and fruit tarts waiting for them, as well as a steaming pot of mint tea.

Tor stationed himself beside a tall yellow rose bush that peered out over the courtyard, and beyond it, the Eshlinn woods. Wren did her best not to look at him but she couldn't help the odd, traitorous flick of her gaze. This time, she noted what she had missed the first time – his impressive sword. The pommel was made from frosted glass, and glinted like an icicle in the sunlight. The scabbard was midnight blue and wrought with silver – the same colours as his uniform.

Gevra colours.

Now Wren really was starting to feel unwell. She swayed on her feet, and Tor's arm shot out to steady her.

'Rose?' Across the table, Ansel's face creased in concern. 'Are you well?'

Wren ignored the soldier's arm, and sank into her chair. 'Just a little warm, that's all.'

Ansel nodded, knowingly. 'I know spring is mild here but after growing up in Gevra, these tepid afternoons feel like a desert to me.'

'Then I'd caution you to steer clear of the Ganyeve. Your face would melt right off,' said Wren, absently.

He raised his eyebrows. 'Didn't you say you'd never been outside the capital?'

'Or so I *hear*,' she added, hastily. 'And if it helps, today is a lot hotter than I was expecting it to be.' She glanced at Tor, then laughed awkwardly. 'Anyway. What do we have here?'

In the centre of the table sat an ornate box full of small, wooden pieces. Ansel inclined his chin towards it. 'I thought instead of embarrassing myself at chess again today, you might like to have a go at a puzzle instead? It is such sweet destiny that we both enjoy the rush of a good board game.'

'Ah, mild, orderly fun,' said Wren, as she reached for her teacup. 'My favourite.'

'Strawberry tart?' offered Ansel, plucking one for himself.

She shook her head as she sipped, trying to figure out why on earth her sister had decided to court a Gevran prince of all people.

'Keeping yourself nice and trim, I see,' said Ansel, approvingly.

Well, that certainly wouldn't do. Prince or no prince, he had no right commenting on how she ate. Wren shot her hand out and shoved an entire tart in her mouth. 'SHANGED SHMY MINDSH,' she said, crumbs flying from her lips. 'MMM, DELSHSSS!'

The prince's bright blue eyes went wide.

Wren chewed expressively while she fished a puzzle piece from the box and set it down between them. A blur of white.

'Then again, a woman who satisfies her appetites can be just as alluring.' Ansel took a puzzle piece out and connected it to Wren's. 'Ah! What an auspicious start.'

Wren swallowed, thickly, and wiped a bit of custard off her mouth. 'I'd *hate* to put you off.'

'Impossible.' Ansel placed a corner piece of puzzle. A smudge of grey. Wren rifled through the wooden box, looking for another. How was this already *so boring*?

'This is the most fun I've had in months,' said the prince, with a sheepish smile. Wren could admit he had nice teeth, even if they were wincingly bright. 'I'm not used to such charming company. With each passing day, I grow ever more thankful to the Kingsbreath for opening his palace to me.'

'I think you mean *my* palace.' Wren pressed two grey blobs together, imagining the sweet cracking of Willem Rathborne's neck as they snapped into place. What business could he possibly have with the bloodthirsty nation of Gevra?

'Yes, well, he has certainly taken great care of it.

Especially after what happened to your poor parents . . .' Ansel rubbed the back of his neck, sorrow pooling in his eyes. 'What awful circumstances. To be murdered in the very place they called home, and then all that horrid war business that came afterwards. You must feel most grateful to the Kingsbreath for taking you in.'

Wren was careful to control her face. *'Bank your temper, little bird,'* cautioned Banba's voice in her head. *'Even if it burns you alive.'*

Wren's parents' story was as tragic as it was romantic, their untimely deaths reverberating in every far-off corner of Eana. Falling in love with the king should have made Wren's mother fear for her life, but the bloodshed of the Protector's War was long past, then – and by all accounts, Wren's father did not bear the same resentment towards the witches as his ancestors. After all, how else could he have fallen in love with one? Banba said it was hope that made Lillith Greenrock open her heart to a Valhart – the possibility of a kingdom finally united by a marriage between two lineages long at war. The dream of a child who would be a descendant of both the Protector and the witches – and one day, a bringer of peace.

But then Lillith was murdered moments after giving birth, and all that hope died with her. King Keir was found poisoned in his bedchamber soon after. Willem Rathborne swore it was a jealous palace witch who did it – a midwife who couldn't stand the thought of one of her own marrying a Valhart – a claim that was bolstered by several witnesses who saw her fleeing across the Silvertongue River not long after.

Rathborne's story contained a clever half-truth. The midwife was indeed a healer witch. And she fled swiftly, across the Silvertongue, but not from guilt. For life. The palace guards who saw her disappear didn't notice the mewling bundle wrapped up in her arms.

They spoke only of the one left behind.

The tale of poor orphaned Princess Rose and her slain parents was all the Kingsbreath needed to usher in Lillith's War, a bloody, futile battle designed to finish what the Protector had started a thousand years ago. To finally stamp out the last of the witches in Eana. Almost all of them – enchanters and healers, tempests and warriors, and even the seers – were decimated within weeks of the Kingsbreath's order. The few fortunate survivors escaped to a secret windswept coastal settlement in the west, which they named Ortha, after the last reigning witch queen.

And for all the years since, nobody – not Willem Rathborne nor Rose herself – knew of the other twin. The girl who had inherited her mother's craft. The girl who had returned all these years later to reclaim her kingdom for the witches.

There was so much more at stake than pride, but Wren couldn't help herself. 'Willem was merely my father's advisor.' *Snap!* Another puzzle piece. 'So, really it was *I* who took *him* in.'

Ansel frowned. 'But you were just a baby.'

'Which makes it even more impressive. No?' Wren

stole another glance at Tor. His gaze was on the distant trees, but she could tell by his furrowed brow that he was eavesdropping. She knitted her hands under her chin. 'But let's not talk of brutally murdered parents. We'll spoil our afternoon.'

A blush rose in Ansel's cheeks. 'I'm afraid I've broached a topic I shouldn't have, my flower. Please forgive me.'

He reached across the table and Wren, masquerading as Rose, had no choice but to take his hand. Its clamminess betrayed his nerves but she pretended not to notice. 'All is forgiven.' She fished another three pieces from the box and slotted them into place . . . *Snap! Snap! Snap!* The greys were bleeding into white.

'I should have known you'd be a champion of puzzles, too,' said Ansel, admiringly. 'I can scarcely keep up with you.'

Please try, thought Wren, as she grabbed another piece. *So this infernal boredom can end.*

A droning bumblebee startled them from their conversation. Ansel yelped as he sprung to his feet, his teacup sailing through the air. Wren lunged without thinking, hooking it on her pinkie finger a heartbeat before it could shatter on the ground.

'My, how impressive!' panted the prince. 'Especially considering you accidentally toppled the chessboard on our last date. Don't you agree, Tor?'

Tor smiled, tightly. 'Good catch, Your Highness.'

Wren stifled a groan. Of course her sister would be a

clumsy fool. 'More like a lucky catch,' she said, gently placing the teacup back on the tablecloth. When she looked up, she gasped. A white blur was bounding out from the rose bushes, and heading straight for her.

'*Rotting carp!*' She stumbled backwards, tripping over her chair in a clatter.

'Elske! Down!' Tor's command ripped through the air like thunder. He leaped towards the blur, which turned out to be a fully grown *wolf*, and curled a strong arm around her before she could pounce on the table.

'I told you to control that beast, Tor!' cried Ansel. 'You've frightened the princess half to death!'

'She meant only to protect you, Your Highness.' He scratched behind the wolf's ears and she licked his face. Wren didn't blame the wolf one bit. 'Elske wouldn't harm a flea unless I commanded it.'

'Even so. This is no place for your wolf to play, Tor. She belongs on a chain. I shouldn't need to remind you of all people that in Gevra, we train our animals to be soldiers, not pets.' Ansel helped Wren to her feet, putting a protective arm around her waist. 'You have nothing to fear, my flower. I would throw myself between you and even the most fearsome of beasts.'

Except the dreaded bumblebee, noted Wren.

Tor stood up, stiff-backed. Wren could see he was affronted by Ansel's words, but he knew better than to defend his beast. Despite everything the prince had just said, Elske was very clearly a pet.

Wren spun out of Ansel's embrace. She had never seen a wolf before, and she was quite taken with the beauty of this one. She knelt to get a closer look. Elske's fur was the colour of freshly fallen snow and her eyes were pale as glaciers.

'Hello, sweet girl,' cooed Wren.

Elske blinked her bright eyes, then rested her head in Wren's lap, where she began to nibble at her skirts.

Ansel cleared his throat. 'Darling, our puzzle.'

'It will keep.' Wren pressed her face into the wolf's fur. She smelled of wild pine and adventure. 'Oh, you're a darling,' she murmured, as she scratched behind her ears.

'Elske does not often warm to strangers.' Wren could feel the soldier's gaze on the crown of her head, and detected a hint of curiosity in his voice. 'Especially in this country.'

'She is a princess.' Wren tipped her head back, her eyes meeting his. For the briefest moment, she felt utterly at sea. 'Like calls to like.'

'Well, this prince is calling to his princess.' Ansel drummed his fingers along the table. 'Come, my flower. We must see our puzzle through to its stirring conclusion.'

Tor released a sharp whistle. Elske lifted her head from Wren's skirts and padded over to her master. Wren rolled to her feet and returned to the table, with the melancholy of a prisoner walking to the gallows.

With remarkable quickness, Ansel returned to boring the life out of her. She threw her remaining energy into finishing the damned puzzle, and with it, their date. After today, she would have to come up with a way to remove any further meetings with the prince from Chapman's schedule. Otherwise she might perish from acute boredom before her coronation. The pieces of greys and whites slowly arranged themselves into a towering fortress, cut into the heart of an icy mountain range. No sun above, just an endless swathe of white sky.

'Grinstad Palace,' said Ansel, triumphantly, as he placed the last puzzle piece. A final *snap!* completed the spectre. 'Once we're married, my flower, this is where we'll summer.'

Wren's heart juddered to a grinding halt. She stared at the prince in silent horror.

Ansel whipped his head around. 'What is it? Is it another bumblebee? Where?'

Wren feigned a cough to hide her grimace but she could do nothing about the violent shock coursing through her body. Since when did Rose have a *hissing* fiancé? And why had he been plucked from Gevra of all places? The more she thought about it, the more uneasy she felt.

'Rose?' said Ansel, worriedly. 'Are you well?'

'I was just thinking about our wedding,' said Wren, weakly. 'Sometimes, I get so excited I'm afraid I might vomit.'

Ansel's grin revealed every one of his pearly teeth. 'I admit the idea that you will soon be my wife gives me butterflies, too.'

Wren exhaled through her smile. She didn't have butterflies. She had scorpions, and right now, they were eating her alive. To her relief, Chapman arrived presently to collect her, with his precious schedule tucked underneath his arm. She said her goodbyes to Prince Ansel, allowing herself a final stealthy glimpse of his guard, before following Chapman back into the palace.

'I need to speak to Willem at once.'

Chapman blinked at her in alarm. 'The Kingsbreath's not taking visitors, and *certainly* not ones that aren't on the schedule!'

'Well, put me on the schedule, then.'

'Oh, and shall I sprout wings while I'm at it?' he scoffed.

Wren glowered at him. 'Please tell the Kingsbreath I wish to speak to him urgently about my wedding to Prince Ansel. I have some thoughts.'

Chapman wagged his finger at her. 'A girl with too many thoughts in her head is not busy enough with her days,' he chided. 'And anyway, today is no good. You're due to go riding with Celeste in an hour.' He stalled at the bottom of the east tower. 'Go up and change. I'll have the stablehand prepare your horse.'

Wren winced. Celeste was Rose's best friend. As the daughter of Rathborne's prized physician, Hector Pegasi, she had grown up in the palace alongside Rose, the two girls fast becoming inseparable. She was going to be the hardest to fool, and after everything she had just learned, Wren was in no fit state to try.

'There's no need,' she said, as she started up the steps. 'I'm afraid I'm going to have to cancel. I've got a terrible headache.'

The headache's name was Ansel. She hadn't come all the way to the palace to betray her sister and steal her life only to end up sharing her crown with some puzzle-obsessed Gevran prince. In the space of an Anadawn afternoon, one thing had becoming abundantly and unavoidably clear: Wren would sooner feed herself to Elske than bind herself to this man – or any other – for the rest of her life.

Rose
CHAPTER 8

With no other choice, Rose followed the bandit deeper into the cave. When the cavern widened out, they came upon a gathering of supplies tucked under a boulder. 'Good fortune. Everything is still here.' Shen picked up a leather sack, removing two apples and a hunk of crusty bread. 'Ha! And no insects got to it this time!'

Rose's stomach growled. By now, she was so ravenous she didn't care that the bread was starting to go stale and the apples were small and mealy. Shen pulled out some tough pieces of dried meat and bit into one with gusto. 'Lamb strips are my favourite. They taste great and last forever.'

He offered one to her.

'I'm surprised you didn't say it was made from special desert lambs.' Rose held the piece of lamb between her thumb and forefinger as she inspected it. 'When you say it lasts forever, exactly how long has this piece of meat been rotting in that bag?'

'Just try a bite.'

She nibbled a bit. 'Chewy but . . . very flavourful. I'll

give you that. Though I don't think I'll be requesting it from the Anadawn cooks any time soon.' Her face suddenly fell. 'Oh. The cooks. They'll be missing me. Most evenings, I go down to the kitchens to try a bit of Cam's newest creation. He's the most wonderful baker. He's always trying new recipes. Lately, he's been working on a Gevran ice cake, and oh, the trouble he's having with it.' She smiled at the memory. Some of Rose's happiest days at Anadawn were spent in its warm kitchens, laughing away the hours with Cam and Celeste. In bed at night, her hair often smelled like icing sugar and she would fall asleep dreaming of sweet spices from faraway villages. 'He'll get it right though. He always does.'

Shen frowned. 'I'm surprised Gevrans even have desserts. Doesn't their brutal king hate everything?'

'Watch your tongue,' said Rose, hurtling back out of the memory. 'I'm betrothed to the brother of that brutal king.'

Shen spat out a piece of lamb. 'You're BETROTHED?'

'Goodness me. Calm yourself, bandit. Of course I'm betrothed.' Rose tossed her tangled hair, with mild frustration. If only she had a brush with her to make it shine. 'Do you really think me so ineligible?'

Shen looked as if he was about to keel over. He sank slowly to the ground.

'I'm a princess,' she went on, smoothing her hopelessly wrinkled nightgown. 'Marrying ourselves to other nations for the betterment of our own is what we do.'

Rose had long known that youth and beauty were

her true power. Willem had taught her that early on. He had been planning her betrothal for as long as she could remember, rifling through potential suitors who would be kind to her *and* to her kingdom, preparing for the day when she would marry for the good of Eana, and have a strong consort by her side to help her rule.

'Wait.' Shen was still trying to make sense of it. '*Who* exactly are you marrying?'

'Prince Ansel Felsing, brother to the king of Gevra.' Rose perched on a boulder, relishing the sight of Shen's deepening frown. Though she couldn't quite figure out why, she sensed she had gained the upper hand. 'I am very lucky to be so well matched.'

She smiled to herself, thinking of the prince. How his blue eyes widened whenever he looked at her – as though she was the most beautiful woman in the world. Rose had loved his easy warmth on their first date and how gingerly he'd held her hand, asking questions about her childhood and laughing at her jokes. She had suspected from his letters that he would make an amenable match, but now that they had finally met each other in person, Rose could imagine them having quite a nice life together.

'I didn't even know the king had a brother,' said Shen. 'Why aren't you marrying Alarik?'

'Because I am in *love* with Ansel,' said Rose, hotly. 'The prince is a prize in his own right. And anyway, Alarik has made it quite clear he is not seeking a bride. His thoughts are on other matters.'

'Such as war, no doubt.'

Rose ignored him. 'With the might of the Gevran army at my beckoning, Eana will be the strongest it has ever been.' She watched Shen squirm, smiling like a satisfied cat. It seemed he was finally starting to regret kidnapping her. 'And Ansel and I will live happily ever after.'

Shen kicked his legs out, disturbing a cloud of golden dust. 'You seem very certain about that.'

'The moment I met him, I knew we were destined to be together.'

'Have you even met any other men?'

'Of course I have, you brute! I am not as cloistered as you seem to think.'

'Name someone you've met outside the palace walls,' said Shen. 'And don't just make up a name.'

Rose threw him a withering look. 'Marino Pegasi,' she said, primly. 'And I assure you, he is as real as my disdain for you. Marino is the brother of my best friend, Celeste. A wealthy merchant sailor, and quite a handsome one at that.'

Shen snorted. 'And what does that have to do with anything?'

'Well, if I were the type to simply fall in love for no reason, which you are implying, I surely would have fallen for Marino for his good looks alone.' She lowered her voice, as if she were telling Shen a secret. 'I think many women already have. Celeste has seen them up at Wishbone Bay, parading along the dock in their best dresses, waiting for his ship to come in. It drives her mad, of course.'

'I'm sure he enjoys it well enough,' said Shen, thoughtfully. 'But we aren't talking about this dreamy Marino. We're talking about your prince.'

'I assure you, Ansel has *many* virtues.' Rose smiled as she recalled the prince's bright blue eyes and long lashes. 'Firstly, he is very well mannered,' she said, pointedly. 'And he understands what it means to be truly royal. To grow up with a hundred pairs of eyes on you at all times. To feel lonely, even when you're surrounded by people. He cares very much for me. I can't imagine I'll ever meet anyone who makes me feel so adored. And he loses graciously at chess.' Shen was infuriatingly silent, waiting for more. Rose frowned, trying to think of what else she loved about Ansel. 'His hair shines like gold in the sunshine. And . . . and he dresses impeccably.'

'Hmm,' was all Shen said.

She huffed a sigh. 'Not that I even care what you think, but what do *you* know of love, Shen Lo?'

'Clearly not as much as you, Princess.' He rolled to his feet. 'My best wishes to you and your groom.' He muttered to himself as he paced the cavern. 'Gevra . . . *Gevra* . . . Good luck with that, Wren.'

Rose's ears pricked up. 'Who is Wren?'

Shen spun around. '*Shen*,' he said, quickly. 'I said, "Good luck with that, *Shen*."'

'Are you feeling frightened, bandit?' Rose revelled in her sudden rush of triumph. 'After all, it's no small task to face the *entire* Gevran army on your own.'

He stared down at her, a smirk twitching on his lips. 'I suspect they wouldn't last a day in the desert. They'd surely melt.'

Exasperated with his smugness, Rose threw her piece of lamb at him. 'Take your rotten mutton meat. I don't want it.'

Shen caught it with ease. 'All the more for me,' he said, tossing it in his mouth. 'And perhaps I was being too nice by sharing. We're not friends. Better for you to remember that.'

'You forget yourself, Shen Lo of the Desert.' Rose's words hung heavy with scorn. 'I may be dependent on you now, but it would behove you to remember who truly holds the power between us.'

She fixed him with a stare so withering, he broke eye contact.

He began to rifle through his pile of supplies. 'We need to sleep. It's too hot to ride.' He tossed her what looked like ragged bedclothes.

Rose batted it away from her. 'What is that supposed to be?'

'It's your bedroll, my lady,' said Shen, with an exaggerated bow.

'It's *Your Highness*,' Rose corrected him. 'And I'm not sleeping on a bunch of rags!'

'It's that or the cave floor, *Your Highness*.'

Rose was certain that nobody had ever hissed her title at her quite like that and she found she did not care for it. She cleared her throat. 'And where am I supposed to lay my head?'

'You've got your pick of any spot in the cave. I'm going to go right here though.' Shen unfurled his bedroll. A spider skittered out of it. Rose bit back a shriek.

She couldn't sleep close to the bandit; it would be entirely improper. But she didn't want to stray too far from him either. She couldn't be alone in a cave that was covered in witch markings.

'I'll go . . . right here.' She unfurled her bedroll on the other side of the boulder. Witch markings stared down at her from the wall. She shivered and sat up.

'Actually, I'll go here.' She scooted back around to where she could see Shen but was still several feet away from him. She felt grateful for the cloak now. As smelly and rough as it was, it worked perfectly as a blanket.

'Sleep well, Princess,' said Shen, with a yawn.

Rose had no intention of sleeping. She was going to wait until he fell asleep and then she would take his horse and return to Anadawn, leaving him to his stale bread and stringy mutton. She could see the map of Eana in her mind, the rolling Ganyeve wide and golden in its centre. Rose didn't know it the way the bandit did, but if she chose a direction and rode for long enough, she knew she would find her way out eventually.

She rolled on to her side and made a show of yawning and stretching. She would use this time to calm herself, she thought, as she closed her eyes and softly hummed the tune to her favourite Eana waltz, imagining herself dancing with her darling Ansel. *Step, glide, twirl* . . . She ignored

Shen chuckling to himself across the cave. He'd be asleep in moments and then she'd be gone, back to her palace where she belonged. Her humming quietened . . . *Step, glide, twirl,* one more imaginary waltz and then surely Shen would be asleep . . . *Step, glide, twirl* . . .

Rose jerked awake. The cave was lit up in dusty pinks and oranges, which meant that somewhere outside, the sun was setting.

Hours had passed.

Oh, crumbs!

She must have been more exhausted than she'd realized. But that was no excuse. She had almost squandered her only opportunity to escape . . .

Thankfully, Shen's snores were rattling through the little cavern. The bandit was still fast asleep.

I'm a fool but a lucky one.

Rose scrabbled to her feet. As she crept past the slumbering bandit, she noticed he had taken his shoes off. Well. Only a fool would venture out into the desert without shoes. She bent down, and then paused mid-reach. She was already taking the horse. It would be cruel to leave him to wander the desert barefoot. It was the queenly thing to do, she decided, to leave him his shoes. And she'd spare his life as well. A fine trade for a fine horse.

Storm was sleeping near the cave entrance.

'Wake up,' Rose whispered in the horse's ear.

Storm snorted, and kept sleeping. Rose prodded her in the side. Storm's eyes flew open. She whinnied in alarm.

'Shush, shush, don't be frightened!' hissed Rose. 'You know me, remember? I'm your princess.'

Storm only whinnied louder.

'I watched you consider taking my shoes,' came a voice from behind her. Rose's heart dropped. 'I'll admit I was surprised when you left them. Rather polite of you. You know what isn't polite? Horse thievery.'

'Neither is kidnapping,' said Rose. 'And you can hardly blame me for trying to escape.' She looked out at the desert, where the sands shifted like golden waves.

'So, you *were* attempting to steal my horse and run off while I was asleep.'

'You are mistaken on one crucial point.' Rose turned to glare at him. 'I'm soon to be Queen of this land. I don't need to *steal* anything.'

'You Valharts do have a tendency to just take what you want and claim it for your own.'

'I am Eana,' Rose reminded him. 'And Eana is me. I could no more steal from my own country than I could steal my own ear.'

'Yes, yes, so you've said. It all belongs to you. Except this horse. This horse belongs to me.' Shen whistled and Storm was instantly on her feet. He leaped on to her back in one fluid motion and twisted to look down at Rose.

'Well? Are you coming?'

She scowled at him. They both knew if she stayed in this

cave she'd die, and she couldn't roam the desert on foot. 'Where are you going?'

'I'll tell you when we get there.'

'That's hardly a compromise.'

Shen's smile was lazy. 'I'm the one on the horse. I don't have to compromise.'

Rose's scowl deepened. 'Perhaps I'll feed you that same line when you find yourself in the Anadawn dungeons.'

'Well, as we're not currently in Anadawn, I don't need to worry about that, do I?' He clicked his teeth and Storm began to amble away from the caves. He looked over his shoulder, his brown eyes molten in the setting sun. 'Last chance to join me.'

Rose knew she would be safer with the bandit than on her own in the desert. And surely they would reach some sign of civilization soon. Once they did, she would leap off the horse and scream for help and then, *oh, then*, Shen Lo would be sorry.

She started after him. 'I *will* return to my throne. *And* my beloved.'

'Not tonight, Princess,' he said, the horse slowing.

But soon, thought Rose, as she clambered on.

'You know,' said Shen, once Storm began to pick up pace, 'you're more spirited than I thought you'd be. Especially for a princess.'

Rose glanced at him over her shoulder. 'How many princesses do you know?'

He laughed, the sound rumbling through his chest and

into her. It made her heart flutter in a way that was not entirely unpleasant. 'You're braver than I thought, too. Or at least you're trying to be.' His voice was close to her ear, his breath warm on her skin. Rose swallowed. 'I can't help but admire that.'

'Oh, to be admired by a shameless, kidnapping bandit,' she said, dryly, and when he laughed again, it sent another burst of warmth through her that had nothing to do with the heat. 'Then again, I suppose you're not as awful as I expected.'

'Does that mean you find me . . . tolerable?'

Rose could hear the smirk in his voice. 'I'd like you a lot more if you took me home,' she huffed.

'Since we've already established why I can't do that, how about I promise to make the rest of our journey as *tolerable* as possible?' He dropped his voice to a whisper. 'You never know, Princess, you might enjoy yourself.'

Beyond the caves, the setting sun painted the desert in a blaze of colours, the shifting sands shimmering like an ocean of violet and gold. It was not a soft beauty like the manicured gardens of Anadawn. Or even a wild beauty like the woods beyond. It was a sharp, fierce beauty that pierced Rose's heart and reminded her how big the island of Eana truly was, and how little of it she had seen.

'I most certainly will not,' she said, grateful he couldn't see the smile that belied her words.

Wren

CHAPTER 9

Wren stared out of the window in the east tower, trying to control her anger. Just beyond the golden gates, on the top of a humpback hill, sat the Protector's Vault – an extravagant marble building domed in glass. It was supposed to be a place of worship, a safe haven from the witchcraft that the people of Eana swore had plagued them for years. Tonight, there was a man hanging from it.

Wren couldn't take her eyes off him. He was a carpenter from the capital city of Eshlinn, according to Agnes. The maidservant had insisted on delivering her dinner to her rooms, upon hearing about Wren's feigned headache. She'd laid out a veritable feast in the side chamber that connected to Rose's bedroom, where floor-to-ceiling bookshelves clustered around a small reading desk. There was roast duck drizzled with almond and pomegranate sauce, buttered greens and fondant potatoes, followed by a freshly baked apple crumble.

Wren hadn't been able to stomach a single mouthful of it. She was too fixated on the dead carpenter, who

Agnes said had been in the employ of the palace until the Kingsbreath's breakfast chair collapsed underneath him three days ago. When the guards found strange markings underneath the seat cushion, the carpenter was dragged in for an interrogation.

'*And was he a witch?*' Wren had asked, barely clinging to her composure.

Agnes only sighed. '*You know what the Kingsbreath says, love. When it comes to the witches, it's better to be safe than sorry.*' Wren must have done a poor job of hiding her dismay, because Agnes began to rub her back in warm circles. '*Best not to think too much about it, if you can help it. It'll only give you nightmares.*'

The second the old woman had left the room, Wren threw her goblet against the bookshelf.

This whole bloody kingdom is a nightmare, she wanted to scream. *We're all living in one!* She stalked back into the bedroom and upended Rose's vanity, toppling her perfumes across the floor. She threw her hairbrush at the unlucky palace guard who'd ducked his head in to see what was going on and then flung every single gaudy ring Rose owned across the room, watching them plink off the wall one by one.

Only then was she able to sit down and force herself to eat. She had to keep her strength up for the weeks ahead, and whatever nasty surprises Anadawn still had in store for her. If Willem Rathborne was going to murder witches right in front of her, she would have a much harder time pretending to be Princess Rose.

Despite telling Chapman that she urgently wished to speak to Rathborne, the Kingsbreath was still too busy to see her. Wren was used to waiting, but that didn't mean she would be idle. Tonight, rather than pacing a hole in the carpet, she decided to find her way to Rathborne's chamber to see what he was up to. She possessed some knowledge of the layout of Anadawn, but now that she was here, the endless hallways and winding turrets all looked the same.

She donned one of Rose's elegant nightgowns for her midnight mission. It was long and crimson, the silk silent as she moved. A bracelet taken from her sister's bottomless jewellery drawer anchored her dagger beneath her sleeve – just in case – while a demure smile and a quick sleeping enchantment took care of the guards in her tower.

Wren's footsteps echoed along the stone floor, sconce-light casting her in shadow and flame. She took the stairs to the third floor and headed in the general direction of the king's bedchamber, the room where her father, King Keir Valhart, had been found poisoned almost eighteen years ago. The room Willem Rathborne had since claimed for his own.

Portraits of past kings and queens looked down on her from the walls – the descendants of the Great Protector unfurling in an endless line of furrowed brows and gilded crowns. There were no memories of the witch queens and kings who had ruled Eana long before them, though Wren was hardly surprised. History belonged to the victors, and so, it seemed, did the winding halls of Anadawn Palace.

When she became Queen, all of that would change. A portrait of Eana, the first witch, and all those who ruled after her would hang proudly from these walls. Magic would be celebrated, not feared, and there would be a role – and a refuge – at Anadawn for every witch who came here in search of one.

On their last day together in Ortha, Wren and Banba had waded out on to the sea-slimed rocks, a howling wind whipping up around them, until it felt as if it was just the two of them pushing ceaselessly towards a new horizon.

'I would raze this whole world to the ground for you, little bird.' Her grandmother had pulled her close, her cloak scratchy against Wren's cheek. *'I would kill a thousand men and more just to keep you from harm, but the time has come to set you free. To send you home. Will you raze a trail through those golden gates for your people? Will you raze a trail for me?'*

Banba had looked at her with such faith in her eyes, Wren had felt ten feet tall. In her, she had found not just a grandmother, but a family. A way to belong to the country that had orphaned her. And so she had said, without hesitation, *'I would do anything for you, Banba.'* And she had meant it.

They had made the best of Ortha but they were sick of it – all of them – of living on the edge of the world, mired in the cold and the damp, shouting over the wind just to be heard. Cowering beneath the cliffs whenever a storm rattled the coastline and always looking up, never knowing when they might be discovered. The witches deserved peace of mind. They deserved to live in a place that was truly theirs. After a thousand years of exile, Wren was going to welcome them home.

'*Do whatever it takes to seize that throne, little bird. Eana will forgive you.*' Banba had dulled the wind with a flick of her wrist, her hand closing around Wren's as they turned for the shore. '*I will forgive you.*'

Wren rounded the corner at the end of the palace hallway and stopped dead in her tracks. *Hissing seaweed!* She had been so lost in thought that she didn't recognize the Kingsbreath's bedchamber until she was before it. Two burly soldiers stood guard, either side of the wooden doors. 'Oi! Who's that skulking down there?'

Wren's stomach twisted. It was too late to turn back now – she had already been spotted. She rolled her shoulders back and relaxed her stride. 'Good evening, gentleman. I was just looking for Willem?'

The guard on the right, who was pale and freckled with a bright red beard, flicked his gaze to the other. 'The Kingsbreath's a bit, er, indisposed at the moment, Your Highness.'

His furtiveness piqued Wren's interest. 'Oh. How so?'

The guard on the left, black-haired and olive-skinned with dark circles under his eyes, raised an eyebrow. 'It's awful late to be wandering about the palace by yourself, Princess. Is something the matter?'

'I had a nightmare.'

The guards exchanged another look.

Wren pouted. 'It was very scary.'

The bearded one caved. 'The Kingsbreath's just left,' he conceded. 'You'd be better off heading down to the kitchens for some camomile tea. Good for the nerves, my missus says.'

It was the perfect excuse for Wren to turn around and scurry away, but now she couldn't help herself. 'Where did he go?'

'Up to the west tower.'

'*Ralph*,' hissed the other one. 'You're not supposed to say *where*.'

'Burning stars, Gilly, it's only Princess *Rose*.'

'Ah, yes, the west tower,' said Wren, mildly. 'I haven't been up there in ages. Is there something I should know?'

Ralph's cheeks went as red as his beard. 'Nothing of note.'

'Certainly nothing for you to worry yourself about, Princess,' Gilly assured her. 'There ain't no threat that'd ever breach the palace walls without *us* knowing.' He winked. 'We're the best in the kingdom. Ain't that right, Ralph?'

Ralph puffed his chest up. 'Nothing gets past us, Princess.'

It was an effort for Wren to keep a straight face. 'Well, thank the Great Protector you two fine soldiers have everything perfectly under control. Perhaps I'll sleep soundly tonight, after all.'

Gilly grinned, toothily. 'I should hope so. You'll need your beauty sleep for the wedding.'

'Goodnight, gentlemen. Keep up the sterling work.'

The soldiers dipped their chins. 'Good night, Princess.'

Wren spun around and strode down the corridor. The second she turned the corner, she flung caution to the wind and broke into a run. When she reached the hallway that led to the west tower, she heard the rumble of distant conversation. She slipped a pinch of sand from her drawstring pouch and uttered one of her well-practised incantations. '*From earth to dust, on this stone ground, may my footsteps make no sound.*' The sand disappeared as it fell, taking the noise of her approach with it. She kept to the shadows as she crept closer.

'. . . not to breathe a word of my nightly visits here to anyone,' came a low, menacing voice. It raked along Wren's skin, and she knew, without ever having heard it before, exactly who it belonged to.

Rathborne.

The nearness of her parents' murderer sent a shock of fear through Wren. She had been preparing to meet this man her entire life, and yet she was struck by the sudden trembling in her fingers, the rattle of her pulse in her ears.

'I won't have my personal business offered up as palace fodder. Is that understood, Chapman?'

'Yes, sir. Of *course*, sir,' came Chapman's reedy voice. 'As ever, you can count on me for the utmost discretion.'

Wren could just make out Rathborne's shadowy figure up ahead. He was tall and thin as a quill, and he moved with unnerving grace. Firelight flickered along his pallid skin, turned the greying strands of his hair amber. Chapman scurried alongside him, like a palace rat. They were surrounded by guards; one at each side, and two at the rear.

'You four are to wait here until I return, and if I catch word of anyone drifting off, I will hang you from the Protector's Vault by your bootstraps.' Rathborne promptly removed a key from a piece of twine around his neck and slotted it into the door to the tower. He paused to look over his shoulder. 'Chapman, patrol the halls for anything untoward. If you feel even a modicum of suspicion, raise the alarm.'

Chapman tucked his scroll under his arm and gave a rousing salute. 'Rest assured. Not even the tiniest moth will get past me.' He sniffed left and right, and then promptly took off on his patrol.

The door to the west tower groaned as it opened. Rathborne swept inside alone, letting it close behind him with a resounding thud. The guards arranged themselves either side of the door, backs stiff and gazes alert.

Wren lingered a while in the shadows, but it soon became clear that Rathborne wasn't coming back out. She took off the way she came, trying to figure out what she had just witnessed. When she returned to the east tower, Chapman's voice was echoing through the stairwell. The little weasel was interrogating the guards outside her room, and while Wren doubted he would go so far as to enter her bedchamber to check on her, she couldn't very well arrive back in the middle of their conversation. It was bad enough that the guards were still half-asleep from her spell.

She quickly descended the stairwell, tiptoeing down into the bowels of the tower, where she waited for Chapman to leave. In the darkness, Wren's anxiety began to fester. She pressed her fists against her eyes and tried to calm her breathing. Rathborne was skulking around the palace as if he was up to something, and though she had no clue what it was, she had a bad feeling about it. Between the Kingsbreath's evasiveness and Rose's surprise Gevran fiancé, everything had suddenly become much more complicated.

The sooner Wren came face to face with the Kingsbreath, the sooner she could figure out what on earth was going on. She hadn't come this far to be foiled by someone else's plotting. She wasn't going to let anything – or anyone – get in the way of her coronation.

A faint breeze tickled Wren's cheeks, rousing her from her panic. It was coming from under the door at the bottom of the stairs. It yielded with a sharp push, and Wren found herself in a disused cellar, full of dusty casks and old furniture. She followed the breeze into the darkness, until she came upon a broom cupboard. Her fingers tingled as she opened it, something deep and primal stirring in her bones. The air in here was laced with old magic and it was calling out to her.

She stepped inside and let the door close behind her until she could see nothing but a pair of white symbols etched into the wall. They shone out into the blackness, like two tiny stars.

Witch markings.

She traced her finger over them, and the wall released a low, keening groan. The stones cleaved apart to reveal a narrow opening. Warm air tickled Wren's cheeks as she stepped through the doorway. The passageway was cold and damp, the darkness feathered by purple flames that flickered from hollows in the walls.

'Everlights,' whispered Wren. They were cast by tempests, designed to burn until they were blown out – however long that might take. Every winter, during the Festival of Flame, Banba would ignite huge silver bonfires along the rocky shores of Ortha. They would blaze for seven days and nights, until it looked as if the sea had swallowed the sky, and all the stars were burning from within.

Wren's steps quickened as she followed the purple lights. Thea had told her about the network of tunnels that once existed beneath Anadawn Palace, but Wren believed – as they all did – that the old passageways had been sealed up by Rathborne when he rose to power eighteen years ago.

Wren's laughter echoed all the way down the tunnel. The arrogant fool had missed one! But of course, it would never have shown itself to him. Not with the witch markings guarding the entryway, those two simple symbols stronger than any lock in all of Eana.

Wren wound her way deep into the underbelly of Anadawn until the tangy scent of river water reached her on the breeze. She started to run, then, and she didn't stop until she got to the end of the tunnel, where the night sky twinkled through the grill of an old storm drain. The wind tickled her face as she shoved the grill aside and hauled herself up on to the riverbank. Mud stained her nightgown as she crawled through the slimy reeds, until finally, she was standing alone on the banks of the Silvertongue.

Wren's laughter soared on the river wind. No matter what obstacles Anadawn threw at her, the witches still protected her. Tonight, they had shown her that. A nearby rustling startled her from her triumph. She whipped her head around just in time to see a familiar white blur bounding through the reeds towards her.

'Elske, NO!' she shouted, but the wolf leaped at Wren like an excited puppy, the full force of her weight toppling them both. Wren giggled and squirmed as the wolf licked her face. It took an age, but she finally managed to push her off. She was still laughing when she scrabbled to her feet and found herself face to face with Elske's master.

Oh, rotting carp.

Captain Tor Iversen regarded Wren as if she were a wraith dredged up from the river. 'Princess Rose? Is that *you*?'

Wren used her sleeve to casually wipe the drool from her face. 'Good evening, soldier,' she said, mildly. 'Pleasant weather we're having, isn't it?'

Tor blinked in confusion. 'What brings you down here at such a late hour, Your Highness?'

Wren felt a strange tightening in her stomach. 'Is it late? I hadn't noticed.' She was all too aware of the blush rising in her cheeks. 'I was just getting a spot of exercise.' She swung her arms for added effect.

Tor's brows lifted as he swept his gaze over her nightgown. It was thoroughly damp and covered in mud. 'Is this what an Anadawn princess wears to exercise?'

'Oh, I know I'm *hopelessly* mucky.' Wren laughed airily, refusing to acknowledge the fact she was quite clearly dressed for bed. She was thankful at least that her nightgown covered her slippers. 'But I prefer to run in the reeds. It's so much better for the knees.' She gestured vaguely at his muscled arms. 'I don't need to tell you that, soldier. You're certainly no stranger to exercise.'

'I'm not familiar with this kind,' said Tor.

'Well, we like to do things differently in Eana.'

'Evidently.'

'Though perhaps it would be best to keep this just between us,' said Wren, as though the thought had only just occurred to her. 'I would hate for Prince Ansel to ever think of me in such a state of . . . disarray.'

Tor's lips flickered, but he resisted the smile. 'As you wish, Your Highness.'

Elske began to sniff at Wren's drawstring pouch. She pressed her hand over it, terrified the wolf might sense, somehow, what was inside. And what that made her. 'And speaking of dear Ansel, you've left your sleeping prince all alone.' She raked her fingers through her hair to draw the guard's keen gaze away from her waist. 'Shouldn't you be at your post?'

Tor stiffened. Wren had clearly caused offence by questioning his sense of duty but she didn't regret it one bit. His frown was exquisite. 'I'm on my way back,' he said. 'Elske was feeling restless so I took her for a walk.'

Wren smiled at the wolf. 'I know the feeling.'

Tor scratched behind Elske's ears and a certain softness came over him, at odds with the sharp lines of his uniform and the menacing glint of his sword. 'She is far from home, but the midnight moon soothes her.'

'And what about her master?' said Wren, unable to help herself. Even as a child, she would stick her fingers too close to Banba's bonfires, relishing the crackle of danger. Besides, in her filthy nightgown on the muddy banks of the Silvertongue, she was practically dancing in the flames already. 'Are you homesick, too?'

'A soldier's home is where his sword is.'

Wren snorted. 'You can't really mean that.'

'I mean everything I say, Your Highness.' He looked at her and Wren noticed the flecks of silver in his eyes. *Well.* 'I apologize for interrupting your exercise.' She wondered if he was making a point about her own truthfulness. 'Would you like me to escort you back to your tower?'

They had lingered too long in the darkness, and the Gevran was uncomfortable. If anyone saw them down here together, questions would be raised. Princess Rose would never let herself get caught in such a compromising position. Wren only wished she had thought of that before she climbed out of that bloody tunnel.

'I'm afraid I'm not quite finished my route yet.' She pointed vaguely over her shoulder, hoping he wouldn't ask where she was going. 'Don't let me keep you from your post, soldier. You've been absent far too long already.'

Tor's jaw twitched as the barb landed. He dipped his chin. 'Very well, Your Highness.'

Wren swung her arms as she flounced away from him. She could feel the Gevran's eyes on her as she waded back through the reeds, her feet squelching in and out of the soupy mud. Only when she was sure Tor had relinquished his curiosity and returned to the palace did Wren sink on to her hands and knees to crawl back into the storm drain. Back in the tunnel, her ancestors' everlights danced as she passed them, and though deep down Wren knew it was her own addled imagination, she could have sworn they were laughing at her.

Rose
CHAPTER 10

Rose and the bandit rode long into the darkening night. The sand went on and on and on, swallowing the horizon. The sky was a velvet tapestry, melting from purple, to indigo, and finally an inky black. The stars came out in full splendour, each one shining brighter than the last as though they were trying to outdo each other.

'Beautiful, isn't it?' said Shen, close to her ear. 'I bet you never knew the desert could look like this.'

'I suppose it is nice,' Rose conceded. 'If you like this kind of thing.'

He laughed, and Rose was perturbed by how familiar the sound had become . . . by how pleasant she was starting to find it. She shifted in her seat, trying to put some space between them. A breeze stirred the end of her cloak and the faint smell of seawater tickled her nose. 'Who does this cloak belong to anyway?'

'A friend,' said Shen. Then he paused. 'A friend who wanted you to have it.'

'Sounds like a loyal subject,' said Rose, drawing the

cloak tighter.

Shen snorted. 'Something like that.'

Riding at night was infinitely more pleasant than riding by day. The cool air kissed Rose's cheeks, the crescent moon grinning over her as if it knew a secret and wasn't telling. Shen hummed as they rode, and even though Rose would never admit it out loud, it was rather a pleasant sound.

And, cheering her even more, in the far distance she could soon make out the moon-shadow of the Mishnick Mountains. They were still impossibly far away but the sight of them bolstered her confidence that they might soon come upon other signs of civilization – a town or village, perhaps.

She clutched the locket around her neck. *I'll be back to you soon, my sweet Ansel.*

By now, she'd already missed their second date. The poor prince must be going out of his mind with worry! Guilt sluiced through her at the thought of how empty Ansel's days at Anadawn would now become after he had journeyed so far to spend time with her. She wondered if he had joined the search party and was trawling through the Eana countryside at this very moment, looking for her. The thought brought a secret smile to Rose's face.

'What is that?' said Shen, leaning over her shoulder. 'That thing you keep playing with?'

Rose closed her fist around the locket. The encrusted diamond snowflakes dug into her palm. 'It's a gift from my beloved, if you must know. He designed it himself and brought it all the way from Grinstad for me.'

'Can I see it?'

'Of course not. This locket is worth more than any trinket you have ever stolen.'

Shen clucked his tongue. 'Rude of you to assume I'm a thief.'

'Considering you have stolen *me*, it is a fair statement.' Rose exhaled loudly. 'Are you always this insufferable?'

'Depends who you ask.' Before Rose even realized what was happening, Shen had slipped the locket off her neck. He held it up to the moon, starlight catching in its diamond snowflakes, then let out a low whistle. 'This does look expensive.'

'Give it back!' Rose twisted in her seat, swiping desperately at the locket. 'That's mine!'

Shen dangled it out of reach. 'Careful, Princess. All that wriggling might make you fall off.'

'I order you to return my locket!' fumed Rose.

To Rose's alarm, he began to pry the locket open. 'Now what has your Prince Charming left for you in here? A portrait of himself? A vow of eternal love?'

'Don't you dare open that!'

The locket popped open in Shen's palm, revealing a ribbon of blond hair. '*Stars above*, Princess. Don't tell me that's what I think it is . . .'

Rose lunged for the locket but he whipped it away. A rogue breeze curled around the hair and lifted it into the air.

'No! My love!' Rose leaped off the horse, her feet sinking

in the sand as she desperately chased after it. The locket itself was a thing of beauty, but the gift of Ansel's hair held far more value. It felt like a promise between them – a promise she was now breaking.

Shen's laughter floated after her. 'That isn't your love, Princess. That's . . . *hair*.'

'It's all I have of Ansel!' cried Rose. 'Perhaps all I'll ever have of him if I never get home!'

Shen fell silent on his horse. He watched her leap around the sand until the golden hair blew off into the desert night. 'Watch your heart rate. You don't want to attract another blood beetle.'

Rose whirled towards him, her words coming through gritted teeth. 'What I *want* is to go home.'

'Just get back on the horse before you hurt yourself,' said Shen. 'I'm sorry about your beloved's hair. These desert winds have a mind of their own.' His lips twitched. 'And here. You may have your precious locket back. Lucky for you, it's not to my taste.'

He dangled it above her.

Rose snatched it back. She sighed as she settled the locket around her neck, then she swung up on to Storm's back and landed neatly in front of Shen.

The faster we get through this desert, the sooner I can escape.

And besides, Ansel had an entire crop of beautiful wheat-blond hair. He could surely cut another lock for her when she returned to Anadawn.

They rode on in silence.

'I'm sorry about taking your locket,' said Shen, after a while. 'It wasn't my finest moment.'

Rose stared resolutely ahead. 'Why don't I believe you?'

'I want to make it up to you.'

'Then take me back to Anadawn.'

'We both know I can't do that. But I can take you somewhere else you might like.'

Rose perked up. This new destination might have people. She might finally have a real chance at escaping. 'I'm listening . . .'

'We're almost there.' Shen guided Storm through two rippling sand dunes and Rose realized with sinking disappointment that 'somewhere else' simply meant 'somewhere in the desert'.

Between the shifting dunes was an unexpected oasis – a mass of desert shrubs and towering cacti covered in small white flowers. And just beyond it, a glittering black pool.

Shen hopped off Storm, waiting for her to follow. 'Be careful of the thorns.'

'My name is Rose,' said Rose, wryly. 'I know my way around thorns.' And wanting to see that shimmering pool up close, she slipped off the horse and followed Shen as he weaved his way through the prickly shrubs.

The pool sparkled like diamonds, reflecting the night sky. Wisps of steam curled up from the water, beckoning her closer. Rose grinned, seized by an unexpected giddiness as she reached the edge. She had found a hidden treasure in the desert, a place she could never have imagined back at

Anadawn. She leaned forward, trying to catch a glimpse of her reflection.

'This is Balor's Eye. It's a natural hot spring.' As with everything in the Ganyeve Desert, the bandit sounded momentously proud of it. 'In all of Eana, there are only a handful of people who know it exists.'

And now I am one of them, thought Rose, proudly.

For I am Eana, and Eana is me.

'It is quite something,' she admitted.

'Just wait until we're in it.'

Rose came abruptly to her senses. 'I'm not getting in there with you!' she spluttered. 'That is . . . I mean, what . . . Who do you think . . . I would *never*. I'm engaged!'

'Calm down, Princess. I'm not trying to besmirch your reputation. I'll sit on the other side of the spring.' Shen gestured at her sand-mussed nightgown and matted hair. 'Unless you'd prefer to go on looking like a dirty desert rat.'

He began to strip off his shirt.

Rose's eyes widened, then she quickly snapped them shut. Surely the first shirtless man she was meant to see was her husband. But for some reason, in her mind's eye she couldn't imagine Ansel in anything but a fashionable doublet, or perhaps an exquisitely tailored frock coat.

'I always stop here when I cross the desert. It relaxes my muscles after riding for hours on end,' Shen went on, casually, as if they were simply talking about the weather and he wasn't currently shirtless. Rose peeked out of one eye and quickly shut it again.

Make that *nearly naked*.

He was only in his undergarments. *Burning stars!*

'You can look now.' Shen's voice was suddenly distant. Rose opened her eyes to find him soaking on the far side of the hot spring, his head tipped back and arms spread wide. He looked obscenely comfortable.

'Well, you enjoy it,' she called out. 'I'm fine. More than fine. I'm *great*. I'll go and wait with Storm.' She gripped her locket as she turned.

'Suit yourself,' said Shen, settling deeper into the steam.

Rose took a step away, and then paused. 'I am . . . rather dirty.'

'You are.'

'And sore.' She sighed. 'I would really quite like a bath.' Surely Ansel would appreciate the importance of good hygiene. He was impeccably kept, after all. And a princess should always be clean. He would understand that. She was Rose Valhart, the famed beauty of Eana, for goodness' sake! It simply wouldn't do for her to traipse across the country looking like a bedraggled desert rat, captive or not. Especially if she was hoping to be rescued sometime soon. She couldn't let her subjects see her in this sorry state. They might not even recognize her!

Her mind made up, Rose dipped a toe in. *Oh!* It was so warm! 'How deep is it?' She flushed. 'I can't swim.'

'As deep as your trust in me,' said Shen.

'It wouldn't come up to my ankles if that was the truth.'

Shen chuckled. 'You'll be able to stand.' When Rose still

hesitated, his expression softened. 'There's no shame in not knowing how to do something, Princess.'

She looked longingly at the steaming water. She was filthier than she'd ever been in her life and sorer than she ever imagined possible. And it wasn't as if anyone would ever find out . . . 'Close your eyes. And turn around. I mean it!'

She was surprised when Shen did as she asked. With a deep breath, Rose shed her cloak and then her nightgown. Beneath it she wore a pink chemise, and her delicate underthings. Last, she took off her locket and laid it gently on a rock. *Oh, Ansel, forgive me.*

Rose stepped into the hot spring, inhaling sharply as the water lapped against her skin. She settled into the warmth, making sure to tug her chemise down. She sighed in pleasure.

Shen cleared his throat.

'You may turn around now. But stay on your side,' said Rose.

Shen resettled himself with a grin. 'I've got to admit, I never thought I'd be bathing with a princess.'

'We aren't bathing together. We're sharing space. *I* am *allowing* you to remain in my presence.'

Shen turned his gaze on the stars. 'Whatever you say, Princess.'

Rose let herself relax, sinking until the water was almost up to her chin. Then she tilted her head back, her hair floating around her like a halo as she looked up at the stars.

They calmed her pounding heart.

For a long time, the only sound was the occasional whisper of the sands and the water lapping against the stones. With only the sky as her witness, and as desperate as she was to return home, Rose could admit to herself that sitting in this steaming hot spring in the middle of the night was, in fact, quite nice. Even with a desert bandit for company. And while she'd never say it out loud to him, it really was the best bath she'd ever had. Even better than the ones Agnes drew at Anadawn, with mountains of bubbles and perfumed soaps.

Anadawn. Not for the first time, Rose wondered what was happening in her absence. The palace must be in uproar. Perhaps all of Eshlinn, too. Her soldiers would be riding all day and all night to find her. Perhaps the Kingsbreath was riding with them, so consumed by worry that he wouldn't dare stop to rest until he found her.

Unless . . .

Rose tried to push the other thought away but it was already burrowing in. She knew how much appearances meant to Willem. Reputation was everything, and Rose's and Eana's went hand in hand. He wouldn't want their arrangement with Gevra to fall apart. If King Alarik got word of the missing princess, he might whisk his brother Ansel back home, and look for a more secure nation to ally with. The Kingsbreath was a clever strategist. He would likely do everything he could to keep this quiet, publicly holding court back at the palace, while sending out the best

Anadawn soldiers to find Rose in secret. Perhaps, then, Ansel did not even know she was gone. Perhaps he thought she had taken ill and was hiding in her tower!

But some people would certainly notice her absence. Celeste would never fall for such a ruse. And Cam and the rest of the cooks would miss her visits. And then there was Agnes. Her beloved maidservant would start asking questions soon, and then she would worry herself into a tizzy. They all would.

Rose had to get back.

And yet . . . As much as she hated to admit it, a small part of her was enjoying the adventure of being out of Eshlinn, of exploring parts of Eana she had never seen . . . Places she might never have known.

Sometimes, in the quiet of the palace, when Rose felt the strands of her destiny tightening around her, she thought she might suffocate. There was something about the desert air – and this hot spring – that felt almost like an antidote. It soothed a part of her she didn't know was ill.

Anyway, it wasn't the worst thing for her to see more of Eana, the country she claimed as her own. If nothing else, this kidnapping was proving to be educational. And who could argue with the merits of—

There was a loud splash across the pool. Rose snapped her chin down to find Shen suddenly on his feet, water sluicing off his shoulders as he bent over. He was swearing softly, and his hands were pressed against his thigh, where the blood beetle had slashed him with its pincer.

The cut looked severe. Rose could tell, even by the light of the moon. And worse, it was still oozing blood.

'You're hurt!' she cried.

Shen groaned. 'I thought the water would help but it's getting worse.'

Rose had never touched a man's leg before – she'd never even *seen* a man's bare leg for stars' sake – but he was clearly in agony, and the sight of all that blood stirred something deep and primal inside her. She wanted to help him. She suddenly *had* to help him, the urge so strong it sent her wading across the pool. 'Let me look.'

Before she knew it, she had knelt in the water and began gently pressing her fingers around the edges of the cut. It was deep and angry, and starting to pus. *Oh, stars!* What was she supposed to do now?

Suddenly, her fingertips began to prickle.

Shen opened his mouth to say something, then blinked in surprise. He pressed his hand down on hers. 'Don't move,' he said, gruffly. 'That's helping.'

Rose left her hand where it was. Her breathing slowed, and she felt a faint pulling inside her. Stars twinkled at the sides of her vision until she thought, for a horrifying moment, she was going to pass out. She gasped as the prickling sensation in her fingers intensified and then, as suddenly as it had begun, it stopped.

'*Ah.*' Shen let out a long, relieved sigh. He lifted his hand.

Rose pulled her fingers away from his leg. She blinked,

twice, then leaped to her feet.

The wound was gone!

The skin had stitched itself back together, leaving behind a light brown line.

She staggered backwards. 'You . . . you did that. It's witch magic! You're a witch!'

Shen's eyes were wide, the word soundless on his lips: *No.*

'*Yes,*' heaved Rose. 'You did it! I saw you do it!'

Shen shook his head, as though he couldn't quite believe it. '*You* did that.' There was a beat of silence, Rose's heart pounding so hard she couldn't think straight. Couldn't *see* straight. And then Shen said the worst five words she had ever heard in her life.

'Rose, you're a *healer witch.*'

'Liar! Take that back!' Panic clawed up her throat, choking her. 'I'm not any kind of witch! I'm not a witch at all!'

A witch, a witch, a witch.

Shen only stared at her.

'It couldn't have been me! It's not possible!' Rose's fear of the witches burned through her body, even as she remembered the tingling in her fingers, the fierce way she had wanted, almost *willed*, the wound to heal . . .

She blew out a steadied breath. No, she was not a witch at all. It was Valhart blood that ran in her veins. Blood blessed by the Great Protector.

Rose was blessed by the Protector.

'I'm not a witch,' she repeated, sensibly. 'I would *know* if I were a witch.' She stared down at her traitorous fingers. She was still light-headed. It was the hot water. And maybe the sight of the blood. '*You* are the witch.'

Shen shrugged. 'Well, you're not wrong.'

Rose began to tremble. Even as she'd thrown the accusation out, she hadn't expected he'd admit to it so plainly.

'But I'm not the only witch in this pool. And I'm definitely not a healer,' he went on. 'I didn't think *I'd* be the one to tell you, but you, Rose of Eana, are most certainly a witch.' He ran a finger along his thigh, tracing the faint pink scar. 'And an impressive one by the looks of it.'

Rose promptly fainted.

Wren
CHAPTER 11

Prince Ansel stood by the window in the drawing room, gazing out at the world. Wren studied the profile of her sister's fiancé and cursed Willem Rathborne in her mind. After sending two more notes marked for his urgent attention, she was still waiting for him to show his face. If the Kingsbreath continued to avoid her, she wouldn't be able to wriggle out of this nauseating engagement and carry on with her plan. The sky was grey and bloated, casting a dreary mist about the palace, but Ansel's mood was unnervingly bright. 'There's something so enchanting about the sound of rain. It reminds me of the pitter-patter of tiny feet.'

Wren pressed her forehead against the glass and tried to think happy princess thoughts.

It was late spring – the days were supposed to be getting warmer, not wetter. But the thunderstorm had turned the palace into a prison, and the hours were crawling by. She had spent the morning pretending to practise her sewing in her bedroom, before stepping out for a brisk walk in the courtyard with Chapman, who nearly chattered her ear off.

After that, it was a lunch of warm soup and crusty bread rolls, followed by an hour of supervised study in the library, where, much to Wren's dismay, most of the books on offer were dense historical tomes about governance in Eana.

It seemed her sister had spent every mind-numbing moment of her day preparing to rule, but Wren had no interest in the last thousand years of Valhart history. It was the time before that – the time of the witches – that would inform her queendom. She would oversee a court of them – enchanters, seers, warriors, healers and tempests all working in harmony together – and Eshlinn would be a place full of magic once more. Banba would help her see to that.

Instead of having a picnic in the woods, Wren and Prince Ansel were cooped up inside. Tor was standing sentry by the door, his wolf snoozing at his feet. Wren had caught his eye once already, and had experienced such a dangerous flare of heat in her cheeks, she had to look away. Their midnight encounter on the banks of the Silvertongue felt like an illicit secret, and though she knew she shouldn't enjoy it, it made Wren feel a bit giddy inside.

'And of course the rain makes a nice change from all the snow in Gevra,' Ansel went on, thoughtfully. 'It's so silent when it falls. Sometimes the world can feel too quiet there . . . it can make one feel quite isolated.'

Wren glanced sidelong at the prince. 'Are you often by yourself, Prince Ansel?'

'I'm sure I spend too much time with my own thoughts.' Ansel smiled, sheepishly. 'Alarik is often busy with military matters. Even when we were children, he spent much of his time practising swordplay or wrestling one of the family's wolves. And while my sister Anika has her charms, she's too much of a spitfire to ever sit still for long.' Wren thanked the stars she was dealing with the mildest Gevran royal. Mercifully, Ansel didn't seem the type to spontaneously wrestle a wolf.

'I suppose it's been worse for you,' the prince went on. 'I can't imagine how difficult it must have been to grow up without a family.' He shook his head, strands of golden hair flopping into his eyes. 'But of course, you have the Kingsbreath. And your Celeste.'

Wren tried not to flinch at the mention of Rose's best friend. She had managed to avoid her once already, but she was running out of excuses. 'I'm lucky to have Celeste,' she said, ignoring the part about Rathborne. 'She has been like a sister to me.'

Certainly, a far better one than Wren.

'In your letters, you said you were looking for something more. *Someone* more.' Ansel bit his lip, his blue eyes full of longing. 'I confess I've been feeling the same way for some time now. As though my life has been . . .'

'Unbearably tedious?' Wren couldn't help herself. 'Monotonously soul-destroying?'

'Stagnant,' said Ansel. A pause, and then, 'Lonely.'

Wren turned back to the storm. So, Rose had found a suitor who pined for the same thing she did – a lasting human connection, someone to belong to. Was that enough for her sister? The barest sliver of common ground upon which she planned to build an entirely new life? The thought stirred a deep sadness in Wren. In Ortha, she had never felt alone. The witches were like one big family to her. And of course, she had Banba and Thea, and Shen, who would gladly cut off his own arm if she needed it.

But Rose had grown up in a world of stone and ceremony, stifled by routine and constant surveillance, with only one true friend to look out for her.

'I suppose I have been lonely, too,' she said, just as she imagined Rose would say it.

'Which is precisely why we should fill our lives with children at the earliest opportunity!'

A scream built in Wren's throat. She played it off as a high-pitched laugh. 'What a novel idea!'

Ansel's face lit up. 'I wonder how many we'll have, my flower? Six feels like a nice round number,' he went on with the confidence of a man who wouldn't have to bear them. 'We can have our own little Gevran army.' He looked over his shoulder. 'What do you think, Tor? You could train them up!'

Tor chuckled, good-naturedly. 'I look forward to it, Your Highness.'

'And perhaps Elske can be their nanny,' said Wren.

Ansel's face turned serious. 'Don't be absurd, my darling. Elske is a wolf.'

Tor smiled at his boots. At least one of them got the joke.

'Let's not get ahead of ourselves with such talk,' said Wren, deftly. 'We still have our wedding to discuss.'

Ansel clapped his hands, leaping to the topic with eagerness. 'It's thrilling to think that in just three short weeks, you will be my wife.'

Three. Short. Weeks.

The words exploded like cannon-fire in Wren's head. Her stomach swooped, and for a heartbeat, she thought she was going to get sick.

She clawed back her composure, her left eye twitching just a little. 'It seems I'll have a husband in time for my birthday.'

'And a great many jewels.' Ansel beamed at her. 'I intend to shower my new bride with the finest Gevran treasures.'

So, Rose is to be married before she turns eighteen. She must wear a Gevran veil before an Eanan crown. But why would Rathborne push Rose into the arms of Gevra mere days before her coronation, and risk losing control over her and the kingdom? It didn't make any sense . . . Which made Wren even more uneasy.

'I only wish my father were still here to see us married.' Ansel pressed his palm against the window, a touch of sadness creeping into his voice. 'He always said a good man is made great by the wonder of love.'

Wren fetched her teacup and perched on the armchair nearest the fireplace, where her parents' portrait hung. 'What a beautiful sentiment. I'm sorry he's no longer with us.'

Ansel turned from the window. 'It's hard to believe it's been seven years since we lost our great king. We haven't had a hailstorm that brutal since, and thankfully, nothing strong enough to sink another ship.' A shudder passed through him, and Wren felt a sudden rush of empathy.

'What a tragedy,' she murmured.

His eyes misted. 'It brought the country to its knees.'

'Your brother too?'

'Not Alarik,' he said, distantly. 'My brother has always been ready to wear the crown.'

'How fortunate for Gevra.' Wren glanced at Tor to find him watching her. As if he was *trying* to make her squirm. 'What was he like? Your father?'

'The best I could have asked for.' Ansel lit up with the memory of his father. Wren let the prince talk, her eyes flitting to the portrait of her own parents. Her mother looked so young – just a few years older than Wren was now. Her smile was wide, her emerald eyes the exact shade of her gown. They were softened by love. Beside her, King Keir looked regal in his golden crown, one hand on the hilt of his sword, the other resting on Lillith's burgeoning bump. His eyes were soft, too.

Too soft.

'*A soft ruler is a dead ruler*,' echoed Banba's voice in her head. '*You will not make the same mistake.*'

No, thought Wren, as she tore her gaze from her parents' portrait. *I will never fall in love.*

What a foolish way to throw your life away.

'. . . my dear mother refuses to leave Grinstad Palace ever since Father died. And she hasn't played a single note in all those years. The truth is, I miss the music. What do you say, Rose?'

Wren blinked.

Ansel was staring at her. 'Will you grace me with a song?' He gestured at the pianoforte that sat gleaming in the middle of the room. 'You did promise me on our first date.'

'I did . . .' said Wren, vaguely.

Ansel beamed. 'And now we have the perfect opportunity.'

'I would hate to drown out the rain,' she said, quickly. 'As you said, it makes for such a soothing backdrop.'

'Leave the rain to the roses. I would rather bask in your musical talent.'

Wren sipped her tea, thinking. Panicking. She was no musician; she had never even *seen* a pianoforte before today. 'I'm afraid I'm feeling quite shy, Ansel.'

There was a noise from the corner of the room. Tor was clearing his throat.

'Come, my flower,' cajoled Ansel. 'It would cast such brightness to this dreary day.'

Wren hesitated. 'I don't—'

'I would like to hear it, too,' interrupted Tor.

Wren threw him a withering look.

He smiled blandly at her. 'I don't mean to be impertinent, Your Highness. I only meant to help the prince convince you. You spoke so passionately of your pianoforte upon our arrival, I have been looking forward to hearing you play.'

Ansel chuckled. 'Well, there you have it. You wouldn't

disappoint *two* Gevrans on this rainy day, would you?'

'Three,' said Tor. 'Elske is particularly fond of music.'

'Is she indeed?' said Wren, dryly.

'That, and the midnight moon.'

Wren swallowed her gasp. Was he blackmailing her? Well! The soldier's smile broadened, a challenge brewing in those stormy eyes, and Wren found – to her surprise – she very much wanted to meet it.

'Well, then. Who am I to disappoint such an eager audience?' She rose to her feet. 'I just need a moment to . . . prepare.'

She turned, keeping her back to the Gevrans as she slipped a stealthy hand into her drawstring pouch. A pinch of sand would have to do. And even then, the spell was not without its risks. For one thing, it wasn't one of her usuals. She had never practised this kind of spell before. And for another, an enchantment could not make something out of nothing. It would only alter that which was already there, to grow it or to take it away. But if Rose had music in her bones, then perhaps Wren did, too. After all, she spent every Bealtaine dancing late into the night. Shen always teased her about her sense of rhythm but didn't enthusiasm count for something?

She lingered beneath the oil painting of her parents.

'The pianoforte belonged to my father,' said Wren, recalling what Thea had once told her. 'They say he played every morning before breakfast. Sometimes he would wake the birds with the sweetness of his song.' She rubbed the grains between her fingers, and cast a hurried whisper into the world. *'From earth to dust, in doubt I pray, please give my fingers notes to play.'* Her fingertips tingled as the sand disappeared. She turned around and strode purposefully towards the piano. 'Let's see what creatures I can wake with mine.'

Ansel draped himself over the lid. 'What composition will you grace us with, my flower? You had mentioned you were an admirer of Nella Plume.' He gestured to the sheet music; inky black blobs that all looked the same to Wren. 'But I see you have been practising Claude Archer's "Flight of the Melancholy".'

'Oh, who wants to be melancholy on such an already dreary day?' Wren slid on to the music bench. 'I thought I might offer one of my own compositions instead.'

Ansel raised his eyebrows. 'Oh.'

Wren flexed her fingers above the keys. Was she supposed to press the little black ones first or the big white ones? Or both at the same time?

'It's a work in progress.' She smiled, sweetly. 'Please be forgiving.'

'Of course.'

The floorboards creaked as Tor moved closer.

Wren placed her hands on the keys. She held her breath and pressed down, wincing at the discordant clang. Her fingers twitched. They found their way to a different chord, this one harmonious. After that, another, and then another. Nimble fingers skipped up and down the pearly keys, moving so quickly she had to snap her head back and forth to keep up. The result was a brisk melody buoyed by a merry staccato. It was a bunny rabbit hopping in a meadow, a butterfly taking flight in spring. Wren's shoulders sagged with relief. She tossed a smirk over her shoulder at Tor.

He had pushed for a song – and she was giving him one.

Until, suddenly, she wasn't.

Wren's fingers sped up, her hands blurring along the keys. *Oh no.* Her heartbeat galloped, and so did the melody, the notes veering off tune and out of sync until it sounded like the drumbeat of battle. And still her fingers quickened. The melody grew louder, the wooden pins making a violent percussion with every strike.

Wren stared at her fingers in horror.

The enchantment was failing.

Ansel, still draped over the lid, was trying his best to nod along.

Tor was so close, Wren could hear his stifled laughter.

Elske had awakened, and was howling as if she were in physical pain.

'RIVER SPIDER!' Wren tore her hands from the keys and leaped to her feet. The bench tipped over in a clatter. 'Help! Somebody, HELP!'

Ansel rushed into action, rounding the piano and scouring the keys. 'Where, my flower? Point him out and he shall be swiftly beheaded!'

Wren pointed vaguely at the piano. 'There! Underneath! Oh, what an eight-legged scoundrel. He's *huge*!'

Ansel got down on his hands and knees to inspect the legs of the pianoforte.

Tor remained unmoving. 'River spiders are harmless, Your Highness.'

'Easy for *you* to say,' wailed Wren. 'I . . . I once swallowed one in my sleep and . . . and . . . nearly choked to death!'

'*Flipping frost!*' cried Ansel. 'How awful!'

Wren sniffed. 'It was the scariest moment of my life.'

Tor raised a questioning brow.

Wren ignored him. Elske was sniffing about her skirts. She pushed the wolf away. 'I'm sorry but I'm afraid I must retire. It's the trauma. I'm sure you understand.'

'Oh no, what a shame.' Ansel wilted. On his knees under the piano, he looked as if he was about to propose. Again. 'I hate to see you go so soon.'

'And I hate to leave you.' Wren dipped into a hasty curtsy. She bolted from the room, her feet hitting the stone passageway with a clatter. Elske followed her out. The wolf nipped at her drawstring pouch, pulling it loose. Wren turned around to wrestle it free, but the bag was already in the wolf's mouth.

'*Hissing seaweed.*' She crouched down, clicking her teeth. 'Good girl. Give it back, please.'

Elske shook her head. Ortha sand spilled out on to the stones. Wren crawled towards her, swiping at the pouch. 'Here, wolfy wolfy.'

A shadow fell across her.

Tor whistled through his teeth. 'Elske, *release.*'

Elske dropped the pouch. Wren snatched it, just as the wolf's paw came down on it. The string snapped, releasing a shower of sand everywhere.

'No, no, no.' Wren tried to catch the grains, but they sifted through her fingers, turning dull and brassy on the stone floor.

Elske sneezed.

Wren cursed.

'What is that?' said Tor, bending down.

Wren retrieved the empty pouch and scrabbled to her feet. 'Nothing that concerns you.'

He gathered the grains on his finger, his brows drawing close. 'It's sand . . .' He snapped his chin up. 'Why do you carry sand with you?'

'It's fertilizer,' said Wren, smoothly. 'For my roses. How do you think they grow to be so fine?'

Tor stood up, slowly. 'But you had it with you last night. Down by the—'

'Tor?' Ansel ducked his head around the door frame. 'Is everything all right out there?'

'It appears Elske is a little restless,' said Wren, clutching the empty pouch to her chest. 'I was just advising Tor to take her for a walk.' She turned around and scurried away, tossing her parting words over her shoulder. 'After all, a little rain now and then is good for a soldier.'

Rose
CHAPTER 12

Rose awoke, soaking wet in Shen's arms. For a heartbeat, everything was still. Almost peaceful . . . And then she remembered.

'Put me down, you . . . you . . . scoundrel! You witch! You scoundrel witch!' She thwacked Shen's bare chest, kicking her legs wildly to launch herself free.

'Have it your way, Princess.' Shen dumped her back in the pool.

Rose landed with a splash, her feet scrabbling against stone as she waded backwards.

'Would you really rather drown than be saved by a witch?'

'I'm not drowning,' said Rose, breathlessly.

'Well, not any more. You're welcome.'

Rose began to do the witch-warding dance again, splaying her arms and sending water everywhere as she hopped from foot to foot.

Shen pinched the bridge of his nose. 'I don't know who taught you that ridiculous dance, but I assure you, all it will do to a real witch is entertain them.'

'And you apparently know all about real witches. Being one yourself!' The words chattered through Rose's teeth and she realized she was shivering hard.

Shen sighed. 'You've had quite a shock. And we've been in this water long enough. Let's get out.'

'If you think I'm going anywhere with a lying, sneaking WITCH—'

'I never lied to you,' said Shen, sharply. He paused, then added, 'Although I will admit to the sneaking part. And yes, I am a witch. But more importantly, *so are you*.'

'Stop saying that!'

'Or what? I'll make it true?' He cocked a dark brow. 'Tell me you didn't feel your gift when you healed me just now.'

Rose crushed her traitorous fingers into fists. The tingling sensation lingered. She took a deep breath, as if she was going to start shouting again, swearing it wasn't true, that she couldn't *possibly* be one of them. But then the fear that had haunted her as a child came rushing back. In her worst nightmares, Rose would dream of power bursting from her like an inferno, blazing through her blood and her bones, until she woke, screaming for her mother. Perhaps, some small part of her had always known there was magic slumbering inside her, waiting to wake up and unravel her careful life.

'No,' said Rose, violently shaking her head. 'I can't be a witch! I won't be! Witches killed my parents. Witches started the war. They are the cause of every bad thing in

Eana and once they are all gone there will finally be peace and prosperity and . . . and . . . and . . . what are you doing?'

Shen was sloshing towards her, his dagger glinting in his hand. Before Rose could pull away, he grabbed her shoulders and pulled her close.

Rose screamed as he curled her fingers around the hilt of his knife. Then she realized the blade wasn't angled towards her. It was pointed at him. At his chest. And she was the one holding it. His other arm tightened around her waist, trapping her against him.

He stared down at her through thick, dark lashes. 'If you are still so intent on killing the witches, why don't you start with me?'

All the air left Rose's body in a single breath.

Shen tugged her closer, until the dagger point met his skin. A bead of blood slid down his chest. 'Do it.'

Rose tried to drop the knife but he curled her hand inside his, holding it steady. 'What is one less witch to you, Princess? At least have the courage to kill the first with your own hand.'

Rose was trembling so badly, her teeth were chattering. A trail of blood marked a line down Shen's chest, and the sight of it made her want to scream. Her magic roiled and thrashed inside her. It felt as if the blade was piercing her own heart, and the same blood was pooling in her throat.

'No!' she heaved. 'I don't want this! Let me go!'

Shen dropped his arms and stepped away from her.

Rose staggered backwards. 'I would never, I could never
. . .'

'Kill a witch?' Shen's smile was blinding in the dark. 'That's what I thought.'

Rose felt as if she might faint all over again. Carefully, she laid the dagger aside and pulled herself up and out of the hot spring. She wrapped herself in her cloak and gazed down at Shen. 'Would you have really let me kill you?'

'If you had *wanted* me dead, you could have done it,' he said, as he hopped out after her. He grabbed the dagger, dangling it by the tip. 'This blade would have gone straight into my heart.'

Rose was silent, then. The bandit had placed his life in her hands. With a blade pressed to his chest, he had looked past everything she stood for as a Valhart, who hated witches more than anything. Rose would rather rip her hands off than use them to harm him. To harm anyone. And somehow he had known that before she did. He hadn't seen the princess; he had seen the healer.

She thought of how naturally the craft had come to her just now, how *right* it had felt when she healed Shen. There was no fear – only purpose, and the spark of something that felt very much like joy. It was too late to go back. Rose had felt the awakening of her magic like a flare inside her and no matter how hard she tried, she knew she would never forget it.

'I had a feeling you didn't really want me dead,' said Shen. 'Lucky thing I'm always right.' Then he smirked.

'Speaking of wanting. You must have *really* wanted to heal me. With any of the five crafts, desire is the most important part.'

A sudden flash of heat crawled up Rose's neck. All the kind thoughts she had been having about him evaporated. 'I am engaged! I should have stabbed you when I had the chance, you *arrogant*, insufferable—'

He raised his hands. 'I didn't mean you wanted *me*. I meant you wanted to *heal* me.'

'I wasn't even *thinking*.' Rose plucked her nightgown from the rocks and shook the sand off it. 'I just wanted the blood to stop. It was making me sick!'

'You must have a whole lot of natural power in you to have healed me so quickly,' Shen went on, undeterred. He let out a low whistle. 'Just imagine what you could do with a little training.'

Rose ducked behind a cactus and slipped her nightgown over her head. 'I'd rather not.'

When Shen didn't answer her, she peeked her head around the cactus. He was already dressed and sitting atop the horse. He really was lightning fast. 'Did you know all this time? That I was one of them?'

'I wondered if you might be an enchanter. Like—' he stopped, abruptly.

'Like my mother?'

'Yes,' he said, after a beat. 'Like your mother.'

'The Kingsbreath had me tested for her craft when I was a child,' said Rose, in a quiet voice. 'Repeatedly.'

Shen's frown was sharp and sudden. '*Tested? How?*'

A shiver passed through Rose. All those hours spent crawling through the dirt in the gardens on her hands and knees. Willem Rathborne pushing her face into the muck under every new moon, studying her for even the barest flicker of reaction – of magic. When that didn't work, he would pack the dirt between her chubby little fingers, closing her fists with his until her fingernails cracked, while the palace guards looked the other way. '*It will be over soon, Rose, darling,*' he would murmur, stroking her hair as she sobbed. '*It hurts me just as much as it hurts you.*'

Each time, when it was over, Willem would let her plant a rose. One for every test she passed. One for every day she proved she was a Valhart.

'*I'm prouder of you now than I've ever been, Rose.*' He would pull her close, then, and press a kiss into the crown of her head, and Rose would close her eyes and thank the Great Protector for the blood in her veins. That she was not an enchanter like her mother. '*You are the jewel of my heart.*'

By the time she was twelve, she had a rose garden. And Willem Rathborne never pressed her face to the dirt again.

'Rose?' called Shen. 'How did he test you?'

'Thoroughly.' Rose fastened her cloak and stepped out from behind the cactus. 'That's all you need to know.'

Shen was silent, then. Unsettled. 'And if you *had* inherited her magic? Then what would he have done?'

'Does it matter?' said Rose, because the truth was, she didn't know. She had always been too frightened to let herself imagine it.

'He's your guardian. The way he treats you matters.'

'Sometimes his fear takes over him. It changes him, and he can't help it,' said Rose, defensively. She thought of how addled Willem had become in recent months. He was always looking over his shoulder and jumping at his shadow on the walls. Something was eating away at him, and there was nothing Rose could do to stop it.

'What will he do when he finds out about you?' Shen interrupted her thoughts, pulling her back to the oasis. 'Will he turn on you, too?'

Rose tried to swallow the new flicker of fear inside her. 'I suppose when you take me back, we'll find out.'

He glanced at the dawning sky. 'We should get going.'

Rose looked up at him. 'You are the thing I am meant to fear the most.'

'*You* are the thing you fear the most.' His face softened. 'And are you really so scary?'

Under the paling moon, everything seemed different. But Eana, blessed Eana, was still the same. 'I am Princess Rose Valhart, heir to the throne of Eana,' she said, more to herself than to Shen. And no matter what had happened in the desert, or inside her, that wouldn't change.

Shen extended his hand to her. 'What if you're more than that?'

Rose stilled. All her life, she had been the princess, an orphan raised to be Queen. To be good and gentle and gracious, to marry and beget heirs that would strengthen her kingdom and its alliances. She had never imagined she could be more than that . . . that anyone would ever *want* her to be more than that.

An eternity seemed to pass, Rose staring at Shen's hand as if she might find a map of her future in it. She thought of Anadawn melting into the distance behind them, of Willem pacing his room in worry.

She thought of the moment when she pressed her fingers against Shen's thigh and sewed his skin back together. Seamless. As easy as breathing. It hadn't felt vile, or wrong. It had felt, well . . . magical. And even though she knew she shouldn't, a small part of her had enjoyed the feeling.

Rose slipped her hand in Shen's. 'What if I don't like what I find?'

'What if you do, Princess?'

Rose squeezed her eyes shut. She was afraid of that even more.

Shen was silent as they rode, his eyes glazed in thought. Rose kept turning her hands over, looking for tell-tale signs, something she could have missed during all those years in her tower, waiting for her life to begin. They felt like the hands of a stranger now.

Witch, witch, witch.

The word tumbled around in her brain.

You are the thing that killed your mother.

You are the thing that killed your father.

As morning dawned and the sun peered over the horizon, the terrain began to change. The dunes were finally flattening out. The sand had stopped shifting, Storm's hooves thumping along the packed earth. In the distance, at the edge of the desert, an enormous tree climbed towards the sky. It was the biggest tree Rose had ever seen, with gnarled and twisting branches that reached out in every direction, as though to gather up as much space as possible. It creaked as it swayed, a distant wind fluttering in its leaves. It seemed as though it was overlooking the entire desert.

Overlooking them.

The back of her neck began to prickle. She didn't know where they were or how long they had been travelling for, but she knew with a chilling certainty that she did not want to go any closer to that tree. Or to the strange shadows rising beyond it.

'You're taking me to the witches.' An old familiar fear awoke inside Rose. They were close enough now to see that the mighty tree marked the beginning of a dark forest. She could almost sense the witches skulking in the shadows, waiting for her. 'They're in that wood up there, aren't they?'

Shen cleared the cobwebs from his throat. 'That's the Weeping Forest, Princess. And there are no living witches to be found there.'

Rose loosed a sigh of relief.

'It's the dead ones who will want to make your acquaintance.'

Wren

CHAPTER 13

Hours after her disastrous piano performance, Wren sent word to Chapman that she would be spending the evening reading about the inspiring life of Thormund Valhart, Eana's longest-serving king. Once she was left to her own devices in the library, she donned her cloak and slipped out of a side door into the courtyard. Thunder rolled across the plains of Eshlinn and the rain was still bucketing down with a vengeance. The sky was starless, the moon skulking behind a thicket of clouds. Save for the occasional fork of lightning, and a lone silver-breasted starcrest circling overhead, the palace gardens languished in darkness.

Wren dug her fingers into the soil beneath the rose bushes, but the earth was too sodden and compacted. She turned on the flowers, grabbing fistfuls of petals instead, stuffing them hastily into her drawstring pouch. Rain dripped off the tip of her nose and the thorns pricked her fingers, but she didn't care. The roses wouldn't be as strong as the Ortha sand, which bore the footprints of the witches, their sweat and songs and tears, but earth was earth, and since she needed it for her enchantments, Wren couldn't afford to be picky. The flowers had grown rooted in Eana soil, so for now, their petals would have to do.

After she stripped the red roses, Wren turned on the yellow bushes. They were taller, winding up to the sky as if they were trying to escape Anadawn. She rose to her tiptoes, reaching for another fistful—

A hand closed around her wrist.

Wren froze.

'What are you doing?' A flash of lightning lit up Rathborne's face, too close to hers. His eyes were narrowed, his frown sharpening the angles of his features.

Fear pooled in Wren's throat. For years she had imagined what it would be like to get this close to the Kingsbreath, but she had never pictured it like this. Alone and unarmed, in a dark and raging thunderstorm.

Rathborne tightened his grip, gently squeezing the bones in her wrist. Wren heaved a terrified breath, trying to regain control of her emotions, but panic flooded her. The petals tingled against her palm, the sudden surge of anxiety coaxing the flow of her magic. 'Rose, darling. Have you lost your tongue?'

'Perfume,' said Wren, weakly. 'I'm . . . m-making a new scent.'

'You know how I feel about you being out here at night.' Rathborne dropped her hand. 'Isn't your prince keeping you busy?'

'I . . . Yes. Of course.' Wren released the petals before

they could betray her, and curled her hand into her chest. She felt injured by his touch, his nearness. She reached blindly through her haze of hatred, searching for the right tone – one of respect, of deference. 'But the truth is, Prince Ansel and I still barely know each other. I . . . we . . . that is to say, the prince and I were thinking, it might be an idea to postpone the wedding by a few months . . .' *So I can get my crown, and with it, the freedom to make my own decisions* 'So we can spend more time together,' she lied.

Rathborne stared at Wren. 'I arranged Prince Ansel's early arrival at Anadawn for *precisely* this reason,' he said, in a low voice. 'I've gone out of my way to grant your request for more time together.'

'But—'

'Rose, darling. You are being very ungrateful.'

Wren frowned. 'It's just I've been thinking a lot about—'

'Don't think, Rose.' Rathborne patted her head, then moved his hand down along the side of her face, his fingers pressing ever so slightly against her jaw. Wren wanted to open her mouth and bite them off. 'I've told you a hundred times, when you think too much, you worry. You're going to make yourself ill.'

Wren exhaled through her teeth, and tried one more time. 'I just think if we wait until after my coronation, then things will be so much clearer. I can decide whether—'

'Did you hit your head?' said Rathborne, abruptly.

Wren blinked. 'Pardon me?'

His eyes flashed, and his voice took on a dangerous

edge. 'You seem to have forgotten who makes the decisions around here, Rose. I have spent too long crafting this alliance for you to cancel it on some mindless whim.'

Wren's anger surged, overcoming the swell of her panic. 'Well, perhaps we should rethink the alliance, too,' she said, boldly.

'Only a fool would renege on a deal with King Alarik,' snarled Rathborne. 'And what would we do about our witch problem, then? Continue to let them fester like a wound in the side of this country? Let them gather and grow until they force another war upon us? Do you want them to take over our noble kingdom and destroy everything it has become?' He shook his head in revulsion, before answering for her. 'No, of course you don't.'

Wren dug her fingernails into her palms and tried to keep her voice steady. 'I just don't see why we have to be so rash.'

'As long as the witches exist in this land, they could strike at any time.' He raised his finger in warning. 'There is always room for trouble, Rose. You should know that better than anyone. So, wear your veil and your white dress and let King Alarik do what he was born to do. After all, there's no army as brutal and unyielding as the Gevrans. It won't be long before we can have peace in Eana at last.'

Wren was swept up in a hurricane of rage as Rathborne's plan came into sharp focus. In return for having a foot in each continent, Alarik Felsing was going to set his army loose on the witches. For a heartbeat, she considered throttling the Kingsbreath right there in the rose garden.

But they were surrounded by guards, and she knew, even in the eye of her fury, that there was a better way to handle this. To handle *him*. Willem Rathborne was clearly not a man to be reasoned with. It wouldn't be wise to waste her breath – or rattle her careful composure – by trying.

'The wedding will stand, even if I have to carry you down the aisle myself.' He leaned in close, until Wren could smell the rancid stench of his breath. 'Do I make myself clear?'

She nodded, mutely.

Rathborne tutted under his breath. 'I don't know what's got into you today. I didn't raise you to be so quarrelsome. Not to mention, Prince Ansel would think you a lunatic if he saw you out here ripping your roses apart. I don't have to remind you how important your good reputation is. *We* have been cultivating it for eighteen years.' Wren didn't miss the way he lingered over the word 'we'. He stepped aside, shooing her like a dog. 'Don't let me catch you like this again. I'd hate to have to lock you in that tower of yours . . .'

He returned to the darkness, leaving the whisper of his threat hanging in the air.

Wren clutched her drawstring pouch as she hurried out of the rose garden, not daring to look over her shoulder. She only allowed herself a breath of relief when she was safely back in her bedroom, shirking her sopping dress and loosening the strings of her corset.

The pathway to the crown had become infinitely more dangerous. Not only did Wren have to contend with a moon-eyed prince obsessed with marrying her, but with

Ansel came a bloodthirsty alliance that would spell the end of the witches for good. Wren couldn't let that happen – she *wouldn't*.

There was only one course of action left. Since Willem Rathborne was intent on making her go through with the wedding and all the brutality that would come with it, she had no choice but to remove his influence over Rose's life as soon as possible. Wren sat at her vanity and dragged a brush through her hair, her green eyes blazing in the mirror. It was time to plot a murder . . .

Rose
CHAPTER 14

The closer they drew to the giant tree, the cooler the air became. Even as the sun rose higher in the sky, the temperature continued to drop. Rose shivered in her cloak, her fear mingling with curiosity. She craned her neck, desperate to know more.

To know what Shen knew. To know more about who she was. What she was. Staying with him was the only way to find out the truth.

'This is the Mother Tree.' He spoke now with quiet reverence. 'It marks the grave of Ortha Starcrest, the last true witch queen of Eana.'

Rose frowned, searching the annals of her mind for the name. 'Ortha . . . Starcrest? Like the birds? I've never heard of her. Or any witch queens, for that matter. From where did she rule? That tree?'

Shen stared at her in disbelief. '*Hissing seaweed.* Do you really not know your own history?'

Rose looked at him, blankly.

'This country belonged to the witches long before your

precious Protector ever set foot in it. He was nothing more than a dangerous, jealous man who feared the witches almost as badly as he envied them, so he overthrew their queen and turned the kingdom against them.'

'Don't be ridiculous. The witches had no such kingdom. They were wild creatures, roaming from country to country, skulking in the forests and mountains and—'

'Anadawn Palace was built by the witches,' Shen cut in. 'The old witch queens and kings made Eana what it is. The Valhart royals have stood on their shoulders for over a thousand years, only to crush their memory deeper and deeper into the earth.' His words were crisp and biting. 'How else could they claim this country for their own?'

To that, Rose said nothing. But her mind was whirring. The idea of witch queens and kings would have seemed preposterous to her only yesterday but she was beginning to think that despite all the hours she spent in the Anadawn library, there was a lot she had yet to learn. Not just about her country, but about herself, too.

As they passed the Mother Tree, Shen bowed his head. Rose shivered in her nightgown, pulling her borrowed cloak tightly around her shoulders. She glanced back with longing at the Restless Sands. The desert might have scared her once but at least she knew what lay behind her.

A softly glowing seed floated down from the Mother Tree and settled on the edge of her cloak. Another followed, and then more gathered, cascading around her like luminous raindrops.

Beyond the sentry tree, the forest opened like a dark mouth. The trees clustered tightly around them, the gnarled limbs twisted around one another so it was impossible to tell where one ended and another began. Tendrils of moss hung from every branch, swaying in the earthen breeze. The vines swept so low they brushed the ground, the trunks bending as though they were bowing.

'I don't want to go any further,' said Rose. 'I've changed my mind.'

'No turning back now,' said Shen, nudging Storm onwards. 'You will see the truth of what happened here. What your Great Protector did.'

Rose had to push the vines aside as they rode through the trees. They reached out and stroked her face, moss trailing along her arms as though searching for something beneath her skin. The wind swept through the forest after them, and as it did, the sound of weeping filled the air.

Rose whipped her head around. 'Where is that sound coming from? And what are these things?' She eyed the luminous seeds that had landed on her cloak. When she reached down to brush one off, a vision exploded in her mind.

A young woman with russet hair and freckled cheeks bent over a broken body. All around her lay the bodies of hundreds more, men and women, wounded and wailing, across a battlefield choked with fire and smoke. Witches screaming as they died. Others lying utterly still. The young woman snapped her chin up, eyes flashing at Rose.

'Please,' she begged. 'I can't save them all.'

A silver arrow came from the sky and pierced the woman's heart. Blood pooled from her chest as she fell, her gaze still on Rose.

Rose gasped as the vision cleared. 'That woman, just now! Did you see her, too?'

Shen gestured past Rose, to the trees swaying around them. 'The Weeping Forest is a graveyard, Princess. The Mother Tree marks the spot where Ortha Starcrest was cut down by the Valharts over a thousand years ago. Many witches were slain here by the Protector and his army.' He held a hand out, a mossy vine trailing between his fingers. 'The spirits of those who died in that war still linger in this forest. Their last memories dwell in the Mother Tree, and float out when they sense a witch nearby. To pass on their story.' He raked his gaze over her cloak. 'And it looks as if many of them are coming out for you.'

Rose tipped her head back. Hundreds of glowing seeds lit up the gloom of the forest like fireflies. They were drifting after her, the keening wind growing stronger.

'*Witchcraft*.' Rose trembled in her cloak as an old and violent terror took hold of her. 'No, Shen. *No*. I have been through enough today. I refuse to be attacked by witches, living or dead.' She scrunched her eyes shut, hoping they might disappear if she didn't look at them. 'Make them stop. Tell them to stop!'

'I can't, Princess.'

'Then I'll run!' Rose flung herself off Storm and landed up to her ankles in mud. She cursed as she righted herself, then quickly drew her shoulders back. Fear would only encourage these dead witches. She mustn't show any of it. 'No matter. A bit of mud doesn't bother me.'

Shen watched her from atop his horse. 'I think you're going to regret that.'

'Shh.' Rose whirled around, trying to find a way out.

The seeds were coming at her from every direction now. As she stepped backwards, a vine curled around her ankle, rooting her to the spot.

'Let go of me!' she shouted into the woods. 'I want nothing to do with you!'

Another seed brushed her cheek, and an old woman barrelled into Rose's mind. Her face was impossibly wrinkled. 'We'll never disappear!' she cried in a hoarse voice as she marched barefoot across a charred field. A Valhart soldier in green and gold charged towards her, sword drawn. With a rallying scream, the old woman flung her hand out and sent a gust of wind spiralling into his chest. He was thrown backwards, his sword flying from his grip. The old woman caught it and drove it cleanly into his neck. Twelve silver arrows pierced her body as she did. She turned back to Rose, blood pouring through her smile as she fell to her knees. 'Eana's rivers will run red with our enemies' blood.' Another arrow knocked the old woman sideways. She fell into the dirt, the light fading from her eyes. 'Not today. But someday.'

She died smiling.

Rose came out of the vision screaming.

'Get these things off of me! Make them stop!'

'This is your history, Princess. And it will be the future unless things change in this country.'

'This isn't what I want!' Rose fell to her knees in the mud, trying to rip the vine off her ankle. Another tightened around her left arm. 'No, please!'

She tried to bat a drifting seed away, but as she touched it, a new vision swept her up.

This time it was a boy. He was no more than ten, with golden curls and crooked teeth. He reached out to Rose, eyes pleading as a soldier pierced his stomach with a spear. He died with the same word on his lips. *Please.*

Rose flinched as she came out of the vision, 'He was only a child!' Bile rose in her throat as another vine seized her right arm. 'And they *killed* him. They didn't even hesitate!'

'Yes, Princess. Your great and noble Protector slayed our children, too.'

The forest was howling now. Rose bucked against the vines as the seeds found her, one after another, forcing their last moments into her mind. Men and women and children, of all ages and crafts, standing against a ruthless army and dying at its feet.

The army that would soon answer to Rose.

The forest knew who she was. What she stood for.

Finally, after what seemed like hours, the last seed left her. The wind was low and keening now. The vines slithered away and Rose curled up on her side in the mud, staring at nothing.

'Rose?' said Shen, anxiously. He slid off his horse, and came towards her, his footsteps light atop the soupy mud. 'I'm sorry. I didn't think there'd be—'

'So many of them,' said Rose, numbly. 'I never knew there were so many.'

Shen said nothing, but when he offered his knee, Rose took it. Once she was back on the horse, she sat in a daze. Shen nudged Storm into a trot and they continued onwards, through the creeping forest. The trees left them to their thoughts, and for a long time, both were silent.

When light began to filter through the branches and a curling mist crept into the Weeping Forest, Shen spoke again.

'Eighteen years ago, this forest saved the last of our kind when Lillith's War turned in favour of Rathborne's army. The witches retreated and hid among the trees. The spirits of those taken centuries before them, back in the Protector's War, saved the ones still living. No Anadawn soldier was brave enough to march through here to capture them.' His laughter was hollow now. 'Consider yourself braver than your entire army, Princess.'

'I was a baby, Shen. I didn't know.'

'But you *do* know. As custodian of *your* throne, Willem Rathborne has made it clear that witches are no longer welcome in the land they planted. Made it clear what will happen if we dare show ourselves inside the kingdom of Eana. Imprisonment, then death.' Shen hardened his jaw. 'These memories show what the future you claim you want will look like. Do you still want it, Princess? Even after everything you've seen here?'

The final moments of all those witches' lives still swam in Rose's head. An ocean of faces and fears, of last words on soundless lips. She knew she'd never forget them. Not a single one.

'All I've ever wanted is to do what's best for Eana,' she said, quietly.

'You have much to learn about the Eana you claim as your own.'

'Perhaps you're right,' Rose conceded.

The mist thickened, hiding the world beyond the trees. The vines stroked her cheeks and tangled in her hair, as though to pull her back. The wind wept. The seeds were drifting after her again, their flickering lights glowing in the fog. Rose squeezed her eyes shut. Her nerves were frayed and her thoughts were reeling. She needed to get out of this cursed place and gather a moment to herself. To think. To *breathe*.

Her eyes flew open, bright and burning. 'I know what you want from me,' she said in a choked voice. 'You want me to admit it.' She could hear their whispers in her ears, feel them tugging at her sleeves. 'FINE! I'm a witch.' Her voice broke. 'I'm a *witch*.'

The wind stopped, and all was still.

The mist parted, revealing the edge of the forest. Beyond it, across a rolling plain of wild grass, loomed the knife-edge of a cliff.

As they treaded onwards, all Rose could see was endless

grey sky. She tasted brine on the wind, salty and tangy on her tongue. Waves crashed somewhere far, far below. A seagull crested the edge of the cliff, looked straight at her, then disappeared with a screech.

Rose looked over her shoulder at Shen, her voice a frightened whisper. 'Why have you brought me to the edge of the world?'

Shen kept his gaze on the cliffs. 'Welcome to Ortha, Princess. Home of the witches.'

Wren
CHAPTER 15

The day after her encounter with Rathborne in the rose garden, Wren's attempts at avoiding Rose's best friend came to a grinding halt. She had taken dinner in the dining room with Chapman, scarfing down braised beef, honey-glazed carrots and fondant potatoes, before departing for the library. There, under the excuse of evening study, she began to plan the Kingsbreath's murder. In a place with so many prying eyes and ears, Wren needed to make a clean kill – something quick and untraceable. It wasn't long before her research led her to poison.

Celeste found her tucked up in an armchair, buried under a mound of historical tomes.

'Got you!' she crowed, as she swept into the library. Wren snapped her chin up, her heart suddenly clattering in her chest. Rose's best friend matched the description she had memorized – she was tall and slender, with deep-brown skin and black curly hair that bounced just a little with each step. She had arched cheekbones, warm brown eyes and lips that were curved and smirking.

Wren shoved the pamphlet about poisonous plants she had been secretly reading down the side of her armchair, just as Celeste plucked a book from her lap. It was a mind-numbing treatise on the trading laws of Eana. She held it aloft by one corner. 'You've been taking this whole coronation thing far too seriously lately,' Celeste said, wrinkling her nose. 'I keep telling you, Rose, a *truly* good queen knows how to let her hair down.'

Wren yanked the book back, pretending to care about the drivel inside it. 'Can't I wait until the crown's on my head first?'

Celeste stuck her tongue out at her. 'I want my best friend back. I miss our sleepovers.'

'Chapman thinks I can't keep anything in my head. I'm trying to send him a message.'

Celeste perched on the arm of Wren's chair. 'Since when have you cared what Chapman thinks?' She was so close now that Wren could smell the jasmine in her perfume. 'You should be far more concerned about my opinion, and frankly, I can't *believe* you've been avoiding me!'

Wren pulled a face. 'I had an awful headache. Didn't Chapman tell you?'

'Oh yes, he told me you were too out of sorts to see your best friend, but you certainly weren't too ill to go on dates with your new *lover*.' Celeste reclined dramatically across the top of the armchair. 'Don't tell me that's important coronation business, too. I feel as if I'm being replaced.'

'Don't be ridiculous!' Wren rolled to her feet and busied

herself putting away the stack of books. 'I tried to get out of seeing Ansel, too, but he's just so . . . *attached* to me.'

'Well, you've changed your tune. You wouldn't stop talking about his floppy hair and *poetic heart* after your first date. You even went and commissioned a cake for him, for goodness' sake.' Celeste's laugh tinkled around them, and Wren relaxed a little. Rose's best friend was a breath of fresh air. It was a shame she had to live in constant fear of being caught out by her.

'Well, of course I *like* Ansel,' said Wren, deftly covering her misstep. 'But I suppose there's more to love than nice hair and pretty words.'

Celeste arched a perfectly manicured brow. 'After all these years, I'm glad to see you've *finally* started listening to me.'

Wren laughed, breezily. 'Only on rare occasions.'

Celeste got to her feet. 'And speaking of good hair and pretty words, I must tell you about my escapades with Archer Morwell, you know, the blacksmith's son? The one with the *shoulders*. I've been meeting him down by the mill.'

'You mean he has *actual* shoulders?' Wren fanned herself. 'Don't tell me he has a nose, too.'

'And *quite* a mouth.' Celeste waggled her eyebrows, and Wren laughed again. Shen was her closest friend in the world but he'd projectile vomit if she ever tried to have this kind of conversation with him. Perhaps she had been missing out.

'Tell me every sordid detail,' Wren said, eagerly. 'I've been starved of gossip.'

Celeste threaded her arm through Wren's. 'I'll tell you on our way to the kitchens. Cam's been asking for you.'

Down in the kitchens, Wren stared in silent wonder at the Gevran ice cake Rose had commissioned. It was a work of art. Five layers of white sponge had been painstakingly sculpted to resemble a glistening castle. It was lavished with ivory frosting, a silver mist curling around its base, while delicately spun sugar dripped like icicles from each mouth-watering tier.

'It's *incredible*,' she breathed. 'It looks *just* like Grinstad Palace.'

Cam, the head cook, stood behind the cake in his apron and white hat, beaming like a proud parent. 'Well, I certainly hope your prince agrees. I told you I'd get it right eventually.'

It was late. The kitchens were empty, save for the three of them, the air warmed by the glow of the ovens and the comforting flicker of firelight. Wren smiled at the cook. She had liked him immediately. He was short and plump, with a round, smiling face, tanned skin and hazel eyes. She was impressed, too, by her easy rapport with him. Against the odds, her sister had managed to find some true friends at Anadawn.

Celeste traced a whorl of frosting. 'So, when can we sample this magical cake, Rose?'

'Hands off the masterpiece!' Wren swatted her hand with a spatula as the fireworks of a glorious plan exploded in her mind. If she was going to poison Willem Rathborne, then she would need the perfect opportunity. 'I'm going to serve it at a special welcome dinner for Prince Ansel in three days' time.' She beamed at her own cleverness. 'It will be a small, private affair.' *With just a sprinkling of poison.* When Celeste's face fell, Wren was quick to reassure her. 'Don't worry, you're still invited, of course. And I'm going to invite Willem, too. I'll send word to Chapman first thing in the morning.'

Celeste's frown only deepened. 'What makes you think the Kingsbreath will come? You know he barely leaves his bedchamber these days. Father says he's gone as skittish as a mouse.'

This only made Wren wonder again about what had set the Kingsbreath so on edge recently, and whether there was a deeper reason for his ill-advised alliance with Gevra. She resolved to find out what was bothering him. For one thing, she was interminably curious about it. And for another, if her poisoning plan failed, she might turn up something she could use against him.

'Of course he'll come to dinner,' she told Celeste. 'Dear Willem is just as invested in this marriage as I am.'

Not to mention, he wouldn't dare risk offending the prince of Gevra – or his fearsome brother – by not attending. In fact, Wren was counting on it. She smiled as she plucked a lemon from the fruit bowl and tossed it in the air. It calmed her to have something to do with her hands.

'If you say so,' said Celeste, uncertainly. She returned her attention to the cake. 'You've really outdone yourself, Cam. How on earth did you get it to sparkle like that?'

'That's the snow dust.' He made a show of dropping his voice. 'Elliott knows a Gevran trader up at Wishbone Bay. Had to give him a twenty-pound tuna for a sprinkle of that.'

'I must tell Marino to keep an eye out for it,' said Celeste. 'He's keen to dip his toe into the spice trade this summer, even though I keep prodding him towards rum.'

'Maybe you should just commandeer your brother's ship,' suggested Wren. 'I've never taken part in a mutiny but I think it would be a lot of fun.' She grabbed a lime and began to toss it back and forth, yellow giving way to green and then yellow once more. She thought of the wrecked trading ships that sometimes washed up in Ortha after a bad storm and wondered if she would ever go treasure-hunting along the beach with Shen again.

'In the meantime, I can have another word with Elliott,' said Cam. 'Let's see what kind of exotic liquor he can barter from the pirates down at Braddack Bay.'

Celeste beamed. 'Is there anything your wily husband can't get his hands on?'

'Depends what you're looking for,' said Cam, with a conspiratorial wink.

'Oh, I don't know,' she sighed. 'A bit of excitement, maybe?'

The cook released a full belly laugh. Wren felt the warmth of it in her fingertips. 'Celeste Pegasi, what could be more exciting than a Gevran prince staying under this very roof? It's been *years* since we've had a wedding at Anadawn.'

She rolled her eyes. 'I meant exciting for *me*.'

'Why don't you take your chances with the Gevran boats when they come in?' Cam waggled his eyebrows. 'Let's see what they bring to Anadawn.'

Wren tried not to picture Alarik Felsing gliding down the Silvertongue. She couldn't think of anything worse than serving the witches up to him on a platter, while chaining herself to his hapless younger brother for the rest of her life. She prayed she'd never have to see that day. She grabbed a plum from the fruit bowl and tossed it in the air as she wandered around the kitchen. 'What about Archer Morwell? Isn't he exciting enough for you?'

'Archer is yesterday's news,' said Celeste, dismissively. 'You know how restless I get.'

Wren snorted. 'Well, I'm sure there are plenty of other fine pairs of shoulders right here in Eshlinn.'

'Then why did *you* go all the way to Gevra for your suitor?'

Why indeed.

Celeste turned from the mouth-watering cake. 'Then again, if the Gevrans are all built like Prince Ansel's guard, I think I'll be in luck. Frankly, it should be a crime to be that handsome. Do you know what his name—' She gasped. 'Rose! Since when can you *juggle*?'

Wren let the fruit drop with three distinct *splats*. 'I can't.'

Cam chuckled. 'And this from the same girl who has to hold her wine goblet with two hands.'

Wren picked up the fruit and hastily returned them to the bowl. 'His name is Tor Iversen,' she said, breezily. 'That's what you were asking just now, wasn't it?'

'Tor.' Cam rolled the 'r' sound with his tongue. 'I like it.'

Celeste was still staring at the bruised fruit.

Wren cursed her own foolishness. In a bid to settle her nerves, she swiped a tart from a nearby tray and shoved it into her mouth. It melted on her tongue, butter and sugar creating a symphony of delight. *'Mmm, so good.'*

'Princess, NO!' cried Cam. 'That one's full of cinnamon!'

Wren stopped chewing.

The cook was flapping about the kitchen like an addled bird.

Celeste was staring at her again. 'You hate cinnamon.'

Oh, rotting carp.

There was an awkward stretch of silence. Wren spat the tart into her hands. 'Oh no! Ew! *Ew!* Get it away from me!' She balled the half-chewed mouthful into a cloth and flung it across the kitchen, where it splattered against the wall.

Cam sighed and shook his head. 'Well, that was unnecessary.'

Wren briefly considered crawling into the oven and bursting into flames until only the ashes of her regret remained. First the juggling mistake and now the bloody tart – she had been trained better than this. She was *supposed* to be clever, careful.

She smoothed the strands around her face. 'Sorry, Cam. It must have crept up on me. Sneaky cinnamon.' She summoned a sheepish smile. 'Where were we? Oh yes! Handsome Gevrans.'

Cam swept his arms wide. 'I was just about to formally

announce that this kitchen is always open for burly Gevran soldiers.'

Celeste turned to Cam, her suspicion softening into wry amusement. 'And what would Elliott say to such a generous invitation?'

'Celeste, darling, Elliott appreciates the finer things in life. That's why he became a trader in the first place.'

'Speaking of fine things.' Celeste scooped a blob of frosting on to her finger and popped it into her mouth. 'I hear Princess Anika is a beauty. They say she's as fierce as a snow tiger. And you know how I like a challenge.'

'Oh, you are bad.' Cam descended into uproarious laughter. Wren joined in, feigning giddy excitement about her upcoming wedding, and finally, after what seemed like an eternity, Celeste started to relax around her again, sharing titbits of palace gossip and delighting in Wren's re-enactment of her disastrous date with Prince Ansel.

'Right,' said Cam, rubbing his hands. 'I'd better get started on this special dinner menu. Three days isn't very much time at all, but lucky for you, I'm an artiste.' He glanced at Wren, his forehead creasing as he studied her. 'And it will give me a chance to feed you up, too. I swear you're wasting away on us, Rose.'

Celeste cocked her head. 'I thought I was just imagining it.'

Wren hugged her arms around herself, trying to obscure the sinewy limbs the Ortha cliffs had given her. 'It's just nerves. With the wedding so close and everything.'

'Well, I have the perfect remedy for that.' Cam removed

a tray of cookies from the oven. 'Almond and butterscotch. Still warm. And on my honour, not a *hint* of cinnamon.'

'Well, thank the Great Protector for that.' Wren grinned around a cookie as she popped it in her mouth. Cam wrapped another one in a handkerchief and slipped it into Wren's pocket. Somehow, it was even better than the tart. Back in Ortha, when the nights were cold and the sea wind was howling through the cracks in Banba's creaky hut, she often wondered what she was missing out on at Anadawn.

On Wren's ninth birthday, Thea had stayed up all night baking a flour cake and Banba had risen before the sun to fetch honey straight from the hives to drizzle over it. The three of them had walked down to the shore together, Banba dulling the wind so all the gulls could hear her sing 'Happy Birthday' to her granddaughter. Wren had held the meagre cake to her chest like a spell that might lift them up and away to better times. To better cake.

'*I would give you all the luxuries in the world if I could, little bird.*' Banba had cut a slice of cake and held it in her sand-stained fingers. There was sand in everything back in Ortha; even in their teeth. '*But for now, let this cake be a promise.*'

'*There are better days ahead, Wren.*'

'*For you, and for all of us.*'

And now, here Wren was, within reach of the crown. She could taste those better days already – the flavour of an oven-warmed treat as it melted on her tongue and the slip of a silk nightgown against her skin. The warmth of a fire in her bedchamber, the bubbling caress of a morning bath. And friends, like these ones, who would gladly chatter away the evening hours in the warm belly of a sugar-laced kitchen.

Rose's life wasn't so bad, after all.

And once Wren had removed Willem Rathborne from it, it would be even better.

After saying goodnight to Celeste, Wren silenced her footsteps with an enchantment and sneaked across the palace to see if the Kingsbreath had made another visit to the west tower. When she spied his guards hovering on either side of the door, she drew back into the shadows. *Curious.* Rathborne confined himself to his bedchamber all day but was keeping a strict nightly routine. Whatever was in that tower must be important to him. Wren made careful note of this discovery in case she might need it when the time came to kill him. If her dinner party failed, she could meet him in his precious tower with a sharp smile and her trusty dagger. Not quite a clean kill, but she would relish it all the same.

She took off before she was spotted by one of Rathborne's guards. Oil portraits turned to silver suits of armour as she shuffled through the halls of Anadawn. She was so distracted by what Rathborne was doing in the west tower that she startled at the sudden thunder of footsteps up ahead.

Wren slipped into an alcove between two towering suits of armour and flattened herself against the wall. The footsteps grew louder, their shadow spilling across the stones like ink. She scrunched her eyes shut.

Don't look to your right.

Don't look to your right.

Don't look to your—

'Princess Rose?'

Wren snapped her eyes open. '*You*,' she breathed.

Tor was standing in front of the alcove, wearing a look of utter bemusement. Elske sat at his feet, her bright blue eyes pinpricking the darkness. 'Exercising again, Your Highness?'

'Oh, yes.' Wren smiled as she smoothed her skirts. At least this time, she was dressed. 'I never miss an opportunity to raise my heart rate.'

'You must be very fit.'

'And you are very bold,' she chastised. She lingered over his damp uniform and the tousled sweep of his hair. 'Were you out in the rain just now?'

'I'm afraid storms never bother Elske.' Tor's lips flickered. 'And I have heard a little rain now and then is good for a soldier.'

'Well, it certainly suits you.' Wren grinned, wickedly. She was dancing in the flames again, but *oh*, it was such fun. And it made a pleasant change from having to plot a murder. 'And it's nice to know you're in the business of taking sage advice. Perhaps I can persuade you to take a treat, too.'

At Tor's look of alarm, she burst out laughing. 'Mind out of the gutter, soldier. That was hardly a euphemism.' However much Wren wanted it to be. She stuck her hand in her pocket and took out Cam's cookie, wrapped in the handkerchief. 'I'm simply offering you one of my cook's delicious cookies.' She held her hand out. 'It might well change your life.'

Tor glanced at the cookie, but didn't move to take it.

'It's almond and butterscotch. I'm sure Cam would tell you he made it with love, too,' said Wren, mildly. 'Although I can't speak to that particular flavour.'

Elske sniffed at the cookie, then looked up at her master.

Tor rested a gentle hand on her head. 'Thank you, Your Highness, but I don't eat when I'm on duty.'

'Sheesh,' said Wren, as she unwrapped the cookie. 'Are all Gevran soldiers so tightly wound?' When Tor didn't reply, she halved the cookie and slipped a piece into her mouth. She closed her eyes as it melted on her tongue, revelling in its buttery goodness.

She swore she heard the soldier's breathing hitch. She swallowed thickly, then opened her eyes, dangling the other half of the cookie between them. 'Are you *sure* you're not hungry?'

Tor's throat bobbed. 'I'm sure, Your Highness.'

'I admire that Gevran restraint.' Wren slipped the other half in her pocket for later. 'Though I hear your King Alarik is lacking in it. He has a dark reputation on these shores, you know. It is said that his only friends are his beasts. He's cruel beyond measure and vicious in war. And he has a block of ice in place of a heart. Is it true?'

Tor's face shuttered at the mention of his king. He stood a little straighter. 'King Alarik has established himself as a strong ruler these past few years. Any country would be foolish to move against Gevra.'

Wren licked her teeth. 'I can practically taste your training.'

A muscle flickered in his jaw. 'You mistake training with loyalty, Your Highness.'

'Well, then Ansel is lucky to keep such *loyal* company. Indeed, not even a mouth-watering cookie can rattle your resolve. Though I have to say, your wolf impresses me far more.' She turned her curiosity on Elske. 'She really is a beauty. I've been thinking I'd like to get one for my birthday.'

Tor's chuckle rippled all the way down Wren's spine. 'Elske was raised for war, Your Highness. She may seem harmless but she is brutal when she needs to be.'

Wren raised her eyebrows. If this soldier was trying to frighten her, he wasn't going to succeed. He was only making her more curious. 'Like her master, then?'

His smile tightened. 'In a manner of speaking.'

Wren's thoughts turned to Rathborne, and what she had in store for him. 'How many men have you killed for Gevra?'

Tor held her stare. A storm moved in his eyes. 'Enough.'

'Did you lose sleep afterwards?'

'There is no sleep in war, Your Highness.'

And of course Gevra was a warring nation. If Wren didn't do something soon, they would bring their famed brutality to these shores. She tried to keep her anxiety from her face but Tor was watching her too keenly now, and her palms were beginning to sweat. 'When *do* you find the time to sleep?' she said, striving for that easy lightness between them.

Tor gestured at the wolf. 'We take turns on the night watch.'

'I'd be lying if I said that sounded effective.' Wren looked at Elske, who was now drooling liberally all over his boots. 'Aren't you worried she might run off while you're sleeping? To play with someone more fun, and say . . . princessy?'

Tor's laugh was surprisingly musical. It made Wren's stomach flip. 'Elske would only leave my side if I commanded it.'

'I can be *very* persuasive.'

'It will take more than a butterscotch cookie, Your Highness.'

Wren dropped to her knees and scratched beneath Elske's chin. 'How much more?' she pretended to ask the wolf. 'Name your price, sweetling. I'm wildly wealthy.'

Tor towered over her, the silver flecks in his eyes alight with curiosity. 'There's something different about you tonight, Your Highness . . .'

The back of Wren's neck began to prickle. 'Oh?'

As if some unspoken command had passed between them, Elske started sniffing at her skirts.

Wren stood up, abruptly. The air changed as Tor took a careful step towards her. Too little too late, she got the sense that she had wandered unwittingly into a storm.

He raised his hand, slowly, and she watched half-frozen as he reached for something behind her ear. 'Your hair . . .'

he said, more to himself than to her. 'I think it's changing colour.'

Wren's heartbeat faltered.

Seize control, hissed a voice in her head.

She slapped his wrist away. 'I would advise you to keep your hands to yourself, soldier.'

Tor blinked. 'Forgive me. I only meant—'

'To touch the crown princess of Eana,' said Wren, with all the iciness she could summon. It was well past midnight and her morning enchantment was wearing off. Those rose petals were weaker than she thought!

Tor raked his hands through his hair, wearing a look of such violent remorse that Wren almost felt sorry for him. He gathered himself in an instant, stiffening as he became a soldier once more – someone to fear, someone to avoid.

Wren was already backing into the shadows, hiding her changing appearance. 'Consider this your first and only warning, soldier. To save yourself from any further embarrassment, I would suggest never mentioning this little run-in again.'

'As you wish, Your Highness.' The Gevran was a statue in the dark. Wren sensed the rising swell of his suspicion with every silent footstep she took away from him.

Banba's scowling face haunted her as she made her way back to the east tower. Wren had gone looking for trouble tonight, and she had found it in the stormy gaze of a Gevran soldier. She was as thoughtless as the witch Lia, who had drowned herself in the Ortha Sea. If she didn't pull herself together soon, the next time Wren slipped up could be her last. And if she doomed herself with her own carelessness, then she would doom all the witches of Eana, too. She cradled that fear as she fell asleep, dreams of Rathborne's snarling face giving way to visions of him twitching and foaming as he died painfully at her feet.

Rose

CHAPTER 16

Rose stared down into the abyss. The ocean churned restlessly below her, spitting strips of seaweed at the cliffs. It was a beast – foaming and frothing as it waited to devour her. The very sight of it made her dizzy and dry-mouthed, and terrified, and . . . 'I can't.'

She stumbled backwards, knocking into Shen.

He grabbed her shoulders, steadying her. 'Careful.'

Rose glanced at the plummeting cliffs and felt her head spin all over again. 'Have you lost your mind?'

'Just my shoes.' Shen dropped his boots at her feet. 'You can't climb the Whisperwind Cliffs barefoot.'

'I don't want to climb them at all! Isn't there another way down?'

'Afraid not, Princess. The witches of Ortha have made their haven almost impossible to reach. Do you see those waves breaking out there? This cove is protected by a rock reef. No boat – not even your finest royal warship – can get past it without being torn to shreds. So, we'll be going cliff side.'

'No, thank you.' Rose backed away from the edge, moving quickly through the grass until something bumped into her leg. She screamed.

The grass bleated.

Shen chuckled as he knelt down. 'Hello, little one.' He glanced up at Rose. 'I didn't realize you were terrified of baby goats.'

Rose cleared her throat. 'It took me by surprise, that's all. I am *not* afraid of goats.'

Shen dropped his voice. 'Even ones that are secretly witches in disguise?'

'I don't believe you.' Rose knelt in the grass and let the goat nuzzle her hand. 'There is no way this is a witch.'

Shen gave her a meaningful look as he stood up. 'I think we've established that you are terrible at spotting witches.'

He tracked through the grass, where rickety stables winked at them through the shifting mist. Storm trotted after him, and then so did the baby goat. Rose eyed the other animals grazing along the cliff edge, goats and horses and sheep, all navigating the fog with a sense of ease that she was sorely missing. Shen returned in his bare feet with an impossibly long rope ladder. He dropped into a crouch and began to knot one end to a jagged flagstone atop the cliff.

'I'm afraid witches don't fly either. Despite what you might be hoping right now.' He winked at Rose over his shoulder, and she couldn't help but notice how his nearness to Ortha made him seem at once more relaxed.

'I meant what I said. I'm not going down there.'

His gaze shifted to the trees behind her. 'Would you prefer to take your chances in the Weeping Forest again? Alone, I might add?'

Reluctantly, Rose crept back towards the edge. This was it – the thing that would break her. Maybe even kill her. She'd survived crossing the Ganyeve. Slept in caves covered in witch markings and almost drowned in Balor's Eye. Discovered she was a witch *and* made her way through the Weeping Forest, barely unscathed. But climbing down these sheer, bottomless cliffs in her nightgown was the last straw. 'I'll fall!'

'Then I'll catch you,' said Shen, as though it were the simplest thing in the world. He looked up at her, the dying sunlight dancing in his dark eyes. 'We've come all this way, Princess. Do you really want to give up now?'

Rose looked back at Storm, grazing happily by the stables. For one desperate moment, she thought about making a run for her, hopping on to the horse's back and riding as fast as she could through the forest, across the desert, and all the way to Anadawn. All the way *home*.

And yet . . . Here she was at Ortha, with a chance to finally find out the truth about her mother.

About herself.

She drew a steadying breath. She was Rose Valhart, heir to the throne of Eana. These cliffs were part of her kingdom. And that meant they were part of her. She would stay for one day. And then she would find a way to escape.

'Very well, Shen Lo.' She narrowed her eyes at him. 'But if

I fall to my death, I promise you my spirit won't linger in that forest. It will haunt you until the end of your days, and then when you die, I will berate you until the end of time itself.'

'I'm flattered that you want to be with me until the end of time.' Shen smirked as he unfurled the rope ladder and kicked it over the edge. 'And I thought you didn't much like me.'

'Oh, you know what I mean!' Rose slipped her feet into his worn leather boots and laced them up, tightly. They were far too big and in poor condition, but there was something strangely comforting about wearing them. In her borrowed cloak and now borrowed boots, she felt a thousand miles from who she was supposed to be.

'Thank you for the boots,' she said after a moment. 'That is kind of you.'

Shen was knotting the rope, making sure it was fastened tight. 'Well, considering I stole you out of your bed and dragged you across the country, giving you my shoes before we climb down a sheer cliff that will most certainly traumatize you is really the least I can do.'

Rose scowled. 'On second thoughts, never mind.'

Shen swung his legs over the cliff. Gingerly, she did the same. For a fleeting moment, the princess and the bandit sat side by side, their shoulders brushing as they looked out over the edge of the world.

And then, as simply as if he were slipping into a lake, Shen dropped off the cliff.

Rose screamed. 'SHEN! The rope!'

His voice floated up from the misty abyss. 'The rope is for you, Princess. Make sure you hold on tight.' As if he could see the horror spreading on her face, his chuckle reached her on the wind. 'On my honour, I won't let you fall from these cliffs.'

Rose clung to the ladder with all her strength as she lowered herself down the sheer cliff face. Her hands burned, the rope chafing the skin on her palms, and still she did not – would not – loosen her grip. Beside her, Shen was scaling the rock with remarkable ease, his fingers barely touching the stone.

As promised, he had managed to remain close by. Sometimes he was to her left, sometimes to her right, and more than once, he'd scrambled down to help her find her footing when the wind toyed with the ladder. When his fingers grazed her bare ankle, Rose felt her heart thump even harder, but she was too focused on not plummeting to her death to linger over why she'd reacted like that.

'I. See. Gravity. Only. Applies. To. One. Of. Us,' she huffed.

Shen threw his head back and laughed: 'You're not the first witch to be jealous of my climbing skills. Wren always—' His eyes widened and he snapped his mouth shut.

Wren. There was that name again. Rose was sure he had mentioned it in the caves, too. But why on earth was he acting so skittish about it?

'Is Wren your sweetheart?' she needled.

'*No way.*' Shen pulled a face. 'Wren is my best friend. That's all.'

'Wren and Shen,' Rose mused. 'What a funny little rhyme.'

'Oh, it's a lot funnier than you think,' he muttered, before returning his attention to the cliff face.

Rose was about to press him on his sudden furtiveness when the wind picked up in a gust, scattering sea foam across her cheeks and casting her hair into her eyes. Her cloak twisted, the clasp pressing against her throat. She tipped backwards, losing her footing.

'Shen, the cloak!'

Shen was behind her in a heartbeat, planting his hands on either side of her arms and pinning her to the cliffs with his body. He rested his head on her shoulder, his breath warm against her ear. 'Don't move, all right?'

Rose squeezed her eyes shut.

With one hand, he deftly unclasped the cloak and pushed it off her shoulders. He let it flutter to the ground, but Rose didn't dare look to see where it dropped. She felt obscenely exposed now, stuck to the side of a cliff face, practically straddling a rope in only her nightgown as the wind whipped around her, threatening to tug it loose.

She wasn't sure if it was the absence of heat or the nearness of Shen's body that made her start to tremble. 'How much further? I'm still trying not to look.'

'Halfway there.'

'You said that last time!'

'Well, this time I mean it. I was worried if I told you the truth the last time that you would have climbed right back up.'

'Are we *really* halfway there?'

Shen pressed his cheek against the cliff face so she could see him without having to turn her head. 'I promise.'

'You keep promising me things, bandit. It's not a good idea to break a promise to a princess.'

'I always keep my promises.' His gaze lingered on hers, until the wind came rushing back with a fierce howl.

Rose clung to the rope ladder.

'One step at a time,' he said, calmly. 'You can do it.'

She narrowed her eyes. 'Why are you being so nice to me all of a sudden?'

'Because you need me right now.' Shen's smile was slow and lazy. 'And I'm enjoying it.'

'You are truly the most insufferable person I've ever encountered.'

'I'm also the person getting you down these cliffs in one piece.'

Rose bit back a smile. '*Shh*. Let me concentrate.'

With the taste of seaweed on her tongue and the wind nipping at her cheeks, Rose continued her slow descent. Her hands ached, the muscles in her legs were screaming – and oh, she was *starving* – but there was a strange new fire kindling inside her – urging her onwards, telling her not to give up. Shen stayed with her every step of the way, coaching her through the steepest parts of the cliffs and shielding her from the fiercest winds.

Towards the bottom of the Whisperwind Cliffs, the rock jutted out from the cliff face in a series of steep ridges. With her body flush against the stone and her footsteps slow and careful, Rose found that she could release the ladder and walk well enough.

After a while, a strange buzzing filled the air.

She whipped her head around. 'What is that sound? Is the cliff moving?'

Behind her, Shen chuckled. 'The sands shift but these cliffs are the bones of Eana. Even the wind can't rattle them.' He gestured past her, to a rocky plateau. 'That sound you hear is the Ortha honeybees. They build their hives in the cliff side.'

Rose gaped at what she saw. They had beehives in Anadawn, too, but they were wooden and orderly, tucked safely away in the mews by the orchard. The royal beekeepers wore hats and nets when they went near, but here, there were hundreds of hives just dangling from the cliff. 'We'll get stung!'

Shen made a barrier of his arm, as though he was afraid Rose would leap from the cliffs in horror. 'They won't bother you if you don't bother them, Princess. They're a bit like the witches in that way.'

Rose threw him a withering glance before seizing her courage and inching onwards. She hadn't come so far only to fail now.

Soon, the cliffs levelled out and the sound of crashing

waves grew deafening.

Rose dared to look.

Ortha unfurled below her, wind-battered and shining in the setting sun.

The cove was curved and golden. There were close to one hundred intricate wooden huts tucked against the cliff edge – just like the beehives – while others were dotted along rocky peninsulas that stretched like fingers into the frothy waves. There were people everywhere – men and women milling about between fishing boats, dragging nets in from the sea. Children were playing along the beach.

The sound of laughter reached Rose on the wind but the relief she felt at reaching the bottom of the cliffs evaporated once she remembered what lay before them.

Witches.

What did they want with her? Why had they sent for her? She swallowed. 'Shen, can you promise me something else?'

Shen dusted his hands. 'Depends what it is.'

'Don't leave me alone with the witches.'

He turned towards her, and Rose was struck by the softness in his eyes. 'You've been alone with a witch for days now, remember?'

'And look where that has led me.'

His smile grew. 'On the greatest adventure of your life?' When Rose didn't smile back, he turned serious. 'I promised no harm would come to you and I mean to keep that promise. You can trust me.' He pulled her down on to the sand and Rose found herself clinging tightly to his fingers. She didn't want to let go. The person she had feared most in the world only two days ago had become her anchor in this vast unknown place, and now she didn't feel safe without him.

Thankfully, her cloak had landed nearby. Shen plucked it from the sand and cast it around her shoulders. 'I told you I'd get you here in one piece.'

Rose tilted her head back to see how far she'd come. The cliffs wound upwards and out of view – into the misty abyss. She wished Celeste could have seen her conquer them. Whenever they stole away to the apple trees, she always climbed higher than Rose. Celeste was fearless like that, not afraid of the fall but of what she might miss at the top. She claimed the best apples came from there. She would toss them down to Rose, who would fill up her skirts with their spoils, before hauling them all the way to the kitchens where they would pester poor Cam to bake them into a pie.

Now Rose would never balk at an apple tree again. Celeste wouldn't believe her when she told her about these cliffs – about all of it. And Rose *would* tell her. After she faced the witches here in Ortha, she would return home to Anadawn. But for now, she rolled her shoulders back, readying herself for the next challenge. Whatever it may be.

Shen was staring at her.

'What?' she said, suddenly self-conscious.

'Nothing. You just seem so—'

'Shen! You're back!' A new voice shattered the rest of

his sentence, and Rose was frustrated not to have heard it. A young girl with fiery red hair streaming out behind her raced down the beach and barrelled into Shen, throwing her arms around him. 'We've been so worried!'

Shen hugged her back. 'You know you never need to worry about me, Tilda.'

The girl turned to look at Rose. She gasped, her mouth dropping into a perfect circle. 'She's just like Wren!'

Rose frowned. 'Excuse me?'

What did Shen's best friend have to do with her?

'Tilda,' said Shen, warningly, but the girl wasn't listening. She was staring so hard at Rose, it seemed she had forgotten to blink. 'I knew you were twins but I didn't expect you to look so—'

'Tilda!' scolded Shen. 'That's enough.'

The girl grinned as she stepped back. 'Anyways, I'm Tilda. I know you, obviously. Princess Rose.' She dipped into a clumsy curtsy. 'Everyone knows you.'

Rose turned on Shen, but he was looking at his feet now. 'Shen,' she said, in a low voice. 'What is she talking about?'

When he looked at her again, his face crumpled. 'The healer thing was overwhelming enough, and I wasn't supposed to say anything. I wanted to, I really did, but Banba ordered me not to. It wasn't my place—'

'You didn't tell her about Wren?' cried Tilda. 'I wouldn't have been able to hold that in!'

'Clearly,' said Shen, with great exasperation. 'Rose, I can explain.'

Rose forced herself to remain calm even as her heart threatened to beat its way out of her chest. It was a misunderstanding – it had to be. 'Please do,' she said, curtly. 'Who, *exactly*, is Wren?'

'Wren is your sister!' Tilda burst out. Her cheeks were bright red and she was bouncing up and down with excitement. 'She lives here in Ortha. Well . . . no, actually. I guess, technically, she—'

'*Stop talking, Tilda!*' snapped Shen.

Rose's breath caught in her throat. She couldn't think. She could barely *breathe*. 'Is that true?'

Shen winced. 'I'm sorry I didn't tell you—'

'You told me I could trust you.' Rose stumbled away from him. Of course she couldn't trust a kidnapping bandit! How could she ever rule a kingdom if she let herself be so easily taken in by a thief with pretty words and a nice smile? She'd been a fool, a terrible fool. 'You've been lying to me all this time!' Over his shoulder, more witches were drifting towards her. Suddenly, it all became too much. She couldn't face them; she couldn't face any of this . . .

Rose tore down the beach, away from Shen and his false words and the grinning red-haired girl, and all those witches swooping down on her, like vultures. Ortha became a blur around her, streaks of browns and blues and gold blending together as she ran. She heard the whispers on the wind, glimpsed faces watching her as she flew past.

Witch, witch, witch.

There was nowhere to run. Nowhere to hide. She would

claw her way back up those cliffs if she had to. She had to get out of here. She lunged recklessly for the rocks, then froze in mid-air.

Rose screamed as a band of wind tightened around her waist, like a rope. She was tugged backwards, towards Ortha. Towards the witches.

'Let me go!' She fought against the wind but it only yanked her harder, until she landed with a thud on the sand. The strange pressure snapped away as quickly as it had come, and Rose found herself blinking up into a fierce emerald gaze.

It belonged to a wiry old woman with creviced skin and short white hair. She wore a forest-green cloak, the silver clasp winking at her throat. 'Forgive me, Rose, but I can't have you leaving when you've only just arrived.'

The woman's voice was deep and earthy, rippling with a power of its own. 'My name is Banba,' she said, as she extended a hand. 'Perhaps you and I should take a walk.'

Rose glared at the woman's hand. 'And why would I want to do that?'

'Because I am your grandmother.' The old woman moved her fingers and the wind tightened its grip around Rose. She was yanked, roughly, to her feet. 'And I'm afraid you don't have a choice in the matter.'

Wren
CHAPTER 17

The secret tunnel underneath the east tower made sneaking out of Anadawn Palace so much easier than sneaking in. This was fortuitous for Wren, who had a pressing, poison-related errand to run in Eshlinn. All she had to do was wait for nightfall, then enchant the guards outside her room, before slipping down the stairwell. Within minutes, she was winding her way through the firelit underbelly of the palace, following the river wind. She clambered out on to the banks of the Silvertongue and picked her way through the reeds. While a lone starcrest circled overhead, she skipped across the bridge and left the ivory palace staking the darkness behind her.

On the other side of the river, beyond the mill, the cobbled streets of Eshlinn shimmered in the moonlight. The smell of sweet smoke and ale wafted from taverns, accompanied by the distant trill of laughter. Wren slipped by unnoticed, the hood of her cloak casting her face in shadow.

She shuffled past the Howling Wolf inn as a red-faced man hollering obscenities was carted out, nose first. From there, she crossed the street, hurrying past the blacksmith's and then the wheeler's, to where the edge of town languished in darkness. But Wren's memory was alight, and Eshlinn still matched the maps Banba had made her study, over and over again. She counted six side streets before ducking down a narrow laneway, where a single candle burned in a cloudy window.

The crooked sign above the door read:

Alvina's Apothecary.

A bell tinkled as Wren pushed it open. 'We're closing,' came a woman's voice, croaky with age. 'Come back tomorrow.'

'Devil's root.' Wren slammed three gold coins on the counter. It was littered with mason jars of dried herbs and dead insects. The shelves on the walls were just as cluttered, with hundreds of glass vessels winding up and out of view. 'And then I'll be gone.'

Alvina stepped out of the darkness. Her hair was long and raven-black, and her dark eyes were ancient. 'Poison is forbidden,' she said, carefully. 'We do not sell it here.'

Wren dropped another three coins on the counter. 'Yes, you do.'

The woman's eyes flickered from the coins to the folds of Wren's cloak, where Rose's purse was concealed inside her bodice. 'That's a lot of coin for a girl so young.'

'Will it be enough?'

The silence lingered, the woman weighing the risk in her head. Then she drew back and swung a ladder across the shelves. She climbed it all the way to the top, where the jars were dusty and unreadable. The one she brought back to the counter was no bigger than a thimble, filled with a fine white powder. 'It's tasteless. Odourless. And quick.'

Wren smiled. 'I know.'

The woman pocketed the coin. 'How does a nice young girl know something like that?'

Wren tucked the devil's root into the pocket of her cloak. 'I've done my research.'

With her free hand, she removed a fistful of rose petals from the pouch at her waist.

The woman smiled, revealing two rows of yellow teeth. 'Be careful, Princess. The poison might be undetectable but the hand that delivers it must be stealthy.'

'It will be.' Wren shot her free hand out and grabbed the woman by the throat. *'From earth to dust, I make your choice, forget my face, unhear my voice.'*

The petals disappeared as she scattered them over Alvina, leaving a faint shimmering behind.

The woman blinked as she stumbled backwards. 'We're closing,' she said, uncertainly. 'Come back tomorrow.'

Wren drew back into the shadows and in the next breath was gone. A gust of cool air feathered her cheeks as she retraced her way through the cobbled streets of Eshlinn, grinning beneath her hood.

She thought of her grandmother, grinning half a world away. Two summers ago, when the days were long and bright and the sea had lost its bite, Banba had sat with Wren along the rocky cliffs and played with her a game of poison. Their bare legs dangling side by side, she had presented Wren with three vials: one filled with bright red liquid, another clear and the final a deep, rippling purple.

'*Choose one for me to drink. And be clever, little bird. I have many years yet to live and just as many things to do.*'

Wren had sat under the blistering sun until her cheeks had burned, debating between the vials. She'd set aside first the red one first, sure it was poison. '*Good girl,*' Banba had said, as she'd tipped it into the churning sea. '*These are the guts of the reef stonefish. They would send me to bed for three days and three nights.*'

Wren had debated between the final two for a long time, sniffing and swirling, before finally chucking the purple vial over the cliff and listening to it shatter on the rocks. With a stirring confidence, she'd handed the clear one to Banba, who'd promptly drank it down. It had only been when her grandmother began to retch that Wren knew she had made a mistake. Banba had curled the empty vial into her hand. '*That was belladonna,*' she'd groaned. '*Enough to harm but not to kill. Now you will take care of me until it passes.*' Wren had lumbered to her feet, shouldering her grandmother's weight as they'd picked their way back down the cliffs, apologizing so much she'd lost her breath. '*Why did you drink it, Banba? You didn't have to drink it!*'

Banba had thrown her arm around Wren, wincing through her discomfort. '*I drank it to teach you a lesson.*' At Wren's look of alarm, she had managed the ghost of a smile.

'*If you choose to play with poison, do your research. And next time you throw my wine in the sea, ask me first.*' She'd turned, then, to be sick on the sand and Wren had averted her eyes, cursing her mistake.

And then she had promised herself, for as long as she lived, she would never let her grandmother down again.

With the vial of poison tucked safely inside her corset, Wren skipped through the town of Eshlinn. Why end such a successful evening so soon? She had wriggled out of Chapman's precious schedule and the watchful eyes of the palace for a night of her own choosing, and she intended to make the most of it. Candlelight flickered from the windows of the Howling Wolf, beckoning her inside. She scanned the room. Bleary-eyed revellers huddled around pints of ale. In the corner, a slender man with hooded eyes licked his lips in invitation.

Wren flipped him a choice finger before settling herself at the bar. She slapped a gold coin on the counter. 'Something with bubbles, please. You can keep the change.'

The barmaid snatched the coin up. 'I've got some Gevran frostfizz, but fair warning, love, it ain't for the faint of heart.'

Wren peeled her lips back. 'Well, neither am I.'

Wren hadn't drunk alcohol since the *incident* with Shen three moons ago. A merchant trader's ship had washed up on the reef near Ortha, surrendering twelve barrels of spiced rum to the choppy seas. The waves – and a little bit of her friend Rowena's tempest magic – had rolled the barrels right to them, and they had spent the evening guzzling it down by the bonfire, singing old sea shanties until their voices went hoarse and Banba came out to wring their necks.

The following day, Wren's head had ached so badly, she couldn't venture outside until the sun set. And still, the evening had found her retching her guts up into the sea, Rowena and Shen on their knees halfway across the beach, doing the same thing.

Ah, friendship.

Wren toasted to them in her mind as she took the first sip of frostfizz.

It was like a shot of ice fizzing through her bloodstream. She knocked it back, grinning at the success of her outing. Now all she had to do was sneak the poison into Willem Rathborne's dinner the day after tomorrow. With the Kingsbreath dead and the palace plunged into mourning, the plans for Rose's wedding would quickly unravel and so, too, would the impending Gevran alliance. Wren would be crowned and the witches of Eana would fall under her royal protection.

She ordered another drink, smiling at the cleverness of her plan. The tavern gradually emptied out around her, the candles in the window burning down to nothing. Wren emptied her third glass, then pushed away from the bar. Her head was swimming but she welcomed the haze. It made her feel as if she was in a delicious daydream. She floated out of the tavern, humming an old sea shanty to herself.

The streets were deserted now, the last of Eshlinn's revellers gone home to their beds, and Wren's sense of direction was fuzzy. She turned down another lane, where the walls were dark and narrow, and the stench of stale alcohol hung heavy in the air. Quickened footsteps sounded behind her. She stole a glance over her shoulder to find the creepy man from the tavern following her.

'Slow down, girlie!'

Wren spun around, wobbling a little. 'Go home, drunkard!'

The man lunged from the shadows, catching her by the throat. 'Give me the coin and I'll let you live.'

'Get off me,' shouted Wren, as she tried to wriggle free.

'Give it here!' He fumbled about beneath her cloak. His eyes lit up at the feel of her drawstring pouch. '*Ah.*'

'*No.* Not that.' Wren tried to snatch it back.

He ripped it free, releasing his hold on her. She flicked her wrist, her dagger sliding into grip. Using a manoeuvre Shen had taught her, Wren slammed down on her assailant's foot, then yanked his collar and brought her knee to his nose. It shattered with a sickening *crunch*. He doubled over with a groan, dropping the pouch. Wren swiped it as it fell, swinging her other hand around in an arc. The man cried out as she plunged the dagger into his thigh.

She yanked the blade out and kicked him hard in the shoulder. He slumped to the ground with a pathetic whimper.

'Thief,' she spat, as she wiped the blade on the edge of her cloak. 'Next time it's going in your heart.'

With her own heart clattering in her chest, she hastily restrung her pouch and hurried back towards the main street. New footsteps sounded in the dark and a figure appeared before her. Wren didn't even hesitate. She lunged from the shadows and slammed her elbow into his stomach. The man stumbled backwards and she seized her chance, ramming him against the wall and pressing her dagger to his throat. 'Don't move,' she hissed.

He lifted his chin. 'Or what?'

'Or I'll gut you.' Wren had to rise to her tiptoes to keep the dagger flush against his throat. Her head was still swimming. The frostfizz caused her to stumble. He moved, quick as lightning, spinning her around. He swiped the dagger, shoving her back against the wall and pinning her there with his arm.

The point of the blade appeared at her chin, while her hood was tugged away from her face. 'Good evening, Your Highness.'

Wren blinked up into a familiar stormy gaze. 'That's *my* knife.'

Tor raised the dagger above his head. 'Then take it.'

Wren looked up. The soldier was far too tall, and she was not about to humiliate herself by jumping for him. 'Do you think you're funny?'

His chuckle warmed the air between them.

Wren jerked her knee up, catching him between the legs. Tor groaned as he crumpled, and Wren yanked the dagger from his slackened grip. She spun on her heel, throwing a withering glance over her shoulder as she stalked out of the alleyway. 'Because I don't.'

The rush of the Silvertongue drowned out the determined thud of Tor's footfall but Wren knew he was following her. 'If you try anything, I really will stab you,' she called behind her.

'I'm *trying* to look out for you, Your Highness,' he called back. 'What are you doing here all alone?'

Wren turned around, her cloak thrown open in a gust of river wind. 'You know how I enjoy a midnight stroll.'

'In the capital of Eshlinn,' said Tor, dryly. 'In a dark alleyway. All by yourself.'

'I find I make for the best company.'

'Your nightly movements are unusual, to say the least.'

'No more unusual than the fact you seem acutely aware of them,' said Wren, pointedly.

Tor raked his gaze over her as he drew nearer, as though he was searching for clues. Wren folded her arms, suddenly conscious of her appearance. She had renewed her enchantment earlier that evening, but she had learned the hard way that the potency of the petals couldn't be trusted.

'What are *you* doing out here?' she said, in an attempt to seize control of the conversation. 'I don't see your wolf anywhere.'

'Sometimes I get restless, too,' said Tor, with a shrug. 'I was going for a walk when I spotted you through the window of the Howling Wolf. That's hardly a place for a princess.'

Wren rolled her eyes. 'Have a day off, soldier.'

She made for the bridge.

Tor jogged after her. 'Who trained you to fight like that?'

'The Anadawn squirrels.'

'The Kingsbreath said you had no training.' He drew level with her, and Wren was once again thrown off by the sheer size of him. The top of her head just about reached his shoulder. 'He told King Alarik the closest you've come to a knife is when buttering your bread.'

Wren snorted. 'Well, I suppose that makes Willem Rathborne a liar.'

'It makes one of you a liar.'

'Believe what you want.' They had reached the bridge. In the distance, Anadawn Palace loomed like a spectre in the moonlight.

Tor caught her arm, pulling her back. 'Tell me something true, Princess.'

Wren stared at his fingers on her elbow and felt a dangerous shiver ripple down her spine. 'What the hell do you think you're doing?'

He released her at once. 'I'm just trying to understand you,' he said, raising his hands. 'To trust you.'

Wren cut her eyes at him. '*Why?*'

'Because I'm charged with the protection of Prince Ansel. I cannot – *will not* – fail in that.' He hesitated, as if he wasn't sure whether to give voice to his thoughts. 'There's something *strange* about you, Your Highness. Something I can't put my finger on . . .'

Wren read the storm roiling in his eyes – caution and curiosity, and something she couldn't place. It felt threatening, like a rogue wind that might sweep her up if she strayed too close.

'Is it my dazzling wit?'

His jaw tightened. 'Prince Ansel might be easily wooed by your beauty but I will need a little more convincing about your character.'

Wren raised her eyebrows. 'I wasn't aware I was on trial but I'm pleased to hear you like what you see at least.'

Tor held her gaze. 'Appearances can be deceiving.'

Oh, you have no idea.

She turned back to the river to hide her smirk, watching the currents leap over each other. 'Do you like stories, soldier?'

Tor hesitated, but he didn't move away. 'Sometimes.'

Wren thought of something true, and offered it to him. 'Two thousand years ago, when the witch queen Mirella ruled Eana, her moods were famous throughout the land. Her consort was as handsome as he was vain, but he was charming, too. The courtiers called him the Silvertongue because of how quickly he could talk the maids into bed.'

Beside her, the soldier was silent. Listening.

'When the Silvertongue fell in love with a lowly baker from the town of Eshlinn, he changed his philandering ways. He decided to leave the queen and his palace conquests for good.' Wren leaned over the river, straining for her reflection. 'But Queen Mirella was so enraged, she used her tears to cut the land in two and made a rushing river to separate him from his lover forever.'

'Witches are not that powerful,' said Tor.

'Not any more,' said Wren, mildly. 'But this was long ago. Back before the Protector came to Eana and slayed Ortha Starcrest. When the land was bright and new, and it belonged to the witches.'

He shifted, uncomfortably. 'I've never heard of such magic.'

'I'm more than happy to educate you,' said Wren.

'What happened afterwards?' he said, with reluctant curiosity. 'I suppose the Silvertongue built this bridge to get to his lover?'

'No.' Wren turned from the water. 'The love-struck fool drowned trying to swim across it. And Queen Mirella watched from her tower and laughed.'

Tor looked perturbed. 'Such a cruel ending.'

'Revenge is a cruel business, Tor. And for that matter, so is love.' Wren took off again, swinging her arms as she crossed the bridge. 'And that's the truest thing I can think to tell you.'

The soldier stalked after her. 'When you talk of love with Prince Ansel, you make it sound as if you believe in it. But you speak of it now as if it's some kind of curse.'

'Sometimes love *can* be a curse,' said Wren. 'It can be prison. Or a death sentence.'

Careful, warned Banba's voice in her head. Through the haze of frostfizz, Wren remembered who she was supposed to be: Rose. She fluttered her lashes at Tor over her shoulder. 'And *sometimes*, love – especially the royal kind – can be a shooting star that blazes into your palace at just the right moment and fills your life with such brightness, you know you'll *never* be sad or lonely or without a rousing board game again.'

A dent appeared between his eyebrows.

Wren flashed her teeth. 'Don't worry, soldier. I won't be drowning dear Ansel in a river. I'm nothing like that horrid witch Mirella.'

Tor caught up to her in three easy strides. 'I'm not sure I believe your tale about her lover. It sounds more like a bedtime story.'

'Bedtime stories have happy endings.'

'Not in Gevra. In our stories, everyone gets eaten by wolves at the end. We like to scare our children at the earliest opportunity. After all, a fearful child is a safe child.'

'That's awful!' cried Wren, but when she glanced at the soldier, she found him smiling. 'Oh, it was a joke. I didn't know you had a sense of humour.'

'You have much to learn about the Gevrans, Your Highness.'

'Why don't I start with you, then,' she said, coyly. 'Where do you come from? And how did you end up on these shores, protecting a prince who loves puzzles?'

Tor was silent for so long, Wren wondered if she had pushed their conversation too far, but then he fell into step with her again and they ambled onwards, side by side. 'I grew up on the isle of Carrig. It's a place of rugged wilderness and little else. A full day's journey from the capital of Grinstad, and that doesn't include the boat ride. It's . . . remote.'

'I bet it reeks of seaweed,' said Wren, dreamily. She was thinking of Ortha, and suddenly missing it with the fullness of her heart. 'What's on Carrig?'

'Farms, mostly.'

'So, you're a farm boy.' Wren slowed her walk, seized by the absurd urge to tell him about the animals of Ortha – how the first time she volunteered to help Banba during lambing season, she vomited on herself. Twice. 'What kind of farm?'

Tor turned to look at her. 'Do you really wish to know?'

'Yes,' said Wren, and the truth of it surprised her.

'A wild one.' She could hear the smile in his voice now. 'My family are wranglers. We raise and train beasts. Snow tigers. Stallions. Foxes. Wolves. Ice bears . . .'

'So, *that's* where the beasts come from,' mused Wren. 'And I suppose then they are trained for your bloodthirsty king and his bloodthirsty wars . . .'

Tor's voice changed. 'It was not always that way.'

Wren stole another glance at him. 'You don't like it, do you?'

'It doesn't matter what I like. I don't live on Carrig any more.'

'But you're still a wrangler?' Wren could sense it in him – the keen-eyed observations, the careful watchfulness. In some ways, he was just like his wolf.

Tor shrugged. 'A wrangler by heart, perhaps. But not by trade.'

The golden gates glittered up ahead, yet Wren found herself dragging her feet. If the palace guards spotted her out walking with the Gevran soldier, Chapman would come down on her like a thunderstorm. She shuddered to think how Rathborne would react. 'Why did you choose to leave it behind, then? Did your father make you enlist?'

Tor slowed to match her pace. 'My father had an accident ten years ago. My mother cares for him and my sisters run the farm in his stead. They are wranglers, too. But they are young, and the beasts can be brutal. The hours are long and the terrain is tough.' A shadow crossed his face. 'Some winters, there is barely enough food to get by.'

Wren stared at the soldier and saw him for the first time. Without his armour, and his suspicion. He was a son. A brother. A protector. That earlier shiver of danger was fading into something else – something warm and fluttering in her stomach. Which was almost certainly worse. 'So, the wrangler went to war.'

'A wrangler is well suited to war,' he said, without much enthusiasm. 'Our natural affinity with animals means not only can we tame them, we can fight like them, too.'

'Is that how you became Alarik's most trusted soldier? Your *natural* talents?'

He shook his head. 'I trained with Alarik as a boy.'

'Wait.' Wren's jaw dropped. 'You're *friends* with the evil king?'

'He was different back then,' said Tor.

'*How* different? I hear he feeds his enemies to his tigers.'

'Grief changes people.'

'Not like that it doesn't,' said Wren. 'Alarik Felsing is psychotic.'

Tor stiffened, and Wren sensed she had gone too far. *Oops.* 'Vicious as we might be in battle, a Gevran always takes care of their own. To the bloody end.' He gestured north to Wishbone Bay and all that lay beyond it. 'You will learn that soon enough, Your Highness.'

Wren frowned. Now why did he have to go and ruin her fun by bringing up the wedding?

'I wonder what fearsome beasts dear Ansel will slay for me,' she said, idly.

Tor's smile softened at the mention of Ansel. 'The prince possesses a bravery of spirit but I'm afraid he is no swordsman.'

'Didn't he ever learn?'

'Prince Ansel has always preferred the company of books to soldiers. He's certainly more of a daydreamer than his brother.' Tor's voice was warm, and Wren sensed in him a protectiveness that extended beyond duty, a kind of brotherliness that made her like Ansel more. 'Ansel would tell you himself he'd prefer to be remembered as a wordsmith rather than a fighter. For as long as I've known him, he has never been able to stand the sight of blood. The wounds of others wound him, too.'

Wren considered the prince in a new light. Somehow, he had survived a childhood in the icy maw of Gevra, not with brute force but with empathy and kindness. Yes, Ansel was hapless, but he was unashamedly himself, and for that, Wren could respect him. 'Very well,' she said. '*You* can slay my enemies and Ansel will read me poetry.'

'Perhaps you can play for us on your pianoforte.'

Wren's smile faded. She had hoped he'd forgotten about that.

Tor stuck his hands in his pocket as they wandered on. 'Tell me, Your Highness. Do you often sneak into Eshlinn alone or is it only when you need to visit the apothecary?'

Wren stopped walking. Suddenly, she felt very sober. The soldier hadn't let his guard down at all. While she had been flirting, he had been waiting to catch her out. 'So, you were following me.'

Tor pinned her with his gaze. 'The vial in your bodice. What is it?'

'Valerian root,' said Wren, thinking on her feet. 'Not that it's any of your business, but I haven't been sleeping well lately.'

'May I see it?'

She raised her hands. 'On my honour as Rose Valhart, Princess of Eana, what's in my cloak is nothing for you to be concerned about.'

Tor reached for her wrist, and Wren, like a fool, let him take it. He held it in place, tracing the pad of his thumb over her callouses. 'These are not the hands of a princess.'

She leaned towards him, until a muscle feathered in his jaw. 'How many princesses have you been this close to?'

Tor released her hand and stepped away from her.

'That's what I thought.' Wren turned swiftly but his foot came down, catching the end of her dress. She tripped, the vial tumbling out of her bodice before she could grab it. She scrabbled towards it on her hands and knees. Her fingers curled around the poison just as Tor lunged for it. In a blind panic, Wren spun on to her back and kicked his ankles out from under him. He collapsed on top of her, bracing himself on his elbows to keep from crushing her.

Wren's breath left her in a gasp. Suddenly, she was trapped beneath him, with her arms pinned above her head.

The soldier's breath bulleted out of him as he stared down at her, both of them stunned into momentary silence. His leg was warm between hers, his hips pressing her gently into the earth. Wren could feel his heartbeat hammering against her own, and watched the heat of his desire gently colouring his cheeks.

The storm in his eyes darkened. 'You tripped me,' he said, in a low voice.

Wren smirked. 'You fell.'

His chest moved against hers as he reached towards her closed fist.

Wren tipped her chin up, until their noses brushed. Tor froze. 'How far are you willing to go for it?' she said, against his lips. 'You already have me compromised.'

Tor blinked as the reality of their entanglement settled in. He reared back from Wren as if she were on fire, and leaped to his feet. He raked his hands through his hair, a look of such bewilderment on his face, Wren almost laughed.

'I would never . . .'

Wren propped herself on to her elbows. 'Never what? Risk your honour?'

'Risk *yours*,' he said, half breathless.

'Good,' said Wren, though deep down, she felt a prickle of disappointment. She had quite enjoyed the feeling of the soldier's body pressed against hers, even if it was entirely reckless.

She rolled to her feet and made a show of tucking the vial *deep* into her bodice.

Tor looked away. 'We should head back to the palace.'

'Go ahead. I can make my own way back.'

'It's late. Let me escort you.' The soldier was so tightly wound, he could barely look at Wren now. He walked on, gesturing for her to follow. 'I insist.'

Wren hesitated. 'What will my guards say when they see you walking me home all alone in the middle of the night?'

'I imagine they'll be grateful that I am doing their job for them,' he said, stiffly.

The Gevran made a good point. Any soldier that told on her would be putting their own head on the chopping block, too. She hurried after Tor. For the rest of the short journey back to the palace, he didn't utter another word. When they parted ways in the courtyard, he offered a stilted goodbye, his pale cheeks still dappled with red.

Wren made her way back to the east tower, heady from the success of her evening. She had secured the poison, kept it secret *and* compromised Ansel's guard dog in the process.

Though she hadn't expected that part to be so *enjoyable*. She had been kissed before – and more than once – but even without Tor's lips touching hers, she had never felt such desire – it was like a flame threatening to consume her. She had almost unravelled right there on the grass beneath him.

But it was only a moment of a weakness. A brief almost-kiss that Wren would hardly remember in the morning. She told herself that as she fell asleep, but in her dreams, Tor found her, and when he leaned down to kiss her, this time he didn't stop.

Rose
CHAPTER 18

Rose was going to murder Shen. That was if this stern-faced old witch claiming to be her grandmother didn't kill her first. How could he have lied about so much, and so *effortlessly*? Her head spun as she was tugged roughly along the beach. The old woman was small and stout but she moved with the gait of a soldier.

Banba.

The rope of wind around Rose's waist tethered her to the witch, who was hauling her back to the fishing village. A crowd was gathering down by the shore, the children clambering up on to the craggy rocks to get a better look at her. Rose couldn't miss how several of the witches weren't at all happy to see her. Some were blatantly glaring, others whispering among themselves.

'I thought my grandmother was dead,' she said.

Banba glanced at her over her shoulder. 'You sound disappointed.'

Rose hesitated. There was something besides the wind binding her to Banba. She sensed it – this strange pull in her chest – even as she tried to ignore it. Was this what it felt like to be with family? This simmering recognition deep within her bones?

'I'm surprised. I thought I was . . .' Rose's voice trailed off.

'Alone?' Banba's face softened, but her voice remained gruff. 'You've always had us, girl.' Then she narrowed her eyes, taking Rose in. 'At least it looks as if they feed you back at that old stone palace.'

Some of the witches were dragging mottled driftwood into a circle, piling it higher and higher. Others carried freshly caught cod in from the sea, the fish still dangling from their lines. Rose spied wicker baskets full of crusty bread and red wine sloshing from pitchers as they were carted across the beach.

Her stomach growled, and the sound was louder than the crashing waves. She winced.

Banba's laugh was like the caw of a crow. 'Don't worry, we'll feed you here, too.'

A prodding thought distracted Rose from the promise of food. One she had often desperately, secretly hoped. 'Is my mother here?' Banba stopped short on the beach, and Rose yelped as the wind went taut around her. 'I just thought that if I have a sister who survived and a grandmother I never knew about, then maybe—'

'Don't be naive, child.' The wind shoved Rose closer to Banba. The old witch bit off a curse as she grabbed Rose's wrist. 'Your mother is dead. And so is your father.' She gave

Rose a measured look. 'And now that you're here, it's time you knew the truth about what happened. Your parents were killed in cold blood by Willem Rathborne, the man who now orbits the throne, pretending it's his.'

Rose tried to shake her grandmother off, but her grip only tightened.

'Willem isn't capable of such a thing,' she said, before she could even consider it. 'It was a witch who killed my parents.' Even after what Rose had seen in the Weeping Forest, this was the story she held closest to her. The one that informed so much of who she was. If it wasn't true . . . then nothing in her life was, and she simply couldn't accept that. She wouldn't. 'The witches were angry at my mother for marrying a Valhart. They were jealous of her. They—'

'Don't you *dare* say such a thing in Ortha!' Banba squeezed Rose's wrist until it felt as if talons were digging into her skin.

'You're hurting me!' cried Rose.

Banba released the wind and Rose stumbled backwards, cradling her wrist to her chest. She looked away sharply, tears burning in her eyes. She didn't know a great deal about family but she felt very certain this was not how meeting your long-lost grandmother was meant to go.

'The witches loved your mother. *I* loved your mother,' said the old woman, fiercely. 'But it was not enough to save her from Willem Rathborne. A man who has always sought to destroy us.'

'What nonsense! Willem is a good man,' said Rose, just as

fiercely. 'He has taken care of me my entire life. He *loves* me.'

Banba gave her a piteous look. 'No, Rose. He *needs* you.' At Rose's silence, the old woman went on, her words like a dagger, twisting and *twisting* in her chest. 'Don't you see? Willem Rathborne had to keep you alive – you were the perfect prop princess that would allow him to rule Eana from behind the curtain. Of course he only needed one of you. He would have killed Wren, too, if he had found her in that chamber.'

Rose pressed her lips together. She knew there was no point in arguing back, in saying what she had always believed. That Willem had burst in just in time to save her. But if that was true, then what had happened to this supposed sister of hers? If Wren was real, then how could Willem's story be real, too?

She looked down at her hands, imagining another pair next to them. *A twin.* Was it truly possible?

'Willem Rathborne is no innocent,' Banba went on. 'He would kill every last witch in Eana if he could. But you already know that, don't you?'

Rose shook her head, even though she knew that part was true. But still, that didn't mean the rest of it was. This old woman could be lying through her teeth, trying to turn her against her closest advisor and sow descension in the palace. Rose needed a minute to think, but Banba was tugging at her again.

'Come. It's time for you to meet the witches you are so afraid of.' The old woman paused and Rose thought perhaps that she was going to offer her a kind word. Something that might ease the stinging in her wrist and make her feel less frightened of this wild place. But Banba only hardened her stare. '*Don't* disappoint me.'

The last rays of amber sunlight were melting along the horizon when Rose and Banba reached the little cliff village. The patchwork of weather-beaten huts peered over them from the rock face, their slanted roofs tilting towards the greying ocean. Wooden steps climbed up and down the craggy cliffs, some planks angled so precariously that Rose was sure a stiff gust would blow a distracted climber straight into the sea.

Down by the shore, a strange silver bonfire was crackling. Witches milled around it, casting handfuls of sand into the flames that somehow made them burn higher and brighter. *Enchanters*. The younger children were giggling as they chased each other around the fire, while the older ones tended to their feast.

Rose scanned the faces in the crowd, searching for her own. Her throat was bone-dry and her heart was thundering so raucously, she could hear it in her ears. 'Where is my sister? I want to meet her. I need to know if what you say is true.'

Banba grunted. 'You'll have to take my word for it. Wren is as far from home as you are, girl.'

Rose frowned, waiting for more, but the old woman tugged her along.

Smoke billowed into the sky, dusting the air with

charcoal. The clouds were rolling in, hiding the stars behind them. Rose wished she could see them so that something – *anything* – might feel the same. She shivered in the sea wind, drawing her cloak tighter.

No. Not *her* cloak.

'Wren.' Rose rolled the name around in her mouth. There was a wildness to it, not like her own that was soft and demure. *Regal.* In all her imaginings as a child, thinking about her mother and her father, she'd never once considered a sister. Someone who could have made her life so much less lonely.

Stop that, she told herself sternly. This was no time for a pity party. She hadn't been that lonely after all – she'd always had Celeste. And Cam.

And Willem.

The witches parted to let her through, watching her too closely. But despite Banba's prodding, Rose's mind was back in Anadawn.

The more she thought about Willem, the less sure she felt. The Kingsbreath had hovered over Rose her entire life, but was it her throne he truly cared for? This thing that could not be untangled from her person . . . her destiny. Was she truly no better than a prop – someone raised to believe a lie so enormous it had hidden her family from her for eighteen years?

Rose was a witch. It was her only certainty in this wild, foreign place. She knew it in her blood and in her bones. But she didn't know if Willem would forgive her for it, and that troubled her. She imagined him pressing her face to the dirt again, only this time she wouldn't earn a rose for her innocence. In her mind, his face contorted, as if for all her life he'd been wearing a mask and now she could glimpse the ugly truth of what lay underneath. Bile rose quickly in her throat and she halted, turning to be sick on the sand.

Banba stood over her. 'Get up, girl,' she said, in a low voice. 'Don't let them see you on your knees.'

Behind her, Rose heard the patter of laughter, a stir of murmurs rippling through the crowd. She caught the words 'soft' and 'pathetic' as she knelt in the sand. For a moment she thought she might collapse and never get back up. Let the rising tide claim her. With any luck, the current would deposit her body back in Anadawn. Where she belonged.

'Rose!'

She looked up, wiping her mouth. Shen was jostling his way towards her. The sight of him was enough to make her stand up straight and dust herself off. Take another step towards the flames, and all those judgmental gazes. She rolled her shoulders back. She wouldn't falter in front of Shen – she would not let him, nor any of these witches, see her break.

'Are you all right?' He reached out to steady her.

Banba smacked his hand away. 'She's not a child, Shen. Let her walk.'

Rose didn't even look at him. 'I have nothing to say to you.'

'*Rose.*' Something inside her cracked at how he said her

name. 'I'm sorry, I really am. I couldn't—'

'That's enough,' said Banba, sharply. 'You're making a scene. Tonight is important for Rose. It's time for her to get to know her people.'

Shen dropped his gaze. 'Yes, Banba,' he murmured, before melting into the crowd.

Rose frowned. Shen had never shown her that kind of deference and she was his future queen. She hadn't even thought him capable of such respect. She eyed Banba more carefully as Tilda came barrelling towards them. Behind her, an older woman with warm brown skin and long white hair walked more slowly. She had generous curves and a round, kind face, and she wore a cloth patch over her left eye.

Tilda grabbed Rose's hand. 'Come on! We've all been waiting for you!' And though the familiarity of it felt strange to Rose, she was glad to find an ally on this beach. 'The fire is high and the feast is ready!'

'Banba,' the other woman called out as she approached. 'I hope you haven't terrified your granddaughter but instead have welcomed her warmly, as she deserves.' Her voice was low and sonorous like a lullaby, and something about it made Rose feel strangely calm. 'And I trust you've told her of the celebration feast we have prepared in her honour.'

Banba stiffened. 'Do not tell me how to best welcome my own granddaughter, Thea.'

'I'll take that to mean you've been scaring the wits out of her.' Thea reached for Rose's free hand. Her skin was warm and soft, and Rose felt for the briefest moment as though the sun was rising in her chest. Her fingers tingled and the ache in her wrist ebbed away. 'It has been a long time, Rose. But it is good to see you again.'

Rose stared at the old woman, trying to place her. 'We've met?'

'Come, let us eat. There is much to tell you.'

Wren
CHAPTER 19

Wren's shoes click-clacked along the Eshlinn cobblestones as she hurried towards the light flickering at the end of the alleyway. Behind her, new footsteps grew louder, closer. She spun around, her dagger raised, but Tor knocked it easily from her grip. He pressed her up against the wall, his hands sliding into her hair.

'Tell me something true,' he growled against her lips.

Wren opened her mouth to his, waiting for the warm caress of his tongue, and then—

'WAKEY, WAKEY, PRINCESS!'

Wren snapped her eyes open to find Celeste standing over her, smirking. 'I hate to interrupt whatever *that* was. You were moaning in your sleep.'

Wren sat up, trying to get her bearings. It was the day after her trip to Eshlinn and she was exhausted. After an afternoon of dress fittings for a wedding she had no intention of attending, she had stolen away to the library for some peace and quiet. 'I must have dozed off. What time is it?'

'Well after dinner but don't worry, I've brought you a present from the kitchens.' Celeste removed a bottle of red wine from behind her back and dangled it in front of Wren. 'Let's go for a walk in the courtyard.'

Wren grinned as she rolled to her feet. 'Yes, *please*.'

Once outside, they hid the wine from the guards as they made their way to the rose garden. Above them, the moon glowed like a lantern in the sky, casting a pallid light across the bushes.

'Ugh. The flowers look haggard,' said Celeste. 'So many of them have lost their petals.'

'Must have been that pesky rainstorm the other night,' said Wren, before taking her first glug of wine. It was deliciously plummy, the sharp edges of her anxiety dulling as she gulped it down.

'*Someone's* thirsty,' said Celeste, swiping it back.

Wren made a mental note to take dainty, princess-like sips in future. 'Well, I did miss dinner.'

They sank on to a bench and laid their heads back, watching the stars.

Celeste drank from the bottle before setting it down between them. 'I had the strangest dream about you the other night.'

'Oh?' said Wren, resisting the urge to take another slug.

'You were by the sea.' Celeste closed her eyes as she pulled the dream from her memory. 'You were standing on the edge of a cliff. It plummeted down into these huge, crashing waves. And you were just hovering there in your nightgown.' She chewed the inside of her cheek. 'You looked so dishevelled. So . . . well, so unlike you.'

Wren masked her unease with a small sip of wine. She thought of Rose, a world away. If Shen had made good time, they would have scaled the Whisperwind Cliffs and reached Ortha by now. But there was no way Celeste could know that. It was a coincidence. A strange, uneasy coincidence . . .

Wren stood up and drifted towards the edge of the courtyard. Beyond it, the Silvertongue was steady, the grey waters meandering silently towards Wishbone Bay. 'I haven't been sleeping well either. Must be the bad weather.'

There was a sudden creaking overhead, followed by the furious flapping of wings. She looked up just in time to see a flock of starcrests burst free from the window in the west tower. The birds swooped and swarmed, their silver breasts shooting across the sky, like stars. In their flight patterns, Wren knew there were whispers of the future but she was not able to read them. She was no seer, after all. For all her time living at Ortha, Wren had never even met one. Banba claimed some still dwelled in the lost village of Amarach in the south, but the towers there were hidden so well, it could take years to find a seer. And that was if you knew where to look.

'I think Willem has a new bird obsession,' said Celeste, who was watching them just as keenly. 'He lets the starcrests fly almost every night now.'

Wren frowned. Was *that* what Rathborne was doing in the west tower? Surely, he wasn't arrogant enough to think he could actually teach himself how to read their prophetic patterns. Or was it his paranoia about the witches that had driven him to collect so many starcrests?

'How strange,' she muttered.

'I bet he's going to put on some kind of bird show for King Alarik when he gets here,' mused Celeste. 'A starcrest murmuration can be quite mesmerizing and the Gevran king does have a fascination with animals.'

'I think you mean predatory beasts,' Wren corrected her. 'And I can't imagine a man who feeds people to his tigers will appreciate a flock of twinkling birds.'

'Alarik might surprise you,' said Celeste, between sips. 'Maybe he's more like Ansel than you think. I bet he has a soft side.'

Wren snorted. Alarik Felsing could have a side as soft as a snow bunny wrapped in a cloud but as long as he intended to kill every last witch in Eana, she wanted nothing to do with him.

She returned to the bench and took the wine bottle from Celeste. It was almost empty already. She tipped her head back for the dregs and glimpsed a face in the window of the west tower. She blinked and it disappeared. Wren lowered the bottle, unease stirring in her gut.

Was Rathborne up there right now, watching them?

'Come on,' she said. 'I want to stretch my legs.' She stowed the wine bottle under the bench and dragged Celeste deeper into the rose garden, past the hideous statue of the Protector, until they were out of view of the west tower.

Celeste kept her gaze on the birds as they walked. 'My mother once told me that when Eana was a young country, the witches called down the stars and turned them into starcrests, so they could read the heavens and see into the future.' She cleared her throat. 'Nonsense, of course, but she loved those silly fairy tales.'

Wren hid her surprise. The starcrest legend was a living tale among witches, a bedtime story parents told their children at night, but it wasn't widely known in Eshlinn – a place that solely worshipped the Protector. 'I think a little silliness every now and then is a good thing,' she said, mildly.

'I haven't thought of that story since my mother died,' murmured Celeste. 'Must be the wine.'

'And the birds,' said Wren, kindly. She sensed Celeste was embarrassed about revealing her mother's interest in the witches. The wine had loosened her memories and her tongue, but in truth, it only made Wren like her more. Not to mention, it made her wonder about Celeste's mother.

'They make me uneasy sometimes,' Celeste confided. 'It's their silver breasts. They get far too bright and when they swarm together it makes my eyes hurt.'

Wren studied Celeste from the corner of her eye as they wandered through the garden. First, there was the mention of her dream of Ortha, and now this strange reaction to the starcrests . . . To even hint at the possibility of her being a seer would doom Celeste to death, so Wren kept her theory to herself, vowing to keep a closer eye on Rose's best friend.

'I wouldn't worry too much,' she said, coolly. 'I'm sure Willem will get bored of them soon.' *Or he'll die.* 'And then they'll all fly away.'

They wandered a while longer, both girls lost in thought as they watched the birds return to their tower. The starcrests landed one by one on the windowsill, and with a final melancholic chirp, disappeared inside.

The tower window shut with a resounding thud, and just when she was about to turn away, Wren swore she glimpsed Rathborne's face again. Then a hand pressed flat against the glass until it slid slowly into darkness.

Wren took the long way back to the east tower, her feet leading her to the third-floor corridor before she could decide whether or not it was a good idea. But of course it wasn't. It was foolish to go looking for Tor, especially after how close he'd come to finding out about the devil's root last night. But her dream from the library was fresh in her mind and the wine wasn't helping.

She had barely reached the top of the stairwell when she spotted him by the window. He was standing in a shaft of moonlight with his hands in his pockets, as though he was waiting for someone. She hated her heart for leaping, for hoping that he was there for her.

'It's never a good idea to sneak up on a Gevran, Your Highness,' he said, without tearing his gaze from the night sky.

Wren smirked. 'Did I interrupt your soulful moon-gazing?'

He turned to look at her. 'It seems your Valerian root isn't working. Can't you sleep, Your Highness?'

'Perhaps I was in the mood for another interrogation,' said Wren, her cheeks tingling under his gaze.

A smile softened the hard edge of his jaw. 'How about a walk instead?'

Wren pretended to consider it. 'Very well,' she sighed. 'But only because I'm feeling generous.'

Tor's chuckle sent a welcome ripple of warmth down her spine. They fell into step, the silvery moon lighting their way as they meandered along the deserted hallways of Anadawn Palace, both of them pretending as if they hadn't been looking for each other.

Rose
CHAPTER 20

As Rose wove her way through the witches, she held her head high. The whispers were not subtle, and the stares were even less so. A huddle of teenagers hissed at her as she passed by. An old woman bared her yellowed teeth, sending nerves skittering up her spine. Still, she held every gaze that met hers. She would not be cowed by anyone, witch or no witch.

I am Eana; Eana is me.

She wished she wasn't in her nightgown. If only her face were clean and her hair untangled. She longed for her best dress of honey-gold, and her most decadent jewellery, so she could mark herself as the princess of Eana, the true ruler of this feral place. Princess Rose Valhart, beautiful and beloved.

But all she had now was her pride, and that would have to be enough.

Banba was pulled away from the crowd by an old witch with a long grey beard while Tilda chattered like a friendly bird in Rose's ear. 'That's where I live, in that hut there, and that big one, right next to it, belongs to Thea and Banba. On rainy days, Thea does her healing there, too. I know because when I broke my arm after I fell from the cliffs, that's where I went.'

Rose turned to Thea. 'You're a healer?'

Thea smiled. 'Shen tells me you are a healer, too.'

'I don't know why Shen thinks he has any right to talk about me at all,' said Rose, quickly. Thinking about that deceitful bandit sent fresh anger coursing through her. 'But I do know that he's a liar.'

Thea raised her eyebrow but didn't push for more.

'Did Shen have to use his craft on your journey?' said Tilda, excitedly. 'I've never seen him *fight* fight. Only practise. He trains me sometimes. The truth is, I'm not a very good warrior yet, but Shen says if I practise every day and eat my bread crusts then one day I might be able to take him down.' She giggled. 'He trained Wren, too. It was much harder for her at the start because it's not her craft. She can't jump very high or climb very well, and one time, she got tangled up in a bunch of seaweed and we had to cut her loose with a tackle knife.' Tilda had to stop to catch her breath, she was talking so fast. 'Anyways, sometimes when Shen's out on the rocks, it looks as if he's *flying*!'

Rose remembered how fast Shen had moved when he'd pounced on the blood beetle to save her life. She should have known right away that his skill wasn't natural, that he was a warrior witch. 'Who would he have fought?'

'Palace soldiers, of course!' Tilda lowered her voice as if she were telling Rose a secret. 'Did you know that Shen can fight ten people at once? Probably more. But the most I've seen is ten and that was only practice, so I don't even think he was trying his best!'

'I'm afraid you will have to ask him yourself,' she said, tightly. 'I was asleep when he kidnapped me.'

Tilda's face fell. 'Oh, that's right . . .'

Thea cleared her throat. 'Tilda, how about we let Rose have something to eat and a moment to settle in before we badger her. I'm sure the princess has had a difficult journey getting here.'

'That's one way of putting it,' said Rose, pointedly.

She wrung her hands as she searched for Shen's face in the crowd. Insolent, sneaky, lying Shen. She guessed there were close to two hundred people gathered around the bonfire now. They wore rough tunics and dark trousers similar to the ones Banba and Thea wore, their hair blowing loose and tangled in the sea wind. It felt strange to be among the people she had feared for so long. Rose reminded herself that just because the witches didn't look threatening, didn't mean they weren't dangerous. She mustn't drop her guard.

'Here, love.' Thea guided her to a woven mat on the sand. 'Sit and steady your nerves. Rowena will bring you something to eat.' She waved over a tall girl with long golden curls and a face full of freckles. She looked about Rose's age, though her scowl made her seem younger. 'I'll be back soon. Tilda, come and help me fetch the wine.'

Rose watched with rising panic as Thea and Tilda disappeared into the crowd. A moment later, Rowena carried over a wooden platter piled with grilled fish and brown bread. She dropped it roughly in front of Rose. 'Don't get used to this, *Princess*,' she said, coldly. 'We serve ourselves here in Ortha.' She threw a glare over her shoulder as she stalked away to join a girl with cropped black hair who was snickering at the edge of the bonfire.

Rose's hand shook as she rescued a sliver of cod from the sand. Never in her life had anyone dared speak to her like that. The witches were already testing her. Gingerly, she took a bite of fish.

'Don't let Rowena get to you,' said a voice close to her ear.

Rose jerked her head around to find Shen kneeling next to her. 'How are you so quiet all the time?' she startled. 'It's unnatural.'

Shen flashed his teeth. 'Witch, remember?'

Rose yanked Shen's boots off her feet and dumped them in his lap. Then she stood and shook out her nightgown. She was suddenly acutely aware of how dirty it was, not to mention the tangles in her hair and the sunburn on her face. 'Please just leave me alone.'

Before Shen could reply, she stalked around the bonfire, where she stood alone by the shore.

The waves lapped at her feet as she stared into the sea, fighting back tears. The desert with Shen had been frightening but sometimes it had been exciting, too. And out in the sands, she'd had a plan. Now that she had scaled those towering cliffs and met Banba at the bottom of them, the possibility of escape seemed almost impossible, and her throne – her *life* – seemed further away than ever.

Rose yelped as something sharp struck the back of her leg. She whipped her head around to find four witches stalking towards her. Rowena and her snickering friend led the charge, followed by two lanky boys. One had brown skin and shorn hair and the other was white, with tight blond curls. They were laughing and nudging each other as they raked their eyes over Rose.

Rowena's smile was feral. She held a fistful of rocks in one hand, and was flinging them carelessly in Rose's direction. Rose craned her neck, searching for Thea – the witch who had been kind to her – or even Tilda. But through the haze of fire and smoke, she saw only strangers staring back at her.

She managed a thin smile. 'May I help you with something?'

'So formal!' Rowena jeered. 'Bryony, did you hear that? The princess wants to *help* us.'

Bryony kicked sand at Rose, forcing her to back up, into the shallows. 'You and your beloved Kingsbreath have already done more than enough.'

Rose's stomach twisted as the young witches converged on her like a pack of wolves. 'I think there's been some misunderstanding . . .'

'The misunderstanding is yours,' said Rowena, flinging another rock. 'If you think a witch-hating princess is welcome here, you're sorely mistaken.'

'What do you think, Cathal?' Bryony smirked at the blond-haired boy. 'Is she a good trade for Wren?'

He rounded on Rose. 'I'd have to taste her to see. What do you reckon, Grady?'

The other boy pretended to retch. 'I'd sooner kiss my own toes than a stinking Valhart.'

'Nah. She's not a patch on our Wren,' said Bryony.

Rose attempted to sidestep them. 'I must get back to the festivities.'

Rowena shoved her towards the ocean. The four witches closed in on her, making a wall of their bodies.

The waves lapped at Rose's knees. 'I . . . I command you to let me pass!'

The witches looked at each other, then burst out laughing.

'You're not our princess,' sneered Rowena.

'And you'll *never* be our queen,' Cathal spat at Rose, the glob hitting her cheek.

Rose furiously scrubbed it away. 'I could throw you in the dungeons for that!'

'I'd like to see you try without your precious army. You wouldn't stand a chance against him.' Rowena nudged Cathal. 'Go on. Show her.'

Cathal smirked as he picked up a fistful of sand and Rose flinched, waiting for him to throw it. But instead he began to speak.

'*From earth to dust, I take from you, every breath until you're blue.*'

He opened his fist, but the sand never fell.

'What are—' Rose wheezed as her lungs constricted. She

gasped for air, but found none. She stumbled to her knees with a splash, clawing desperately at her throat.

They all began to laugh, and though there were older witches watching through the flames, no one came to her aid. Rose crawled through the shallows, her head pounding as her vision darkened at the edges. She was going to die on this beach, with these witches cackling at her. She would never make it home and she would never be Queen. The world slipped out from under her – and with it, her future – until all she could hear was the cruel echo of their laughter and the slow thud of her heartbeat as it gave up.

And then suddenly, Shen was pushing his way through.

'Get back. *Move*. Rose? Rose, can you hear me?' He lifted her up and she sagged against him, too weak to stand on her own. He took one look at her, then spun on the others. 'Fix it. *Now*.'

'I'll do it.' Bryony grabbed a fistful of sand and flung it at Rose, uttering a hurried incantation under her breath.

Rose's lungs expanded with a painful wheeze. She found her footing, gulping hungrily at the air as the world shifted back into focus.

Shen cracked his knuckles. 'Who did that to her?'

'Aw, come on, Shen,' said Cathal, backing up. 'We're just having a bit of fun.'

Shen's voice was dangerously quiet. 'It didn't look like fun to me.'

'We weren't going to take it all the way,' said Rowena, blithely. 'She would have been fine.'

Shen's eyes flashed. 'She's Wren's *sister*.'

'You know she hates us,' said Rowena. 'We'd all be dead if she had her way.'

'And what do you care anyway?' challenged Grady. 'Didn't Wren tell you not to seduce her sister?'

'She also told me to protect her.' Shen stepped forward, putting himself between Rose and the witches. 'If you have a problem with that, take it up with Banba.'

At the mention of Banba's name, the group fell still.

Bryony turned on Rose, her dark eyes going wide. 'You won't tell Banba, will you?'

Rose scrubbed the drying tears from her cheeks. As her lungs filled with new breath, her fear turned to a bright and blazing anger. She'd never hated anyone as much as these four witches. And the others – the ones who had stood by and watched, the witches who would sooner see her suffocate than lift a hand to help her. But one day – and that day would come soon – Rose would no longer be alone, and with the power of the crown of Eana on her head and the might of its army at her back, she would return to them as their ruler. And they would bow to her.

'I am not a child who tells tales,' she told them, and she meant it. 'But I will not forget this.'

Bryony sagged in relief.

'Good,' said Rowena, crisply. 'You shouldn't.'

Shen led Rose away from the ocean. 'Are you all right?'

'I'm fine.'

'I'm sorry, Rose. I promised you wouldn't get hurt.' He

raked his hands through his hair, pulling at the dark strands. 'I knew there was resentment here towards you but I never thought anyone would dare act on it.'

Rose folded her arms. 'Don't pretend to feel sorry for me. It's *your* fault I'm here.'

'I'm not pretending . . .' Shen sighed, giving up on whatever he was about to say. 'You should sit down. Have some more fish. Food will calm you. And then perhaps we can talk?'

'*Calm* me?' fumed Rose. 'How can I be calm when a witch just stole the breath from my lungs and left me for dead? How can I *possibly* even begin to—?'

'Rose! There you are!' Tilda scurried over, carrying a jug of wine and some dusty glasses. 'I brought this for you!'

'Thank you, Tilda. Your timing is impeccable.' Rose poured herself a large glass of wine. She finished it in one gulp, then swiftly poured another.

'Go easy there,' said Shen, taking the jug from her.

'Let me be,' said Rose, snatching it back. 'If I have to be here for one minute longer, then I intend to make it bearable.'

'You'll be here a lot longer than that,' said Tilda, cheerfully.

'Hardly.' Rose poured another generous glass. 'I intend to be home in time for my coronation.'

Somehow. Some way.

Tilda clutched the jug to her chest. 'But that's Wren's job now. I know she's not as princessy as you but once she gets the hang of wearing dresses and remembers not to chew with her mouth open or swear all the time, I think she'll make a wonderful queen.'

Rose spat out a mouthful of wine. '*What?*'

'Tilda,' Shen groaned. 'I was just about to tell her about the switch.'

Tilda's smile was toothy and wide. 'Haven't you figured it out yet?'

Before Rose could formulate a sentence, or indeed a single thought, Banba came striding towards them. 'Ah, there's the wine!' She took the jug from Rose and raised it high. 'Tonight is a cause for great celebration. We will feast and drink until we fall asleep full-bellied and bleary-eyed underneath the moon. That Rose is here with us means our Wren will soon sit on the throne of Eana.' Her words carried across the beach, strong and fierce as a winter gale. 'Upon the full moon, we will have a new witch queen, and our time as outcasts will be at an end. By the grace of Ortha Starcrest, the golden gates of Anadawn will open to us after a thousand years, and the Silvertongue will run red with our enemies' blood. The tides of fate are finally turning, my brothers and sisters. The time of the witches has come again!'

Rose swayed dizzily as Banba raised the jug to her lips. The old woman drank deeply as a roaring cheer rose up on the beach, as high and bright as the bonfire flames.

Wren
CHAPTER 21

'You are as exquisite as a snowflake tonight, Rose.' Prince Ansel made moon eyes at Wren from across the dining table. 'Truly, your face is a thing of rare beauty.'

Not as rare as you think.

Wren offered a demure smile. 'And *you* look as handsome as a . . . uh . . . glacier.'

Beside her, Celeste rolled her eyes. 'And *I'm* as hungry as an ice bear. Not that anyone seems to care.'

'We have to wait for Willem.' Wren glanced at the door, where Tor was standing guard. She winked at him and to her wicked delight, he blushed. Their walk last night had been entirely innocent, not to mention all too brief, but in the darkness when there was no one else around, it felt as if something forbidden had begun to stir between them. Something Wren was quite enjoying.

Celeste sighed dramatically. 'Five more minutes, then I'm starting.'

'Chapman said the Kingsbreath would be here.' Wren twisted the napkin on her lap, trying to calm her nerves.

Everything hinged on tonight. If the Kingsbreath didn't show up, she would have to find another way to poison him, and that could take days, or even weeks.

The formal dining room was bedecked in splendour. A stately fireplace crackled at one end of the room, casting a warm glow about the table, where four places had been set. Crystal candelabras dangled from the high ceiling, twinkling along the rich battle tapestries that hung from the walls. Wren's gaze was drawn to a depiction of the Protector's War, ghoulish-faced witches burning in the background while the Valhart army raised their swords in victory.

She looked away only to find herself caught in the storm of Tor's gaze. She shifted in her seat. The vial of devil's root was cool against her ribs but her cheeks were flaming hot.

Ansel noted her discomfort, and misread it. 'Tor is part of the furniture, my flower. Pay him no mind.'

'That's some armoire,' declared Celeste, just as the door to the dining room swung open. Willem Rathborne stalked inside, followed by two palace guards.

'You're here,' said Wren, relief bringing a smile to her face. 'I was worried you wouldn't come.'

Rathborne didn't apologize for his lateness. He glazed over Wren with a brief nod, settling his attention instead on the prince. 'Good evening, Your Highness.'

Prince Ansel stood to shake his hand.

Rathborne looked wretched in the flickering candlelight. He was thin as a spindle, and his pale skin had adopted a greyish hue. Shadows pooled beneath his eyes and the hair around his temples was fraying. It was obvious he wasn't sleeping at night, and Wren knew from Celeste that he'd been anxious about something. Well, the only thing he *should* be nervous about was *her*.

'Willem looks like a corpse,' whispered Celeste.

Wren hmm'd in agreement. *After tonight, he'll be one.*

The feast began with appetizers – delicately whipped salmon mousse topped with chives and served in a flaky crust of pastry. Celeste moaned when she took a bite, and though Rathborne insisted his guard test-taste the first mouthful for anything untoward, he eventually devoured three in quick succession. Wren was too anxious to eat her fill. She was so close to Rathborne their elbows were brushing, and the vial of poison was like an ice cube against her skin.

It didn't help that Tor's attention was glued to her, the towering soldier hovering just a few feet from the table.

'I must thank you for hosting such a delightful dinner in my honour, Rose,' said Ansel, between courses. 'I may be but a prince but tonight you have made me feel like a king.'

'You're most welcome, Your Highness,' said Rathborne, taking the praise for himself. He turned his hawkish gaze on Wren. 'I have raised Rose to be thoughtful, like her father.' He patted her hand, and the unexpectedness of his touch built a scream in Wren's throat. 'She is as agreeable as they come.'

A sudden choking sound came from Tor's direction. 'Excuse me,' he muttered.

'What *else* do you like about Rose, Prince Ansel?' probed Celeste. 'Apart from her beauty, of course.'

'Well, the princess is an excellent chess player . . . not to mention a spirited pianist!' Ansel winked at Wren as he tapped his fingers along the tablecloth, re-enacting her disastrous runaway melody. 'I can assure you, my flower, there are no dastardly river spiders in Gevra. You will be free to fill the halls of Grinstad Palace with your music.' He smiled at Celeste. 'You needn't have any worries about Rose. She'll come to enjoy her new life in Gevra just as much as I am enjoying my time here. Give it a few moons and she'll be revelling in the cold.'

Wren stiffened in her seat.

'Wait a moment,' interrupted Celeste. 'What do you mean Rose's *new life* in Gevra?'

Rathborne cleared his throat. 'Well, I suppose the cat is out of the bag now.'

Ansel bit his lip. 'Oh dear. Me and my big mouth. I know you wanted it to be a wedding surprise.'

That was certainly one way of putting it. The depth of Rathborne's betrayal shouldn't have surprised Wren but she found herself struggling for words.

She turned on the Kingsbreath. 'You intend to ship me off to Gevra?'

'Oh, come now, Rose, darling. Where did you think you would live once you were married?'

'Here in Eana, surely,' said Celeste, beating Wren to indignation. 'Rose can't be an absentee queen. And Ansel isn't even the king of Gevra!'

'Well, not all of us aspire to such dizzying heights.'

Ansel smoothed his napkin on his lap. 'I'm perfectly happy being a prince.'

'Then why aren't you moving to Eana?' said Celeste.

Ansel looked to Rathborne. 'I . . . er . . . well, it was decided.'

Celeste narrowed her eyes. 'By who?'

'By the Kingsbreath,' said Wren, who was staring hard at Rathborne. 'Clearly, he has other plans for me.'

Rathborne plucked a speck of dust from his sleeve. 'I know what your parents wished for you, Rose,' he said, calmly. 'A safe life. An honourable husband. And one day, a family of your own. There's no reason why you can't have that in Gevra.'

'I shall make sure of it,' said Ansel, as he reached for Wren's hand. She pretended not to see it.

'What about Rose's life here?' reeled Celeste. 'Her friends? Her duty? Her coronation?'

The Kingsbreath shot Celeste a warning look. 'There will be no need for a coronation. So much faff and ceremony, and for what? A political headache,' he said, as if Rose's destiny were a tedious chore he was saving her from. 'No. Rose will make her new life in Gevra, and I will continue to take care of the throne here. Of course, King Alarik will oversee everything from Grinstad.'

And there it was – the fullness of Rathborne's scheme laid out before them. In return for having a foot in each continent, Alarik Felsing was going to help the Kingsbreath stamp out the last of the Eana witches for good. And he was going to do it in the most brutal way imaginable. By the evening of her eighteenth birthday, Wren would possess no crown at all, while Alarik Felsing would hold two.

Celeste leaned towards Wren. 'Why aren't you saying anything about this?' she whispered. 'Surely this isn't what you want?'

Wren looked at her hands. She was minutes away from killing Rathborne. If she ruffled too many feathers now, she may not get another chance. 'It's all come as such a surprise,' she said, meekly. 'I suppose I'll have to think it over.'

Celeste flopped back in her chair. 'What is there to think about? Becoming Queen has always been the most important thing in the world to you,' she said, in mounting disbelief. 'It's your birthright, Rose. You've talked about it ever since we were children.' When Wren didn't answer, Celeste turned to Ansel. 'And what about *you*? Do you really see no issue with stealing Rose away from her country? Her people?'

Ansel's smile faltered. 'Surely, we can share her?'

'She's not a bloody bread roll!' Celeste took an angry slug of wine. The alcohol was making her too brave. 'This all sounds more like a banishment than a betrothal to me. Sending Rose away to a sunless land. Far from her throne and her home.'

'That's *enough*,' seethed the Kingsbreath. 'This is none of your business, Lady Pegasi.'

'Of course it is! Rose is my best friend.'

'The next word on this will be your last.' Rathborne slammed his fist on the table, and the temperature in the room plummeted. 'Curb your tongue or you'll be sleeping in the dungeons tonight.'

'Just leave it alone,' hissed Wren. Rose's best friend was dangerously close to ruining everything. Wren stepped on her foot under the table, then plastered a smile on her face. 'Celeste is just upset because she knows how much she'll miss me. I'm sure we'll all feel better about this once we eat.' She clicked her fingers impatiently. 'Bring out the next course, please. I'm *ravenous*.'

Celeste looked at her strangely, before drinking deeply from her goblet.

Rathborne's mood perked up when the soup arrived. 'Ah, winter parsnip,' he said, as his guard performed another taste test. 'My favourite.'

'And a Gevran recipe,' said Ansel, delightedly.

'There are a great many things to admire about Gevra,' said Rathborne, taking a big soupy slurp. 'For starters, the Gevran army is second to none.'

Wren dropped her napkin. 'Oops.'

When she bent down to pick it up, she slid the vial of poison from her bodice and settled it on her lap, beneath her napkin. She returned to her soup, using her free hand to gently work the stopper free.

'My brother has devoted particular attention to our army since his coronation.' Ansel nodded in Tor's direction. 'They are not just soldiers but hunters. We are man *and* beast, ferocious in all things. There is nothing hidden that cannot be found by us.'

'Let's hope Rose never tries to escape, then,' muttered Celeste, as she stood up. 'If you'll excuse me a moment, I think I'll take a turn to the privy chamber.'

Wren used the fleeting distraction to scoot her chair closer to Rathborne. His body was turned towards Ansel now, both men mired in discussion of the Gevran army. 'It's the beasts I admire most. How does King Alarik get them so disciplined?'

She planted her elbow on the table and rested her cheek on her palm. She made moon eyes at Ansel as he answered, her other hand inching towards Rathborne's soup.

Wren could feel Tor's gaze on the side of her face, so she untucked her hair and used it as a curtain. Her fingers grazed the rim of Rathborne's soup dish and then—

'BOOM!' Ansel slammed his hands down on the table. 'THE FOX FLEW RIGHT OUT OF THE CANNON.' The plates shook and a mouthful of hot soup sloshed over the rim, on to Wren's wrist. She hinged backwards, trapping a curse between her teeth as she hastily returned the vial to her lap.

Rathborne threw his hands up in uproarious laughter. 'What a blunder!'

'On the contrary,' said Ansel, through his own pealing laughter. 'He survived the entire ordeal. My sister, Anika, was so impressed, she kept him as a pet.'

Rathborne wiped his eyes with his napkin. 'I suppose beast warfare is not without its follies. Though I look forward to seeing it in action.' He pushed his soup away, and Wren's heart sank. 'King Alarik has promised me the full spectacle.'

Ansel's face turned sombre. 'Ah, yes. For your witch problem.'

'Terrible creatures,' said Rathborne, clucking his tongue. 'Your brother has assured me his soldiers will make quick work of them after the wedding. He may have his pick of the witches and let the winter wolves at the rest.' He chuckled, darkly. 'I hear he has quite a fascination for them.'

Wren crushed her fingers into her palms. In that moment, she wanted nothing more than to drown Rathborne in his parsnip soup. She glanced at Tor. He was frowning at the turn in conversation. She hoped that meant he was as uncomfortable with it as any sane person would be. But then again, he was a Gevran . . .

Ansel looked guiltily at Wren. 'I am just relieved Rose will never have to worry about meeting the same dreadful fate as her parents. Or anything so unpleasant as another war under our reign.'

Rathborne clapped his hands, summoning the next course just as Celeste swept back into the room. 'I hope you're not still discussing war. If you are, I'll get drunk and sing something inappropriate.'

Ansel had the good sense to look ashamed of himself. 'Celeste is right. Let's talk not of war tonight. It can make for upsetting conversation.'

'It doesn't upset me. It *bores* me.' Celeste took another swig from her goblet. 'Which I think you'll agree is much worse.'

The Kingsbreath glared at her.

'I'm sure my brother will be happy to discuss his plans for the witches in person once he arrives,' said Ansel, deftly.

Wren couldn't help herself. 'He'll have a hard time finding them.'

Rathborne's smile was slow and curling. 'The desert witches might be lost to us but my spies have come to discover a sizeable settlement in the west.' He leaned towards Wren, dropping his voice to a whisper, as though the secret – and its triumph – was theirs to share. 'Not even the Whisperwind Cliffs and that blasted reef will be able to save them this time.'

Wren went rigid in her seat, the rush of her panic sweeping in to claim her.

No, no, no.

Her heartbeat thrummed in her ears, drowning out the rest of the room. She forgot to blink, to breathe.

Celeste grabbed her knee under the table, jolting her back to life. 'What is it?'

But Wren couldn't speak.

'They've turned themselves into sitting ducks. What a feast they'll be for King Alarik's beasts.' Rathborne laughed brashly, but no one joined in.

Ansel broke the lingering silence in a strained voice. 'Speaking of ducks, I saw the most charming little ducklings on my walk down by the river this morning.' When no one said anything, he went on, braving the awkwardness. 'And what about birds! Ah, *birds*. I've heard the ones in Eana are remarkable. The starcrests are of particular interest to me. I wonder when I might see one of their famous murmurations?'

Rathborne adjusted his collar, and Wren caught a glimpse of the golden key hanging from his neck. 'The starcrests at Anadawn are caged. As all rare birds should be.'

Silence hung heavy as a thundercloud. Wren was afraid if she opened her mouth she might scream, so she said nothing. Beside her, Celeste had lost all interest in conversation and was drinking away the strangeness of the evening. The mood had turned and it seemed not even Ansel could think of a platitude absurd enough to salvage it.

The main course arrived presently. It was roast pork with orange herb sauce, creamy garlic potatoes and seasoned green beans. Cam had excelled, of course, but Wren's stomach was full of bile. She gripped the poison in her lap and pushed her food around her plate, waiting for the others to finish.

When the Gevran ice cake marked the arrival of dessert and the final course of the night, Ansel stood up and pressed a hand to his chest, as if he were welcoming a foreign dignitary. Cam laid it down in the centre of the table, and basked in the prince's praise.

'It is truly a work of art. Should you ever want a job in Grinstad, we would be thrilled to have you!'

Rathborne shook his head. 'I'm afraid I could never part with my best cook.'

'Just Rose, then,' said Celeste, bluntly.

Wren admired her bravery. She suspected if Celeste's

father wasn't Rathborne's personal physician, she would have been marched to the dungeons by the second course.

'You know what would go down delightfully with this?' said Wren. 'A glass of Gevran's finest frostfizz.'

Ansel threw his hands up. 'What an inspired idea!'

Rathborne clicked his fingers and made it so. A moment later, their glasses were full of fizzing alcohol, and his own had passed his poison test. Wren caught Tor's eye as she raised her goblet. 'Why don't we give your soldier one, too, Ansel? He looks thirsty.'

Tor smiled, blandly. 'You're kind to think of me, Your Highness. But I don't drink when I'm on duty.'

'A fine soldier,' grunted Rathborne.

'Fine indeed,' said Wren.

Ansel leaped to his feet. 'A toast!'

While the prince waffled on about kingdoms and friendship and Rose's unfailing beauty, Wren unstrung her drawstring pouch and slipped a few petals free. She let her gaze roam, until it fell on the sconce nearest the window.

She crushed the petals in her fist, using her free hand to cover her whisper.

The petals turned to dust, and across the room, a candle flame flared for the briefest moment. The drapes erupted in a sudden blaze.

Celeste shrieked.

Ansel leaped on to his chair and waved his arms about in a panic. 'FIRE! FIRE IN THE DINING ROOM!' He wobbled as he lost his balance and the chair went flying backwards, knocking him to the ground, where he landed like a winded starfish.

Rathborne raced for the kitchens, while the palace guards ran after him like headless chickens. Celeste followed them. Tor jolted into action, stalking across the room and ripping the drapes to the floor before the ones beside them could catch fire.

He cursed as he stamped the flames out, and Wren, finding herself unwatched for the first time all evening, tipped the vial of devil's root into Rathborne's goblet, before stashing the empty vessel in her pouch. By the time the others had returned from the kitchen carrying jugs of water, the fire was out and Tor was on his hunkers, wiping the sweat from his brow.

Ansel dragged himself up from the floor and peered over the table to make sure it was safe. Then he leaped to his feet. 'What a furore! Apologies, my flower, I'm afraid I took a little tumble before I could rescue you.' He put his hands on his hips. 'Well done, Tor. I knew you'd have it well in hand. Calm as a slumbering ice bear and as prepared as a snow fox in winter. As ever.'

Wren fanned herself. 'Thank goodness everyone is safe.'

Rathborne examined the tattered drapes. 'What on earth happened?'

Tor rolled to his feet. He licked his bottom lip, as if he could taste something in the air. His frown deepened as he tried to make sense of it. 'It must have been a wayward flame.'

'And caught just in time! What a heroic effort!' Wren

raised her goblet. 'I suggest we all drink to this soldier's quick-thinking.'

'To Tor,' said Ansel, raising his goblet.

'To Tor,' said Celeste, joining in.

Rathborne raised his goblet. 'To Gevran competence. May we see more of it in the weeks to come.'

Ansel took a swig of his frostfizz. '*Ah,*' he said, wiping his mouth. 'That certainly does settle the nerves.'

Wren watched Rathborne over the rim of her goblet.

He sipped gingerly, then winced. 'That is strong.'

'Best to down it all in one go,' advised Ansel. 'That's how my brother drinks his. But then again, Alarik has a tolerance like no one I've ever met.'

'Is that so?' said Rathborne, and Wren could have leaned across the table and kissed Ansel for egging him on so beautifully.

The Kingsbreath raised the goblet to his lips and drank deeply. Wren's heart began to beat furiously. Celeste crashed into her shoulder, sending her flying into Rathborne. The goblet flew from his hand and catapulted to the floor.

Wren watched in horror as the rest of the poisonous frostfizz bubbled into the rug. She whirled on Celeste. 'You shoved me.'

'I feel faint,' she said, sinking into her chair. 'It must be the fumes.'

'I don't think I've *ever* encountered such a dramatic evening before,' announced Ansel. 'And that includes the time Anika hurled an ice sculpture at my mother. There must be something in the air tonight.'

'Must be,' said Wren, tightly.

Then Rathborne groaned.

She spun around. 'Willem?'

He wrapped his arms around his stomach and began to retch.

A wild, maddening hope took hold of Wren. 'Are you feeling all right, Willem?'

'I . . . think . . . the . . . fizz . . . was . . . too . . . strong . . . for . . . me.'

'You only had the barest sip,' said Ansel, with a small giggle.

Rathborne pushed away from the table.

Tor rushed to his side as he staggered to the door. Wren could tell the soldier was studying Rathborne – the colour quickly draining from his pallor, the sweat beading on his brow. Another minute and that pesky Gevran might figure out what she did.

She jostled Tor out of the way. 'Stand back. Let his guards through.'

Tor stepped back, and the palace guards promptly escorted Rathborne from the room.

Wren followed them out into the hallway.

'Tell Chapman to fetch Hector. *Ah*. There is such a twisting in my stomach. It *burns*.' Rathborne winced. 'She warned me . . . the flames are inside me . . . the *burning* . . . *ah* . . . but the moon is not yet full, *oh*, the moon . . .' He trailed off, into senseless muttering.

Wren reached for his hand. 'Let me help you, Willem. You can trust me.'

Rathborne pushed her away. He retched again, this time bringing up a mouthful of blood. 'The enemy wears two faces, Rose . . . We must come for the witches before they come for us . . . And they are coming . . . they will burn us . . . the flames . . . I can see them . . . I can taste them . . .' A violent shudder passed through him and he retched again. 'May the Great Protector watch over us now.'

He staggered away, still muttering feverishly to himself. Wren watched him go, wondering who had told him those strange things and what on earth they meant.

'Rose?' Celeste was standing in the doorway to the dining room. 'What the hell is going on?'

'It looks as if the frostfizz didn't agree with poor Willem.' Wren clutched her stomach just as Tor appeared behind Celeste, wearing the same look of bewilderment. She stepped away from both of them. 'Come to think of it, I don't feel too good either. I really should retire.'

Before either of them could say another word, Wren hurried away, the clatter of her footfall filling the halls as she ran for the safety of her tower. Tonight had been a disaster, but if she was lucky – if the fates were watching over her – then that mouthful of poison would be enough to finish Willem Rathborne off for good.

Rose

CHAPTER 22

The sun rose over Ortha, bathing the cliffs in bright golden light.

'*Nnngh.*' Rose rolled over on the scratchy hay mattress but it was no use trying to go back to sleep. The sun was too bright and Banba's snores were practically shaking the entire hut. Even from their height on the cliff, Rose could hear the waves crashing against the rocks and the piercing cries of the gulls.

What she would have given for the gentle silence of her bedroom back in Anadawn Palace, the rustle of silk against her skin and the promise of a lavender-scented bath bubbling nearby. To make matters worse, her head was pounding awfully. It felt like an egg that might crack open at any moment.

The celebration had gone on late into the night, with singing and dancing and drinking – *so much drinking* – and she had watched it all, feeling dizzier by the moment. Shen had stayed by her side, practically daring anyone to try to harm her again. Rose had wanted to send him away for lying to her about Wren but she was too frightened to face the witches by herself. She couldn't forget that awful *whoosh* as the air left her lungs, nor the ratcheting panic that came after, so every time a jug of wine passed by, she'd reached for it and drunk deeply. Far more deeply than she ever would at home.

That had been a mistake.

She vaguely remembered Shen catching her as she stumbled along the beach, away from the bonfire. He and Tilda had carried her up the cliff side, into Banba and Thea's creaking hut. The floor had been unsteady under her feet, though Rose wasn't sure if that was from the wind rattling the wooden slats or the wine rattling her head.

Banba and Thea had come home later, their arms wrapped around each other and their cheeks rosy from drinking. Thea had tucked Rose into bed as if she were a child. Banba had put an empty pot next to it and warned Rose not to vomit on the floor.

Mercifully, Rose had managed not to vomit in the night, but as the wind howled through the little hut, sloshing the liquid in her stomach, she thought she might not be so lucky this morning.

'I'm glad to see you survived the night.' Thea was awake, and sitting in her rocking chair. Her long white hair was pulled back in a braid, and she was smiling.

'Good morning,' croaked Rose. Her headache flared at the sound of her own voice. Goodness, is *this* what drinking did to a person? She felt as if she'd been dragged through the Ganyeve and then left in the sun to bake.

'Since you're awake, I thought you might want to join me for some early morning fishing.'

The mere mention of fish made Rose's stomach roil. 'I'm afraid I'm not feeling my best.'

'The sea air does wonders for a person.' Thea's dark eye crinkled. 'Especially if that person has perhaps indulged in too much wine.'

Rose winced. She did not care to be teased while in such a fragile state.

'Or you can stay here until Banba wakes,' Thea went on, serenely. 'But I should tell you she tends to be at her grumpiest in the mornings.'

Rose sat bolt upright and swept the tangled hair out of her face. 'I'll come with you.'

Rose dressed in one of Wren's drab grey tunics and matching trousers and hastily braided her hair before following Thea down the narrow cliff path, holding her breath until they were safely back on the sand. It was early yet, and Rose was relieved to see they had the beach to themselves. She didn't know if she could face any of the witches just then. Or maybe ever again.

As they drifted towards the shoreline, she flinched at the reflection of the morning sun on the water. Her footsteps slowed as the pain in her head worsened. She didn't want to be here, in this desolate place, so far from the comforts of home and the people she had left behind. She hated feeling so afraid and alone. And then there was the pressing matter of her twin sister, a veritable thief who was planning on stealing her crown!

'You look just like Wren when you scowl like that.'

Rose turned her glare from the too-bright sea and settled it on the woman next to her. She sensed from their meeting last night that Thea was inherently kind, and something about that kindness – offered so freely and without expectation – made everything worse. It was easier to remain steely in front of her fierce grandmother but Thea's warmth made Rose want to curl up into her and cry, and she *could not* do that. The yearning to do so made her even angrier.

'I wouldn't know,' said Rose, hotly. 'Since I've never met her.'

'Ah,' said Thea, in that irritatingly soothing lilt. Before she could say anything more, Rose kicked the sand, sending it flying everywhere.

'I don't know anything, apparently!' she fumed. 'I don't know about stupid witch queens and kings. I'd never even *heard* of Ortha – the place *or* the person – or Banba for that matter! Everything I thought I knew about my own mother was wrong, and to top it all off, I didn't even know the most important thing about myself! That I'm a bloody witch!' She kicked the sand again and hit a rock instead. Rose swore as she lost her balance, staggering into the cold water. The icy bite of the Ortha Sea brought back bad memories of last night.

'It's not my fault, you know!' She stomped through the water, sending sea foam flying everywhere. Her voice got shriller as she whirled on Thea. 'That I'm not precious, clever Wren! That I was raised in the palace instead of this place! Everyone here hates me for something that I had no control over!'

Rose took a shuddering breath. There. Letting out some of her anger had helped, if only a little.

Thea, who had patiently endured her tantrum, simply smiled. 'I know it isn't your fault, Rose. And everyone here doesn't hate you.' She stepped into the sea. 'I think it might help if I did something with that headache of yours, don't you?' When Rose didn't respond, only glared harder at her, the old woman raised her hands, slowly, as though Rose were an animal in danger of startling. She placed them on Rose's head, her thumbs lightly grazing her temples. 'Close your eyes, Rose. Breathe in the sea air and breathe out the pain.'

Rose bristled. 'I really don't think—'

'Hush now.'

Rose did as Thea asked, if only to get it over with. One breath in, another breath out. Again, and then again. Her shoulders relaxed, and a strange rush of warmth coursed through her. The edges of her mind began to tingle and then suddenly – so suddenly she almost missed the moment when it happened – the pain disappeared. And along with it, the rage that had overtaken her.

'*Oh.*' Rose opened her eyes and realized the sun didn't hurt any more. 'Perhaps I should learn how to heal myself next time.' She grimaced at the thought of ever drinking again. 'Not that I plan on there being a next time.'

Thea released her. 'I'm afraid a healer cannot work on themselves, Rose.' She ran an absent finger along the edge of her eye patch and Rose cringed at her own thoughtlessness. 'With each of the five crafts of magic, there must be a balance, and this is ours.'

Rose tried not to stare, but she couldn't help her stirring curiosity.

As if sensing her thoughts, Thea said, 'I lost it in Lillith's War. I'm afraid healers don't often make good fighters. We feel pain too deeply. Our own and others'.'

'I'm sorry,' said Rose, and she was.

'I'm glad I was there.' Thea smiled, sadly. 'I wouldn't have wanted to be anywhere else.'

Rose wondered how many other witches here possessed stories like Thea's. Had their lives changed forever because of the war Willem had declared in her mother's name? Did Rowena and her ilk try to punish Rose for it last night, or did their hatred towards the Valharts run deeper, older?

The water lapped at her ankles as she helped Thea unmoor a small fishing boat from the rocks. The old woman pushed it into the waves, then hopped into it with surprising sprightliness.

Rose waded through the shallows after her. This thing was not strictly a *boat*. It was little more than a raft, browbeaten by the wind and half chewed by the sea. On the rare occasions she'd travelled on the Silvertongue it had been on the Anadawn Royal Fleet, and those boats were so large you barely noticed you were even on the water. Which was exactly how Rose liked it.

'I can't swim,' she said, sheepishly. Better for the witch to know now.

'Well, lucky we are going fishing and not swimming. Come. You'll be safe with me.'

Safety and *witches* didn't exactly go together in Rose's mind, especially after what had happened last night, but when she glanced back at the shore, she saw others emerging from their huts. She had a feeling she would be safer out on the water with Thea than by herself on the beach, so she gathered her courage and hopped into the boat.

While the witches of Ortha rose to face a new day with sore heads, Thea took both oars and rowed Rose away from the shoreline.

They drifted out to sea, and when Thea began to grunt from the effort of rowing, Rose flushed and reached for one of the oars. 'I can help.'

Thea laughed, tilting her head back and showing two neat rows of greying teeth. 'Rose, to teach you how to row would take more effort than rowing myself. But thank you for the offer. Your helpfulness is appreciated.' Her amusement settled into a quiet smile. 'Your mother was like that.'

Rose sat up straighter. 'Did you know her well?'

Thea set the oars to rest. The boat bobbed up and down, the morning waves splashing against the side and sprinkling them with seawater. 'This is as good a place as any to catch some fish, I suppose.' She cast the net over the side and then turned back to Rose.

'Everyone in Ortha knew Lillith. And I knew her more than most. I went with her to Anadawn when she married your father. I promised Banba I would look after her . . .' Her smile faltered. 'I was your mother's midwife. I was the one who first held you and welcomed you into the world.'

Rose gripped the sides of the boat, a distant panic rising inside her. All her life, she had been told that the witch who delivered her had killed her parents. And now, here she was, sitting across from that same woman. She recoiled from Thea, the little boat sloshing dangerously as she scrabbled backwards.

'You needn't be frightened of me, Rose. I was not the one who killed your mother.' Thea's one eye was unblinking, her face unusually grave. 'I believe you now know who it was.'

Rose pressed a trembling hand to her chest. She knew in her bones it couldn't be Thea – this soft-eyed woman, who carried the healing gift within her.

Which meant it was Willem. It had always been Willem.

She tilted her head back until black spots swam in her vision. She felt as if the sunlight was burning away the lies she'd always been told. Always believed. 'Did you see my mother die?'

Thea's silence was answer enough. 'Your mother knew it was coming,' she said, softly. 'But she didn't know how it would happen.'

Rose snapped her chin down, blinking the healer back

into focus. 'How did she know?'

'A seer from the Amarach Towers sent word to Lillith that she had seen her fate in a vision. That she would not survive to see her babies grow up, and that her death would cause a devastating war.' Thea looked past Rose, to where the sun painted the cliffs gold. 'Your father was a good man but he was no witch, Rose. He believed he could stop the seer's prophecy. Keir doubled the guards at the golden gates. He had soldiers stationed at every passageway and alcove inside the palace. And outside the birthing chamber, too.'

Her face tightened. 'Not one of them thought to question the movements of Willem Rathborne. He was the Kingsbreath after all – one of the most important men in Eana, and your father's closest advisor. In many ways, his closest friend. After Rathborne poisoned Keir, he came straight to the birthing chamber. He said he was checking on Lillith on behalf of the king.' The old woman's voice broke, and she looked away. Her tears slipped soundlessly into the sea. 'I should have known then that something was wrong. Keir would never have sent a messenger. But your mother trusted Willem Rathborne right up until he took out the knife.'

Rose flinched. 'I don't want to hear any more.'

Thea reached for her hand, and a trickle of warmth came with it. 'You should know, Rose of Eana, that your mother had made her peace with death. Her last wish was for you and Wren to be safe. She named you before you were born.'

Rose's eyes burned. 'Willem said she whispered my

name with her dying breath.'

'The only honourable thing that rotten vermin ever did was give you the name your mother wanted.'

A tear slid down Rose's cheek. 'Why did you leave me with him? Why didn't you take me, too?'

'It had to be that way, Rose. Everyone in Eana knew Lillith was pregnant. Nobody but your parents, the seer and I knew that there would be two babies. A secret blessing.' Thea's smile was watery. 'And you were the one he saw. Your mother told him your name.'

'And then he killed her.'

'I was bathing Wren in the next chamber when he drew the knife. I knew then that I had one chance to escape, to save the child in my arms and the one in his.' Thea's face crumpled. 'I wish I could have taken you. I've wished that every day for almost eighteen years. But you were so loved, Rose. Even from afar.'

Rose drew a shuddering breath. She felt as if she couldn't get enough air, as if all the lies were filling up the space in her lungs. All her life, she thought she was blessed. But she'd been wrong.

'Your mother named you such because she wanted you to grow where you were planted,' said Thea. 'And one day, she wanted her children to bring the witches back home to Anadawn. It must be a shock to know you will not be Queen, but you see, it has to be Wren. A witch who knows what is best for her people; a witch ready to welcome us home. Only then will there be peace – *true* peace – in Eana.'

'It doesn't sound as if Banba wants peace,' said Rose, bitterly. 'She wants revenge.'

Thea laughed. 'Peace will come after.'

'Willem is too clever. He'll see right through Wren and when he does, he'll come looking for me with two armies at his back.'

When Thea didn't respond, Rose went on. 'Wren will never make it to the throne. She'll be lucky to escape with her life.'

Thea gave her a pitying look. 'You don't know our Wren.'

Rose bristled at those words. *Our Wren*. That was what the witches who had attacked Rose last night had called her sister, too. Wren was precious to everyone in Ortha. She had been blessed with a family of witches. They had raised her, taken care of her, and loved her for exactly who she was. She had everything Rose never had and it still wasn't enough for her. She wanted the throne of Eana, too.

My throne, said a voice inside Rose's head. A spark of anger ignited inside her at the thought of giving up what rightfully belonged to her.

Wren had the witches. Let her keep them.

And let Rose keep the throne that was her birthright.

After all, she had not grown up in a palace, starved of true love, living with her parents' murderer for nothing. If this was the trade-off, so be it. Wren did not get to have it all. She did not get her family and Thea and a lifetime of magic *and* the throne of Eana. It wasn't fair. None of this was fair!

Rose glanced at the shore, and as though she had summoned her with her thoughts of last night, Rowena came striding down the beach, her long blond hair streaming through the air behind her. She was watching Rose and Thea in the boat, her arms folded across her chest.

Thea followed her gaze. 'I'm afraid it's no secret here how you feel about the witches, Rose.'

'Can any of you blame me?' said Rose. 'I have spent my whole life believing that witches are responsible for every bad thing that has ever happened to me. And I'm not alone in feeling that way. If someone so much as sneezes in Eana, they say a witch must be passing by. When the corn crops failed last autumn, everyone said it was the witches who did it. When an Eshlinn boy drowned in the Silvertongue River, his mother swore a witch had cursed him. Every time a violent storm blows in, we fall to our knees and pray to the Great Protector to keep us safe from the witches.'

'And do you believe such rumours now?'

Rose wrung her hands. 'I don't know what I believe. But I don't feel safe here,' she said, her eyes darting back to the shoreline. 'These witches want me dead.'

Thea weighed her words, carefully. 'There are some who think it would be easier that way.'

Hearing it so bluntly sent a new fissure of fear through Rose. 'Why did Shen bother to bring me here, then? Why didn't he just kill me in the desert and be done with it?'

'Because Shen, despite his craft, is no ruthless killer. And more importantly, for every witch here that may wish you ill, there are many more who want to welcome you home. And no one more than your grandmother, though Banba may have a hard time showing it. You will get used to her ways.'

Rose was about to say she had no intention of getting used to anything here in Ortha when a piercing screech rang out. 'What *is* that?'

Thea turned her head, sharply. 'That sound, young Rose, is pain.' She pointed towards a cluster of rocks jutting out from the cliffs. 'There. Do you see it?'

On one of the rocks, a wounded gull was thrashing. Even from a distance, Rose could see its wing was bent. Every time the bird tried to lift itself into the air, it shrieked in agony.

Her heart clenched. 'The poor thing won't last very long out here.'

Thea eyed her carefully. 'You could heal it, you know.'

Rose shook her head. 'I want no part of magic.'

Thea raised a brow but didn't question her. Instead, she rowed towards the crying gull, the fishing net drifting with them. The bird squawked as the boat drew level with the rocks.

Rose covered her ears, but her heart clenched, painfully. The pull towards the injured bird was difficult to ignore. 'Hurry up and heal it.'

Thea set the oars down. 'I'm not going to heal it.'

Rose glowered at her. 'Then you are just being cruel.'

'No crueller than you. You can heal the bird, too.'

'*You* are the healer.'

'We are both healers, Rose.' When Rose didn't respond, only glared harder, Thea reached over and scooped the flailing gull into her hands. She held it out to Rose. 'Your gift moves inside you. It is time to accept it. It is time to know this part of yourself.'

Rose squeezed her eyes shut. 'No. And you can't make me.' She sounded like a spoilt child but she didn't care. What had happened with Shen in the hot spring had been an accident, a memory she desperately hoped to forget in time. But if she healed something again, on purpose and with intention, it would mean she had chosen to live as a witch.

'Then we will let it suffer.' The gull let out a pitiful cry as Thea laid it in her lap. 'It will die eventually. Either it will starve or another bird will come along and eat it.'

Rose opened her eyes. The poor bird had fallen still. She sensed defeat in its beady eyes, and it made a part of her soul ache. She knew it was just her magic toying with her emotions, but it felt real. It felt painful.

Thea cupped her hands underneath the bird. 'Or we can simply toss it in the water and give it to the fish.'

'No!' Rose flung her hands out. 'Give it to me.'

'Only if you are sure, Rose. After all, intent is . . .'

'I know, I know. Intent is what matters most,' said Rose, impatiently. 'I want to heal the bird. All right? I don't want it to be in pain any more.'

The corner of Thea's mouth twitched as she settled the bird in Rose's lap.

Rose laid her hands on the quivering creature. She could

feel its tiny heartbeat fluttering against her fingertips. Its wing was bent so badly that bone was piercing through its feathers.

'I . . . I don't know what to do. When I healed Shen, I didn't even think about it.' Rose flushed at the memory of her hands on his bare leg. 'I just put my hands on the wound, and then it healed. Like . . .'

'Magic?' said Thea, wryly. 'You must have wanted to heal him so badly that you did it without realizing how. Try that now. Focus on the bird. Let your desire guide you.'

Rose closed her eyes. She saw the bird's life like a golden thread in her mind, short and dimly glowing. She reached towards it.

The gull twitched in her hands.

Calm your heart, anxious one. Let me heal what is broken.

Her fingers began to prickle. Beneath them, she felt the fine bones knitting themselves back together, one by one. In her mind, the golden thread grew stronger, brighter.

'Good,' said Thea, in a low voice. 'Now gently set the wing.'

Barely breathing, Rose let her instincts guide her. She moved her fingers, slowly, gently. With a small click, the wing slid into place.

Her eyes flew open. 'I did it!'

The bird flapped suddenly, its mended wing whacking Rose in the face. She laughed and let go. With a resounding squawk, the gull lifted into the air. It glided in a circle above them, before taking off for the shore.

Rose flopped backwards, her rush of exhilaration quickly followed by a wave of fatigue. She had *healed* something. On purpose!

'You'll find that healing is exhausting. You must be mindful of your limits.' Thea patted her knee. 'I'm proud of you, Rose. Shen was right, you are a natural.'

Rose beamed with pride. She'd never been told she was a natural at anything. It felt nice to be good at something. Even if that something was magic.

'And fitting, too, that you healed a bird out here in the ocean,' Thea mused. 'You do know the origin of Eana, don't you?'

'Of course,' said Rose. 'The Great Protector founded Eana over a thousand years ago. He came here from the Eternal Kingdom in a ship full of gallant knights and beautiful maidens, and together they cast out the witches and freed the land from dark magic. The Protector established a ruling monarchy that— What? Why are you looking at me like that?'

Thea hmm'd. 'That is a pretty story but I'm afraid it is not the truth. And it certainly does not explain why our island is shaped like a bird.'

Rose laughed. 'Shaped like a bird? What are you talking about?'

'Haven't you ever seen a map?'

'Of course I have! But Eana simply looks like Eana.'

'Next time, look closer.' Thea swept her finger through the air as if to draw it. 'Our land marks the shape of a bird in flight. Right now, we're tucked neatly under its wing.'

Rose gave Thea a polite smile. 'That's a nice image.'

'It is this way because our land was once a bird.'

Rose laughed again, more uncomfortably this time. She was beginning to wonder about the old witch's mind, and if perhaps she might need some healing of her own. 'I'm quite certain Eana is made of earth and desert and rivers, much like any other land.'

Thea went on as if she hadn't heard Rose. 'Eana, of course, is not the bird itself. Rather, it is who this land is named for. Eana was the first witch. Many thousands of years ago, she lived among the stars, flying from one to the next on the back of her green-tailed hawk. But one day she grew tired of flying in the sky. She wanted to settle somewhere, to feel sand on her feet and the spray of saltwater against her skin. And so, she bid her hawk to land in the sea, and with her magic, turned him into land. In time, others like Eana came, and the land grew to welcome them. She ruled as the first witch queen, and the gift of her magic was passed down from generation to generation.' Thea nodded at Rose, a sudden knowing look in her eye. 'The blood of Eana runs through every witch. That is why we are fated to rule this island.'

Rose didn't know if it was exhaustion from healing or the weight of another truth settling on her shoulders but she found she was trembling again. 'I am Eana; Eana is me,' she whispered.

'Exactly,' said Thea. 'Exactly.'

They drifted in the sea a while longer, Rose staring at the changing horizon and thinking about the blood of Eana that ran in her veins.

Thinking about the truth of what had happened to her parents.

And about the sister she had never met, who now wanted to steal her throne.

Rose knew she would be a good queen. To all of Eana, including the witches. Wren may know about being a witch, but she knew nothing about ruling.

Or sisterhood, for that matter. What kind of sister would steal her twin's entire life?

When the wind picked up in a sudden flurry, Thea cast a worried glance towards the shore.

Banba was pacing back and forth with her hands in the air.

The wind howled as another violent gust jostled the boat. Rose gripped the sides, yelping at the sudden spray of saltwater.

'Time to go home.' Thea hauled the net up and dragged it into the boat. It was full of silver fish, wriggling and thrashing at Rose's feet. 'It looks as if we'll have a bit of help today.'

Another gust swept under the boat and pulled them towards the shore.

Rose stiffened as they picked up speed. 'Does she always do this?'

'Throw the wind around for no reason? Only when she's

anxious.' Thea frowned. 'We haven't heard from Wren yet. Your arrival is the first sign that the switch even happened. Banba is getting worried about her. In truth, we all are.'

Even though they'd never met, and Wren was clearly no friend to Rose, a prickle of unease crept up the back of her neck. She thought of her sister, alone in the palace, trying to fool one of the smartest men in Eana. No matter how much she thought she knew about Rose's life, or how much magic she used to try to take it from her, Wren would never fool the man who had raised Rose as his own daughter.

When Rose returned to shore, she clambered out of the boat, looked Banba straight in the eye and said, 'You're right to be worried.'

Wren

CHAPTER 23

Wren stood alone on the cliffs of Ortha, screaming for her grandmother. Banba couldn't hear her. She was scrabbling through the sand on her hands and knees as a mighty snow tiger prowled after her. Across the cove, witches were wailing, the sea frothing with their blood.

'You promised you would save us!' Banba's voice reached Wren from the howling abyss. 'You promised us a new world!'

Wren's terror burned in her throat as she clawed her way down, down, down. But the cove was empty now and the sand was stained red. She knelt over her grandmother's body, pressing her fingers against the puncture wounds in her neck. The green of Wren's cloak turned white, her skirts spilling out in endless reams of lace as a menacing growl rolled in from the sea. The waves turned to beasts before Wren's eyes, with fur like snow and fangs dripping with blood. Behind them, Ansel sauntered through the surf in an ivory doublet inlaid with golden brocade.

He offered her his hand, the same blood dripping from his fingers.

'Shall we dance, my flower?'

Wren woke up screaming.

The bedroom door pounded then swung open, and a palace guard came sweeping in, his sword drawn. Wren sat bolt upright in bed, pulling the duvet up to her chin. 'Get out!' she said, in a strangled voice. 'It was just a nightmare!'

The guard gave her a worried once-over before hastily backing out of the room.

Wren flopped back on to her pillow, her breath whooshing out of her. She was safe. In Anadawn. As far from Ortha as she'd ever been. She'd never been more grateful not to be a seer. To know that her vision of Banba was just a nightmare, and nothing more. But still, it had unsettled her. She had to send word to her grandmother.

Wren rolled out of bed and reached for the pitcher of water on the nightstand, gulping it straight down without bothering to find a glass. Then she stared at herself in the mirror. She looked like hell, the shadow of her nightmare pooling underneath her eyes. Her hair was streaked with her own fading golden strands, and even though the sun-warmed hue of her skin was naturally wearing off, her freckles were stubborn. She quickly recast her enchantment before choosing a flowing lilac day dress from Rose's wardrobe.

A short while later, Agnes arrived with breakfast. 'You don't look well at all, Princess,' she said, as she laid the breakfast tray down.

Wren picked distractedly at a bowl of berries. 'Never

mind about me. How is Willem?'

Agnes shook her head, sombrely. 'No improvement, I'm afraid. Hector's been with him all night.'

'I'm so worried.' Wren's words were truthful, though not for the reasons Agnes suspected. With Rathborne clinging to life, the wedding was still hurtling towards her at full speed, and with it, the Gevrans' imminent invasion. She needed the Kingsbreath to die – and *fast* – so she could finally be in charge of her own decisions. She would cancel the wedding, send Ansel on the first ship back to Gevra and throw a coronation so grand, no one would even remember the Gevran prince's name.

But if Rathborne didn't die – if he somehow managed to recover from her attempted poisoning – then Wren would have to find a way to kill him all over again. And after the disaster that had been the dinner party, she had more than one suspicious pair of eyes already trained on her. Tor's curiosity was one thing – he was, after all, a stranger in this land – but with the backing of her father Hector, Celeste's mistrust could sink Wren.

It could sink all of them.

Wren's failure wouldn't just doom herself. It would doom the witches, too. Once Alarik Felsing gained his foothold in Eana, his beasts would savage the beaches of Ortha, tearing the witches limb from limb. All of this planning – these long years of preparation and hope – would be for nothing.

They would all die screaming.

Wren pushed her food away. 'I think I'll go for my morning

walk. You'll find me if anything changes, won't you?'

Agnes regarded her with doleful eyes. 'Of course, Princess. In the meantime, try not to worry yourself sick. The Great Protector will watch over the Kingsbreath. After all, dear Willem has been a protector of this country in his own way, too.'

Wren slipped from the room and hurried down the tower stairwell. Out in the courtyard, she smiled tightly at a pair of palace guards, who seemed equally out of sorts. Though the day was warm and bright, a heavy cloud of expectation lingered about the palace. One that might break apart to bring sunshine or shatter in a rail of thunder, depending on Rathborne's fate.

Wren found her way to the mews, a row of wooden huts tucked around the back of the palace, where the grass was long and bright with wildflowers. Inside, messenger birds watched her through the wires of their cage. Chapman was going through one of his endless scrolls with the guards here, taking notes with his feather quill.

Frustration roiled inside Wren. Every time she came down here, that busy little weasel was hovering nearby. Chapman kept a close eye on everything in Anadawn, even the falcons. No message could be sent to the skies above Eshlinn without his approval. Even if Wren waited until he left to send a bird, she couldn't risk it turning around and delivering her message straight to Rathborne.

She marched back towards the rose garden, where she paced among the haggard bushes. The statue of the Great

Protector stared down at her with blank, marble eyes. Wren couldn't wait for the day she could finally take a mallet to it.

She sank on to the bench and stared up at the sky. 'I need help,' she said, to the wind. 'I need a way to reach my grandmother.'

For a while, there was nothing but the breeze frittering about her ears. Then came a distant creak as the window in the west tower opened, just enough for a lone starcrest to step out on to the ledge. It dropped from the tower in a glint of silver and landed neatly on the statue's head.

Strange. If Rathborne was on his deathbed, then who was that tending to his birds?

'Go on,' said Wren, willing it to shit on the Protector. 'I won't say a word.'

The starcrest chirped once, then swooped down to land on the bench.

Wren stared at the bird.

The bird stared back.

She had never seen a starcrest up close before. Its beady eyes were as bright and unyielding as the full moon. It almost felt as if the bird recognized her, sensed the craft moving in her bones and knew they were one and the same: magic-born creatures trapped together in this stifling place. Wren glanced up at the west tower, searching for its sender. There was nothing but the sheen of sunshine on the glass.

'Looks as if it's just you and me, little one. Perhaps you can do me a favour . . .' She removed the note she had written that morning from the bodice of her dress and rolled it up tight. It contained a quick and furious warning to Banba, Wren's panic spilling out on to the piece of parchment, before she could stop it. Still, it was best to be honest, to warn the witches of what was coming. She unwound the ribbon from her hair and used it to tie the message to the bird's foot. The starcrest stilled beneath her as she crushed a handful of petals over its black feathers, magic devouring them as they fell. *'From earth to dust, where seagulls roam, please guide this message safely home.'*

The starcrest chirped one final time before lifting off the bench.

'Fly fast and true.' Wren sent the words up like a prayer, watching the bird until it turned west and disappeared among the clouds. Then she left the rose garden and returned to her bedroom where she found a different note waiting for her.

Wren's heart sank when she read it.

Meet me at the baths at noon – Celeste

Celeste was already in the palace baths when Wren arrived. The room was hot and humid, plumes of steam gathering in its domed ceiling before pearling into beads that raced each other down the mosaicked walls. The steam did little to soothe Wren's anxiety about the meeting, but she was careful not to show it on her face. Celeste was sitting on the edge of a marbled basin, her legs swinging back and forth in the water. She was wearing a white bathing robe, her dark curls twisted into a bun at the crown of her head. She waved at Wren through the steam. 'I see you got my message.'

'Interesting suggestion for a meet-up.' Wren settled herself across from Celeste. She had commandeered a blue silk robe and a pair of slippers from Rose's closet. She kicked them off now and dropped her feet into the water, revelling in the fizzle of bath salts between her toes.

'Is it?' said Celeste, raising a brow. 'We often meet here.'

'I know,' said Wren, quickly. The steam was curling the tendrils of hair around her face, and she was suddenly conscious of her enchantment. 'But it's a lovely day outside. I thought maybe we would go for a walk instead.'

'I want to talk where we won't be overheard.' The steam thickened, casting a thick haze about Celeste's face, so Wren couldn't read her expression. 'Father says the Kingsbreath is gravely ill. He fights for every breath.'

Wren tensed at the reminder. 'Poor Rathborne. I've been *so*—'

'Willem,' said Celeste.

'What?'

'You called him Rathborne just now.' Celeste's dark brown eyes flashed through the steam, keen as a hawk's. 'You never call him that.'

Wren swallowed. 'Willem, then.'

'Father can't find a cause for his sudden illness,' Celeste continued. 'He suspects he might have been poisoned.'

A bead of sweat trickled down Wren's spine. *'Really?'*

'He even asked for my account of the dinner.'

Wren went very still. She recalled how Celeste had knocked her into Rathborne, sending the frostfizz flying everywhere. She had been hoping it really was an accident, but the back of her neck was beginning to prickle. 'And what did you tell him?'

'I told him I didn't see anything.'

Wren exhaled through her nose. 'Perhaps Willem is allergic to frostfizz. Whatever it is, I'm sure we'll get to—'

'But I think I did see something.' Celeste pitched forward, her face appearing in a cloud of steam. 'You tampered with his drink.'

'What?' A strangled laugh seeped out of Wren.

'I thought I imagined it at first,' said Celeste. 'It was so quick, so unexpected. But then I watched you watch him. It was as if you were *willing* him to drink.' She planted her arms on either side of Wren, pinning her to the seat. 'I was already suspicious, of course. You were acting strangely all night. You've been acting strangely for a while now.'

Another bead of sweat dripped off Wren's nose and pooled in the hollow between her collarbones. She felt suddenly as if she was in a heat-addled dream. She dipped her hands in the water and splashed some on her chest. 'I think the steam is toying with your memories, Celeste.'

Celeste's frown sharpened. 'Who *are* you?'

'I'm your best friend,' said Wren, but anxiety trilled in her voice. Her composure was slipping. The steam was stinging her eyes and filling her throat and she was finding it hard to breathe.

Celeste was steely-eyed in the heat. 'You are *not* Rose.'

'You're being absurd, Celeste.' Wren stood up, abruptly. 'If I don't get out of here now, I think I'll evaporate.'

Celeste shot to her feet and grabbed her shoulders. 'What's my horse's name?'

'Lady,' said Wren, without missing a beat.

'What are you most afraid of?'

'Drowning.'

'What am *I* most afraid of?'

'A life without adventure.' Wren guessed that last one but she could tell by the disgruntled look on Celeste's face that she was right.

Celeste tightened her grip, her nails digging into Wren's collarbones. 'Remember after my mother died, you decided we should sneak into the kitchens when everyone was asleep and eat our fill of pear tarts, and the following morning, when Cam found me asleep by the stove and covered in crumbs, you leaped to my defence and swore on all the stars in Eana it was the palace rats that did it.'

'Of course,' said Wren, without blinking. 'How could I forget something like that?'

Celeste pursed her lips. 'That never happened.'

Hissing seaweed.

'You tricked me,' said Wren, indignantly.

'How about another one, then.' Celeste's voice dripped with sarcasm. 'When's my birthday?'

Suddenly, Wren was glad of the steam gathering between

them. It hid the look of sheer panic on her face.

Celeste released her with a shove. 'It's today.'

Wren squeezed her eyes shut, dread sinking like a stone in her gut. How had she forgotten something so important? What a fool she was! 'Happy birthday?' she said, weakly.

'Don't even bother,' snapped Celeste. 'In all the years we've known each other, you've never once forgotten my birthday. And last night, you threw a dinner for your prince and served cake in *his* honour.'

'*Oh*,' was all Wren could manage. She was well and truly scuppered. In fact, she had been since the moment she'd planned that cursed dinner.

Celeste wasn't done. 'I've known Rose Valhart all my life. I know her every expression, her sense of humour, her heart. I know *her*. And I don't know you. You might be a good imitation but you are not good *enough*.' She prodded Wren in the chest. 'I'll give you one chance, here and now, to be honest with me. If you lie one more time, I'll scream for the palace guards and have you hauled to the dungeons. Who are you, really?'

Wren raked the damp hair from her face, the heat of her panic mingling with the steam. She contemplated lying.

'Don't even think about it,' warned Celeste.

Wren wilted. It was over, and they both knew it. Her ruse had come to a crashing end. If she let Celeste walk out that door, Wren would be marched to the dungeons before morning, or worse, left hanging from the Protector's Vault. She sank down into the bath. The water lapped at her waist, her robe floating around her like a brightly coloured water lily. 'My name is Wren. Rose is my twin sister.'

Celeste stood over her. 'How is that even possible?'

'Eighteen years ago, Willem Rathborne murdered my parents,' said Wren, raising her head so Celeste could read the truth in her eyes. 'The midwife escaped with me moments before Rathborne killed my mother. He only kept my sister alive so he could keep control of the throne. He's still trying to keep control of it.'

'That's not what happened,' said Celeste, firmly. 'The midwife—'

'Everything you've heard is a lie,' said Wren, flatly. She knew it wasn't Celeste's fault for being hoodwinked like the rest of Eana, but she couldn't help the sudden bite of her anger. 'The midwife, Thea, was part of my mother's family. She came to Anadawn to protect her.'

Celeste shook her head. 'No. That can't be true.'

'Then explain *me*.'

The silence stretched, the steam thickening between them.

'I can't explain you,' said Celeste, uneasily. 'It doesn't make any sense.'

'It does if you listen to my version. The *correct* one.'

'What have you done with Rose?'

'She's safe.'

'Where?'

'Far away.' Wren pointed in the general direction of west. 'She's in a village by the sea.'

Celeste slowly lowered herself on to the ridge. 'Are there cliffs there?'

'Towering ones,' said Wren. 'The sight of them alone would steal the breath from your lungs.'

'I think I've seen that place in my dreams,' murmured Celeste, more to herself than to Wren.

'It's where our mother grew up.'

'You're like Lillith, aren't you? You're a *witch*.' Celeste's voice caught on the last word.

Wren offered the ghost of a smile. 'I suppose it takes one to know one.'

'Don't you dare call me that,' said Celeste, through her teeth. 'I'm no witch.'

Wren rolled her eyes. 'You think your visions of Rose in Ortha are some kind of happy accident? Come on, Celeste. You're smarter than that. Haven't you been wondering why you're so sensitive to Rathborne's starcrests?' Wren could tell by the horror on Celeste's face that she had never even considered that a possibility. If Wren's suspicions were true, then Celeste's craft must be half buried in her bones, stifled by years of fear and denial.

Now was clearly not a good time to prod her on the matter.

Celeste gripped the edge of the bath. 'Why are you *doing* this?'

'I have to save the witches from the Kingsbreath.'

'And you really think wrecking Rose's marriage and stealing her crown is the only way to do that?'

'Yes,' said Wren, evenly. 'And it's not as if you even want

the marriage to happen either. In case you hadn't noticed, Rose is being tricked. The second she says "I do" to Ansel, she'll be shipped off to Gevra, and this kingdom will remain under the control of Willem Rathborne.'

Celeste didn't deny her concerns. 'If you really cared about Rose, you wouldn't have delivered her to the witches.'

'It's the Gevrans you need to worry about.' Wren stood up, sending rivulets of water everywhere. 'But I can stop them, Celeste. I can stop all of this.'

'By trying to kill the Kingsbreath, you mean?' Celeste shook her head in disbelief. 'Are you out of your mind? That's treason!'

Wren flashed her teeth. 'Only a little.'

Celeste tightened her robe and stepped out of the bath. 'I have a good mind to turn you in right now.'

Wren grabbed her by the wrist. 'If you send me to the dungeons, you send Rose to her death in Ortha.'

'Ansel would never let his soldiers kill his bride.' Celeste shook Wren off and stalked towards the door. 'He'll scour every inch of the country for her first. *After* he sees you punished for your deception,' she said, over her shoulder. 'You know, the Gevrans use common thieves as chew toys for their beasts. I can't *imagine* what kind of torture betraying a prince of the realm will earn you.'

'Ansel won't get to Rose before Banba does!' Wren called after her. 'My grandmother has spies in every corner of this palace. How do you think I got in here so easily? If you turn me in, she'll kill Rose.'

Celeste stopped walking. 'You're lying.'

'Risk it, then.' Wren kept her voice steady. It was a bluff, but it was the only thing she could think to do – to barter Rose's safety for her own and pray that Celeste's loyalty to her friend was stronger than her hostility towards Wren. She stepped out of the bath. '*Or* we could go about this a different way. Preferably one in which neither I nor Rose has to die.'

Celeste turned around. 'If you think I'm going to let you run around Anadawn with your schemes and your poison, you are sorely mistaken.'

'I'm only after the Kingsbreath. Rose deserves to be free of him. We all do.'

Celeste's nostrils flared. 'If you really cared about Rose, you wouldn't be stealing her life. You just want to usurp the throne.'

Wren shrugged. There was no point in denying it. 'Can't both things be true?'

The silence grew thick and hazy, both girls glaring at each other through the steam.

'Three days,' said Celeste, at last. 'You have three days to return Rose safely to Anadawn. If you don't bring her back to me, I'll turn you in.'

Wren pretended to consider the deal. Even if she wanted to bring Rose back to the palace, which of course she had no intention of doing, the princess had travelled far beyond her reach. She would need a horse as quick as Storm to fetch her. And there was only one of those in all of Eana.

But Wren wasn't bargaining for her freedom. She was bargaining for time. And for now, three days was enough to come up with a way to deal with Rose's best friend.

'Very well, Celeste.' Wren brushed the tendrils from her face and met Celeste's gaze with bold conviction. 'In three days' time you will be with Rose again.'

Celeste pulled her arms around herself, studying Wren for a long moment. 'It's the strangest thing,' she said, at last. 'You look so much like Rose that my instinct is to trust you.'

Wren smirked as she bent down to retrieve her slippers. Perhaps Celeste wasn't a seer after all.

Rose
CHAPTER 24

The witches were nothing like Rose had imagined. There was so much laughter in Ortha. And dancing and singing, and storytelling. Not that Rose took part in any of it. She was as wary of the witches as they were of her. Every day, she felt their hardened stares and heard their judging whispers, but she held her head high, making sure to keep her distance from Rowena and her hateful friends.

Each night, Rose watched the moon grow fuller in the sky and knew she was running out of time. Her coronation was fast approaching. She would not let Wren steal her throne from her and hand it to the witches. What would that leave for Rose in the end? She refused to live out the rest of her days in Ortha, reeking of seaweed and brine, pretending to be something she was not. *She* was the princess of Eana, and she had spent her entire life preparing to be Queen. That destiny belonged to her, and her alone.

The thought of confronting Willem made Rose feel ill, but with her eighteenth birthday looming, the Kingsbreath's sway over her was finally waning, and she was no longer a little girl, afraid of the world beyond the golden gates. She resolved to return to Anadawn at the earliest opportunity and face the man who had lied to her, no matter how much it terrified her. It was time he gave up his grip on the throne.

And so, as the days passed, she grew more observant. She learned as much as she could about the movements of the Ortha witches, and quietly, carefully, planned her escape.

The day after her arrival, Banba had told Rose to start making herself useful, and Rose had quickly learned how few useful skills she possessed. She couldn't cook or fish, nor could she clean or gut the fish without retching. She had no idea how to forage for plants or weave rope, and once, when she tried to mend an old tunic with Thea, she somehow managed to sew her own hair underneath the hem.

Tilda had been the one to suggest Rose help with her chores. So, each morning Rose donned Wren's old clothes and worn leather boots and braided her hair, before heading down to the beach to help the young witch gather driftwood.

'My best friend, Celeste, would be shocked if she saw me now,' she told Tilda when they were looking for crabs in the surf one morning, almost two weeks after Rose had arrived in Ortha. 'She's always harping on about the virtues of trousers, but I'm afraid a queen and her noblewomen simply cannot be so informal.'

Tilda laughed as she skipped through the waves. 'Wren has never worn a dress in her life. Not even on Candlemas! I think she will be a different kind of queen.'

'I'm sure she will,' said Rose, mildly.

Tilda peered at her over her shoulder. 'Are you sad to be missing your wedding? I heard Shen telling Banba at the bonfire about your special prince.'

Rose stiffened. 'That's none of his business.'

'I suppose it's Wren's business for now.' Tilda wrinkled her nose. 'If it helps, Wren always says she'd rather drown in the sea than ever get married, so I don't think she will steal your sweetheart from you. Maybe you can have him back after all this coronation business is over.' She grinned, toothily. '*Or* you could find a new sweetheart here in Ortha instead!'

'Tilda!' said Rose, aghast.

The little girl pealed into laughter.

'That's quite enough chatter,' said Rose, in a bluster. In recent days, she hadn't been thinking very much about Prince Ansel. She hadn't even considered the possibility that her sister would steal her throne *and* her fiancé. And anyway, the prince would surely be understanding when Rose returned to Anadawn and explained the whole sorry tale to him. Especially since he had undoubtedly already figured out that Wren was not who she was pretending to be.

After Tilda ran off to help with lunch, Rose glanced over her shoulder to make sure nobody was following her, then crept towards the Whisperwind Cliffs. She had expected the witches to pay close attention to her, but most of the time, they seemed completely unconcerned with where she was or what she was doing. It was clear they thought her incapable of doing anything that required a measure of strength and fortitude, that a lifetime of being served by others at Anadawn had made her fearful and helpless. Well, all the better for her. She had been climbing the cliffs in secret for days now – a little bit at a time – trying to build confidence in her footing. Today, with the wind so calm, she made it higher than she ever had before. She was contemplating going all the way up and not turning back, when she bumped straight into Shen.

They faced each other on a narrow ridge. 'What are you doing all the way up here?' she said.

Shen arched a brow. 'I should be asking you the same thing.'

Rose's cheeks burst into flames. 'I . . . I wanted a moment to myself.'

'At such dizzying heights?' Shen's dark gaze roamed her face. He gestured to her neck. 'What happened to your locket?'

Rose blinked. 'What?'

'The one from your Gevran. You know, the sacred glittering repository of his delicate golden hair?'

'Oh.' Rose pressed a hand to her neck and only then realized she wasn't wearing Ansel's locket. That she hadn't been wearing it for days. And worse than that, she had no idea where it was.

'I've hidden it,' she lied. 'Under my pillow. I didn't want to risk it being stolen by a witch.'

'How sensible of you.' Shen's eyes danced and Rose knew he suspected the terrible truth – that she hadn't been thinking all that much about her beloved.

'Not that it is *any* of your business,' she added, as an afterthought.

'Do you miss him?'

'Who?'

Shen grinned. 'Your snowy prince.'

'Oh! Yes. Of course.' Rose frowned. She did miss Ansel, didn't she? Perhaps it was a bit strange that she'd barely thought of him this past week, but then she'd been so distracted. Her thoughts had been taken up with the witches and her plans for escape.

'Anyway, if you'll excuse me, I'll be on my way,' she said, trying to scoot past Shen. 'I'm sure you have somewhere to be. Someone to kidnap, perhaps.'

Shen moved in front of her. 'Rose. I've missed you recently, you know.'

Rose started at his candour. It did something to her heart, made it feel as if it was going far too fast and much too slow all at once. Though she hated to admit it, a small part of her had missed him, too. It was that musical laugh, and the stories he told. And maybe it was even the way he said her name. As if it were a precious jewel.

'I'm sure you say that to all the girls.'

'I don't.'

'Well, you forget your word means nothing to me.'

'You can't be mad at me forever, Rose.'

She pursed her lips. 'I think you'll find that I can.'

'How about today you give me a reprieve? I'm on my way to the hives, and I'd like to show them to you.' He offered her a half-smile. 'You can be angry at me again tomorrow.'

Rose faltered. To her deep, unsettling surprise, she realized she did want to accompany him to the hives. She'd never felt this way before about anyone. Never missed them. Never wondered what they were thinking about. Never wanted to face the collective intimidation of ten thousand bees just to spend time with them.

Oh, crumbs.

Well, she reasoned with herself, she really did have a royal duty to taste this honey. For research purposes. And for Cam. Yes, Cam would certainly want to know what Ortha honey was like. He was fascinated by new delicacies, always fawning over the treats and spices his husband smuggled home from his trips.

'Well, Princess? What's it to be?'

Rose chewed on her bottom lip. Then her face split into a mutinous grin. 'I'm feeling generous today, bandit. You may have your reprieve. But tomorrow, I shall return to being mad at you.'

'Forever, right?' said Shen, teasingly.

'Forever.'

The hives were higher still. Rose had the uncanny feeling that Shen could have scaled the cliffs in minutes if he'd wanted to but he let her set the pace as they climbed the narrow ridges. The wind picked up and gusted around them, but Rose had learned to press herself against the rock whenever it whistled by.

She kept her eyes on her feet so she wouldn't stumble. 'These cliffs are certainly well-named!'

'The first witch, Eana, named them long ago,' said Shen, from behind her. 'Careful.' He shot out a steadying hand just as Rose slid on a scattering of loose shale.

She yelped as she flattened herself against the rock face. 'I thought I was getting better at this.'

'You are,' said Shen. 'And it must be easier to climb in those trousers rather than your nightgown.' Though Rose wasn't looking at him, she could hear the smirk in his voice.

'It may sound frivolous to you but I miss my real clothes. Their frills and lace; the fullness of my skirts.' She sighed, wistfully. 'My dresses have always felt like a kind of armour to me. When I wear them, I feel stronger, somehow. Braver.' She bit her lip. 'You must think that very silly indeed . . .'

To her surprise, Shen didn't laugh. 'Not at all,' he said, contemplatively. 'I imagine the battles a princess must fight don't often call for knives and swords.'

'No,' said Rose, feeling glad to be understood. She gestured at the tunic she was wearing. 'And even though this is quite drab and shapeless, I suppose it is an improvement from my nightgown. I don't think my maids would even recognize it now. It was absolutely filthy and it reeked.'

Shen laughed. 'In Ortha, we wash our clothes in the sea so we can never escape the smell of it.'

Rose glanced back at him. 'But you love the sea, don't you?'

Shen shrugged. 'I like it well enough. But not like I love the desert. The sands will always be my first home.' His voice turned wistful, and Rose glimpsed something in him that she had not noticed before – it was sadness. It moved like a shadow behind his eyes.

'The desert is very beautiful,' she conceded, and something in Shen's face softened.

'The Ganyeve possesses its own special kind of magic,' he said, his gaze turning distant. 'Legend says that before Eana brought her hawk to land in the sea, she and the sun were lovers. And when she left for another life in a new world, the sun came down from the sky to kiss her goodbye. But while Eana could withstand the heat, the land could not. The kiss scorched the earth and the desert was born. It was a gift to this new land, sun-warmed and golden. A gift to the witch who made it. But the desert never forgot the sun. That's why the sands are always moving, always shifting – they're trying to go home.'

Rose came to a stop, entranced by the tale. Where once she might have thought such a story ridiculous, she found she wanted to hear more. 'I've never heard these legends before.'

Shen turned back to the cliffs. 'The Valharts have always feared our tales. After all, the legends speak of power they can never hope to have. The best way to kill a memory is to stop speaking it aloud.' He pressed a hand against Rose's back, nudging her on. 'But we will never stop speaking our stories. And you deserve to hear them, Princess.'

Rose tried to ignore the feeling of Shen's hand on her lower back, his breath on her neck. The path narrowed, climbing steeply up the cliffs, and it took all of her concentration now to steady her feet.

When another gust came howling, Rose stumbled. Shen caught her in the same heartbeat, his arm tightening around her waist.

'Oh!' Flustered, she quickly stepped back. Her foot dangled in mid-air.

Shen yanked her into his chest and twirled her until her back was flush against the cliff. 'Careful, Princess.'

They stared at each other for an aching moment, almost nose to nose, before he loosened his grip. He passed a hand across his jaw, his expression unreadable. 'We're almost there. The alcove's just up ahead.'

'It's a shame I can't control the wind the way Banba does,' said Rose, striving for breeziness.

Stop being silly, she scolded herself. She'd ridden on a horse with Shen for two days. She shouldn't be so affected by him grabbing her for a moment out of sheer necessity.

'Growing up, Wren always envied your grandmother for that,' said Shen, fondly. 'She badly wanted to be a tempest.'

'Doesn't an enchanter have their own charms?'

'Of course. Just as healers do.'

'And then that leaves you, Shen Lo.' Rose stole another glance at him. 'The warrior witch.'

Shen flattened his hand on the cliff side, then kicked his legs out over the edge, clicking them together at the heels.

Rose shrieked. 'Shen!'

He landed neatly on the ridge, then dropped into an elaborate bow. A strand of black hair came loose, dipping into his eye. 'At your service,' he said, sweeping it away.

Rose pressed a hand to her chest to calm her thundering heart. She was sure it was about to gallop right out of her chest. 'Don't *ever* do that again.'

Shen's smirk revealed his dimple. 'Weren't you impressed?'

'*No*,' lied Rose.

A low droning up ahead alerted them to the nearness of the hives. Rose kept her eyes on her feet and her curiosity on Shen. 'Tilda told me you two are the only warriors left in Eana.'

'Luckily for her, I am an excellent tutor.' Shen's smile was short-lived. He had that faraway look in his eyes again. The shadow of sadness Rose couldn't guess at. 'There used to be more of us, once.'

She let the silence linger, hoping he'd fill it.

'Many of my people were warriors,' he went on, after a moment. 'We lived in the Sun-kissed Kingdom in the heart of the Ganyeve Desert.'

Rose recalled the tale he had told her in the Golden Caves, of a kingdom that had been swallowed by the desert. It had sounded like a fairy tale, then . . . or at least some half-embellished legend from long ago. 'You mean you've seen this place with your own eyes?'

'I was born there, Princess.' Shen moved so swiftly Rose

didn't realize what he was doing until he had pulled the dagger from his boot. He flipped it in his hand, holding the blade flush against his wrist. The hilt was pure gold and inlaid with a row of delicate rubies. 'After Lillith's War eighteen years ago, Banba found me wandering alone in the desert. I was just a child, then, with nothing but this dagger in my hands.'

'You were all alone?' said Rose, aghast. 'With *a dagger*?'

Shen nodded, grimly. 'I have few memories of the Sun-kissed Kingdom, but enough to know it is real. Or at least it was. I remember great halls of shining gold. A sun dome so high and bright, it flooded the entire palace with light. There was a throne fashioned in the shape of a sand beetle, with mighty pincers and hulking rubies for its eyes.' His voice softened. 'I remember a woman with long black hair singing me to sleep. A little girl chasing me across the sands. The sweet smell of candied pears baked by an old lady with a wheezing laugh.' He closed his eyes, as if he could hear it. 'A tall man with smiling eyes showed me how to mount a horse, and then fling myself free of it without injury. I think he was my father. And there was a boy. He was older than me, and a lot mouthier. I think he was a warrior, too. He taught me my first fighting stance. And then . . .' Shen opened his eyes, his voice turning quiet. 'They were all gone. And I was alone.'

Rose's heart ached. For the boy who had lost his home and his family. For the young man who stood before her now, baring so much of himself.

She took his hand. 'I know how it feels to be alone as a child.'

Shen looked at her hand in his. 'I was lucky Banba found me. She took me back to Ortha, and they welcomed me. I've never had to want for anything here. They're not the people of my past but they're my family now.' He gave her an uncharacteristically serious look. 'They can be your family, too, Rose.'

To that, she said nothing.

The hives were nestled in a natural alcove halfway along the next ridge. As they drew closer, the buzzing intensified. A handful of honeybees flew around them, but before Rose could startle herself off the cliff, Shen began to sing. It was a lilting, unfamiliar language, and as the notes washed over her, Rose felt strangely calm. The bees droned lazily, as if they were falling asleep.

Shen pulled her into the alcove.

Before them, dozens of hives hung from the cliff face, each one teeming with thousands of honeybees. The space was tight, and Rose found herself half pressed against him. She was suddenly conscious of where their arms were touching, and how his leg brushed against hers. There was no sea breeze in here, only the heady honey-scented air. Still singing, Shen reached into a hive and deftly broke off a piece of honeycomb.

Rose's eyes went wide as he held it to her lips. She felt

as if she was in a trance as she took a bite. Honey spilled into her mouth and dribbled down his fingers. Keeping his eyes on hers, Shen licked them clean. Rose felt as if not only was she eating honey, but she was floating in it. Her limbs felt deliciously heavy. A bee landed on her shoulder, but she didn't even flinch.

She didn't want to break whatever spell Shen had cast on her by speaking. Because that was surely what was happening. Why she felt like this. Why she wanted to close the sliver of space between them and press her mouth to his and taste the honey on his lips.

Oh, how badly she *wanted* that. Her head was spinning, her heart fluttering like a bird in her chest. What on earth was happening to her? This strange yearning . . . it was new, and frightening. Had she ever felt such a thing with Ansel?

Ansel! Oh, stars!

Rose stepped away from Shen, and backed out on to the cliffs. Away from the hives and the sweet scent of honey, the touch of his leg pressed against hers and his dark eyes drinking her in.

The rest of the world came rushing back. The furious crash of the waves, then the piercing cry of a gull. Rose returned to her senses with a violent blush. Had she really eaten out of his hand just now? Like some sort of squirrel?

'Rose? Are you all right?' Shen came after her and, *oh no*, Rose couldn't face him, not after what she had done.

'I'm fine!' she called over her shoulder, as she hurried

along the cliff path. Back to the beach, and to reality. 'I just remembered, I promised Banba I'd help her with . . . um . . . some cooking!' She shuffled faster, nearly tripping over herself as she turned sharply around a steep curve.

'Hello, traitor.'

Rowena was suddenly standing before her.

Rose froze.

Rowena's eyes flashed. 'I've been wondering when I'd catch you on your own.'

'I'm not alone,' said Rose, quickly. 'Shen is right behind me.'

'Of course he is. Besotted with you, clearly. Although I don't know why.' Rowena craned her neck to look over Rose's shoulder. 'But he's not here now, is he?'

She raised her hand to her mouth, and for a fleeting moment, Rose thought she was blowing her a kiss. Then she felt the sharp gust of wind. It hit her squarely in the chest.

Rose didn't even have time to scream before she realized she was falling. She tumbled through the air, plummeting down, down, down, towards the roaring sea. The waves swallowed her in a shock of cold, snatching the breath from her lungs as she sank like a stone in the darkness.

Wren

CHAPTER 25

The summer sun hung high above the Eshlinn woods, sending golden light spiralling through the trees. Wren hummed to herself as she followed a well-worn trail deep into the forest. The saddle was stiff beneath her and she was not yet used to the jangling stirrups, but the steady hoof beats helped settle the riot of her pulse. She had braided her hair and chosen a soft yellow dress, and though her dagger was carefully stowed in her boot, to all who saw her that morning, she looked like a perfectly innocent princess.

She nudged the horse into a light canter, and after a while, the ancient Eshlinn woods parted to reveal a silver-blue lake in the shape of a horseshoe. It was here she spied Celeste's beloved piebald mare, Lady, tied to a gnarled oak tree.

Wren's hands were sweating as she slipped off her horse, her spelled footsteps silent on the trail. Nerves swilled in her stomach. She had tossed and turned for the last two nights, wrestling with what she was about to do, but her resolve had come steady as the dawn light. There was no other way, but the blade.

It had been two days since Celeste had threatened to expose her in the palace baths. Wren had been careful to avoid her since then but she knew her grace period was about to run out. She had made a promise she couldn't keep. Celeste was expecting to see Rose tomorrow, and when the princess didn't magically reappear at Anadawn, she would make good on her threat and turn Wren in.

No, Celeste would never let Wren make it to the throne. She had become an obstacle and now Wren had no choice but to get rid of her. Her life and the lives of all the witches of Eana depended on Wren becoming Queen. She had made a promise to them, after all, and she would see it through – to the bloody, bitter end.

Celeste was sitting cross-legged by the lake, reading a book. A slant of sunlight cast her in spotlight, the warm breeze rippling in her skirts.

Wren wiped her hands on her dress and slipped the dagger from her boot. She crept up behind Celeste, like a wildcat stalking its prey.

A rogue wind swept through the trees.

'*Do whatever it takes to seize that throne, little bird,*' whispered Banba's voice in her head.

Celeste giggled at something in her book, then eagerly turned the page.

Wren smiled without meaning to. Then her face fell. Her fingers trembled around the knife.

Celeste was Rose's best friend.

Her *Shen*.

Wren's palms were sodden, her breath swelling in her throat. She could take the throne from her sister but could she take away the only family she had ever known? The only person at Anadawn willing to fight for Rose? Celeste had interrogated Ansel to make sure he was a worthy suitor for her. She had even risked the Kingsbreath's wrath to stand up for her at dinner.

'Eana will forgive you,' urged Banba's voice in her head. 'I will forgive you.'

Wren took another step, and faltered.

How could I ever forgive myself?

Now that the reality of her decision was upon her, Wren couldn't face it. Killing an evil man was one thing, but murdering Celeste – whose only crimes were her cleverness and her loyalty – was quite another. It wouldn't just stain Wren's hands, it would stain her soul, too. And when Rose found out . . .

No. Wren had to find another way, even if it was riskier. She owed that to her sister. She owed it to Celeste, who, after all, was not so unlike her. She couldn't kill Rose's best friend, which meant she had no choice but to try to enchant her.

Wren dug her fingers in the dirt, her mind whirring as she searched for the right words. She had never done a memory enchantment this intricate before. If the spell was too broad, it wouldn't hold. Too narrow, and it wouldn't be enough.

Her skirts rustled as she stood, and Celeste looked up from her book. She frowned. 'What are you—' Then she noticed the dagger in Wren's hand. Her eyes went wide. '*Don't*. Don't you dare.' She tried to scrabble away, but Wren loomed over her.

'*From earth to dust, set your suspicions free. Forget all that makes you mistrust me.*'

Celeste cowered as Wren cast her fistful of earth, but the dirt never fell. The air around Celeste shimmered and then she went very still.

Wren held the dagger behind her back, while her breath ballooned inside her.

Celeste blinked up at her. 'Rose?' she said, uncertainly. 'When did you get here?'

Wren loosed a sigh. 'Just now. I was out for a morning ride when I spotted Lady by the trees.'

Celeste looked at her lap. 'I was . . . reading . . . I think.'

'So you were.' Wren bent down to retrieve Celeste's book, subtly returning the dagger to her boot. 'I think you've lost your page.'

Celeste thumbed through the book, then looked up at her again. Her brows drew close. 'Are you staying?'

'I'm afraid I can't,' said Wren, regretfully. 'I only came out to get some fresh air. Now that I have, I should head back and check on dear Willem.'

Celeste's eyes glazed at the mention of Rathborne. 'Yes . . . that's right . . . Willem is ill.'

Relief prickled in Wren's cheeks. She hadn't completely obliterated the last week from Celeste's memory, just the parts that incriminated herself. So far, so good. 'It's positively wretched. May the Great Protector watch over him.'

Celeste nodded, absently. She opened her mouth to say something, then forgot whatever it was.

'I'll leave you to your novel. Happy reading, Celeste . . .' Wren waggled her fingers as she backed out of the clearing, leaving Rose's bewildered friend alone in her cloud of confusion.

When Wren mounted her horse, her fingers were still shaking. It was a risk doing it this way. The enchantment had worked but she had no idea how long it would last.

Still, it was better than the blade. She told herself that as Banba's scowling face floated through her mind. If luck was on Wren's side, her grandmother would never find out about it.

When she returned to the stables, she was surprised to find Tor saddling Ansel's spectacular snow stallion. Celeste wasn't the only person Wren had been avoiding these past two days. She hadn't seen the Gevrans since the disastrous dinner party. She had used her worry over Rathborne's lingering illness – and the wretched sickness it was causing her – as an excuse to wriggle out of seeing the prince.

Tor looked up at the sound of her approach. 'I was wondering when we might cross paths again,' he said, as if they were old friends.

A rush of giddiness coursed through Wren but she was careful not to show it. 'Have the midnight halls of Anadawn been lonely without me, soldier?'

Tor's gaze lingered on hers. 'I think Elske has been missing you.'

'The feeling is mutual.' Wren leaned down towards Tor, enjoying the blush that coloured his cheeks. She glanced around, furtively. 'Where is dear Prince Ansel this morning?'

'The prince is having his mid-morning nap.' Tor was doing his best to ignore her sudden closeness but Wren didn't miss the way his throat bobbed or how tightly coiled the muscles in his shoulders had become. 'I came to saddle the horses ahead of our ride.'

'Dutiful as ever,' murmured Wren.

Tor's gaze darted suddenly to her left shoulder. 'Don't move, Your Highness,' he said, in a low voice. 'There's nothing to be frightened of. It won't harm you.'

Wren glanced sidelong, spotting the brown river spider on her shoulder. It must have dropped from a tree in the forest. 'Pesky little thing,' she said, brushing it off.

Tor watched the spider scuttle away. 'I'm pleased to see you've conquered your crippling fear of spiders.'

He looked up at her and Wren realized too late she had made a misstep. She bit her lip. 'Your bravery must be rubbing off on me.'

Tor frowned and Wren sensed that old familiar suspicion creeping over him again. The warmth that had been stirring between them quickly evaporated. He was every bit a soldier again, his loyalty to Gevra flashing in the storm of his gaze. He pinned her with it. 'I'm glad we ran into each other this morning, Your Highness. I'd like to talk to you about what happened at dinner the other night.'

'Oh, let's not revisit that dreadful evening,' said Wren, morosely.

'I've heard a rumour that the Kingsbreath may have been poisoned. I am interested to know your thoughts on the matter.' He took a step towards her and in her panic, Wren hinged backwards, yanking hard on the reins. Her horse reared up on to its hind legs and she shrieked as she lost her balance. She twisted on to her side, her foot tangling in the stirrup as she clung to the saddle. 'HELP!'

Tor reacted at once, grabbing the reins and clicking his teeth. The horse settled and, as all four hooves hit the ground, he laid a gentle hand against her muzzle. 'Easy girl,' he murmured, putting his nose against her own. 'All is well.'

The mare went perfectly still. Wren managed to right herself but she was trembling awfully. Perhaps she had never truly stopped. Her fate – and that of the witches – now hinged on a tenuous memory enchantment and the uncanny instincts of a Gevran soldier. She had the sudden sensation that the world was tilting and everything was slipping away from her – her careful plan, her longed-for coronation, the lives of her people. Banba had given her a destiny that was crushing her and then had left Wren alone to bear its weight.

Tor swept his gaze over her. 'Are you all right? You're shaking.'

The concern on his face was so raw it caught Wren off guard. Despite everything, he had come to care about her, and the sudden sureness of it touched a part of her she had been hiding – the soft underside of her soul. The part that was terrified every moment of every day, that threaded nightmares through her dreams and buried screams in her throat. For a dangerous, fleeting moment, Wren thought she might break down. *No, I'm not all right,* she wanted to tell him. *I'm all alone and I'm frightened as hell.*

But those words would damn her just as surely as her tears would. '*People only cry for two reasons, little bird,*' echoed Banba's voice in her head. '*Guilt and weakness.*' Wren inhaled through her nose and blinked away the stinging in her eyes. When she spoke, her voice wavered. 'Can you help me down? I'm afraid I might fall.'

Tor opened his arms for her without a beat of hesitation. Wren swung her leg over the saddle and slid off the horse.

He caught her easily, his arms strong and sure as they enveloped her. Wren wrapped her legs around his waist and clung to him, her heart hammering so loudly, she swore he could hear it. He didn't set her down. He held her to him, as if he could sense, in that moment, how badly she needed it.

Wren buried her face in his neck.

Tor turned his head towards hers, his nose brushing against the shell of her ear. 'I've got you,' he whispered.

She shivered against him. He slid his strong hands along her back, searing his heat into her skin. For a moment, there was nothing but the ragged sound of their breath heaving in perfect unison.

Wren pressed her forehead against his, waiting, wanting.

Tor's gaze came to settle on her lips, fear and desire warring in those stormy eyes. His shoulders slackened as his lips parted, and then—

Footsteps pattered nearby.

He went rigid beneath her.

'It's just the stable hand,' said Wren, not caring if it was or not. She was lost in lust, craving the press of his lips against hers, the release of all that fire surging through her veins. They were so close, *so close* . . .

But Tor's demeanour had already shifted. He was a loyal Gevran soldier once more and Wren was the forbidden princess.

'Forgive me. You make me forget myself,' he said, deftly untangling her legs from around his waist.

He set her down with aching tenderness as though she were made of glass, and Wren wanted to rail her fists against his chest to show her that she wasn't breakable or frightened of getting caught, that he could kiss her any way he wanted to.

She grabbed the lapels of his coat. 'You're a Gevran,' she said, pulling him to her. 'Don't you enjoy danger?'

'Not when it puts you at risk, Your Highness,' he said, gently removing her fingers. Before Wren could figure out what to say to that, the stable doors swung open and Prince Ansel came striding in, fresh-faced and sprightly after his morning nap. Tor stepped away from her and turned to busy himself with the horses.

'Rose, my flower, I wasn't expecting to see you here this

morning!' Prince Ansel jogged to meet her, strands of his shiny blond hair flopping into his eyes. 'What a wonderful surprise.'

Elske padded after him, the white wolf keeping a watchful eye on her charge.

Wren smiled at the oblivious prince. 'It has been a morning of surprises! I just ran into Tor. He says you two are off for your ride soon.'

'Indeed. We're going to the border of Eshlinn today. I hear there's a river there where you can watch the salmon jump. We're going to catch our dinner! Isn't that a lark?' Prince Ansel took her hand in his and Wren was struck by the sudden searing absence of her desire. Her blood cooled in her veins and her head cleared in an instant. The storm had passed but she had no interest in the blue sky behind it. 'You should join us, my darling. It will be all the better in your company.'

Wren glanced at Tor, who was pretending to examine a stirrup. She swept her gaze over his muscled shoulders and tried not to imagine how they would move under her hands . . . how she could make him groan if given half the chance. 'Oh, I'm not sure I should intrude.'

'Nonsense.' Ansel tossed the notion aside. 'Tor, you don't mind, do you?'

'No, Your Highness.' Tor turned back to them. He looked at Wren with such naked desire in his eyes, it took her breath away. 'Come with us.'

Wren heard the words for what they really were.

Come with me.

She was surprised by how badly she wanted to.

'Very well,' she said, lifting her chin. 'It's a date.'

'Wonderful! I'll send word to Chapman at once.' Ansel's face brightened but it was Tor's smile that made Wren's blood sing.

Rose

CHAPTER 26

The world was dark and cold and clawing. Rose's lungs were so tight she felt as if they would burst. Her limbs were impossibly heavy, sinking, sinking, as the ocean wrapped her in its frigid embrace. Her head swam with sinister thoughts. They told her to open her mouth and let the water rush in, let the tide take her. It would be over, then – all this pain, this heaviness . . .

And then, just when she was about to give in to the sea, an arm tightened around her waist. She was pulled up, up, up – back to the surface. Back to the light.

Air.

Rose gulped it down, heaving and coughing as her lungs expanded.

'Slow down, Princess,' came a familiar voice, somewhere in the waves. 'Deep breaths. You're safe now.' Shen shifted her on to her back, one hand flat against the base of her spine, her head cradled in the other.

Rose coughed up a stream of seawater. Her nose stung and the back of her throat was achingly raw. 'I feel anything but safe,' she croaked.

Shen brushed a strand of wet hair out of her eyes. 'I need you to hold on to my shoulders so we can swim to shore. I can't tread water out here forever.'

'Some warrior witch you are,' said Rose, as she twisted towards him. She tried to clamber on to his back, pushing down on his shoulders and accidentally submerging him completely.

He came up spluttering. 'Don't drown me in the process!'

'It was an accident!' she yelped, still clinging to his shoulders. 'I don't know how to swim!'

Shen looped her arms around his neck, then hitched her up until her body was flush against his back and her head rested in the crook of his shoulder. 'Now, wrap your legs around me.'

Rose's cheeks burned. 'Like this?' she said, adjusting herself.

'Just like that.'

The waves rippled around them as Shen swam her back to shore, the water cresting just beneath his chin. By the time they staggered on to the sand, sopping wet from head-to-toe, a crowd of witches had gathered on the shoreline.

Thea ran to them, scooping Rose into her bosom, as if she were a small child. 'Oh, Rose. I'm so glad you're safe.' She rubbed her back in circles and Rose felt her lungs relax, the lingering ache in her muscles slowly melting away. 'Don't worry, love. We'll get you out of those wet clothes and in front of a crackling fire.' When Thea released her, she looked sharply at Shen. 'What happened?'

'Rowena happened.' He peeled off his soaking shirt, revealing the golden-brown planes of his chest and the ring that hung from his neck. His skin was smooth and muscled, and . . . Rose realized she was staring. She looked away, quickly, to where Tilda was tearing down the beach.

'Rose! Rose! Banba is coming!'

Banba stomped after the young witch with a face like thunder. The crowd parted for her. Her gaze hardened as she looked Rose up and down. 'Are you all right?'

Rose tried to swallow the tremble in her voice. 'Barely.'

Banba unclasped her cloak and slung it around her shoulders. 'Warm yourself, girl. I will deal with this.'

She spun around, searching the crowd. 'Rowena Glasstide, show yourself!'

Rowena was hauled to the front of the crowd. Banba took one look at the witch and backhanded her across the face. 'How dare you attack one of your own? Do you think you are above the rules of Ortha? Above *me*?'

Rowena spat blood on to the sand. Then she raised her chin and met Banba's gaze. 'It's not my fault I'm the only witch in this damned place who's brave enough to give her what she deserves. Rose is a witch-hating traitor. We all know she'd kill every one of us if she had half the chance!'

'Nonsense,' said Thea, calmly. 'Rose is no killer. She has been blessed with the craft of healing. She is one of *us*.'

'She will never be one of us!'

'Well, not if you kill her!' shouted Shen. 'Give her a chance!'

'What use have we of the princess?' challenged Cathal. 'The switch has already been made!'

Banba raised her fists and a howling wind ripped across the beach. The witches fell silent. Rowena kept her jaw clenched, but Rose saw that she was trembling now.

'You do *not* decide justice here, Rowena Glasstide.' Banba's voice soared on the wind, until it was everywhere all at once. 'With your actions, you shame your ancestors. You shame your craft. You shame yourself.' She dropped her hands and the wind disappeared in a ragged howl. The sudden quiet felt even deadlier. 'I punish you for what you have done. I punish you for defying me. And more than that, I punish you for the attempted murder of one of your witch sisters.'

'*And* your princess!' cried Rose, unable to stop herself.

'You will never be my princess,' Rowena hissed back.

'SILENCE!' Banba raised her hands, and with them, she silenced not only the witches but the crashing waves and the shrieking gulls. Until only her voice could be heard. She looked hard at Rowena. 'You will hang by your wrists from the cliffs until sunrise tomorrow.'

Rowena was swiftly hauled away. She didn't protest, nor did she struggle. She went willingly to her fate, and Rose found herself squirming as she watched her.

Banba glared at the rest of the witches. 'Take this as a warning to all of you. Rose is my granddaughter. My blood. Do not forget it. I decreed she would live, and so she shall.'

Back in the hut, Rose shivered in front of the hearth, trying to get warm.

Thea brought her a steaming cup of ginger tea. 'Drink this, love. It will help with the shock.'

The floorboards creaked and Banba appeared in the doorway. 'Thea, my light in the dark, I'd like to speak to my granddaughter alone.'

'Of course, my sky.' Thea kissed Banba on the cheek as she bustled past her. 'I'll be back within the hour.'

Rose did not relish the idea of being alone with her grandmother but she was too cold to leave the fire.

Banba sighed wearily as she settled in her rocking chair. 'Do you think me a monster?'

'No . . .' Rose chose her words carefully. 'But I think that kind of punishment could be considered monstrous.'

Banba released a short, sharp laugh. 'You must know that a strong ruler must sometimes be cruel. You cannot allow others to take advantage of you, Rose.' Her chair creaked as it rocked back and forth. 'Rowena wanted you dead. And she is not alone in that desire. She got off lightly today. As leader of Ortha and your grandmother, I could have drowned her myself. And maybe I should have. To make it clear that no one in Ortha should defy me. That nobody should harm you.'

Rose took a sip of tea to settle her nerves. 'How did you become so powerful?'

'Sixty years of practice and vengeance.' Banba smiled, her teeth yellow in the firelight. 'You truly know nothing of witches, do you, Rose? I thought – I had *hoped* – that somehow our stories would have reached you in the palace.'

Rose put down her tea and stared hard at Banba. 'You underestimate Willem Rathborne. He has scrubbed the palace, scrubbed all of Eshlinn, of any truth to do with witches.'

Banba sighed. 'Perhaps you're right. The last time I underestimated the Kingsbreath, he killed my daughter.'

Rose stilled at the mention of her mother, at the flash of pain in the old woman's eyes. 'Thea said my mother knew she was going to die. That a seer told her so.'

'The seer was my sister, Glenna,' said Banba, with a confirming nod. 'Before the war, she lived in the Amarach Towers in the south. It was in those skies that she foresaw Lillith's fate. But the vision did not sharpen in time. She didn't see the man who wielded the dagger until it was too late.' Banba closed her eyes, the lines in her face deepening as the memory aged her. 'Glenna couldn't save Lillith, nor indeed herself. Like so many of our kind, my sister was killed in the bloodbath that came after.'

'Oh,' said Rose, quietly. She could think of nothing else to say to pierce the loss that seemed to fill up the space between them, dark and heavy as a thundercloud.

Banba snapped her eyes open. 'You think I am powerful, Rose. If only you knew how we witches used to be.'

The fire seem to crackle in agreement. And a kernel of curiosity awoke in Rose. 'Tell me,' she said, leaning closer.

Banba lifted her hand and a cool breeze stirred about

the room. The fire began to dance. Flame shadow crawled across the wall, and in it, Rose glimpsed the figure of a woman wearing a crown.

'A thousand years ago, Eana blossomed under the rule of Ortha Starcrest, the last true witch queen. We were at the height of our power, then – not bound to just one strand of magic. The crafts were not separate. There were no warriors nor healers, tempests nor enchanters, no seers. The witches held all the strands of power as their own – they had everything. They *were* everything.'

Rose could scarcely imagine power like that. It sounded almost . . . other-worldly.

The shadows danced and in them, another woman emerged, side by side with the first. She, too, wore a crown. But when Rose blinked, she disappeared, leaving her wondering if she had imagined the second figure entirely.

'Ortha Starcrest was a good queen, a fair queen and a wise one,' Banba went on. 'But that was not enough to pacify the Protector and his followers who feared her power, who had spent long years plotting against the witches. They found a way to curse Ortha, to splinter her magic into five separate strands, leaving only one for herself.'

In the shadows, Rose saw a five-pointed star shatter into pieces. A queen ripped of her crown, as she fell to her knees. 'They weakened her.' Rose glimpsed the Mother Tree, rising alone over the desert, and felt the sudden urge to weep. 'And then they killed her.'

'They stole our queen, they stole our throne and then

they stole our kingdom.' Banba's face darkened and so too did her voice. 'Our magic remained broken, splintered forever into five separate crafts. A paltry echo of what they had once been. We were driven out of our own country, forced to live in the frigid corners of Eana, with nothing but the memory of what we once were to keep us warm. To keep us fighting.'

Banba closed her fist and the shadows went out.

Her green eyes flashed. 'Reclaiming the throne is the first step to reclaiming the fullness of our power. The witches will return to our former glory and the rivers of Eana will run red with the blood of all those who tried to stand in our way.'

Rose looked away from the intensity in her gaze. 'It sounds as if you wish you could be the one on the throne.'

Banba cackled, but offered no denial.

Rose squirmed uncomfortably. Something else was tugging at her. She stared into the flames, trying to find what she had glimpsed before. 'I swore I saw another shadow beside Ortha just now. Another woman.'

Now it was Banba who looked away. 'Ortha Starcrest had a twin, too. But we do not speak of her.'

Later, when the moon was high and Banba's snores echoed through the little hut, Rose crept out into the night. The wily old witch had told her that a strong ruler must sometimes be cruel, but Rose knew that there was just as much strength in mercy. She intended to be a just queen, a *good* queen.

It didn't take long to find Rowena. Her golden hair was like a candle flame in the dark. She was hanging halfway down the cliffs. Her wrists were bound to the rock above her head, her feet dangling loose above the churning sea.

Her head lolled to one side when she spotted Rose creeping along the path towards her. 'Here to finish me off, Valhart?'

Rose removed Thea's tackle knife from her tunic. 'Maybe.'

And for a moment, she relished the fear that clouded Rowena's face, the power it gave her. Then she knelt down and grabbed hold of her arm as she cut the rope around her wrists. Rose held on tight to Rowena as the binds fell away and then hauled her up, over the cliff edge. Rowena clambered on to the path. She rubbed her chafed wrists, staring up at Rose with a wild look in her eyes. 'I could knock you off again, you know.'

'You could,' said Rose, carefully. 'But I don't think you will.'

'My allegiance is to Wren.'

'I'm not asking you to choose.'

Rowena staggered to her feet. 'Why are you helping me?'

'Because a good leader rules with compassion, not cruelty. My grandmother might own these sands, but Eana belongs to me.' Rose levelled Rowena with a dark look. 'You would do well to remember that.'

Rose smiled to herself as she walked back across the beach. Her blood was warm inside her, and her hands were tingling, but it wasn't magic that set the new spring in her step. It was power. She had held it firmly in her grasp just now as she looked down on Rowena, and despite her anger and resentment, she had used it in the right way. With mercy, and justice.

For the first time in her life, on this ragged little beach at the edge of the world, with sand in her hair and salt in her teeth, Rose felt like a queen.

A queen, who was ready to face anything and anyone that stood in her way.

When she returned to the hut, Banba was sitting in her rocking chair. 'I know what you did.'

Rose squared her jaw. 'It was the right thing.'

Banba snorted. 'I should hang *you* from the cliffs for disobeying me.'

'Then go ahead.'

The old witch sighed and shook her head. 'Your mother had the same kind heart. And it got her killed.' A sweeping sadness came over her, and for a terrifying moment, Rose thought her grandmother was going to cry. She took a step towards her but then something in the old woman shifted. Banba's gaze hardened, and so did her voice. 'I won't let that happen to you.'

Early the next morning, the sound of scratching woke Rose

before the others. She tiptoed to the door and opened it, expecting to see Tilda.

Instead, a starcrest stared up at her with bright, beady eyes. It had a letter tied to its left leg. Rose recognized the ribbon as one of her own, and knew at once who it was from. She retrieved it with trembling fingers, and as the bird returned to the dawning sky, she read the name scrawled on the letter.

Banba.

She looked over her shoulder to make sure her grandmother was still snoring. Then she stepped out into the sea air, crept down to the beach and opened the letter.

I can't stop the wedding.
The Gevrans are coming.
Run.

Wren

CHAPTER 27

The following days in Anadawn passed under bloated skies. Wren chewed her fingernails down to nothing and paced herself to exhaustion while the Kingsbreath lay in his bedchamber, suspended between sleep and wakefulness, under the watchful eye of Hector Pegasi. His condition hadn't improved but it hadn't worsened either. Each morning Wren woke to the fear that she might pass him in the courtyard, looking as well as ever, or open her door to find the palace guards waiting to arrest her for what she had done.

She had been avoiding Celeste, for fear her memory enchantment would fail and she would return to her senses – and her suspicion. Thankfully, Chapman's schedule kept her busy, Wren's allotted time with Prince Ansel providing the perfect excuse to avoid Rose's best friend while finding excuses to be close to Tor. On their horse ride to the Eshlinn border, Wren had reclined on the riverbank, laughing uproariously as the prince and his soldier tried to outdo each other catching leaping salmon with their bare hands.

After that, she saw Ansel for three more lunch dates and once for a meandering walk in the woods, where the prince failed on several occasions to hold her hand before turning his attention to feeding the ducks in the lake. Wren spent these meetings exchanging furtive glances with Tor, wanting nothing more than to pull him into a dark corner and finally kiss him senseless.

Sometimes she would pretend to fawn over Elske just to get close to him without arousing suspicion. It was a dangerous game but she couldn't help herself, and even though the Gevran carried himself all too professionally – standing stiff-backed and remote by his wolf – she would sometimes catch him watching her with a look of such naked desire, it sent a thrill rippling up her spine.

A week before the wedding, when the moon was almost full again, Wren woke to the distant blare of horns. She sprang out of bed in a fright and threw on a dress. Agnes was nowhere to be found and neither was breakfast, for that matter. When Wren descended the east tower, she almost crashed straight into Chapman, who was racing about in a panic.

She caught him by the arm. 'What's that noise? What's going on?'

'It's the Gevrans!' he shrieked. 'They're halfway down the Silvertongue!'

Wren stiffened. 'They're *here*?'

'And ahead of schedule!' Chapman waved his scroll about in a bluster. 'With the Kingsbreath ill, we've had no time to prepare a welcome procession. I need to assemble the honour guard at once. And the prince! Oh!' He took off in a rush. 'Someone has to tell the prince!'

The second Chapman disappeared from view, Wren picked up her skirts and made for the passageway underneath the east tower. Her hurried footsteps thundered in the damp silence, the everlights of long-dead witches lighting her way towards the river. By the time she clambered out through the storm drain, her skirts were covered in mud.

Down on the banks of the Silvertongue, the townsfolk of Eshlinn were gathering by the mill. Some had spilled out across the bridge and were craning their necks to get a look at the ships. Wren crept along the nearside of the river, keeping to the shadows. When she reached a gnarled tree that hung low over the water, she rolled her sleeves and started to climb it. It was trickier with her dress cinching her ribs and her skirts bunching around her ankles, but she got the hang of it, scrabbling up the trunk like a squirrel.

The horns sounded again. Wren rolled her eyes. The Gevrans were clearly intent on waking every man, woman and child in Eshlinn.

Soon, she was high enough to make out the sharp nose of the first ship, cutting through the river mist. It was a thing of monstrous beauty. Its sleek black hull moved swiftly and gracefully, and its billowing sails were a deep, shimmering grey. The Gevran crest was emblazoned in bright silver along each one – a mighty ice bear mid-roar – so there could be no mistaking the proud vessel or whom it carried. Wren inched along an overhanging branch to get a better view of the people out on deck. The tree groaned as it tipped towards the river but she held on tight, her knuckles white against the bark.

She could make out faces now. They belonged to soldiers; men and women, dressed in the same midnight-blue uniform that Tor wore, heavy black boots and tailored frock coats, fastened with shining silver buttons. They seemed to be just as tall and well-built as him, too. A nation of steely giants. They were all standing eerily still, broad shoulders rolled back, square chins upturned towards Anadawn Palace as though it were a challenge, rather than a destination. A thread of unease uncoiled inside Wren.

She climbed to a higher branch. Her legs trembled as she crept up, up, up, through the leaves of the canopy, until she could see the next ship gliding in the procession.

'*Hissing seaweed.*' The second ship was full of beasts. Towering ice bears roamed among fearsome snow tigers and silver-fanged wolves, and not a single one was chained.

Tor's family of wranglers had trained them well.

A shudder passed through Wren as she imagined these terrifying creatures bearing down on the witches of Ortha after the wedding. Time was a noose closing around her neck. Every breath Rathborne took was one closer to an alliance that would spell the end of the witches. And even if he did die, now that the Gevrans were here in Eshlinn, how on *earth* was she going to send them back?

She could only hope Banba had received her letter and

was herding the witches to safety.

The Silvertongue Bridge was teeming with townsfolk now. A quick glance over Wren's shoulder alerted her to an envoy that had been dispatched from the palace. Tor was marching out in front, the auburn strands of his hair shining in the morning sunlight. Ansel followed close behind, sporting a large grey hat with a tall silver feather affixed to the top. They were flanked by a flustered-looking Chapman and two palace guards.

Wren cursed when she realized they were coming her way. She hugged the branch in an attempt to camouflage herself but there weren't enough leaves to hide the pale pink of her dress – *why* had she chosen the pink dress? – nor the rest of her, for that matter. All she could do now was press her cheek to the bark and hope for the best.

The third ship glided out of the mist like a swan. It was smaller and sleeker than the ones that came before it, its slim sails a bright silver-white. Out on deck, nobility milled about in lavish stoles, decadent hats and trailing fur coats. There was a full-figured girl standing up on the bow, as though she were about to launch herself into the water. Her hair was long and crimson-red and her face was ghostly pale. She was cradling a small white fox in her arms.

Princess Anika Felsing.

Even from a distance, Wren could see there was a kind of wild beauty about the Gevran princess, and a challenge in the set of her jaw. She was looking at the white towers of Anadawn the way a predator might size up its prey before devouring it. If Anika was here, that meant Alarik was close at hand, though there was no sign of the Gevran king out on deck. Wren scooted along the branch to get a better look. The tree creaked ominously.

'Princess Rose? Is that *you*?' Chapman's voice rang out in alarm. 'By the Great Protector! What are you doing down here without a chaperone?'

Wren squeezed her eyes shut. *Rotting carp.*

'And more to the point, what are you doing up in that tree?' added Prince Ansel, with great concern.

Wren looked down through the twisting branches to find the prince peering up at her, the feather on his hat fluttering dramatically in the breeze. Beside him, Chapman looked as if he was halfway to a heart attack.

She waggled her fingers at them. 'I was just . . . uh . . . trying to get a better look at the boats.'

Tor stepped into view just as a gust of wind rattled the tree. Wren tried to scoot backwards but her skirts snagged on a knot and the sudden shifting of her weight sent a crack fissuring down the centre of the branch. She yelped as it tipped towards the water. 'Oh no, oh no, oh no.'

Chapman screamed.

'Don't move!' yelled Tor but it was already too late. As the Gevran horns blasted again, the rest of the branch tore away from the trunk, taking Wren with it. With a final cleaving and a strangled cry, she plummeted down into the Silvertongue River.

The water swallowed her up. It was *freezing*, but Wren

was used to the icy bite of the ocean. She stilled her body, her skits floating around her like a jellyfish as she waited for the chill to pass. When she broke the surface, she lay on her back and spread her arms wide.

There was chaos on the riverbank.

Chapman was shouting himself hoarse. 'The princess can't swim! She's going to drown! Someone get in there now!'

'I can't swim, Gilly!' yelled one of the guards.

'Well, don't look at me, Ralph. Neither can I!'

Perhaps a little too late, Wren realized that Rose should be drowning.

She flung her hands up, splashing about in the water. 'Help! I'm drowning! I can't swim! Oh, help me! Ahhh! I'm going to die!'

'Tor, for the love of Grinstad! DO SOMETHING!' cried Ansel.

Wren let the water gargle her pleas while Tor tore his boots off and shed his coat. The last thing she saw before she let herself sink beneath the waterline was the Gevran soldier launching himself off the riverbank. She let herself go limp in the river, her hair floating eerily about her face as he weaved towards her.

The Gevran was a good swimmer.

But Wren was pleased to note that he was not as good as her. And certainly not as graceful.

He reached her in a matter of moments, his arm tightening around her waist as he hoisted her up above the waterline. Wren broke the surface in a dramatic gasp. Then she spluttered and flailed for good measure. Tor pulled her against his body until her head flopped back against his shoulder.

'Thank you,' she heaved, as she lay in his arms. 'You saved me.'

The soldier used his free arm to swim them back to the riverbank. 'You can drop the act. I know you can swim.'

Wren fluttered her lashes. 'I don't know what you mean.'

'If you want a moment alone, there are better ways to go about it.' Tor's lips were cool against the shell of her ear. 'I saw you float at first. You looked as if you were enjoying it.'

'I was in shock,' said Wren, mildly. 'Everyone knows I'm terrified of water.'

He turned to look at her. Droplets hung like beads from his lashes, the grey of his eyes the exact shade of a thunderstorm. 'Liar,' he whispered.

Feeling reckless and overcome with desire, Wren turned her face and pressed a kiss to his neck.

A shiver passed through Tor and she felt him harden against her.

Wren rolled her head back and closed her eyes, smirking just a little as he ferried her back to the riverbank. She was pulled out of the water by the palace guards, who both looked rather sheepish. 'It's fine. I survived,' she assured them. 'You can catch your breath now.'

Ansel jostled his way through. He cupped Wren's face in his hands, his palms warm and clammy against her cheeks.

'Are you all right, my flower? Your lips are positively blue.'

'I'm lucky your soldier swims like a fish,' said Wren, through chattering teeth.

Behind her, Tor was shaking himself off like a wet dog. His hair was sopping wet and plastered across his forehead, and his white shirt had gone completely see-through. *Oh, stars.* Wren tried not to stare at his biceps as he wrung himself out. Tor caught her looking at him. His gaze dropped, first to the column of her neck, then slowly to the rest of her body, where her sopping dress clung too tightly to her curves.

His throat bobbed. Then he plucked his frock coat from the ground and handed it to her. 'For your modesty, Princess.'

'Well, thank the Great Protector for good sense!' Chapman whirled on the palace guards. 'In case either of you two hapless imbeciles are wondering, that is what a *competent* soldier looks like.'

The guards hurried to remove their frock coats. 'Here, have mine, Your Highness!'

'No, take mine! I just shined the buttons this morning!'

'Just one will do, thank you,' said Wren. Tor's coat dwarfed her, coming to just above her knees, and yet the smell – of alpine and adventure – pleasantly tickled her nose. She pulled the collar around her.

Ansel toyed with the feather on his hat, looking anxiously towards the approaching boats. 'My countrymen are almost upon us.'

Chapman turned on Wren. 'You should return to the palace at once. The king of Gevra must be introduced to the princess of Eana in the proper forum, not to mention in her finest regalia and at her fullest beauty.' He clucked his tongue. 'Not like the quivering river rat you are now.'

Wren fought the urge to shove Chapman into the water. 'Of course,' she said, meekly. 'I'll go at once.'

'It's too late,' said Tor, who being considerably taller than the others, could see much further. He wasn't looking at the first boat of Gevran soldiers but to the one gliding directly behind it. The one full of beasts.

Wren frowned. 'Is that—?'

'Yes,' said Ansel and Tor at the same time.

King Alarik was standing alone at the bow of the ship, his beasts roaming freely around him. He was tall and slender, wearing an immaculate white coat trimmed with fur and inlaid with silver brocade. His skin was pale as winter's snow and his hair was the colour of summer wheat, a single dark line streaking through it like a lightning bolt. It was swept away from his face by an elaborate silver branch crown that lent him the impression of a proud stag.

Behind him, a mighty ice bear reared up and released an earth-shattering roar.

Alarik Felsing didn't even flinch.

'So, the king rides with his beasts?' Wren couldn't tear her eyes off him. There was a kind of terrifying beauty about Alarik – a delicacy that belied his brutal nature – and his unexpected presence on the river had inspired an icy kernel of fear to take hold inside her.

'He trusts them more than his men,' said Tor, darkly.

Ansel shifted uncomfortably.

'Well, that's . . . disturbing,' she muttered.

Alarik jerked his head as though he had heard her. His gaze came to rest on their drenched huddle by the riverbank. There was a breath of confusion, his brows drawing close as he made sense of the scene, then he pulled his lips back, the scythe of his smile revealing his sharp canines.

Wren felt that smile all the way down her spine, cold and unforgiving as ice.

Rose
CHAPTER 28

Rose had made up her mind – she was leaving Ortha tonight.

She had let Willem Rathborne poison her mind long enough. She had not only allowed, but had abetted his scheme to wipe out the witches, and while she was certainly still wary of some of them, she would never forgive herself if the Gevrans descended on Ortha. The impending alliance was a precarious matter that required diplomacy and careful negotiation, and judging by her sister's panicked note to Banba, Wren, raised in rags and seaweed, was clearly *not* equal to the task. It was time to reverse the switch.

If Rose left tonight, with any luck, she would make it back in time for the official Welcoming Ball, or perhaps the Gevran Feast the following night. It was at one of these important events that she intended to change the course of her destiny. And the fate of her country.

Down on the beach, word had spread quickly that she had helped Rowena last night.

Rose didn't miss the new nods of approval from witches who had previously snubbed her. Even Grady offered her a careful smile, Cathal looking awkwardly at his feet as she walked past him. The most surprising change came from Bryony, who sought Rose out after breakfast, carrying a basket of bright purple berries.

'I misjudged you, Rose Greenrock.' She held out the basket. 'I would like to apologize for that.'

Rose didn't move to take it. For all she knew, it was some kind of trick.

Bryony shifted uncomfortably. 'I wanted to cut Rowena down myself but . . .'

'Nobody defies Banba?' said Rose. 'Well. Nobody defies me either.'

'I guess you two have that in common.' Bryony cleared her throat, looking everywhere but at Rose. 'I didn't know Rowena was going to blow you off the cliffs. Honest. I would have told her not to do it. I know what we did to you on your first night was unkind but I never *really* wanted you to die.'

Rose arched a brow.

'All right, *fine*, I *may* have wanted you dead before I met you,' Bryony admitted, sheepishly. 'But you were just some faraway evil princess wearing Wren's face and I thought you spent your days in a big, fancy tower plotting to kill us all.'

Shame flared in Rose's cheeks. Bryony's description wasn't too far off who she had been. Or what she had wanted.

'And I'm really not trying to poison you either. Here, I'll prove it.' Bryony plucked a purple berry from the basket and tossed it into her mouth. The juice spilled over her lips as she chewed. 'See?'

'Moonberries! But Samhain isn't for ages yet!' Tilda barrelled into their conversation and plunged her hand into the basket. 'Can I have one?'

Bryony swatted it away. 'Mind your grasping, Tilda! These are a gift for Rose and once she believes I'm not secretly trying to kill her, I think she'll enjoy them.'

Tilda blinked up at Rose. 'Don't they have moonberries at Anadawn Palace?'

Rose thought of all the wonders Cam could make with such a brightly coloured fruit. 'It must be one of the few things we lack.'

'They only grow by the light of a full moon and when you eat them you feel the love of all the stars in the sky.' Tilda flung her arms wide, as if she were trying to hug the air. 'That's why we only get them on Samhain. Try one!'

'We don't celebrate Samhain at Anadawn either,' said Rose, plucking a berry from the basket. She bit down on it, gingerly, her mouth filling with a burst of tart juice. Her lips began to tingle and she felt a spark of joy radiate through her. '*Oh!*'

'See?' Bryony was smiling broadly. 'Now you really are one of us.'

Rose returned her grin, and a different kind of joy that had nothing to do with the moonberry spread from her fingers to her toes.

Long after sunset, when the witches of Ortha had retired to bed, Rose set her escape plan into motion. If she wanted to get all the way back to Anadawn in one piece, she was going to need a horse. And as luck would have it, there was one, in particular, that she had her eye on.

Guilt churned inside her, but she shoved it down and focused on the crown – *her* crown – as she sought out Shen. His hut was nestled at the edge of the cove, where the land jutted into the sea. She found him sitting out on the rocks, whittling a piece of driftwood.

'I looked for you today,' he said, tilting his head back to look at her. 'I wanted to make sure you were feeling all right after what happened. But every time I spotted you, you were with someone. And you were smiling. It was nice to see.' His grin pressed a dimple into his cheek, and Rose ached at the sudden thought that after tonight she might never see it again. That he might hate her forever for what she was about to do.

She tugged on the end of her blue tunic. It was the nicest one she'd been able to find among Wren's things. Despite everything, she wanted to look nice tonight. She wanted him to think she looked nice. 'You don't need to check up on me all the time, you know. I'm not as helpless as everyone here thinks I am.'

Shen's dark eyes widened. 'I don't think you're helpless at all, Princess. Quite the opposite.'

'Still, I never thanked you properly for saving me.' Rose bit her lip as she held out the amber bottle she'd found under Wren's bed. 'I was wondering if you'd like to come for a walk with me? We could have some of this.'

Shen raised his eyebrows. 'Rum?'

'Yes,' said Rose, confidently, even though she had no idea what was in the bottle, only that it smelled like bonfire fumes.

'Well, I never say no to rum.' Shen rolled to his feet, his eyes never leaving hers. 'And to be honest, Princess, I think I'd find it hard to say no to you at all.'

Even though the night was cool, Shen's words sent a delicious heat buzzing through Rose. 'Good,' she said, coyly. 'It's about time you started paying me the respect I deserve.'

Shen threw his head back and laughed, the sound dancing around them like fireflies. Rose let herself enjoy it as they ambled along the beach together, their fingers almost brushing. In the moonlight she could better appreciate his profile – his strong jaw and proud brow, the gentle curve of his lips that made it seem as though he was always smiling. He must have sensed her looking at him, because he turned suddenly, piercing her with his gaze. His dark eyes looked like fallen pieces of the night sky. 'What is it?'

She reached for something to say. 'Tilda tells me it's rare for you to stay in Ortha for weeks at a time. She says usually you are running back to the desert every chance you get.'

Shen shrugged. 'Ortha is my home, but the desert still calls to me.'

'Is there any particular . . . reason you've stayed so long this time?'

He flashed his teeth. 'Someone has to keep you alive.'

'Well, I think I can take it from here.' Rose looked at her feet, hoping he couldn't hear the guilt in her voice.

'I don't doubt it, Princess.' He moved a step closer and her breath caught in her throat. 'All the same, I can be a good friend to you in Ortha.'

Oh.

A friend.

Rose told herself it didn't matter how he thought of her. Her mind was already made up. She was leaving tonight. Not to mention she was engaged! And yet . . . for some reason, that word – *friend* – stung. Whatever this was with Shen didn't feel like friendship to her. It felt like a glimpse of something more. Something she'd never imagined was possible.

'What are you thinking about?' he asked. 'You've got the strangest expression on your face.'

Rose's breath whooshed out of her. 'I . . . was just wondering about your chain.' She pointed at the glint of gold around his neck.

'Oh.' Shen frowned as he tugged it free, revealing the ring dangling on the end. Up close, Rose could see it held an engraving of the sun, with a small ruby shining in its centre.

'Are you . . . is it . . .' She searched clumsily for words. 'Are *you* betrothed?'

'Me? No. This is . . . no.' Shen smiled. 'No, I'm not betrothed, Princess.'

Rose tried not to look relieved. 'I just thought . . . well, it's a magnificent ring.'

Shen turned the ring in his hand. 'I was wearing this the day Banba found me.' His voice quietened as he slipped it back under his shirt. 'I like to imagine it belonged to my mother.'

Before Rose could overthink it, she took Shen's hand in hers and squeezed tightly.

He didn't let go.

They had strayed from the village and far from the glare of its huts, to where the moon bathed the cliffs in silver light and the waves crashed wildly against the shore.

'Here seems as nice a place as any to drink some rum.' Rose reluctantly dropped Shen's hand before sinking on to the sand. She raised the bottle to her lips and took a careful sip. It burned all the way down, then settled like an ember in the pit of her stomach. '*Mmm* . . .'

'Easy there, pirate,' said Shen, sinking down beside her. 'You don't want to make yourself sick.'

Rose handed him the bottle. 'Show me how it's done, then.'

He smirked as he took a long sip.

Guilt twisted Rose's stomach as she watched him drink. She didn't tell him to slow down.

'You're nothing like what I was expecting, you know,' said Shen, when he passed the bottle back. 'I thought you would be cold.'

'You must be confusing me with a Gevran princess.' As soon as the words left her mouth, Rose regretted them. She didn't want to think about Gevra tonight. She took another minuscule sip of rum before returning it to Shen.

She watched the apple of his throat bob as he drunk, deeper this time.

'Wren and I have been friends for years. I've only known you a matter of weeks and yet . . .' Shen looked out to sea, as if he were searching for words in the waves. 'And yet, I already feel as if I know you almost as well as I know her.' He turned back to Rose, his brow furrowing. 'Is that strange?'

'Maybe it's because you know her so well that you feel as if you know me.'

A laugh sprang from Shen. 'Trust me, you two are *very* different. I think you would get along though. I mean, you *will* get along. You'll have to meet eventually, right?'

'Eventually.' Rose pushed the rum back to him. Then she tilted her head to the sky. 'I never used to look at the stars back in Anadawn. I didn't know there were so many.'

'Do you miss the palace?'

'Yes and no.' Rose was surprised by her honesty. Perhaps the rum was working on her, too. Or perhaps the nearness of her retreat was making her bolder. 'I miss my best friend, Celeste. And the food, of course.' She laughed a little. 'And baths. Proper baths. With mountains of bubbles and scented soaps . . .' She let her voice trail off and then bit her lip as she met Shen's gaze. He coughed and then tried to cover it with a generous swig of rum.

'But in some ways, I feel as if my life before all of this

was just a dream,' Rose went on. 'And now I'm awake, I see things more clearly than I ever have. Including myself. It's as if . . . everything is sharper. I'll never be able to go back to how I was. And I think that's a good thing.' She took another sip, just enough to burn her lips. 'Of course, I would have rather *not* been kidnapped in the middle of the night.'

Shen wiped his mouth with the back of his hand. 'Did I ever properly apologize for that?'

'It seems you are always apologizing for the past or making promises for the future,' teased Rose. 'Now that I've met Banba, I understand the pressure you were under.'

Shen chuckled, softly. 'I don't have many fears. But your grandmother is certainly one of them.'

'That is one thing that we have in common.' Rose found herself laughing, too. She set the bottle in the sand. 'Is it strange if I say I'm glad it turned out the way it did? That I got to see the wonders of the desert. That I gazed upon the Mother Tree and learned the stories of the witches. That you brought me here to Ortha. That . . .' Shen was leaning towards her now, a strand of black hair dipping into his eye. Rose couldn't tell if it was because of her words or the rum but they were so close now, their noses were almost touching. He smelled like the sea air, something fresh and wild and untameable. She swallowed. 'I'm glad that I'm here right now with you.'

Shen watched her from beneath thick, dark lashes, and Rose felt certain he was listening to the riotous beating of her heart. 'I'm glad you are too, Princess.'

Her cheeks began to prickle. 'I prefer it when you call me Rose.'

'Rose.' Shen's voice was low, and Rose felt it within her bones.

His gaze dropped to her lips.

'Rose,' he whispered again.

Rose's breathing hitched as he moved closer.

Remember what you came to do.

Remember what's at stake.

She grabbed the bottle and held it up between them. 'More rum?'

Shen blinked. His shoulders sagged as he took the bottle. 'Thanks.'

Rose sat up straight. 'You know what I've missed, or I should say, *who* I've missed, more than I thought I would?' She tried to keep her voice light. 'Storm. I thought I'd see more of her here in Ortha.'

'Don't you worry about Storm – she's happy as can be grazing on top of the cliffs,' said Shen, between swigs. 'And I go and visit her in the mornings.'

'I truly think that horse is your one true love.'

'The Ganyeve gave her to me when she was just a foal. One day, she climbed out of the shifting sands like a shadow and galloped straight for me. I thought it was a trick of the light at first but Storm was a gift from the desert. I'm sure of it.' Shen smiled at the memory. 'She's been a loyal friend to me ever since.'

Rose chose her next words carefully. 'She certainly does seem to adore you. As much as a horse can adore a man. And you never seem to give her much direction.'

Shen settled back in the sand, propped up on his elbows. 'I just know how to talk to her, that's all.'

'I hear you've got a gift for sweet-talking horses and women.'

He raised an eyebrow. 'And who told you that?'

'A small, chatty friend we both know.'

Shen shook his head. 'I should have known Tilda would tell you all my secrets.' He took another languid sip. 'What she doesn't know is that the secret to wooing Storm is all in a little whisper.'

'What is it?'

Shen pressed a playful finger to his lips.

'Try it,' said Rose. 'Perhaps it will work on me, too.'

Shen's laugh revealed the pearly glint of his teeth. 'Very well, Princess.' He leaned towards her, his breath tickling her cheek. '*Hush, hush, rush*.'

Rose snorted. '*Hush, hush, rush?* Is that some sort of silly spell?'

'If you call good horsemanship a spell. It's nothing more than years of training. Storm knows when she hears those words it's time to go.'

'She must trust you very much.'

'I've never given her reason not to.'

'Well, we've found the difference between me and Storm, then.'

'I can think of a few more.' He raised a finger to her cheek. 'Ortha has given you freckles, Princess.'

Rose swallowed, thickly. 'I can't remember the last time I looked in a mirror.'

'They're beautiful,' he said, gently tracing them. 'Like a constellation.'

Rose felt as if she might dissolve under his touch. 'Can you read my future in them?'

'I'm no seer,' said Shen, drawing back. 'But I hope you'll feel at home here soon. And know that you are . . .' His voice trailed off.

Rose gazed at him. 'Among friends?'

He laughed a little ruefully. 'If that's what you want.'

'This . . . this doesn't feel like friendship to me,' said Rose, boldly.

Shen raked a hand through his hair. 'No. I suppose it doesn't . . . I guess what I meant to say earlier was, I would like to be there for you. However you'd like me to be.'

Oh. Tingles that had nothing to do with the rum danced through Rose's body.

She tried not to think of how much he was going to hate her in the morning, or of what she was about to leave behind. Here was the possibility of a life she had always dreamed of, where adventure entangled with love, and freedom – *true* freedom – rolled in from the sea and kissed her cheeks every morning. She cleared her throat. 'Spoken like a faithful subject at last.'

'If that's what you want to call it.' Shen scooted closer

to her. 'I'm just glad you've decided not to be mad at me forever.' His words were slurring now, the rum slowly taking hold of his senses.

Rose let her head rest against his. It was only because she was leaving tonight that she allowed herself this moment. 'Today is merely a reprieve, Shen.'

He laughed softly and she felt the rumble of it in her bones. 'I thought you said yesterday was a reprieve.'

'And so it was. Forever starts again tomorrow.'

'Until tomorrow, then,' said Shen, taking a long swig. 'And all the days after that.'

When the rum had been drunk and his lids had grown heavy, Rose tucked his cloak around him and helped him lie down on the sand. She stayed with him until he fell asleep, then she curled up Wren's letter and stuck it in the top of the empty rum bottle, where he wouldn't miss it.

Once she started climbing the Whisperwind Cliffs, Rose never looked back. After hours of practice, her feet knew where to go and she was quicker now, braver. She almost wished Shen could have seen her. When she reached the top, she dragged herself on to the grass and looked up at the same stars she'd been watching with him. She felt the strands of her destiny tugging at her, leading her back to Anadawn.

To Wren.

She knew she didn't have much time. But she had

conquered the cliffs, and no matter what lay before her, she would not be stopped. '*I am Eana; Eana is me,*' she whispered before getting to her feet.

Storm seemed happy to see her, nuzzling Rose's hand as she led her from the stables. Out in the cool night air, she climbed on to the horse's back. 'Take me home to Anadawn, Storm.' She curled her fingers in her mane, holding on for dear life as she whispered, '*Hush, hush, rush.*'

Storm took off like thunder, carrying Rose into the night.

Wren
CHAPTER 29

The evening air in Eshlinn was unnaturally cool. It was as though the Gevrans had dragged the icy winter with them across the Sunless Sea. It nipped at Wren's cheeks as she sank on to a bench in the rose garden, the silver moon glimmering overhead. It was almost full again. The arrival of King Alarik yesterday morning had thrown the palace into chaos, sending servants skittering back and forth through the halls of the guest wing, and the cooks working all through the night.

Chapman was in such a panic he had thrown Rose's schedule to the wind. Wren hadn't seen him since yesterday when he had called her a river rat and sent her swiftly back to her tower. She had done exactly as she had been told, and had stayed in her bedroom ever since, spiralling deeper into her own panic.

Willem Rathborne was still clinging to life and now King Alarik was at Anadawn Palace. Wren could feel the maw of Gevra closing around her like a ravenous ice bear. The pressure had sent her running to the gardens where she hoped a morsel of fresh air might help her find another plan in the tornado of her terror. But the cold seared into her bones, and under the haggard skeletons of her sister's rose bushes and the mournful gaze of a single starcrest perched atop a nearby trellis, Wren felt more hopeless than ever.

The Gevrans were here and if the wedding went ahead in three days' time, their soldiers would go on to track the witches, and they would die screaming without ever knowing how sorry Wren was for failing them. The thought of Banba and Thea perishing on that wind-ravaged beach was too much to bear. She dropped her head in her hands and squeezed her eyes shut but she couldn't stop the sudden rush of her tears, fear and frustration rising within her like a tidal wave.

'I don't think I can do this any more, Banba,' she whispered, between sobs. 'I'm sorry. I'm so sorry.'

For a long time, there was only the staccato of her breath and the salty wetness of her tears. Then the wind changed, ever so slightly, and Wren felt something soft and warm brushing against her legs. She dropped her hands to find Elske sitting at her feet, her head cocked in concern.

'Hello, sweetling,' sniffed Wren. 'What are you doing here?'

As if in answer, Elske laid her head in Wren's lap and snuffled at her skirts. Wren scratched behind the wolf's ears, losing herself in the loveliness of her snow-white fur and those wide pale eyes. Slowly, slowly, her tears dried. For the first time since she glimpsed those fearsome boats gliding down the Silvertongue yesterday morning, Wren felt as if she could breathe again. 'If only all Gevrans were as lovely as you,' she murmured.

She looked up, then, past the bushes and the hideous marble statue of the Protector, to find Tor loitering at the edge of the rose garden. He was standing with his hands behind his back, his gaze on his boots as if he could see his reflection in their polish. In the silvery moonlight, he looked more like a god than a soldier, tall and broad and impeccably dressed, the angles of his jaw chiselled to near-perfection. And here was his beloved wolf nuzzling into Wren's lap, offering the comfort that he could not give her himself. Not under the watchful windows of the palace.

The coldness in Wren's bones ebbed away. 'Is she an early wedding gift?' she called out. 'Really, Tor, you shouldn't have.'

The soldier chuckled. 'You overestimate my generosity.'

Wren returned her attentions to Elske, trying not to dwell on how the Gevran had seen her in her weakest moment, weeping alone in the rose garden. 'Can't you be persuaded to give her up?' she said, striving for lightness. 'I'll give you every free elk in Eana. You'll eat like a king for the next ten years. You can mount their heads on all your walls and use their antlers to clean your teeth.'

'As appealing as a home filled with elk carcasses sounds, I'm afraid I could never give Elske up,' said Tor, his smile gleaming as he drifted closer. 'It would be like cutting out my own heart.'

'So dramatic,' said Wren, but she was smiling, too.

Tor loitered by the statue, his hands dug deep into his pockets as he studied the tear tracks on her face.

Wren looked at her hands, embarrassed. She hadn't cried in front of anyone since she'd been a child, not even last summer when she'd taken a tumble off a rocky peninsula while training with Shen and ended up shattering her ankle. She had gritted through the pain as they hobbled back to shore, biting into a pillow as Thea methodically set the bones, one by one.

'King Alarik is only a terror to his enemies.' Tor's voice pulled her from the memory. He was closer now, the heat from his body gently warming the air between them. 'You don't have to be afraid of him. There is nothing that matters more to the king than family, and you will be family soon enough.'

Wren looked up at the Gevran soldier. He had misread her pain but instead of pressing her about it, he had decided to try to remedy it. First with the wolf and now with his words.

'I'm not afraid of your king.' She didn't know if that was strictly true or not, just that it had little to do with the swell of anxiety moving inside her. Things were far graver – far bigger – than Tor could ever guess at. 'And I am *not* his family.' If Tor thought Wren would ever feel anything but utter repulsion for Alarik Felsing, then he didn't know her at all.

Tor's brows lifted. 'I thought that's why . . .' He trailed

off at the sight of her grimace. 'Forgive me. I just wanted to put your mind at ease.'

'A wasted effort, I'm afraid.'

'Is it that you're worried for the Kingsbreath?' he said, uncertainly. 'There are Gevran healers here now. I'm sure they will be able to offer some kind of—'

'Please stop,' said Wren. It was exactly what she didn't need to hear – that Rathborne was inching closer to life, not death. That the Gevrans had arrived just in time to save his fate and seal hers. The wedding was still hurtling towards her and with it, a new life in a foreign land without her throne. Without her people. 'I don't want to talk about that. I don't want to talk about anything.' She pressed her face into Elske's fur and inhaled her glorious alpine scent. 'I just want to cuddle your wolf.'

Tor took a careful step backwards. 'As you wish,' he murmured.

The silence stretched around them like a bubble, the lone starcrest returning to its tower as a brisk breeze stirred the rose bushes. Wren drew her cloak tighter but the cold chattered through her teeth.

'There is a place in Gevra that winter doesn't touch,' said Tor, quietly. Wren looked up at him again. 'It's tucked away in the northern hills, a full day's hike from civilization, but it's worth every footstep. The Turcah Valley is a place of rare beauty. The land there is as deep and green as your eyes.' He swallowed, thickly. The storm in his gaze had settled into a moonlit silver and in its spotlight, Wren felt as if she was glowing. A blush rose in her cheeks. 'You will like it there,' he said with unerring sureness. 'The sun will shine on you whenever you're missing home.'

She smiled, ruefully. 'You make it sound so simple.'

'It can be,' he said, a note of pleading in his voice.

Wren shook her head. She would need more than a valley to sort out the mess she was in, but she couldn't tell him so, no matter how badly she wanted to. 'And what is your remedy for a life with Prince Ansel?' she said, instead.

Tor exhaled through his nose, relief flitting across his face at her admission – that she was bound to Ansel not by feelings but by duty. 'Prince Ansel will be good to you.'

'What if I don't want good? What if I want passion? What if I want freedom? What if I want . . . ?' She let the rest of her sentence hang in the air.

In her heart, she said, *Eana*. She *screamed*, *Eana*. Wren had only ever wanted Eana. She told herself that as her breath shallowed in her chest, as the air between them felt as if it was crackling. She looked at her hands and thought of Banba half a world away. Waiting for the life Wren had promised her. 'It's not enough, Tor.'

He made to reach out to her, then stopped, instead curling his hand into a fist and pinning it to his side. 'Elske will be at Grinstad,' he said, hoarsely.

Wren understood what he meant. Where Elske roamed, so did her master. He was offering her a lifeline, another reason to walk down the aisle and bind herself to Ansel. But the crown was Wren's destiny. Even if there were times she wished it wasn't. Even if in the quiet darkness of the last few weeks she had found herself pining for a simpler life in a safer place, without her grandmother's prodding finger pushing her towards the throne.

'It takes great courage to face the unknown,' said Tor, when she didn't reply. 'And from what I know of you, Your Highness, you have no shortage of that.'

Courage. The word was like a life raft in the storm. Tor was right. Wren had come to Anadawn with all the courage of the witches. She was the granddaughter of Banba Greenrock, the fiercest witch she had ever known, who had trusted her – and her alone – with the future of the witches. She had not raised Wren to cower at the first sign of danger, nor to quit at the sudden changing of a plan.

Wren raised her chin, meeting the molten silver of Tor's eyes, and offered the truest thing she had ever said to him. 'You're right, soldier. I can't think of anything worse than living a coward's life.'

Which was why she was going to get the crown she had come here for, no matter who or what stood in her way.

Rose
CHAPTER 30

Storm was faster than Rose remembered, her hooves barely hitting the ground. If Rose hadn't seen the plumes of dirt churning around them as they raced through the night, she might have thought they were flying. She clung to the horse for dear life, the strands of her mane whipping her face as the wind galloped alongside them.

When they reached the Weeping Forest, Storm slowed to a walk and lowered her head in deference. Rose squeezed her thighs around the horse's middle, urging her onwards, but Storm's pace was careful and plodding, as if something in the mist was stopping her.

Or, perhaps, someone.

The glowing seeds soon found Rose in the forest, the first one landing on her cheek. It was a new memory, but no less violent than the others had been. A raven-haired tempest flung whorls of wind at the Protector's advancing army, casting them from their horses and up into the air. The witch laughed as she tossed the burly soldiers like rag dolls in a storm. But then a dagger, thrown with deadly aim, came from above and pierced the hollow of her throat. Blood spurted from her mouth as she collapsed, lightning crackling in her fingertips as she gurgled her last breath.

Rose came out of the memory grasping at her own throat, sure she had felt the point of the dagger against her skin. But it was another trick of the forest, memory and reality blurring as the souls descended on her like raindrops. She suddenly, desperately missed Shen and his steady presence behind her, the comfort of his hands around her waist. She had only her courage now, so she raised her voice and used it as a shield.

'I am one of you,' Rose called to the forest, to the sweeping trees and the floating seeds, to the witch spirits that lingered in the mist. 'I have seen your stories and felt your pain as my own. I mean the witches no harm. Not today, nor any day. Please, let me pass.'

The forest stilled, as though it were listening. Slowly, quietly, Storm trekked onwards, and this time, the seeds floated around them, like fireflies. Rose loosed a sigh of relief. She had survived this haunted place before when she was its enemy. She would survive it now as a friend.

After what seemed like a lifetime, they reached the edge of the forest, where the Mother Tree stretched towards the sky, mighty and uncowed by time. Beyond it, the sun was rising over the Ganyeve Desert. As they passed the great tree, Rose was struck by the sudden urge to press her palm against it and pay her respects to Ortha Starcrest, the last witch queen of Eana. To tell her that another witch would soon sit on her throne and rule this land in her memory.

Rose nudged Storm towards the Mother Tree, bowing her head as she placed her hand against the trunk. She could have sworn she felt it move, as though it were taking a breath, taking her in. The air warmed and a faint breeze tickled her earlobes. Rose looked up, through the branches of the tree, and gasped. The largest seed she'd ever seen was floating down from the canopy, the soul of Ortha Starcrest, bright and glowing like a star.

Without thinking, Rose stuck her hand out and caught it in her palm. She tensed, waiting to be thrown into another memory, but nothing changed. She was still sitting atop Storm at the edge of the forest. The wind was whistling through the trees and dawn was breaking in beautiful brushstrokes of amber and pink.

She was about to open her hand and set the soul free when a bellowing cry split the air in two. A man in silver armour stepped out from the other side of the Mother Tree and came charging towards her. He was tall and broad with a large chin and a heavy brow, and though Rose had never glimpsed the angry brightness of his eyes, she knew him at once from his portraits.

It was the Great Protector.

'DIE, WITCH!' Spittle spewed from his mouth as he lunged at her. 'YOU HATEFUL, FOUL CREATURE!' Rose recognized his sword in the split second before he swung it at her – the revered Sanguis Bellum that lived under lock and key at Anadawn, confirming her suspicions. She screamed as she lurched backwards, toppling from the horse and landing in the dirt.

Rose scrabbled away from the man she had worshipped her entire life, his face distorted with rage and bloodlust as he stalked towards her.

'Please!' she cried to the spirits in the forest. 'Someone, help me!'

But there was no one alive to hear her. Even Storm had disappeared, and she couldn't see the Mother Tree beyond the Protector's looming shadow. He stood over her now, hatred dripping from his words as he raised his sword. 'Your end has come, Ortha Starcrest. May your soul and the souls of all the witches die with you.'

Rose flinched as his sword came down. It sluiced through the air and sailed past her left ear. There came the sickening sound of steel tearing through flesh and blood and bone, and then a new voice cried out beside Rose.

She whipped her head around. A woman wearing Rose's face lay pinned to the ground beside her, Sanguis Bellum now embedded in her chest. Blood pooled around her body, seeping into the earth as quickly as it flowed out of her.

Her emerald gaze slid past Rose, to the man still standing over her. 'Our souls will never die.' Her final words were a faint rasp, but Rose swore the ground trembled as she spoke. 'Some day, the witches will rise again and the rivers of Eana will run red with your blood.'

The Protector threw his head back and laughed, and before Rose could think better of it, she flung herself at him, ready to tear the sound from his throat. Her hands met nothing but air, and when she landed, her knees sang with pain. She looked up, not into the eyes of an evil man but the bough of a great and weeping tree. The Protector had disappeared. When she turned around, the body of Ortha Starcrest was gone, too, and Rose was alone again.

It *had* been a memory, she realized with sickening relief. The worst one yet. She collapsed at the base of the Mother Tree and began to sob. For Ortha Starcrest and for her mother; for all the witches who might have lived if things had been different, fairer.

Storm, who had been hovering nearby all along, returned to Rose's side and gently nudged her shoulder, as if to say, *It's over.*

Rose trembled as she got to her feet. She pressed her forehead against the trunk and offered a promise to the soul of Ortha Starcrest. 'When I get home, I will change everything in Eana,' she whispered. 'And when I am Queen, I will rule in the name of all witches, under the banner of your legacy.'

With shaking limbs, she climbed back on to Storm, her heart burning with hatred for the man she had been taught to worship. He was no hero. He was nothing but an evil, hateful wretch who had killed ceaselessly and ruthlessly for power he could never truly own.

As Rose set off across the rolling dunes of the Ganyeve Desert, she resolved to put all thoughts of the Protector behind her, but she couldn't shake the memory of Ortha

Starcrest's face, nor the fear in those wide emerald eyes that looked so much like her own.

The desert was blessedly silent and for that, Rose was grateful. She trusted Storm to lead the way but after hours of riding beneath the blistering sun, there was still no sign of the golden mountain where Shen had taken her to rest.

'To the caves, Storm,' she urged, with as much authority as she could muster with a throat that was painfully parched and tight with panic. 'We have to get out of the sun!'

If the horse heard her, she showed no sign of it. She galloped onwards, into the golden abyss. Sweat dripped down Rose's back and pooled under her arms. She was achingly hot, and the sun was still climbing in the sky. If they didn't reach shelter soon, she would perish from the heat.

And then she saw it. A grove of trees, shimmering just beyond the next dune. They stood out in stark relief against the sand, their dark green canopies beckoning. She swore she heard the sound of running water, too, spied droplets hanging from the pillowy leaves.

'Storm! That way!' she rasped, nudging the horse towards the trees. 'Quickly!'

Storm tossed her head and made for the opposite direction.

'*Hush, hush, rush!*' hissed Rose, pointing ahead. 'Don't you see them?'

The horse dug her hooves into the sand and stopped walking.

Rose patted her side. 'What on earth is wrong with you? GO!'

But the horse was still as a statue now, her brown eye watching Rose.

'Fine,' she huffed. 'You can stay here. I'm going to nap in the shade.'

The horse whinnied in alarm as she slid off her back. Then moved in front of Rose as if to block her way.

'Oh no, you don't! I am *hot* and I need a rest. And for that matter, so do you!' Rose pushed past the horse. 'I swear you're as stubborn as your master,' she muttered, as she made for the oasis on foot. But with every step she took, it seemed to get further away.

Strange.

Rose pushed on, desperation quickening her footsteps. The trees began to sway, which was stranger still. There was no wind in the desert, no reprieve from this insipid heat.

'Oh no.' Her heart sank as realization set in. She had been fooled by a mirage. There was no glade, only her own eyes playing tricks on her. What a fool she was! Rose was so busy berating herself that she didn't notice the sands trembling at her feet. She lost her footing and fell with a strangled yelp. When she tried to stand up again, she couldn't find her balance. The dunes weren't just shifting, they were *whirling*. Around and around they went, growing faster and deeper. Without warning, they began to pull her down, down, down . . .

Rose opened her mouth to scream and sand poured into it. She flapped her arms, trying to break the surface, but she was caught in the desert tide, and the dune was a whirlpool now, determined to swallow her up.

She gagged as the sand filled her nose, the last of her energy quickly ebbing away. She flung her hand out desperately, and just as the desert folded over her, she brushed against something solid. She grabbed on to it, twining her fingers in a familiar black mane.

With a determined whinny, Storm pulled her from the jaws of the Ganyeve Desert. Her hooves were firm on the restless sand, her gait steady as she dragged Rose to safety. Back on the dunes, she coughed the sand from her lungs, and used the last morsel of her energy to clamber up on to the horse's back. As they set off in a thundering gallop, towards a gold mountain rising in the distance, she curled her arms around Storm's neck and wept with gratitude for the desert horse that had just saved her life.

Wren
CHAPTER 31

Wren dressed in gold for the official Welcoming Ball. It was to be the first of three celebrations, which would culminate in her wedding to Prince Ansel, and though she had no intention of making it to that particular ceremony – or indeed the Gevran Feast that would fall the night before it – she still wanted to look her best tonight.

After all, she was the crown princess of Eana. More or less.

She had renewed her enchantment with careful precision that afternoon, banishing the freckles along the bridge of her nose and the strands of honey in her hair before Agnes arrived to help her with her dress. It was truly a thing of beauty, the tight corset rendered in delicate black and gold lace, the skirts cascading around her like melted sunlight. Soon, every inch of Wren was cinched to discomfort, her breasts so high she could practically rest her chin on them. Agnes had arranged her dark hair in loose curls that tumbled artfully down her back. The apples of her cheeks were tinted with soft blush, a rosy hue to match her lips, while her eyelids were shadowed in a shimmering bronze that made the green of her eyes shine even brighter. As she stood in front of the mirror, primped and preened to perfection, she almost didn't recognize herself.

She felt . . . well, *ravishing*. Her dagger, which she had tucked discretely against her hip alongside her pouch of earth, made her feel deadly, and it was that which brought the smile to Wren's face. After her conversation with Tor in the rose garden last night, she had resolved to take back control of her destiny. Tonight, while the noblemen and women of Eana danced and mingled with the Gevrans, she was going to slip away and deliver Rathborne's death, swiftly and silently.

A nation in mourning for their beloved Kingsbreath couldn't possibly celebrate a royal wedding in two days' time. There would be a funeral instead of a wedding, and as Alarik Felsing's best-laid plans fell away, Wren would reinstate the coronation she was owed and seize control of Eana. Once she was Queen, with her fate and that of Eana resting firmly in the palm of her hand, there would be no alliance at all. She would send the Gevrans back to their sunless land with their feral king and frightening beasts.

Agnes stood back to look at her. 'Oh, Princess Rose, you are truly the jewel of our nation,' she crowed. 'I dare say King Alarik will envy his brother when he sees you tonight.'

'I almost envy him myself.' Wren swished her skirts to and fro. 'I'm a *vision*.'

It was certainly an improvement on the other morning,

when Alarik had seen her shivering and sopping like a river rat. Wren had chosen the fanciest of Rose's dresses to repair that awful first impression. Once Chapman relaxed at the sight of her glowing like the sun and the icy Gevran king was taken up with the evening's festivities, she would slip away and find her way to Rathborne's bedchamber.

All being well, she would make it back in time for the waltz.

The ballroom at Anadawn Palace was a feast for the senses. It was a sprawling chamber in the heart of the palace, its arched windows peering out at the finest gardens in all of Eshlinn. The walls were lavished with beautiful art, gilded frames climbing towards a glass-domed ceiling that welcomed the full spectacle of the night sky. Tonight, the stars sprinkled pinwheels of silver light along the floors, while candelabras burned brightly from the inside, casting a dreamlike glow about the room. Servants milled among the gathering court, carrying platters of bread and cheese and finely sliced meats, carafes of heady wine and goblets bubbling with frostfizz.

The minstrels were already playing from the balcony when Wren arrived. Members of the Anadawn court, dressed in their finest splendour, bowed to welcome her, while Celeste skipped over in a trailing sapphire dress. Her curly hair was pinned away from her face with delicate gold hairpins and her lips were painted a deep crimson.

'Rose! There you are!' she said, breathlessly. 'Have you been hiding from me? I feel as if I haven't seen you in forever!'

Wren stiffened without meaning to. She hadn't been this close to Celeste since the day she had enchanted her by the lake. Now she was terrified that one wrong word might raise enough suspicion to break the spell. She quickly summoned a smile. 'I'm so sorry, Celeste. I'm afraid Ansel has been keeping me busy,' she said, breezily. 'True love can be *so* time-consuming.'

Celeste arched a manicured brow. 'Listen to you! You're hardly in love with him already, are you? It's only been a few weeks.'

'What can I say? When you know, you *know*.'

Celeste's smile faltered. She looked a little closer at Wren. 'When you know, you know,' she repeated, more to herself than to Wren.

Wren took a careful step away from her. Celeste opened her mouth to say something else, but thankfully, she was interrupted by Chapman, who came skittering towards them in an elaborate green frock coat. 'What are you two chatter merchants doing over here by yourselves?' His face twitched as he waved his parchment scroll around. 'For goodness' sake, go and *mingle*.'

He shooed Celeste towards a gaggle of Gevran noblewomen who were laughing raucously by the dance floor. '*Mingle!*'

Then he turned back to Wren, the end of his quill tickling

her nose as he jabbed it at her. 'It's *imperative* that you make a good impression tonight, Rose. The Kingsbreath will be counting on it!'

Wren flashed her teeth. 'I'll make it a night to remember.'

Just then the ballroom doors swung open, welcoming a parade of new faces. The Gevran soldiers came with their beasts, grey wolves and white leopards and prowling snow tigers leashed in iron chains. They turned their watchful stares on the crowd, their canines glinting golden in the flame light. Eanan nobles gasped and recoiled in horror, while some faint-hearted courtiers set their goblets down and scurried swiftly from the room.

'By the Great Protector!' breathed Chapman, whose moustache had begun to tremble.

Wren glanced sidelong at him. 'What's the matter, Chapman? Didn't you invite the beasts?'

His face paled. 'I thought their forbiddance was *implied* by the very nature of the event,' he said in a strangled voice.

Wren snorted. 'Then you must know very little of Gevra.'

He threw her a withering glance.

'Oh, cheer up,' she said, brightly. 'Maybe the beasts can dance.'

Privately, Wren was glad of the added distraction. The less attention everyone – especially Celeste – paid her tonight, the better. And if it took the menacing growl of a wolf or the thundering roar of a snow tiger to allow her to slip away unnoticed, then so be it.

The Gevran soldiers didn't seem to notice the alarm

they were causing or perhaps they simply didn't care. They were stern-faced as they moved purposefully through the mingling crowds, ignoring the jaunty music and the passing platters of food. They posted themselves along the walls, each with one hand on the head of their beast, the other resting on the glittering hilt of their sword.

When Tor entered the ballroom, his gaze found Wren's almost immediately. He swept it over her dress, his jaw tightening. For a fleeting moment, he looked ravenous. Wren felt a blush rise up from her toes and settle in her cheeks. Suddenly, she was ravenous, too.

'Music,' muttered Chapman, spinning on his heel. 'Protector save us! Why has the bloody music stopped?' He took off towards the minstrels but Wren was too busy staring at the Gevran soldier to care. Tor looked away first and she felt the absence of his gaze as if the sun itself had turned its back on her. She ran her fingers through her hair. 'I need a drink,' she murmured.

'A fine idea.' Celeste appeared at her side, holding two goblets of frostfizz. 'Chapman could probably do with a couple of these, too. As if I'm going to spend tonight with some random Gevran gossips instead of my best friend.'

Wren smiled into her goblet, careful not to make eye contact this time. She downed her drink in one go, silently encouraging Celeste to do the same. She was about to reach for a second goblet on a passing tray when the ballroom doors swung open once more.

Anika Felsing, the crown princess of Gevra, waltzed

into the room, with all the feline grace of a snow leopard. Celeste's mouth fell open. 'Rose, we have been blessed by the Great Protector tonight.'

Anika wore a plunging silver gown that looked as if it had been sewn from the stars themselves. It clung tightly to her generous curves and, with her crimson hair pulled away from her face in decadent waves, she caught the eye of everyone in the room. Around her shoulders, she wore a white stole, and in her arms, a tiny snow fox was slumbering like a baby.

Wren whistled under her breath. 'What an outfit.'

'What an *entrance*,' murmured Celeste, who was starry-eyed. For once, it had nothing to do with Wren's enchantment.

Like her brother, Ansel, Anika's nose was dainty and her eyes were ice-pale. They were rimmed in long dark lashes that made her roving gaze all the more noticeable. She wrinkled her nose as she swept through the room as though the full spectacle of Eana's hospitality had fallen drastically short of her expectations, and Wren was seized by a sudden unexpected defensiveness of this place she barely knew.

'I don't think I like her,' she said.

'You don't *know* her yet.' Celeste drifted towards the Gevran princess, like a moth drawn to a flame.

Wren grabbed her arm. 'What do you think you're doing?'

'Being welcoming.' Celeste grinned. 'Isn't that the point of this evening?' She waggled her fingers at something over

Wren's shoulder. 'Your fiancé's waving at you. You should go and see to that. I think he might also be drooling.'

Wren summoned the dregs of a smile but when she turned to look for Ansel, she found herself caught in the snare of King Alarik's gaze.

Hissing seaweed.

It was like being caught in a blizzard.

The king of Gevra stalked into the ballroom like a proud stag, and as if alerted by a frigid wind, every single person turned to look at him. The minstrels slowed their music as he strolled purposefully towards Wren. He was taller at close range, like a statue cut from pristine marble. His perfectly coiffed hair shone golden in the flickering light, the lightning streak in the middle the same colour as his fine black coat.

Wren sensed a challenge in his pale blue eyes and decided she would meet it head-on.

The Gevran king might be used to inspiring fear in people but she was no coward. She had been raised by Banba Greenrock after all, trained on the unforgiving cliffs of Ortha and sung to sleep by howling winds and raging seas. Yes, Alarik was a king, but he was still only a man.

She offered him her most ravishing smile as she dipped into a curtsy. 'Your Majesty, it's an honour to host you and your countrymen here at Anadawn. You are most welcome.'

'The honour is all mine, Princess Rose,' purred the Gevran king. He bowed low, revealing the smaller figure of Prince Ansel, who was hovering awkwardly behind him. He waved enthusiastically at Wren before being eclipsed once more. 'My little brother is a lucky man indeed.'

Wren tried not to balk as a passing snow tiger brushed its tail against her skirts. 'I am cheered to see your beasts have settled in well.'

Alarik flashed his teeth. 'You needn't be frightened of them. We'll keep them on their chains tonight.'

'I'm not afraid of them,' said Wren. 'In fact, they fascinate me.'

His eyebrows rose. 'Do you have many beasts here in Eana?'

'Oh, you'd be surprised.'

Alarik's lips curled. 'Would I indeed?'

The *click-clack* of heels announced the arrival of Princess Anika, who jostled in front of her older brother. 'So, *this* is Ansel's blushing bride?' She unashamedly examined Wren from head-to-toe. '*Interesting.*'

Wren smiled thinly. 'Welcome to Anadawn, Princess Anika. I hope you find it to your liking.'

Anika humph'd. 'Your palace is certainly impressive in size, although some of the decor is a bit . . . dated.' She looked meaningfully at Wren's dress.

'I like your pet snow fox,' said Wren, sweetly. 'Are you wearing his brother around your shoulders?'

Anika's eyes flashed, and the ghost of something feral passed over her face.

'Your fox truly *is* a darling,' Celeste cut in, gracefully, before the Gevran princess could retort. She offered a goblet of wine to Anika. 'Is he always so well-behaved?'

Anika's eyes glittered as she took it. 'Hardly. He has a fierce temper.'

'My sister exaggerates,' said Alarik. 'Her fox is tamed like all of our beasts. They know to obey their masters.'

Wren's eyes found Tor's across the room. His jaw was clenched, his shoulders stiff. 'Perhaps some beasts should never be tamed.'

'I've never known a beast that can't be broken. In fact, the same goes for humans.' Alarik's laugh was cold as a winter wind, and Wren felt the shiver of it in her bones. 'Your witches will learn that soon enough.'

'Oh, you and your obsessions, Alarik. Can't we have a night of fun?' Anika pouted. 'I want to dance! Who will indulge me?' She looked at Celeste, a sudden gleam in her eye. 'You're certainly dressed as if you know your way around a dance floor.'

Celeste smirked. 'Well spotted.' She glanced at Wren, no doubt to make sure she wasn't crossing enemy lines. Wren winked at her, quickly deciding that a distracted Anika Felsing was far more preferable to the one who had just jostled into her conversation. And besides, a little distraction would be good for Celeste, too.

Celeste drained the wine in her goblet and held out her arm to the Gevran princess. Anika took it, both girls cackling wickedly as they sauntered away.

Ansel, who had been nervously loitering close by, slid out from behind his brother. 'Speaking of dancing, would you like to indulge *me*, my flower?'

'Gladly.' Wren snatched his hand without a second thought and even though she wasn't in the mood for dancing, she was relieved to be swept away from King Alarik and his talk of the witches.

As it turned out, Prince Ansel was a terrible dancer. And despite Thea's best efforts to teach her over the years, so was Wren. They ambled clumsily around the dance floor, giggling like children every time they stepped on each other's feet. 'I had pictured this going a little more gracefully,' Ansel admitted, sheepishly.

Wren laughed, breathlessly. 'But then it wouldn't be half as much fun!'

'Indeed not!' said Ansel, stomping on her pinkie toe for the third time. Wren could see Tor over Ansel's shoulder, watching them. He was smiling now – just the gentlest curve of his lips.

'Ah, Tor, my faithful shadow,' said Ansel, following her gaze. 'After all these years, I'm not sure I could imagine my life without him.'

'You are lucky to have him,' said Wren, and she meant it. She couldn't help but imagine what it would be like to dance with the soldier instead of Ansel. How strong his arms would feel around her, how tight he would hold her, how his breath would flutter against her neck, how—

'May I cut in?' Alarik stepped in front of his brother and offered his hand to Wren. 'I was feeling left out.'

'Oh.' For a heartbeat, Prince Ansel looked crestfallen but

he deftly covered his disappointment with a smile before shuffling out of the way, and Wren understood that although Alarik had phrased it as a request, it was not that at all.

She swallowed her revulsion as she took the king's hand. 'I should warn you, I'm not much of a dancer.'

'So I've witnessed.' Alarik looked down at Wren through the column of his nose. 'Perhaps you just need the right partner.'

Wren was distracted by Celeste's pealing laugher. She and Anika were cavorting around the dance floor, downing goblets of frostfizz like water.

'Am I not interesting enough to hold your attention, Princess Rose?'

Wren blinked up at Alarik. 'Excuse me?'

His frown sharpened, adding a savagery to his handsomeness. 'You are looking everywhere but at me.'

'I'm simply waiting for you to lead.'

Alarik's fingers tightened around hers and Wren tried not to wince. He swept her in a circle, moving so fast, her feet almost left the dance floor. Just as she was catching her breath, he spun her again. She caught a flash of Tor before the room blurred.

Her head began to spin. 'What are you doing?' she gritted out.

'I am leading.' Alarik pulled her roughly against him, his hand pressing into her back. 'As you asked.'

The room twirled around Wren, again and again, and again. She glimpsed Tor standing stiff-backed by the wall, then Celeste with her head thrown back in laughter. She tried to get her attention but Anika was commanding every drop of it and Wren quickly found herself marooned in a dance that had far outpaced its musical accompaniment.

'I'm feeling a bit dizzy,' she said, trying to pull away.

Alarik pretended not to hear her. He twirled her like a spinning top, Tor's face giving way to Ansel's. Then there was Celeste and Anika, laughing in blurs of blue and silver, and as they glided closer to the windows, Wren thought she caught a glimpse of something out in the gardens. A figure moving in the darkness.

But . . . *No*.

She spun away, sure she had imagined it. The incessant turning was toying with her mind. She was impossibly dizzy now and it was causing her to hallucinate.

But then she saw it again.

Wren tried to blink the face into focus. Was it her own reflection staring back at her? A trick of the lights or the frostfizz toying with her mind? Her stomach roiled as the world spun again, and a distant panic started to inch up her throat.

'*Stop*,' she said, digging her heels in. 'I'll be sick.'

'Say please.'

Wren slammed the heel of her shoe into Alarik's foot.

The king cursed as he released her.

'Oops.' She leaped backwards before he could grab her. 'I told you I was clumsy.'

Wren quickly lost herself in the milling crowds, winding

her way towards the dessert table, which was as far from the dance floor as she could get. She slumped into a chair by a tower of cupcakes and massaged her temples, trying to regain control of her senses.

She looked to the windows, where the world outside was perfectly still. A sigh unfurled from her. 'I knew I was seeing things.' She started to laugh at her own absurdity . . .

And then glimpsed that face again.

Wren's amusement died, quick and strangled, in her throat.

She was sure of it this time – there was a figure moving in the bushes outside.

'No,' said Wren, rising to her feet. 'It isn't possible.'

She jolted into action, her skirts bunched in her fists as she weaved around prowling leopards and growling wolves, hurrying from the ballroom without looking back.

The palace guards in the hallway regarded her curiously. 'Everything all right, Princess Rose?'

'Too much waltzing,' said Wren, fanning herself. 'I just need some fresh air.'

Out in the courtyard, she scoured the darkness. 'I know you're here!' she hissed. 'Come out before you get us both killed!'

There was a stretch of silence. And then a faint rustling.

Wren stared in horror as Rose stepped out from behind a hydrangea bush.

She raised her chin and glared at her sister in the moonlit dark. Wren glared right back, the same emerald-green eyes boring into each other. Rose was a world away from the princess she had been almost one moon ago. She was wearing a bedraggled tunic and her boots were falling apart. Her face was mussed with dirt and sand and sun-borne freckles, and her hair, now streaked with gold, was as tangled as a bird's nest.

It was Wren who shattered the silence. 'What the hell do you think you're doing here?' she demanded.

Rose balled her fists, her face flashing with pure, undiluted fury. 'I could ask *you* the same question.'

Then she leaped at her.

Rose
CHAPTER 32

Rose pinned Wren against the wall, away from the glare of the ballroom windows. She studied her long-lost twin. It was like looking into a mirror and seeing the reflection of how her life had been only a few weeks ago. But it wasn't just the resemblance that startled her. Rose was overwhelmed by the strange pull inside her. It was like some innate part of her recognized Wren and was trying to answer back. Her blood was hot and her pulse was racing, and for a fleeting moment, she felt as if her heart might burst open.

Her sister was silent. Unblinking.

Rose searched her face for the barest difference – a mole, perhaps, or even a stray eyebrow hair – but found none. 'You look *just* like me.'

Wren's lips twisted. 'And *you* look like hell.'

And just like that, the spell of silence – this strange reverence – was broken.

Rose pulled back from her sister, all the stress and exhaustion of her journey home rearing up in a swell of anger. 'I've *been* through hell and back,' she hissed. 'First, I had to climb those forsaken cliffs. *Then* I had to trek through the Weeping Forest with all those ghosts trying to claw at me, cursing me with visions of the Protector himself, who I *swear* nearly skewered me with his sword!' She shuddered at the memory of Ortha Starcrest's death, then pulled a twig out of her matted hair and flung it at her sister.

Wren caught it easily.

Rose wasn't done. 'Then I had to ride through the Restless Sands, which *by the way* are restless *all the time*. And just when I thought I was through the worst of it, the desert tried to *swallow* me. Because apparently that's a thing it can do!'

Wren raised her eyebrows.

Rose shook a deluge of sand out of her tunic, making sure it landed on her sister. 'I rode all night and all day wearing nothing but this . . . this . . . *awful* tunic. I am thirsty. And hungry. And dirty. And exhausted.' She jabbed an accusatory finger at Wren – this imposter who thought she could be Rose simply by putting on her clothes. '*That* is my best dress! And you've spilled frostfizz on the sleeve!'

Wren lifted her sleeve, noting the tiny stain with mild interest. 'Well. Barely.'

Rose was so full of anger, she felt as if she might explode with it. And worse, there seemed to be no emotion at all coming from Wren – just a simmering impatience that pinched the corners of her lips.

'There are more important things to worry about right now, Rose,' she said, sharply. 'And your ridiculously large and *frankly unnecessary* collection of uncomfortable dresses is not one of them. What are you even doing here? You're supposed to be in Ortha.'

'No. *You're* supposed to be in Ortha. *I* am the princess.'

Wren's eyes flashed. 'You're going to ruin everything.'

The twins glowered at each other for a long moment, their chests heaving in perfect harmony. There was so much to say and somehow it was all crowding together on the back of Rose's tongue, her anger warring with disbelief, old pain and new longing, all mixed up in confusion and frustration.

Then came the unmistakable patter of approaching footsteps.

Wren opened her mouth to say something, and Rose slapped her hand over it, stuffing the words back in. 'Shh. Someone's coming.'

She pulled her sister away, moving quickly across the courtyard.

'You need to get out of here. *Now*,' Wren hissed.

'No, *you* need to get out of here.' Rose pulled her sister through the side door that led to the library. It closed behind them with a groan, and then there was nothing but Rose Valhart and Wren Greenrock seething at each other between the winding stacks of a thousand leather-bound books. Moonlight slipped through the windows, casting silver pinwheels along the furniture. Rose glared at the pearl-drop necklace around Wren's neck. *Her* necklace. 'This life does not belong to you and neither does the throne of Eana!'

Wren folded her arms. 'If the throne is so important to you, then why are you in such a hurry to give it away? You bartered your freedom and the fate of the witches for a life with *Ansel*? What were you *thinking*?'

'Not that it's *any* of your business, but I was thinking we might make a good match,' said Rose, sourly. She had not come back here to defend herself to this poor excuse for a princess. 'I was thinking that I might not want to rule this kingdom all by myself.'

'Well, now you're not going to rule it at all!' fumed Wren. At Rose's look of alarm, she shook her head. 'You really had no idea that you were going to be shipped off to Gevra the moment the wedding was over? That there was no longer going to *be* a coronation?'

Rose recoiled from her sister's words. Shock coursed through her as she searched for a response, but her mind was reeling. The floor felt unsteady beneath her, as if the entire world had shifted on its axis.

'You're lying,' she said, hoarsely. It was just a bluff, surely, a way to get Rose to flee Anadawn and leave Wren free to steal her life.

But then her sister curled her lip, and Rose knew by the furious blaze in her eyes that it was true. 'You let Rathborne trade your crown for a Gevran veil,' she said, scornfully. 'You don't deserve to be Queen.'

Rose felt as if she had been slapped in the face. Her own anger – vicious and biting – bubbled to the surface. 'And you do? Oh, please! You aren't fit for anything other than casting silly little spells and fishing on small, smelly boats! You know nothing about ruling a nation!'

Wren jabbed her finger at Rose. 'I know you don't ally yourself with a bloodthirsty king unless you want blood on your hands.'

'The Kingsbreath's spies said the witches were plotting against Anadawn,' Rose shouted. She'd never wanted to smack someone so much in her life. 'And *furthermore*, you *were* plotting against me!'

They fumed in silence, the tension so thick Rose could almost taste it. She took a moment to gather her composure. She should not have stooped to Wren's level and raised her voice just now. It was positively unregal. 'But it didn't work,' she said, calmly. 'I'm back and I *will* be Queen. No matter how you, your witches or Willem Rathborne seek to conspire against me.'

'And what about Gevra?' challenged Wren. 'You won't be Queen of anything unless you cancel your wedding.' Her lips twisted. 'Which is easier said than done, by the way.'

'That's precisely what I intend to do,' said Rose, adamantly.

Wren snorted. 'By all means, go right ahead, Rose. I'm afraid Rathborne won't be at the ball tonight. He's had a little poisoning mishap, which has left him feeling rather ill,' she said, with no small amount of satisfaction. 'But good luck renegotiating the terms of your ill-conceived alliance with King Alarik.' Wren smiled, blandly. 'He's a *real* delight.'

'I'll handle everything this very evening.' Rose refused to be cowed by her sister's taunt. 'You will see how a true princess gets things done.' She rolled her hand, expectantly.

'I'll need my dress back.'

'Why don't I just use one of my *silly little spells* to make you one?' Rose startled as Wren leaned over and reached into the pocket of her tunic. She removed a fistful of sand and rubbed the grains between her fingers. 'Hold still, dear sister.'

Rose shifted nervously. 'Don't you dare turn me into a goat.'

'Shh. I'm focusing.' Wren shut her eyes and muttered an incantation. Then she sprinkled the sand over Rose's head. The grains never landed.

As the dent between her sister's eyebrows deepened, Rose's skin began to tingle. Her tunic shifted, and when she looked down at herself in the dimness, she found it was glowing. Slowly, seamlessly, the tattered material transformed into a sumptuous gold dress, the exact twin of the one Wren was wearing. 'Oh, my stars!'

As the dress settled on her curves and tightened around her waist, Rose's face began to prickle. And then her hair, as though an invisible hand were running a brush through it. The strange glow settled into a gentle shimmer and then it was done.

Wren opened her eyes and smiled so wide, Rose could see all of her teeth.

Suddenly, Rose was smiling, too.

Wren tucked a manicured curl behind Rose's ear. '*Wow*, I'm good.'

'I'll grant you that. I *do* look divine.' Rose surveyed

herself with delight. 'Although you forgot one important detail.' She yanked the pearl necklace from her sister's neck and fixed it around her own. 'Now you stay here, and don't cause any more trouble than you already have.'

Wren flashed her teeth. 'I'll be on my best behaviour.'

Rose swiftly left the library and flounced across the Anadawn courtyard, relieved to be wearing her best gown, to feel beautiful once more. There was a rightness to it, a sense that the world was settling around her, exactly as it should be. Up ahead, a towering figure hurried through the darkness towards her, his boot buckles clinking in time with his footsteps.

'There you are. I was beginning to worry.' The moonlight shifted, and Ansel's personal guard appeared before Rose. He reached for her hand, then stopped suddenly. 'Rose?' he said, uncertainly.

She smacked his hand away. 'What on earth do you think you're doing? How dare you touch me!'

The soldier stiffened. 'Forgive me, Your Highness. It's so dark out here.' His frown deepened as he studied her. 'I thought maybe . . . No. I don't know what I thought. I'm sorry.'

'Never mind,' said Rose, brushing past him. 'Lucky for you, I have more important matters to deal with.'

And with that, she swept into the palace and stepped back into her life.

Wren
CHAPTER 33

Wren stood in the middle of the library, listening to the sound of her sister's fading footsteps. She would slip away once Rose was safely inside the ballroom. Her bullheadedness was already working in Wren's favour. Though her sister's efforts with King Alarik would surely come to nothing, Rose was unwittingly providing the perfect alibi by presenting herself at the Welcoming Ball, leaving Wren free to pay the Kingsbreath a visit in his bedchamber.

She traced the dagger fastened at her hip with still-tingling fingers.

Her magic was warm in her blood, her heart hammering with the success of her spell. In all her years as an enchanter, Wren had never felt power like that. She had never *created* something as fine as Rose's dress and from nothing but a ragged tunic! It had turned out perfectly, every ruffle the exact double of the one Wren wore.

Rose had no idea that Wren wasn't expecting the enchantment to go so well. She had simply expected Wren's magic to be impressive. That made Wren chuckle as she paced the room. Perhaps it was the combination of Ortha sand and desert sand on Rose's tunic that had strengthened the spell. After all, earth taken from magical places worked better for enchantments. But there was only one way to know for certain. She found a vase of wilting roses on a table by the window. She stood over them, gathering the fallen petals in her hand. They were half dust already.

She crushed the petals over the roses. *'From earth to dust, what was once alive, make it grow again and thrive.'*

The vase exploded. Wren gasped as the flowers doubled in size and then doubled again, winding up along the walls, like greedy vines. Two more lurched for the window, growing and twisting until they choked the moonlight from the room. She stumbled backwards, tripping over her dress and falling on the floor. 'No, no, no. Stop growing. *Please.*' She frantically did another enchantment.

The roses stopped crawling, but not before the window groaned and then shattered in a hail of glass. She ducked as the shards rained down on her. The pitter-patter of falling glass soon faded into silence, and Wren's breath loosened in her chest. When she finally looked up, Tor was standing in the doorway.

She covered her face. 'Please tell me you didn't just see that.'

The door closed behind him with a groan. He glanced at the floor, where twisting stalks and bloated roses mingled among the splintered glass. 'I knew there was something off about you,' he said, under his breath. 'I should have listened to my gut.'

Wren rolled to her feet, trying to ignore the look of betrayal on his face. She grasped for the connection that had been blossoming between them. 'You sniffed me out, like a good little Gevran wolf,' she said, coyly. 'Perhaps I should give you a treat.'

The floorboards creaked as he came towards her. 'I'm not playing this game with you.'

'But you want to,' said Wren, boldly. 'Isn't that why you came looking for me?'

Tor's face shuttered. He was every bit the soldier now, stiff and unyielding. He gestured to the mess she had made. 'Explain this.'

Wren's gaze flitted to the shattered window as panic inched up her throat. She wished she could get out of this room and rip off this stupid sparkly dress. It felt even tighter now, as if all the air in her body were being squeezed out, breath by breath.

'Speak,' said Tor, in a low growl.

She bit off a curse. 'I'm thinking.'

'Of a good lie?'

She sagged against a desk. There was nothing to say. She couldn't hide from this and they both knew it. 'I don't think there's a lie good enough to explain that explosion. And even if there were, you're not stupid enough to believe it.'

'I'm glad we agree on something.' Tor stopped a couple of feet from her. 'And while you're explaining things to me, why don't you tell me why I just walked past someone who looks exactly like you outside in the courtyard?'

Rotting carp. He'd seen Rose, too.

'Wait. How did you know she wasn't me?'

He pinned her with his gaze. 'Because I pay attention to you.'

Wren looked away, sharply. She wasn't frightened by the soldier's nearness, but the sight of him standing before her, waiting for her to untangle herself from this unholy mess she had made instead of running back inside to report the explosion – not to mention the unexplained twin sister – unsettled her in a different way. It was more than she deserved.

She briefly considered an enchantment. But what if she harmed him? Or worse – killed him. Her craft wasn't exactly stable right now.

'I suppose I owe you the truth.' Wren looked up at him from beneath her lashes. 'But can I trust you with it?'

His face was unreadable as he watched her. 'That depends.'

'You can't tell anyone. Not Ansel. Nor your awful king or even your darling wolf. If you do, I'll be strung up in the Protector's Vault for the crows to come and peck my eyes out. And I don't think you want that . . .'

A muscle feathered in his jaw. 'No.'

Wren knew there would be no turning back once she told him the truth but they were halfway there already. She might be able to conjure an explanation for the absurd explosion around them but she couldn't explain her sister.

He had already witnessed too much and a small, reckless part of her wanted him to know her – not as Rose, but as herself.

She blew out a breath. 'Here is your something true, Tor. My name is Wren. Rose is my twin sister and *she* is the princess of Eana. Not me.' She stared at the silver buttons on his coat, seized by a mixture of relief and trepidation. There. It was done and there was no taking it back.

'Wren.' Tor said the name as if he were tasting it. 'Like the bird.'

She tilted her head back to look at him. 'The one that flew away.'

'Small creatures, wrens,' he said, watching her too closely. 'Though they have remarkably loud voices. And good survival instincts.'

Wren huffed a laugh. 'Not good enough, it seems.'

'You are not engaged to Prince Ansel, then.'

Wren shook her head. She could have sworn the tension in his shoulders eased, that he looked a little relieved, too. 'Where do you come from, Wren?'

'A faraway place.' Banba's face flashed through her mind and Wren winced. If her grandmother could see her now, spilling all her secrets to a Gevran, she would drag her back to Ortha by her hair. She glanced at the doorway, wondering what he would do if she decided to run from the rest of his questions.

As if sensing her thoughts, Tor leaned down and placed an arm either side of her. 'Why are you here now, Wren?'

'I wanted a change of scenery.'

'Lie,' he whispered.

'Fine,' she said, wringing her hands. 'I wanted to meet Willem Rathborne. The Kingsbreath knew my parents.'

Tor narrowed his eyes. 'That is a half-truth.'

Wren couldn't help but be impressed by his instincts. 'You're good.'

'And you are stalling.'

She shoved him away as she slid off the desk. He let her wander over to the bookshelves where she fingered the spine of a dusty tome.

'Do you intend to harm Prince Ansel?'

'Of course not. That would be like kicking a puppy.' Wren looked at him over her shoulder so he could read the truth in her eyes.

'And the king?'

'Your king is the harmful one.' Wren grimaced at the memory of their dance, of Alarik's fingers pressing into the small of her back, the casual cruelty in how he spoke about the witches. 'He makes my skin crawl.'

Tor's gaze darkened, but he said nothing.

'Are you no better than a beast?' she challenged. 'Can't you speak against your master?'

'I am a soldier of the Gevran army. Bound by honour and loyalty,' he said, gruffly. Perhaps it was Wren's imagination but the buttons of his uniform seemed to shine a little brighter in the moonlight. He rested a hand on the pommel of his sword. 'I came here in service to my country. To protect my prince, my king and Gevra from unseen threats. From imposters like *you*.'

Wren folded her arms. 'Well, then you are not very good at your job.'

'You used me.' Tor shook his head, and he suddenly looked so crestfallen that Wren had to look away. 'You made me think that . . .' He trailed off, swearing under his breath.

'Betraying Ansel would be worth it?' said Wren. 'If you really cared about your prince, you would have kept your distance from me.'

'I should have,' said Tor, ruefully. 'You're nothing but a liar.'

Wren hated how much that word stung her. But there were things – and people – she hated more.

'*You* are the liar, Tor. You didn't only come here for Ansel. You and the rest of your soldiers came to Eana to slaughter innocent people,' she seethed. '*I* didn't bring a bloodthirsty army to Anadawn. I came here *alone* to settle a family matter. Your king is the dangerous one here. Not me.'

'But you are a witch,' said Tor, matter-of-factly.

Wren glared at him. 'That's irrelevant.'

The soldier's laugh was hollow. 'Wren.' He crossed the room in four easy strides. 'I would wager it is the most important thing about you.'

Wren cursed her own stupidity. 'Why did I have to go and do that damned enchantment?'

'I suspected long before tonight.'

'Liar,' she said, again. 'What does a Gevran such as you even *know* of witches?'

'I know magic.' This time when Tor closed the space between them, Wren didn't move. He braced himself against the bookcase and brushed his nose against her neck. 'I can smell it on you.'

Wren closed her eyes as every part of her went taut. '*Please*,' she whispered, but she didn't know what she was asking.

'If Alarik finds out you're a witch, he'll make you his new plaything,' breathed Tor.

Wren snapped her eyes open. 'I could hurt you, you know . . .'

'You mean with this?' He lowered his hand, finding the dagger hidden beneath her skirts. He pressed it gently against her hip. 'Try it.'

Wren's cheeks flamed. 'I have other weapons in my arsenal.'

Tor pulled back from her. 'I'm not scared of you, witch.'

'And I'm not scared of *you*, wrangler.' She tilted her chin to meet the storm in his gaze. 'You caught me out with luck, not skill.'

'I would have caught you a lot sooner if you hadn't kept distracting me.'

Wren laughed in his face. 'Oh, please. You enjoyed it. You *wanted* it. You want it even now.' She pressed herself against him. 'I can *feel* it.'

Tor swallowed whatever he was about to say.

Wren didn't move. It would have to come from him. 'If you want it, take it. I've made it more than clear how I—'

With a rumbling growl, Tor took her face in his hands and kissed her. It was like being swept up in a storm. For a moment, Wren lost her senses entirely. She let the Gevran devour her, his tongue finding hers in an explosion of fireworks. His arms tightened around her waist as he pressed her up against the bookcase. She ran her fingers through his hair, nipping gently at his bottom lip as she ground herself against him. Tor groaned in pleasure and she drank it down.

She forgot what they were arguing about – only that they had wasted precious time sniping at each other when they could have been doing *this*. They should have been doing this all along. The kiss deepened, growing fast and urgent until they were both gasping for breath. Wren tore his coat off and then his shirt, running her hands along the hard planes of his chest. Tor kissed her neck, skilfully trailing his tongue along the shell of her ear as he loosened the ties on her dress.

Wren was hungry for every brush of his lips against her skin, the warmth between them getting hotter and hotter until she felt as if she would burn up inside it.

The bookcase trembled at her back but she barely noticed. Tor tangled his fingers in her hair, kissing her hungrily, but this time, when he moved his body against hers, the bookcase gave way entirely. A shower of books rained down on them. The first one thwacked Wren hard in the shoulder, and Tor grabbed her waist and spun her out of harm's way, before the rest of the case came crashing down.

She shrieked as it hit the floor in a clatter, sending books flying everywhere.

When the dust finally settled, they stood in a puddle of history, gasping for breath.

Wren pressed a hand to her swollen lips. 'Oops.'

'That was . . . unexpected,' said Tor, hoarsely.

Wren stared at his bare chest. 'Which part?'

He ran a hand through his tousled hair. 'Was that magic just now? Is that what it feels like?'

'No,' she said. 'That was no spell.'

Tor's face was stricken. Wren couldn't tell if it was regret or longing warring in his eyes; all she knew was if he kept looking at her like that, she would fling herself at him and tear the rest of this place down.

She surveyed the mess instead. There were books everywhere, shelves broken and splintered where they had hit the ground. Everything was destroyed beyond repair. What on earth had come over her?

A leather spine cracked as Tor took a careful step towards her. 'I should . . . return to the ball. Prince Ansel will be looking for me.'

Wren whirled around, feeling a little lost. Her evening was unravelling around her and she couldn't seem to stop it. 'And I have somewhere else to be . . .'

Tor took another step. 'Do you need help with . . . ?'

'My dress?' Wren looked down at the loose ties. 'I think I can do it.'

Another step.

She heard the staccato of his breath in the silence. His lips parted, as if he wanted to say something.

'What is it?' she said, softly.

But Tor couldn't find the words. He reached for her and she went to him.

And then they were kissing again.

This time, they didn't stop.

Rose

CHAPTER 34

Rose held her head high as she marched towards the ballroom. She paused for a brief moment at the door, gathering her courage. Then she swept inside, and barrelled straight into King Alarik.

While Rose had not yet met the fierce Gevran king, she recognized the crown on his head and his pale blue eyes – they were Ansel's eyes, but somehow the king's gaze seemed sharper. Crueller. She dropped into a curtsy to avoid it.

'King Alarik,' she said, demurely. 'Pardon me, I didn't see you.'

The king placed a cool finger beneath her chin and tilted her head up. 'You should be apologizing for your absence of decorum,' he said, in a dangerously low voice. 'Firstly, for stamping on my foot and then for disappearing in the middle of our dance.'

Rose blinked.

At the very least her sister could have warned her she'd been dancing with the Gevran king, and that she'd already managed to gravely offend him!

'You must forgive me. I wasn't feeling myself,' Rose simpered. 'My corset was too tight, but I've taken some fresh air and I'm feeling *much* better now. Truly.'

'Well, in that case, we have a dance to finish.' Alarik curled his arm around her waist and dragged her on to the dance floor, where she nearly tripped over a snow tiger lounging at the feet of a Gevran soldier. Rose swallowed her scream.

She was so distracted by the roomful of beasts that she nearly lost her footing when Alarik spun her much too fast. But the princess was a seasoned dancer and she refused to be twirled like a spinning top in her own ballroom. She dug her fingers into his shoulder and curled her other hand tight around his to anchor herself. Alarik flashed his canines as he spun her again.

Stay calm, she told herself. *Stay focused*. One dance to smooth things over, and then they would discuss the wedding. Wren may have been defter at stealth and spells, but if Rose knew about anything, it was diplomacy. She schooled her features into a pleasant smile as she picked up her footwork and pretended that being hauled across the dance floor like a rag doll by a surly Gevran king was exactly her idea of a perfect evening.

When they reached the middle of the ballroom, the minstrels broke into a traditional Eana waltz. To Rose's relief, Alarik relaxed his pace and they fell into step with one another. She felt increasingly aware of their onlookers, but was mindful to keep her gaze on the king. She suspected he would not like to share her attention.

Alarik frowned at her. 'Why is your countenance so changed? And your steps. You now know how to dance?'

'As I said . . .' Rose gracefully spun out of his arms and then back in, keeping her shoulders firm and her neck elongated as the dance required. 'It was simply a matter of loosening my corset.'

'I see.' Alarik eyed her waist as he twirled her again, gentler this time.

Now that Rose was in the king's arms, she found herself lost in a sea of Gevran soldiers, their beasts stalking ever closer. She spotted Celeste by the dessert table, relief guttering through her at the sight of her best friend. She couldn't wait to tell her everything. But who was that woman making her laugh so much? Rose saw with some surprise that it was Princess Anika, her cascading red hair and voluptuous figure setting her apart as the famed beauty of Gevra.

Alarik followed her gaze. 'Do not think because my sister runs as wild as her beasts that all women in Gevra are permitted to do the same,' he said, darkly. 'Our courtly women may be strong-willed but they obey their masters.'

Rose understood with sudden clarity how Wren had not lasted long in the king's company without stamping on him.

Alarik lifted a finger to trace her jaw. 'A delicate name for a delicate face. We'll see if a rose so fair can survive the Gevran winter.'

Rose sensed the opportune moment, and reached for it with both hands. 'That reminds me, there is something I wanted to speak to you about.'

'Oh?' Alarik sounded amused.

She steeled her nerves. 'I fear we may have ventured into this arrangement too hastily. Your brother is the most wonderful man, truly – a prince of princes. But I fear we haven't yet spent enough time together to fully test our compatibility and so I wondered if it might be better if we waited until *after* my coronation to finalize our union . . .' Rose trailed off at the sight of Alarik's expression. He looked as if he was going to open his mouth and rip her head off.

He stopped dancing. 'You wish to postpone the wedding?'

Rose quailed. 'Well . . . yes.'

The silence that followed was torturous, Rose wound so tightly she almost forgot to breathe.

And then the king of Gevra threw back his head and laughed. And laughed, and laughed. And laughed.

The sound of it made Rose's skin crawl. She stood trapped in his arms, with a hundred gazes suddenly boring into her.

Alarik stopped laughing with unnerving abruptness, the last of it dying in his throat. 'No.'

Rose blinked. 'No?'

'*No*,' he growled. 'You should be kissing my feet for the pleasure of this union.'

'I mean no disrespect, Your Majesty,' said Rose, hastily. 'I only thought that being such a prize himself, perhaps Prince Ansel may prefer a little more time to consider whether—'

'*Enough.*' Alarik dug his fingernails into her waist. 'It is for me to decide who is best suited to Ansel. And I say that person is *you*. And besides, without this union, I don't get any witches for my collection . . .' He paused and licked his teeth. 'And I *want* them.'

An image sprang up in Rose's mind of Banba and Thea holding hands in front of a roaring bonfire. Suddenly, her fear for them and all of Ortha rang in her ears like a gull's cry. 'I'm afraid the witches are no longer part of the deal.'

Alarik grabbed her jaw and pulled her close until they were nose to nose. 'If I were you, Princess Rose, I would take that back. You do not want to see what happens when you renege on a deal with a Gevran.' He dropped his hand. 'Back home, witches are nothing more than a bedtime story. A tale to frighten our young, and yet I have always wondered what truth lies in those tales. What *power* . . .'

The waltz ended and Alarik released her, bowing once at the waist, before brushing his cool lips against her hand. 'Thank you for the dance, and for the entertainment. I haven't laughed like that in such a long time. Until tomorrow, Princess.'

He sauntered away and Rose stared after him with such hatred burning inside her, her cheeks turned bright pink.

Then Ansel appeared. 'My flower! You have been waltzing with my brother for positively too long. Surely it must be my turn again? And I must say, it looks as if your dancing has improved remarkably.' He cast a nervous glance at the king's retreating figure. 'Alarik is quite good at that. Inspiring improvement.'

'He certainly has a firm grip,' muttered Rose, as she massaged her jaw.

'When I was a boy I refused to ride the palace ice bear because I was terrified of its teeth, but after Alarik made me rest my head in its open mouth for an entire afternoon, I found I was no longer afraid of the creature at all!' Ansel giggled, nervously. 'Alarik is a good king. A strong king. And a good brother, too! Of course, being King is more important than being a good brother.'

Rose stared at the babbling prince, trying to remember why she had ever thought herself in love with him. He felt like a stranger to her now. Perhaps he had always been a stranger, and she'd been so eager for love – for extraordinariness – that she had painted in the edges of him, and turned him into someone else entirely. Someone she thought she could love. But now that she had tasted the desert air with Shen and watched the stars dancing in his eyes as he looked at her, she knew she had never loved Ansel. And she certainly couldn't marry him. Of that, she was unerringly sure.

She was struck by a surge of pity for poor Ansel, growing up in the shadow of someone like Alarik. She took his hand in hers. The unprompted touch silenced the chattering prince, who stared at their hands in muted surprise. A blush rose in his cheeks.

'Alarik is lucky to have you as a brother, Ansel.'

Ansel swept his golden hair from his face, his blue eyes bright with joy. 'It is I who am the lucky one. What a good brother Alarik is, to arrange for me to marry the most beautiful and unique woman in all of Eana. You will be adored in Gevra, Rose. You'll see. The love of our people will keep you warm in the long winter months.'

Rose smiled faintly. She might have steeled herself for their wedding if she had truly believed it was what was best for Eana. She would do whatever it took to protect her kingdom, to ensure the prosperity and peace her people deserved. But this union was not the answer.

She could see now it never had been.

Ansel tugged her towards the dance floor. 'Shall we dance, my sunbeam?'

'I'm afraid I can't right now.' Rose stepped away from him just as the doors to the ballroom opened. She gasped as Willem Rathborne stepped inside, looking like a ghost who had come to haunt her. *Oh no!* Suddenly, everything was going wrong.

Although Wren was mistaken about how close the Kingsbreath was to death, Rose could tell, even from a distance, that he was not well. The sight of his gaunt face and sallow skin evoked no kindness in her heart. She knew him now for the monster he was. The monster he had always been. 'I must speak with the Kingsbreath.' She flashed Ansel her most radiant smile. 'When I return, you and I will raise a glass to the future of both our great countries.'

And how they may never be joined, she thought to herself, as she seized her courage, lifted her skirts and marched towards the Kingsbreath.

Willem scowled at Rose as she approached, and the sight of his displeasure made her feel like a child again. On instinct, she curtsied. 'I'm so pleased you have recovered from your illness, Willem.'

'Mind your tongue,' he hissed. 'I will not have the Gevrans hear another word about my illness. It's bad enough that I missed their arrival on the Silvertongue. I told Chapman to keep things running smoothly in my absence, which begs the question, *why* aren't you over there waltzing with your prince?'

Rose raised her head and met the gaze of the man who had murdered her parents. The man who had raised her, had pretended to love her, had taught her how to cower and bend her whole life, not for Eana but for him.

She wished for a knife to run into his heart.

Be careful, she reminded herself. There was no sense in revealing what she had learned about Willem yet, nor the existence of her twin sister. Despite Wren's betrayal, they shared a common enemy. She was more than just her sister. Wren was her ally.

With King Alarik's laughter still echoing in her head and the Kingsbreath standing before her, Rose decided to appeal to him one last time. 'I do not intend to dance with Prince Ansel again, nor will I make a life with him,' she said, steadily. 'After careful consideration, I no longer believe that a Gevran alliance is what is best for Eana. Alarik seemed to disagree, but perhaps if both you and I speak to him—'

'I will *not* go over this with you again, Rose.' Willem's eyes flashed in warning. 'You are marrying Prince Ansel and that is final.'

Rose stood her ground. 'I want to become Queen and find my own suitable match when the time is right. One that is good for me and for my kingdom.'

'Rose, darling,' he said through his teeth. 'You are simply having pre-wedding nerves. You will be a beautiful bride and you will make me and your country proud. And more than that, you will make your dear parents proud. Now. We will not speak of this again. Am I understood?'

Rose squeezed her hands into fists, her fingernails cutting half-moons in her palms. She had stood up for herself and it wasn't enough. What more could she do? With mounting despair, she realized how little control she had over her own life. She was no princess. She was a puppet. And Willem Rathborne would sooner ship her off to Gevra than cut her strings.

'Rose? Am I understood?'

Rose nodded, her eyes filling with tears.

'That's my good girl. Now run along back to your fiancé. He's waiting for you by the dance floor.'

Rose did not return to Ansel. Instead, she waited until Willem's back was turned then slipped out of the ballroom.

Once outside in the courtyard, she raced through the shadows until she reached the library. She burst inside in a panic. 'Wren! Are you still in here? It didn't work. We have a huge— *Burning stars!*'

Ansel's personal guard had her sister pinned against

the wall.

And her sister looked as if she was very much enjoying it.

No wonder he had acted so familiar with her in the courtyard! Rose had never seen anyone kiss like that – it looked as if they were trying to crawl into each other's mouths. And he was *shirtless*. And there were books *everywhere*. And glass. And splintered wood. And giant, creeping roses!

Rose slammed the library door with a resounding bang. They didn't stop.

She picked up a book and flung it at the Gevran. 'WREN!'

The soldier spun around, his eyes wide and darting.

'Oh, *good*,' said Wren, smoothing down her now very wrinkled dress. 'It's only you.'

'You're lucky it's me!' fumed Rose. 'What if anyone else had walked in here? They . . . they would have thought I was you! Kissing *him*!' She flung a finger at the Gevran. He had plucked his shirt from the floor and was fumbling over the buttons. 'Think of my reputation!' Rose's cheeks were bright and burning. 'And what are you even doing kissing him anyway?'

Wren bit her lip. 'I might have got a little carried away.'

The soldier plucked his frock coat from the floor and shrugged it on. 'I should go.' He nodded at Rose, his gaze lingering on Wren, before he slipped out of the library.

Rose turned on her sister. 'I leave you for ten minutes and the next thing I know you're undressing the enemy!'

'Well. Only the top half,' Wren pointed out. 'And Tor

isn't the enemy.'

'For all we know, *Tor* is strolling back inside to tell Alarik that there are now two of us! And if that horrid king catches wind that we're witches, we'll both be on the first ship back to Gevra!'

'Tor won't say a word,' said Wren.

'And how do you know?' Rose paused. 'Wait. Did you enchant him?'

Wren sighed. 'I trust him, Rose.'

Rose threw her hands up. 'Oh, well, in that case we have *nothing* to worry about.'

'Leave the Gevran solider to me,' said Wren, calmly. 'Now. Did you succeed in calling the wedding off?'

Rose cleared her throat. 'I'm afraid there's a better chance of Alarik feeding me to one of his beasts than agreeing to cancel the wedding.'

Wren collapsed into an overstuffed armchair. 'So, you failed. As I knew you would.'

'Well, so did you,' said Rose, unable to help herself. 'Willem Rathborne is alive and well. He's at the ball.'

Wren stared at her in horror. '*What?*'

Rose groaned as she sank into a matching chair. 'Now what do we do?'

Wren buried her face in her hands. 'I have no idea.'

Wren
CHAPTER 35

Wren stood in squalid darkness, rattling the bars of her cage. She screamed but no sound came out. The shadows shifted and Rose appeared before her. Her smile was wide and mocking but when she spoke it was with Banba's voice. *'You have failed, little bird.'* She reached through the bars of Wren's cage and yanked the crown from her head. She settled it on her own, the gold gleaming in the darkness. *'You were always going to fail.'*

Banba's voice became Alarik's, then, his laughter so cold it chattered through Wren's teeth. In the darkness, witches clawed at her ankles. There were no beasts now, only death. Between them, Banba's corpse lay curled on its side.

Wren lunged for her sister, grabbing her through the bars. Something jolted inside her and a spark of magic erupted between them. It became a wild, roaring fire, devouring everything – the fear and the darkness, Banba's lifeless body and the witches crawling at their feet, and finally, mercifully, the rest of the nightmare.

Wren woke with a gasp. She blinked into the dimness,

trying to piece together where she was and why her body was aching. She grimaced as memories of last night came flooding back. Rose had returned to Anadawn and everything was spiralling out of control. Now Wren was lying on the floor, covered in dust and blinking up at creaking wooden slats.

Her nose tickled and she sneezed.

'*Shh,*' hissed Rose from above. 'Someone will hear you!'

Wren scooted out from under her sister's bed to find a familiar pair of emerald-green eyes glaring down at her. In the morning light, the twins' similarities were even more astonishing. Rose's time in Ortha had speckled her nose with freckles, the desert sun casting streaks of honey in her chestnut-brown hair.

Wren grunted as she stood up. After coming to an uneasy truce borne of having a common, looming enemy in the Kingsbreath, the girls had stayed up late into the night, trying to figure out how to deal with Rathborne now that he was up and about again. Rose had quailed at the idea of committing outright murder in the heart of Anadawn Palace, and in the absence of any alternate ideas, Wren had become increasingly frustrated at her sister's squeamishness. The wedding was tomorrow, only one day before the twins' eighteenth birthday, and with Rathborne more determined than ever to see Rose off to Gevra before then, there was no time for hesitation.

When their conversation eventually dissolved into exhausted bickering, Rose had stormed out to fetch herself a camomile tea in the kitchens. Wren had fallen asleep to the distant roar of Gevran beasts and, in the darkness under Rose's bed, she had dreamed of her own failure, over and over again.

She brushed the hair from her eyes. 'Next time you see one of your maids, ask them to clean under your bed once in a while. I'll be coughing up dust for days.'

If Rose felt bad for her sister, she didn't show it. 'I'll make a note about the dust,' she said, sinking back into her pillows.

'My back is sore, too.' Wren reached for her sister's hand. 'Will you heal it?'

Rose swatted it away. 'And undo all the good resting I did last night?' she whispered. 'Certainly not.'

'I suppose that makes you the evil twin, then.' Rose's healing gift had come as a surprise to Wren. She had grown up wondering why their mother's enchantment had only manifested in her but had never considered that Rose might in fact be a different kind of witch.

Wren considered her sister in the glaring morning light. In her high-necked pink nightgown and surrounded by piles of goose-down pillows, she looked like a doll. There was a delicacy about Rose that Wren did not – had never – possessed. Rose had inherited the noble gentleness of the Valharts but Eana needed a witch queen – someone steely-eyed and fearless, who was not afraid to carve her way into the dark heart of Anadawn Palace and bleed the poison from within.

It needed Wren.

'Why are you frowning like that?' Rose interrupted her sister's thoughts. 'You'll give yourself wrinkles.'

'Nothing a little enchantment can't fix,' said Wren, airily. 'And if you must know, I'm frowning because I don't see why we can't just share this giant bed of yours!' She leaped on to the bed and began bouncing up and down. 'This mattress is much too big and it's not as if you get any nightly visitors.'

'Except for you and Shen, you mean. Speaking of, this is for kidnapping me.' Rose whacked Wren with her pillow, setting a handful of feathers loose. 'And for goodness' sake, keep your voice down!'

Wren tried to wrestle the pillow from her sister. 'Are you afraid the palace guards will think you're talking to yourself?'

'My reputation might mean little to you but it's important to me,' said Rose, refusing to let go. 'Honestly, Wren. All these weeks pretending to be me and you still haven't learned a basic modicum of decorum.'

'And *you* haven't learned how to relax.' Wren yanked the pillow free and hit her sister back, much harder. A laugh sprang from her at the sight of Rose's dazed expression and she realized with a start that she was enjoying herself. That this – having a sister – even one who was a spoilt, stubborn princess was . . . well, quite nice.

Rose blew the tangled hair from her face. 'When Agnes comes with my breakfast, you have to hide.'

'Why can't *you* hide? I'm ravenous.'

Rose glared at her. 'Because *I* am the princess. And technically speaking, *you're* a criminal.'

'Technically speaking, we're *both* princesses,' said Wren.

'Don't even joke about that!' Rose leaped off the bed and crossed to her dresser, where she sat in front of the mirror and roughly dragged a brush through her hair. 'I still can't *believe* you took a Gevran lover in my name.'

Somewhere outside, a wolf howled.

Wren grabbed her drawstring pouch from under the bed and stalked to the dressing table. 'Actually, I used my own name. And you're just jealous you didn't think of seducing Tor first.' She yanked the hairbrush from her sister and tossed it aside. 'Here, let me fix you up.'

Two enchantments later, Wren and Rose looked like a pair of prim and proper princesses. Despite the waning potency of the rose petals, somehow Wren's spellwork was better than ever. She couldn't trace a single freckle along the bridge of her nose and her hair had fallen into perfect loose curls, the exact same shade and length as her sister's.

Huh. I must be a better enchanter than I thought, Wren told herself, ignoring the prickle of unease that walked down her spine.

Rose admired herself in the mirror. 'Perhaps we can find a way to let you stay on here as my personal lady's maid.'

'You couldn't afford me,' said Wren, dryly.

Rose gave a wide smile. 'You underestimate my exorbitant wealth.'

'*Our* wealth.' Wren skipped towards the wardrobe. 'So, which one of us gets to be Rose today?'

Rose threw her a withering glance. 'That's *not* funny.'

Wren flung the wardrobe open and began rifling through the dresses. 'Don't forget, there's still work to be done, Rose,' she said, as she pulled out three at once. She held a shimmering violet one up to her neck. 'And by *work*, I mean the swift and brutal disposal of—'

Wren fell out of her sentence as the door to the bedroom swung open. She froze with the dresses clutched against her chest. Celeste stalked into the room, beautiful and fuming in the morning sunlight. She slammed the door behind her, looked once between the twins and then whirled on Wren. 'You!' she hissed, in accusation. 'You messed with my memories!'

Wren looked at Rose, straining now to keep her voice low. 'You *told* her?'

Rose folded her arms. 'Of course I told her. She's my best friend.'

'*When?*' reeled Wren, but then she remembered Rose's midnight trip to the kitchens. Clearly, she had gone to see Celeste instead. 'And you think *I'm* reckless!'

'You are reckless!' said Celeste, as she came towards Wren.

Wren felt like a naughty child about to be punished. 'Now, Celeste, I can explain.' She flung a lavender dress at her to keep her at bay. 'We can't afford to make a scene.'

Celeste batted it aside. 'There's only one of me, Wren. I

can do whatever I want.' She slipped off her shoe and returned fire. Wren ducked at the last second, dropping another dress in her haste as the shoe clattered against the wall.

'*Shhh!*' said Rose, fanning her arms wildly. 'We'll get caught!'

Celeste removed her other shoe. 'Your guard is taking his privy break.'

'Sound still travels!' said Wren, as she backed away.

'Well, so does my shoe.' Celeste let it fly and this time it hit Wren squarely on the shoulder.

Wren threw the final dress at Rose as she climbed on to the bed. 'Tell your best friend to stop chasing me!'

'Only if you tell *your* best friend not to kidnap me,' said Rose, as she picked up the dress and shook out the wrinkles. 'Oh, wait, too late.'

Celeste laughed as she clambered on to the bed. She flung her arms out, as if to tackle Wren. 'I'll stop chasing you when you apologize for what you did.'

'You were too clever. You were going to turn me in,' said Wren, hoisting a pillow in defence. 'What was I supposed to do? Just give up and be done with it?'

Celeste's eyes flashed. 'I didn't hear the word *sorry* in there.'

Wren leaped off the bed and hid behind Rose. 'I did what I had to do,' she said, over her sister's shoulder. 'I didn't *want* to wipe those memories, but really, Celeste, would you have preferred me to kill you?'

Rose shook herself free from Wren's grasp. 'Have you lost your mind?'

'You did magic on *my* best friend,' said Wren.

'Yes! To save his life!' snapped Rose. 'You're *welcome*, by the way.'

Wren stilled as her pride faltered. She heard herself properly for the first time, defending something that she knew was wrong. Rose had saved Shen's life in the desert and Wren had almost taken Celeste's from her in the woods. If Shen were here now, he would be ashamed of her.

Celeste towered over Wren from the bed, the sunlight streaming over her shoulders and picking out the threads of amber in her dress. Beneath the fury in her face, Wren could see hurt and confusion, too. Pain she had caused.

She dipped her head in shame. 'I'm sorry, Celeste,' she said, and she meant it. 'I was desperate that day in the woods but I shouldn't have done it.'

Celeste stood her ground. 'Promise you'll never use your magic against me again.'

'I promise,' said Wren, and she meant that, too.

Celeste stepped down off the bed. 'Now make the same promise to your sister.'

Wren blinked at her. 'Excuse me?'

Celeste jerked her chin towards Rose, who seemed just as surprised by the request as Wren was. 'Promise you won't use your magic against your sister either.'

Wren's lips twisted. It was a bold request. After all, once Rathborne was out of the way and the Gevrans were sent packing, Rose would be the single biggest obstacle on her way to the throne. The way Celeste was staring at Wren made it clear she had already come to that same conclusion. She knew how badly Wren still wanted it, how meeting Rose – her own sister – hadn't changed her ultimate goal.

Rose turned to look at her. 'Wren? Why are you hesitating?'

'I promise,' said Wren, after a beat. 'Of course I promise.'

Celeste blew out a breath, the fire in her gaze banked. For now. 'Good. Now fill me in on everything.'

So they did. And together, the three of them began to plot.

'I still don't see why we can't just kill him in his bed and be done with it,' said Wren, as she reclined against Rose's headboard.

'Because it's reckless,' said Rose, impatiently. 'Willem's already doubled his personal guards since you tried to poison him and who knows how many more he has *inside* his chamber? You'd never be able to enchant them all and if you're caught, then it'd be over.'

Wren closed her eyes. Though it pained her to admit it, her sister was right. 'Fine. No bedroom assassination.'

'If you ask me, I think you're getting too caught up in the murder aspect,' Celeste interjected.

Wren rolled her head around to face her. 'What other aspects are there, Celeste?'

'Why not seek the Kingsbreath's exposure first?' suggested Celeste. 'Once the country sees him for what he really is – a liar and a usurper – then you can have your retribution. Hang him from the Protector's Vault, if you like.'

Wren sat up straight. 'Keep going.'

Celeste's smile curled. 'I say you do it at the wedding tomorrow so every Eanan noble and official can witness the moment you expose him for all of his lies. And what better way to do that than to introduce Willem Rathborne and the rest of the congregation to you, Wren? The royal twin that got away.'

Rose began to nod. 'The royal twin that the witches of Ortha protected.' She looked at Wren, eyes alight with triumph. 'We can change the way Eana thinks about witches, show them they were wronged by Willem eighteen years ago, too.'

Wren was still chewing on the idea, but she certainly liked the way it tasted. Exposing Willem Rathborne in public would go a long way to rebuilding the witches' poor reputation in the capital and sowing the seeds of change ahead of her own reign. But would that be enough to satisfy Banba? Or would she still insist on tearing down Anadawn in revenge for Lillith's War and filling the rivers of Eana with the blood of all those who'd once supported it?

And then there were the Gevrans to worry about. Without a wedding there would be no alliance but Wren doubted King Alarik would go quietly after coming all this way for the witches.

She quickly banished the thought. They could worry about that once the wedding was cancelled. First, they had to deal with Rathborne. 'And *then* we can kill him, right?'

'Once Rathborne's exposed, you can punish him any way you like,' said Celeste. 'And you can do it under the sun, sanctified by Eanan law. A true justice.'

'I like it,' said Wren, slowly. In fact, she loved it.

'It's *genius*, Celeste,' said Rose. 'All Wren has to do is stay hidden until the wedding tomorrow. Willem won't know what's coming. Not until it's too—'

TAP! TAP! TAP!

She froze at a sound from outside. The girls whipped their heads around to find a lone starcrest sitting on the window ledge. It tapped its beak against the glass, watching them with its bright beady eyes.

A trickle of unease snaked down Wren's spine. She rolled to her feet and went to the window. The starcrest launched itself into the air, circling once before gliding back towards the west tower of Anadawn. She watched it go and this time, when she glimpsed the face in the window, she gasped.

Rose was on her feet in an instant. 'What is it?'

'There's a woman in the west tower.' Wren leaned out of the window, trying to get a better look at her. Her face was pale and gaunt, dwarfed by reams of cloudy white hair. Then it was gone again.

'*She warned me . . . the flames are inside me . . . the burning . . . ah . . .*' Rathborne's words echoed in Wren's head and she was reminded of him doubled over in pain after the poisoning.

'She warned him,' Wren murmured. She plucked the rest of his ramblings from her memory as a new horror dawned inside her. *'The enemy wears two faces. We must come for the witches before they come for us . . . And they are coming.'*

'What are you talking about?' said Rose, in mounting alarm.

'Oh no.' Behind her, Celeste had already pieced it together. She came to the window, giving voice to Wren's thoughts. 'Willem's got a seer.'

'It was never just the birds,' said Wren, cursing her own stupidity. Somehow the Kingsbreath had done the impossible – he had got his grasping hands on a damned seer. 'Someone's been whispering to him about the future.'

Warning him, thought Wren, angrily. 'No wonder he's been so skittish.'

She stepped away from the window. 'A seer's vision sharpens over time. As a prophecy draws nearer, there's always more to know. More to see,' she told them, urgently. 'If Rathborne truly has a witch at Anadawn, we won't be able to hide from her for much longer. Not now that you've come back here, Rose.' She couldn't help the hint of accusation in her voice.

'We need to get the seer out of here before she can expose us,' said Rose.

Celeste blew out a breath. 'It might already be too late. He visited her last night after the ball. I saw his guards outside the west tower.'

The three of them glanced at the door at the same time, half expecting the Kingsbreath to barrel through it and arrest them. There was only the distant stirring of maidservants rising to face the day and the faraway growl of Gevran beasts as they paced the courtyard.

Wren ground her jaw, thinking. 'If not last night, then tonight.'

Rose and Celeste exchanged a worried glance. 'We could free her before then,' said Rose.

'And find out what she knows,' added Celeste. 'What she's been telling him.'

Rose nodded. 'The Gevran Feast begins at sundown. Willem will have to be in attendance. That gives us some time.'

'He won't take his eyes off you tonight,' warned Celeste. 'The guards will be watching your every move.'

Wren's smile was slow and creeping. She felt the tides of destiny rippling around her and glimpsed a plan floating in its waves. 'But no one will be watching *me*.' She could easily make it to the west tower with the help of her magic. She just needed a way to get inside the turret without arousing suspicion. 'I'll need the key to the tower. The one he wears around his neck.'

'I could steal it from him at the feast,' said Rose, clenching her fists as she summoned her courage.

Celeste looked at Wren. 'I could take it to you.'

Wren nodded. 'I'll have it back before he even notices it's missing.' She turned to Rose, then. 'Just make sure you dance with every Gevran in attendance. Be bright and bubbly. No one can suspect a thing.'

'Why don't we start the subterfuge right now?' said Celeste, as she skipped across the room. She plucked the violet dress from the stool by the vanity and tossed it to Rose. 'Let's go for a morning stroll in the courtyard. The more people who see you acting normally today, the better.'

'And what about me?' demanded Wren. 'What am *I* supposed to do?'

Celeste smiled, thinly. 'You can go back to not existing for a while.'

Within minutes, both girls were gone and Wren was alone again. She turned to the window, resting her elbows on the ledge. Outside, the flag of Eana was rippling in the summer breeze.

When she was Queen, she would rip it down and restore Eana, the first witch queen, to the crest. This land would be ruled by her descendant and the halls of Anadawn would sing with magic once more. Freedom was coming at last and it would be granted by a Greenrock witch, born and raised on the sands of Ortha. Not a pampered Valhart who barely had a handle on her own magic. No matter how Wren's plans had been altered by Rose's return, her mission had not.

'*I'm so close now, Banba*,' she whispered to the wind. '*I will not fail you.*'

She closed her eyes and pictured herself sitting on the throne of Eana, surrounded by the witches. When she opened them again, Wren looked to the west tower and wondered if the seer saw that same future, too.

Rose
CHAPTER 36

'I don't trust her,' said Celeste, as they walked arm in arm through the courtyard. 'You need to keep your guard up.'

'You needn't worry about Wren.' Rose deftly arced around a Gevran soldier who was out walking his snow leopard and smiled at a silver fox rustling in a nearby bush. 'She's on our side.' She gestured to the golden gates, where four soldiers were stationed at each post, while another six patrolled the nearby gardens. 'Just look around you, Celeste; she *needs* us.'

Celeste's frown deepened as they wandered into the rose garden. 'She might be on our side now but that doesn't mean she always will be.'

They passed beneath the garish statue of the Protector. Rose scowled up at his marble face, the memory of him hunting down Ortha Starcrest passing through her like a violent shudder. She turned abruptly down another path, tugging Celeste with her. 'Wren won't betray me. Not now that we want the same thing,' she said with simmering confidence. 'After all, I'm not just her sister. I'm a witch, too. Wren knows when I am Queen, I will do what's best for them. For all of us.'

'Have you had that conversation with her?' asked Celeste.

'More or less.' Rose waved her hand in breezy dismissal. 'We'll work out the finer details after tonight.'

Celeste looked at her with lingering disbelief. 'I still can't believe that you, Rose Valhart, are a witch.'

'And a healer, at that,' said Rose, proudly. 'It's clearly the best kind to be, if you are going to be one at all.' She couldn't quite believe how much had changed since she last walked among her rose bushes. One moon ago, she would have balked at the idea of magic living inside her but now she treasured her power. She liked helping people, making them feel good. It made her feel like she belonged to something bigger than herself. Not a kingdom, but a purpose. 'Healing brings about peace and happiness. My magic isn't tricky, like Wren's. Or scary, like our grandmother's. It makes things better.'

Celeste hmm'd in agreement, and not for the first time since her return, Rose was seized by a rush of affection for her. She had told Celeste everything last night during her midnight visit, and she had weathered it all with remarkable calmness, as though deep down, a part of her had been expecting it, *bracing* for it. Rose was grateful for her openness, and relieved that the revelation about her magic didn't frighten Celeste one bit. Her friend's reaction had filled her with hope for the future. If Rose was lucky, the people of Eana would be just as accepting of her craft. Eventually.

'What about the handsome bandit you told me about last night?' needled Celeste. 'He's a warrior witch. Born to fight. Isn't that basically the opposite of a healer?'

Rose flushed. 'Shen only uses his craft for good. To protect people. To protect *me*.' She smiled, coyly. 'Oh, Celeste, if you could only see the way he moves. He's like a shadow, as quick and silent as the wind. Even that first day out in the desert, when he saved me from that awful blood beetle, I couldn't take my eyes off him.'

Celeste snorted. 'I'm glad to see the desert didn't change you. You're still a hopeless romantic.' She gently nudged Rose in the ribs. 'Wasn't it just last month you were waxing poetic about Prince Ansel? Who, by the way, is going to be utterly heartbroken when not one but *two* Roses reject him.'

'That was different,' said Rose, finding the truth in the tide of her guilt. 'How I feel about Shen is nothing like what I thought I felt for Ansel.' They wandered deeper into the garden, past the red roses which had been plucked to ruin. She glanced around to make sure they weren't overheard. 'My feelings for Ansel were as real as they could have been at the time. But they were like a painting of . . . oh, I don't know, a basket of fruit. Nice to have, but never truly *satisfying*. And Shen.' She smiled, without meaning to. 'Well, my feelings for Shen are like *real* fruit. A whole mountain of fresh fruit! Apples and berries and pears and bananas . . .'

'Bananas?' Celeste arched an eyebrow. 'What do you

know of men's bananas, Rose?'

Rose burst into a fit of giggles. 'You have a filthy mind, Celeste Pegasi!' she said, swatting her arm. 'I just mean that my feelings for Shen are real. *Really* real.'

'And clearly delicious.'

'I just wish I'd kissed him when I had the chance.' Rose pressed her fingers to her lips, trying to imagine what it would feel like – to be kissed for the first time in her life, by Shen, a man who moved like the night air and laughed like a song.

'Well, maybe some day you'll get the chance,' said Celeste, encouragingly.

'Oh yes, between cancelling my wedding, exposing the Kingsbreath, reintegrating the witches into Eana and becoming Queen, I'm sure I'll find time to sneak off to Ortha to kiss Shen.' Rose shook her head, thinking of her last moments with him. 'I doubt he ever wants to see me again. Not after what I did to him.' It was bad enough that she had stolen his beloved horse and then set her loose in the Eshlinn woods. She had no way of knowing if Storm had managed to make it back home.

'I'm sure Wren would happily pretend to be you again if you ever wanted to slip away and . . . say *sorry*.' Celeste lingered over the last word, and Rose could tell by her smirk she meant a lot more than a simple apology. 'Speaking of your wily sister, what is she planning to do when you become Queen?'

Rose traced the petals of an unspoilt flower. 'Whatever

she likes, I suppose. She can go back to Ortha. Or I can find her something to do in the palace. She does have quite a knack for enchantments,' she said, mildly. In truth, she hadn't given much thought to what Wren would do after the coronation. Apart from sulk, probably.

'Rose.' Celeste grabbed her arm, pulling her attention from the flowers. 'Can't you see that Wren still wants the throne for herself?'

'Well, she can't have it.' Rose folded her arms. 'I'm here now, and I am quite plainly the *real* heir to the throne. So, unless she plans on kidnapping me again—'

'I wouldn't put it past her.'

'We have to trust her, Celeste. What other choice do we have? We need her to expose Rathborne. It's the only way to stop this wedding.' Rose's face brightened. 'And don't forget, I have you on my side. You are the cleverest person I know.'

'Too clever for my own good, apparently,' Celeste muttered. '*You* don't forget that my cleverness nearly got me killed.'

'Wren isn't truly capable of that. I know it in my heart.'

'Just like you know she's not going to backstab you after tomorrow?'

Rose sighed, as she threaded her arm through Celeste's. 'If it makes you feel better, I'll talk to her.'

The bells in the clock tower began to chime. A new day had dawned, and there was much to do. 'We should get back,' said Celeste, through a sprawling yawn. 'I'm sorely in need of a nap. We stayed up far too late last night, and I want to look my best for the feast later.'

'You'll look radiant, as you always do.'

'As long as Princess Anika notices,' said Celeste, with a glint in her eye. 'She's the only Gevran I'll miss when those ships depart.'

'Now who's the hopeless romantic?' teased Rose.

'Still you,' said Celeste, as they headed for the palace. 'It's always you.'

They laughed as they parted in the hallway, the two girls peeling off to opposite wings to get ready for the Gevran Feast.

Rose made her way to the east tower, thinking again about Wren. It was preposterous for her sister to think she would still be Queen. That she was even *fit* for it in the first place. Wren was far too brash, not to mention she swore like a sailor and had horrendous manners. The very idea of her wearing the crown, much less trying to rule with it, made Rose chuckle to herself.

She was still laughing when she stepped into the stairwell, and was seized by a figure waiting in the darkness.

Wren
CHAPTER 37

Wren grabbed her sister and pulled her into the shadows, a hand pressed to her mouth to keep her from screaming. 'It's Wren,' she whispered, as Rose struggled against her. 'Come with me. I want to show you something.'

In the dimness, Rose's eyes were wide and frightened. They slid to Wren's and the fight seeped out of her. She relaxed her shoulders and Wren removed her hand from her mouth.

'Do you have a death wish?' Rose hissed. 'What are you doing down here? You're supposed to be hiding in my bedchamber!'

'I got bored,' said Wren, defensively.

Rose glared at her. 'I almost screamed just now.'

'Good thing I'm quicker than you.' Wren winked as she tapped the pouch at her waist. 'And anyway, the tower guards are asleep.' She had spelled them both with ease before winding her way down the stairwell, where she had been waiting impatiently for her sister's return.

'I have a good mind to fire them for their incompetence,' muttered Rose.

'If you want real protection, you should seek it from the witches,' said Wren. 'Didn't you learn that in Ortha?'

Rose's lips twisted. 'The last time one of your witch friends used magic on me, it wasn't to protect me. It was to kill me.' She shivered at the memory and Wren was seized by a sudden, violent protectiveness.

She curled her hands into fists. 'Who tried to kill you?'

'Rowena,' said Rose, in a quiet voice. 'She threw me off the Whisperwind Cliffs.'

'Why didn't you tell me this last night?'

Rose shrugged. 'Would you have cared?'

Wren stared at her sister in alarm. Did Rose really think she meant so little to Wren? That she was too callous to care if her only sister *died*? 'Of course I care,' she said, biting off a curse. 'When I see Rowena again, I'll wring her neck. I left *explicit* instructions that you were not to be harmed.'

Now it was Rose's turn to look surprised.

'Come with me.' Wren grabbed her sister's hand and led her down the rest of the spiralling steps, where the shadows rose up like waves to claim them.

Rose clenched Wren's fingers. 'What are we doing in this dusty old cellar?'

'You'll see.' Wren pulled her sister deep into the cellar until they came upon the old broom closet. Inside, the witch markings glowed like twin stars in the dark. Rose gasped, leaping behind Wren on instinct. She twined her fingers in the back of her dress as though to pull her away from the danger.

Wren chuckled at her sister's horror-stricken face. 'You

don't have to be frightened,' she told her. 'This place is a secret gift. It's *our* secret gift.'

She pressed her hand against the stone and felt a familiar heat buzzing against her palm. The wall parted with a groan and Rose whimpered as the passageway revealed itself, its hollow darkness feathered by the faraway glow of the everlights.

'Well?' said Wren, over her shoulder. 'Are you coming?'

Rose's green eyes shimmered with curiosity. She rolled her shoulders back and raised her chin. 'Well, it is *my* palace,' she said, as she stepped out from behind Wren. 'Of course I'm coming.'

With her fear suddenly consumed by wonder, Rose slipped through the opening without so much as a backwards glance. Wren followed her sister into the passageway, their footsteps echoing around them as they fell into step.

Rose drifted towards the first everlight and swished her hand above the purple flame. 'What are these things?' she said, looking up to where the rest of the flames flickered along the tunnel.

'They're called everlights.' Wren told her how they were made and how long they had been burning. 'They're relics from the witches who once lived here.'

Rose was silent for a long time, staring into that purple flame as if she could glimpse a whisper of the past inside it. 'They're still here,' she murmured. 'After all this time.'

Wren glanced sidelong at her. 'You can't destroy magic, Rose. It will always find its way home.'

Just as I have.

Rose looked up, and Wren was struck by the sadness in her face. She felt the same melancholy inside her and was overcome by the urge to throw her arms around her sister and make it go away. 'I never knew what we took from them,' said Rose, in a cracked voice. 'I swear I never knew about any of it.'

'How could you?' said Wren, softly. 'You only knew what Rathborne taught you.' Without meaning to, she took her sister's hand and curled it in her own.

Rose's bottom lip began to wobble.

Wren gently squeezed her fingers. 'It's not your fault.'

'It's not that,' said Rose, her face crumpling. 'It's just . . . Wren, you're my *sister*.'

Wren's throat constricted. 'Don't you dare cry, Rose.'

Rose took a shuddering breath as her eyes filled with tears. 'I'm n-not c-crying.'

'Stop that,' said Wren, as her own eyes began to prickle. 'I mean it, Rose.'

Hot tears slipped down Rose's cheeks. 'How could you have known about me for all these years and just left me here? Left me with *him*.' Her voice broke again. 'Didn't you want to meet me? To *know* me?'

'Of course I wanted to meet you,' said Wren, and when her own tears fell she scrubbed them away, wishing she could erase the unpleasant feelings that came with them. Guilt and loss, and this new yearning for the life they might have had together if things had been different. *If only* things had been different. 'I thought about you every day of my life, Rose. You're my sister. I just . . .'

'Wanted to steal my throne first?' said Rose, wiping her nose.

Wren offered her a watery smile. 'It's nothing personal.'

Rose sniffed again, and just when Wren thought her sister was going to admonish her, she flung her arms around her neck and buried her face in her shoulder. 'I have a *sister*!'

Wren bristled, and then slowly hugged Rose back. It felt nice. It felt *right*. Her chest warmed and her tears dried and when they pulled back from each other, both girls were wearing the same smile, one borne of gentle hope.

They ambled onwards, past flame after flame.

'I always wondered what it would be like to grow up here,' said Wren, after a while. 'When I was little, I used to wear Thea's favourite tablecloth around me like a dress and make Shen have afternoon tea with me up on the cliffs. We'd drink it cold from cracked mugs with our pinkies out, and pretend we were in the courtyard at Anadawn, looking out over our kingdom.'

'I can picture that perfectly,' said Rose, with a giggle. 'When I was young I used to dream of faraway cliffs that teetered over the ocean, imagining what it would be like to tiptoe along them with the wind blowing in my hair. Agnes said she could always tell when I was dreaming of adventure because I would wake with a smile on my face.'

Wren grinned at her sister's confession. 'Now that you've seen those cliffs, did they live up to your dreams?'

Rose bit her lip. 'To tell you the truth, they frightened the life out of me. I clung on to Shen like a terrified squirrel.' Wren could have sworn her sister was blushing but perhaps it was a trick of the everlights.

She laughed, brashly. 'It took me ten years before I could climb those cliffs on my own.'

'I climbed back up them all by myself,' said Rose, proudly.

Wren couldn't help but be impressed by Rose. She had made the journey home to Anadawn all alone, through the howling forest and the restless desert, galloping ceaselessly across the rolling plains of Eana on a horse that didn't answer to her, all to save the country that didn't yet belong to her. A country that never would.

But Wren pushed that truth away. Why ruin a perfectly lovely morning with talk of what lay beyond tomorrow? For now, she would save all thoughts of betrayal for Rathborne.

They came to the end of the passageway, both girls craning their necks to catch a glimpse of the sky through the ancient storm drain.

'I can't believe this tunnel has been right under my nose all these years,' said Rose, rising to her tiptoes. 'And worse. That *you* discovered it within days of coming here.'

'It pays to be nosy,' said Wren, with a shrug. 'And don't forget, I've always known how to sniff out magic. I'm probably the only one in Anadawn who does.' She thought briefly of Celeste's uncanny instincts but decided not to mention her suspicions. That girl had enough against Wren as it was. She curled her fingers around the grate, jiggling it loose and then sliding it to one side. 'I wanted to show you this place before tonight just in case anything goes wrong. Now that there are two of us here, we're in real danger. If Rathborne's seer even gets a whiff of—'

'Wren.' Rose laid a gentle hand on her arm. 'It's going to be fine.'

'You don't know that.'

'We have a plan.'

Wren huffed a frustrated sigh. 'Plans can change in an instant, Rose.' She had learned that well enough since coming to Anadawn. She couldn't afford to make one more miscalculation. 'I'm not going to be at the feast tonight. So, please, just promise me if something goes wrong – if Rathborne starts to suspect something or I get trapped in the tower – that you'll run. That you'll save yourself.'

'Very well,' said Rose, calmly. 'As long as you can say the same.'

Wren nodded. 'This place is our secret, Rose. Just you and me.'

'Just you and me,' promised Rose. 'Thank you for sharing it with me.'

Wren released the storm drain, her shoulders sagging in relief. The thought of something bad happening to her sister was deeply unsettling. No matter what happened after tonight, she wanted her to be safe. Always.

This time, when they turned from the drain, it was Rose who led the way, tugging Wren back through the winding passageway and into the belly of Anadawn Palace once more. The everlights flickered brighter as they passed, the purple flames high enough now to lick the stone. Wren felt the nearness of her magic buzzing in her bloodstream and wondered if Rose felt it, too.

When they reached the wall, and with the witch markings glowing before them, Rose turned to Wren. 'I'm so glad we got to meet each other. It's wonderful that after all these years of yearning for family, my wish has come true. I've found a sister. I've found *you*.' Her smile was as radiant as the sun. 'No matter what happens tonight or tomorrow or in the weeks and years after that, you'll always be my sister. My blood. I want you to know that from now on I'll fight for the witches. I'll bring them home again.' Her smile faltered, then, and her voice hardened. 'But I also need you to know that the day after the cancelled wedding, when we turn eighteen, it will be me who is crowned Queen of Eana, not you. There can't be any confusion about that.'

Wren stared at her sister, taken aback not just by her boldness but by the sureness in her voice. Before she could think of a response, Rose pressed her palm against the witch markings and opened the wall. She flounced through it and though Wren couldn't see her sister's face, she heard the satisfaction in her voice. 'I'm *so* glad we had this talk, Wren. I feel much better about everything now.'

That afternoon, when both girls were safely back in Rose's bedroom rifling through potential dresses for the Gevran

Feast, a knock at the door startled them both.

'Hide!' hissed Rose, but Wren was already scrabbling under the bed.

Agnes bustled into the room, tea tray in hand. 'Afternoon, Princess. The kitchens have sent up some soup and sandwiches ahead of the feast. We gather you'll be needing your energy for dancing!'

'Oh, you're a treasure, Agnes. I really can't wait for tonight,' crowed Rose, and lying in the dust under her sister's bed, Wren smirked to herself.

'Aye, the Gevrans have certainly added a lot of excitement around here. But I could do without those awful snow tigers snapping at my heels! One of them went right for your tray in the hallway just now.' She set it down with a thud. 'And speaking of the Gevrans, this arrived just this afternoon for you. Courtesy of King Alarik himself.'

'What is *that*?' Wren heard her sister say.

Agnes cleared her throat. 'Well, I expect this kind of dress is all the fashion in Grinstad.'

'But it's barely more than a piece of fur! In fact . . . it *is* a piece of fur!'

'There are these, too, Princess,' said Agnes, nervously. 'What an . . . interesting pair of hairpins. And look at this. Oooh! Now that's a lovely silver brooch.'

'With a snarling ice bear on it!' cried Rose. 'I don't want to wear that horrid Gevran crest.'

'Well, I fear you'll need *something* to hold this . . . dress together.'

Wren thought she might perish from curiosity as she hid underneath her sister's bed. She had never in her life been so interested in a dress. She scooted across the carpet, trying to get a better look, but all she could see was the trailing end of what appeared to be a wolf's tail.

The dressing table groaned as Rose sagged against it. 'I *cannot* wear that!'

The next few minutes felt like an eternity but when Agnes finally excused herself, Wren rolled out from under the bed at such a speed she gave herself carpet burn.

'Where is it?' she said, leaping to her feet. 'Show me the outfit!'

Rose had flung the dress on the bed. It did indeed look like an overgrown wolf's tail. It was warm and plush, strands of black and grey and silver intermingling in the afternoon sunlight. It was the tiniest dress Wren had ever seen – even her underthings covered more than this – and it smelled faintly of blood.

She snatched it up, whipping it around her neck like a scarf as she pranced around the room. 'Really, Rose. It's so versatile! Just be careful not to move too vigorously.'

Rose had gone deathly pale. 'Oh, Wren, this might be the only time in my entire life that I wished I were *you* instead of me.'

Wren cackled wickedly. 'And I think this might be the only time in *my* entire life that I feel truly and thoroughly relieved not to be you.' She flung the wolfy dress at Rose. 'This one is all yours. It truly is fit for only a princess such as yourself.'

Rose

CHAPTER 38

The courtyard at Anadawn Palace had been transformed for the Gevran Feast.

Enormous ice sculptures lined the entranceway, towering over the guests, and in the centre, atop the pale stone fountain, stood the most impressive one of all: a mighty ice bear with glistening teeth. It loomed over figures of a man and a woman peering up at him in frozen awe. Caged fires roared from every corner, as a nod to the long Gevran winters.

While the flames were caged, the beasts were not. Tonight, they weren't even leashed. White wolves prowled by the sides of Gevran soldiers, while three regal snow tigers sprawled on a raised dais, watching over the festivities. Winter foxes leaped mischievously from table to table, threatening to topple the wine goblets and startling several members of the Anadawn court. Even Alarik's ice bear roamed freely, its neck adorned with a collar of rubies. A fur-clad priestess wandered alongside it, her soothing hand resting on its massive paw.

The tables were laden with meat and poultry, all freshly

killed in honour of the evening. Huge slabs of Eanan elk, skinned rabbits, legs of lamb, and whole pheasants glistened in the firelight. And on a table of its own, the Gevran delicacy: a squid so large, its tentacles spilled over the sides. It had been caught by the Gevran fleet on their journey across the Sunless Sea and had been roasting over an open fire all afternoon.

Rose hovered at the edge of the courtyard, listening to the thunder of the Gevran drums. She could feel them pounding against her feet, bidding her to enter. She desperately wished she had a cloak to cover herself.

Whoever had called this thing she was wearing a 'dress' had an interesting sense of humour. After hours of primping and preening, she still wasn't certain she was wearing it right. Two lengths of silver fur criss-crossed her chest, barely covering her breasts, before meeting in a knot at the nape of her neck. Another darker piece encircled her waist, then spilled across her hips, where the Gevran brooch pinned the paltry material together. The dress stopped several inches above her knees.

Rose could barely walk without fear of the entire thing falling off, never mind attempt one of the notoriously dramatic Gevran dances. But she couldn't refuse to wear it and risk causing offence. No, tonight everything had to go perfectly. And that meant she had to look perfect. She wore her hair long and loose, cascading down her back and pulled away from her face with bone hairpins that looked unnervingly like fangs.

One more night of playing the simpering princess, and then everything would change. Forever. The thought of being able to decide her own destiny, to make her own choices, suddenly made Rose feel brave. A shiver danced down her spine and she wasn't sure if it was the chill of the wind against her half-naked body or the thrill of what the future held, but it was enough to nudge her onwards, into the mouth of the feast.

'*Yoo-hoo!* I spy my winter rose!'

Rose's jaw fell open. 'Oh, Ansel.'

The prince was standing in the middle of the courtyard, wearing a skinned ice bear like a cape. The jaws of the bear had been prised open, so the eyes and snout were resting on Ansel's head, as if it were about to devour him. He swayed a little under its weight as he waved at her. 'My darling! Over here! Don't you recognize your ice-bear prince?' He held up his hands like claws and attempted a roar.

Rose wished her sister were here to see this. What would her life have been like, having fierce and fearless Wren always next to her? Rathborne had taken that from her. He had taken her parents and with them a whole life she would never know. Anger flared inside her, as hot as the flames crackling in their cages.

As if she had summoned him, the Kingsbreath appeared at her side. Unlike her, he was dressed in traditional Eanan attire – a slim-fitting suit of forest green, trimmed in gold.

'Your prince is calling you. It won't do to leave him waiting.' He prodded her in the back. 'I expect perfect behaviour from you, Rose. Nothing like how you were last night.'

Swallowing her revulsion, Rose offered him her warmest smile. 'I don't know what came over me yesterday. But I'm feeling much more myself now. I hope you can forgive me for speaking out of turn.'

'As long as you do as you're told, all is forgiven. You know I always have your best interests at heart.'

Rose made her bottom lip tremble. 'I don't know how I'll ever thank you for taking such good care of me, Willem.' Then, before she lost her nerve, she flung her arms around his neck.

The Kingsbreath stiffened. When Rose pulled back from him, the key was curled safely in her fist. Wren had enchanted her nails, so they could cut easily through the twine around his neck, and for a moment, Rose wished she could use them to claw the skin off his face, too.

'I must find my prince,' she murmured, as she scurried away. As she moved through the courtyard, she passed Alarik and Anika. Like Rose, Anika was wearing an eye-wateringly revealing outfit, but the fur of her dress was jet black, making her crimson tresses stand out even more.

The king was almost as naked as his sister. He stood pale and shirtless before Rose, wearing fitted leather trousers and his glistening silver crown.

Burning stars! What do the Gevrans have against shirts?

Rose averted her eyes and dipped into a shallow curtsy. Alarik raked his gaze along her body, his grin turning feral. 'Perhaps you will fit in better than I thought. Our furs suit you.'

Anika threw her head back and laughed. 'Alarik, you wicked beast, don't toy with Ansel's bride. The poor thing is clearly petrified.'

A snow leopard padded out from behind the Gevran princess and caught the edge of Rose's skirt in its teeth.

'Oh no!' Rose clutched the paltry material, trying desperately to hold it together.

'Voldsom! You are as naughty as Alarik!' Anika clucked her tongue. '*Release!*'

The snow leopard obeyed at once, and with her cheeks burning, Rose hurried away.

Alarik's laughter followed her all the way across the courtyard.

As she approached the elaborate ice sculpture, Rose spotted Celeste moving through the crowd. She was wearing a magnificent purple dress trimmed in thick white fur, and holding a glass of frostfizz aloft. When her best friend sashayed past her, Rose slipped the key into her waiting hand. Celeste winked at Rose over her shoulder, and then nodded up at the ice sculpture. 'The likeness is uncanny. Some might even say it's your *twin*.'

Then she swanned off towards the drinks table, smiling at anyone who looked her way, as though she didn't have a care in the world. Celeste didn't need magic, Rose thought as she watched her friend melt into the crowd; she had enough charm to enchant anyone.

Now that she was alone, Rose tilted her head back to examine the sculpture more closely. Oh, *stars*. Was that meant to be *her*? And the male figure . . . was that—

'There you are, my frosty little flower!' Ansel ambled over to her, looking as unsteady under his ice-bear ensemble as Rose felt in her fur. 'I see you've noticed my special surprise! That's us, Rose. Carved in ice, under our Gevran god, the Great Bear, Bernhard. It's a blessing for our future together.'

'It is . . . truly . . . something,' Rose managed.

'And just think, this time next year we may have our own cub pitter-pattering around.' Ansel laughed, gaily. 'And when I say *cub*, I of course mean *baby*. How do you feel about the name Ronsel? In honour of both of us.'

He looked expectantly at her.

'*Ronsel?*' she said, weakly.

Ansel nodded, his eyes so big they looked like pools of seawater. Rose felt an awful twinge of guilt for how she was going to end their betrothal tomorrow, but to tell the prince now would scupper their chances of bringing Rathborne to justice. There had to be a wedding in order to expose him. She could only hope that one day Ansel would forgive her for ruining it.

She placed a gentle hand on his arm just as something across the courtyard caught her eye. 'My darling, it looks as if they're about to cut into the roasted squid. Isn't that your job?'

Ansel gasped. 'Too right you are! It's the groom's duty to

cut the first ceremonial slice of squid!' He turned promptly on his heel, jostling his way to the table.

Rose exhaled. The pungent smell of roasted squid mingling with the scent of wet fur and raw meat was suddenly too much to bear. And the beat of the drums hammering against her skull was starting to give Rose a headache. Glancing over her shoulder to make sure nobody was watching, she slipped out of the courtyard to steal a moment alone.

The rose garden was blessedly empty. Rose drifted into the heart of it and sank on to her favourite bench. For a luxurious moment, all was silent. And still.

Then came a sudden *whoosh* from somewhere over her head, followed by a rippling breeze. The roses trembled.

The bench groaned under a new weight.

Rose whipped her head around.

And found herself staring into Shen Lo's night-dark eyes. 'Hello, Princess. Miss me?'

Wren

CHAPTER 39

Wren was sitting under a tree in the orchard, frowning at the key in her lap, when she heard footsteps behind her. She had retrieved the key from Celeste only moments ago, slipping through the shadowy gardens and around the east wall so as not to be seen by any wandering Gevrans or their beasts. Except this one.

Even though it was dangerous – not just for her but for Rose, who was expertly playing her part at the feast – Wren had been secretly hoping that Tor might find her tonight. The reckless part of her still yearned for his company, burned for his touch. She tipped her head back at the sound of his approach, the end of her braid grazing the grass. 'I had a feeling you'd sniff me out sooner or later.' She glanced around, making sure they were alone. But the soldier was careful. Far more careful than her.

Tor watched Wren from the stone entranceway, one hand resting on the crystalline pommel of his sword. Tonight, he was dressed in full Gevran regalia, the collar of his navy frock coat lined in velvety grey fur. Elske was at his side. The midnight moon turned the white of her coat a soft, shimmering silver. 'What are you doing out here by yourself?' he said, in a low voice.

'Where should I be?' said Wren, just as softly. They both knew there was no place for her at Anadawn. At least not yet. 'My sister and I can't exactly dance with Ansel at the same time,' she said, as she stripped off another strand of bark. Beside Rathborne's golden key in her lap, a strip of rosewood lay twisted into a near-perfect imitation – close but not close enough. 'I think that might give the game away.'

'You look different tonight,' said Tor, his gaze roaming. Wren was wearing her old shirt and fitted trousers – the ones she'd hidden in Rose's room on her first night in Anadawn. Her face was bare and her hair was pulled into a simple trailing braid. Tonight, beauty didn't matter to her. She needed to move swiftly and freely.

'Now you truly have discovered the real me.' She flicked her braid, ignoring the unwelcome flicker of her self-consciousness. 'Do you like what you see?'

'Always,' said Tor.

Wren bit back her smile.

'You're doing magic again.' There was a note of caution in his voice as he drifted into the orchard, his wolf padding softly at his side. 'Show me.'

'Say please.'

He hunkered down beside Wren and she was struck by the freshness of his alpine scent and the memory it conjured.

She tried not to think of him shirtless in the library, crushing his lips against hers. 'Please,' he said, in a low rumble.

The word rippled down Wren's spine. She glanced sidelong at Elske. 'I don't want your wolf to eat me.'

Tor patted the wolf's head. 'She's just curious.'

'Like her master.'

'Yes.'

'Fine,' said Wren. 'But only because I feel like showing off.'

Tor's lips flickered. 'I'm glad you're feeling like yourself.'

'Hush.' She closed her eyes, trying not to smile. 'I need to focus.'

He went so still so quickly, Wren half wondered if he had evaporated into thin air until she heard Elske sniffing about beside him. She held the strip of bark in her hand and the golden key in the other. To offer earth in exchange for a spell was one thing but to mould something *from* the earth was quite another. It was a more complicated kind of enchantment.

She began to whisper, feeling the tendrils of her magic gathering in her palm. The enchantment set itself to work, twisting and bending the bark until it took on the shape of the key.

Wren snapped her eyes open. And frowned. '*Hissing seaweed.*'

Tor plucked the rosewood key from her hand. He traced the grooves with the pad of his thumb. 'The indent is weak. It needs to be—'

'I know,' groaned Wren. 'The spell is perfect. For some reason my power is stronger than it's ever been but the stupid wood won't hold the enchantment.' She curled the golden key in her fist until her palm ached. 'I don't understand why it's so hard.'

'Actually, it's too soft.' Tor adjusted his sword and sat back on the grass, kicking his legs out until his thigh brushed against her knee. Elske padded once in a circle before dropping her head into his lap. 'It doesn't matter how many times you try. The wood won't keep its shape.'

Wren scowled. 'It's the strongest wood in Eana. Yes, it will.'

Tor crossed one ankle over the other. 'It won't.'

'Whatever,' she mumbled. 'What do you even know?'

'I know the difference between wood and metal.' He plucked the golden key from her hand. 'I know this key opens the west tower. And I know that it belongs to the Kingsbreath. He wears it around his neck.'

Wren was forced to concede her surprise. 'Wrangler indeed.'

He grinned at her and the unexpectedness of it – the pearly glint of his teeth and the wideness of his smile – nearly knocked her sideways.

A shiver of wind rattled the leaves, allowing a shard of moonlight to slip through. They sat in a puddle of it, sizing each other up.

'So, it's not just me you were watching,' said Wren. 'Now I don't feel half as special.'

Tor turned his gaze to the white walls of Anadawn. 'Alarik sent me here to keep a close eye on Ansel but it was the Kingsbreath he was most wary of. He struck him as agitated and desperate in their correspondence. And a man who does not possess full control of himself cannot be trusted.'

'Your king is surprisingly observant.'

'A Gevran trait.'

'If utterly and completely contemptible,' Wren added, pointedly. 'Do you know he's walking around in there completely shirtless?'

'Perhaps that's another Gevran trait.' Tor's laugh was breathy . . . dangerous, and Wren was again seized by the memory of their kiss, her hands sliding against his bare chest, his lips moaning her name as he . . . *Stop that*. She quickly gathered herself but the soldier was smirking at her now as if he could read her thoughts. It was risky enough that he was here with her at all – she couldn't afford to let tonight go any further than this.

She cleared her throat. 'So, you came to Eana to watch Rathborne and somehow you wound up hounding *me* instead.'

'I found a new vocation.'

'Stalking me?'

'Wanting you.'

Wren's cheeks flared. *Damn*. She looked away, sharply. 'I can't think about that tonight.' She hastily peeled another strip from the bark. The silence swelled until Wren felt as if she could pop it with her finger. '*Stop*,' she hissed. 'I can *feel* you thinking about it.'

'Wren, I can't stop.'

She pulled her hair around her face. 'A man who does not possess full control of himself cannot be trusted, Tor.'

He inhaled through his teeth. 'Very well, then.' His gaze fell upon the golden key and then in a completely different voice he said, 'So, it's the Kingsbreath you're after.'

Wren turned the piece of bark in her hands, relieved to have something else to talk about. 'First, I'm going to free his caged bird,' she said, thinking of that face in the tower window. 'Once I help his seer escape Rathborne will lose his connection to the future and any glimpses of what might happen to him. Then, I'm going to strip him of his precious reputation.' She clenched the key in her fist until the grooves stung her palm. 'And after that I'm going to send him straight to hell.'

'For plotting against the witches of Ortha?'

'That.' Wren hesitated. 'And for murdering my parents eighteen years ago.' She hardened her voice, all too aware of the soldier's sharpened attention, the sudden clenching of his jaw. 'It's time Eana knew the truth. It's time I freed this country from his grasping, greedy hands.' She thought of her sister inside the courtyard, wearing that ridiculous strip of fur as she danced for her life. 'And it's time I freed Rose, too.'

'I didn't know he killed your parents.' Tor's voice was carefully controlled but his eyes were alight with a quiet fury, the silver streaks like lightning cutting through thunderclouds. Elske lifted her head from his lap as though she had sensed the change in his demeanour, felt the storm brewing inside him.

'Tomorrow all of Eana will know.' Wren looked up at the trees, trying to ignore the nearness of her own pain. Through the swaying canopies, she spied the west tower of Anadawn winding towards the stars. 'But first I need to get into that tower.'

Tor held up the wooden key. 'Not with this you won't.'

'Do I really need to remind you that *you* are the soldier and *I* am the enchanter,' said Wren, impatiently.

He flung the twisted key into the trees. 'Then cast your spell, witch.'

So Wren did.

Again.

And again.

And again.

Tor watched her work, so quiet and still she wouldn't have noticed him at all if it wasn't for the heat rolling off his body. After six more failed attempts, she flopped back against the grass. She could feel the Gevran drums pounding in the earth, like a clock running out of time.

Tor peered over her. 'Do you want my help?'

'No.' Wren sat up. She blew her hair out of her face. 'Fine. Yes.'

He smirked. 'Say please.'

She didn't know if she wanted to kiss that smirk or slap

it off his face. '*Please.*'

Tor snapped the topmost button off his frock coat. Wren's heart leaped but the soldier was all business now. 'This is Gevran iron. Strong as steel and mined straight from the earth.' He folded it into her palm and Wren pretended not to notice the way her fingers tingled beneath his. 'This time don't think of the Kingsbreath. Your hatred will cloud your focus.'

'How did you know I was thinking of Rathborne's stupid, sneering face?'

'Because I can read you like a book.'

'You can *read*?'

He gave her a hard look. 'You're all talk, witch.'

'Oh yeah? Watch this.' Wren held the button in her palm. Rathborne's golden key rested in the other. She loosened a breath, focusing now on the rhythm of her pulse. She felt it fluttering against Tor's button. Her skin began to prickle. Magic coursed through her, leaving one hand and gathering in the other. Tor guided her breath with his own and this time, even before she opened her eyes, Wren knew the enchantment had worked.

She grinned as she held both keys up to the moonlight: one silver and one gold. 'Well, look at that. Twins.'

'You're welcome,' said Tor.

Wren winked at him. 'My spell; my glory.'

The Gevran chuckled.

'I like that sound,' she said, as she rolled to her feet. 'You should make it more often.'

Tor stood up, too. He kicked the failed keys away, scattering them into the orchard. 'I'll try to find something to laugh about.' He dug his hands into his pockets and without the top button of his frock coat, he looked dishevelled. He looked past her, towards the tower. 'How will I know if you've succeeded in your task?'

'Will the suspense keep you up tonight?' teased Wren.

'Yes,' he said, without an ounce of humour.

'Just listen for the sound of me merrily skipping down the hallways.'

His gaze darkened. 'Be serious, Wren.'

'Fine. If you don't see me at Prince Ansel's wedding tomorrow, you'll know I failed miserably and am likely dead in a stairwell somewhere.' She prodded his chest. 'And in that unlikely event, you must spend the rest of your wintry days protecting my sister with your life.'

Tor grabbed her waist before she could pull away.

Wren's body erupted in a blaze of heat. She flicked her gaze to Elske. 'I'm not kissing you in front of your wolf. I'm afraid that's where I draw the line.'

'So, there is a line.'

'I'm as surprised as you are.'

But Tor's face had grown serious. 'Aren't we going to talk about it?'

'Talk about what?'

'This. *Us.*'

'Don't do that,' she said, warily. 'Don't act as if—'

'I have feelings for you?' he said, unflinching.

Wren inhaled, sharply. The soldier felt more dangerous now than last night when he had caught her in a spell. The way he was looking at her . . . the things it was doing to her insides. *No.* No. She was not going to end up like her parents. She was the strong twin. Banba had made her strong. And she was so close now to the rest of her life. She would not risk it for something so fleeting and pointless, no matter how good it felt. No matter how the Gevran plagued her thoughts. 'You should know I have no interest in love.'

Tor raised his eyebrows.

'I don't even believe in it,' she said, firmly.

He trailed his fingers down her wrist, gently pressing his thumb against her racing pulse. 'Forgive me for thinking there was something between us, Wren. I must have misread your moans.'

She swallowed, thickly. 'You must have.'

'Liar,' he whispered.

Wren scowled at him. 'If you want to talk about your feelings, go and write a poem in a dark corner. I can't think about any of this right now.' Overhead, a cloud moved in front of the moon, casting them in shadow. It was late and the west tower was calling. Not to mention Rose still had to return Rathborne's key before he noticed it was missing. 'I have somewhere else to be.'

Tor's hand lingered on her wrist. 'Then meet me here tomorrow. At sunrise.'

Wren couldn't stand the hope in his eyes. 'Tor, you are a Gevran soldier. And I am an Ortha witch. You are loyal to the king who wants to destroy us, and when Rathborne is exposed at the wedding tomorrow and his precious alliance is cancelled, our truce will be over. You know whose side you will choose and so do I.' Wren stepped out of his embrace, blinking the tears from her eyes. 'There is no future for us beyond tonight.'

He looked at her for a long moment. His face was torn, desire and duty warring in that stormy gaze. When he looked away, Wren knew it was over. He might have feelings for her but he wouldn't fight for her. Not against his own people.

And Wren didn't expect him to. It was nothing serious after all – just a stolen evening in the library, and the whisper of something that might have been in another life. Let him keep his feelings. She didn't want them. She *couldn't* want him. She told herself she didn't care as she backed away from him, even as her heart clenched painfully.

Tor's parting words floated after her on the wind. 'Be careful, witch.'

'I always am,' muttered Wren, as she made her way back to the palace.

'*Because a careless witch is a dead witch,*' said Banba's voice in her head.

Rose
CHAPTER 40

Rose leaped up from the bench and grabbed Shen's hand, pulling him with her. 'This way! Before anyone sees you!'

'You've certainly become a lot more forward than the last time we met,' he said under his breath, as he followed her. Rose led him deeper into the garden, treading a path towards her favourite childhood hiding place. Behind a trellis dripping in roses, the garden appeared to meet the stone wall. She brushed aside the hanging ivy and pulled Shen into a hidden alcove. It was narrow and leafy, the roses twisting above them, as if they were trying to grow up to reach the stars.

Rose stared at Shen in the darkness. He was dressed all in black and his face was obscured beneath a cloak. With trembling fingers, she pushed the hood back. Time stilled around them, and for one precious moment, she forgot all about the Gevran Feast and everything that hinged on tonight. There was only Shen and his night-dark eyes and those quirked lips and the way his skin smelled like—

'You stole my horse.'

The moment shattered.

Rose winced. 'It was really more of a borrowing.'

'*After* you left me snoring on the beach and reeking of rum,' he added.

'Oh, about that . . . it was merely a precaution.'

'To guarantee you could steal my horse.' Shen wagged his finger in admonition. 'I had to ride *another* much less impressive horse, until I came across Storm in the Golden Caves.'

Rose sighed in relief. 'I *knew* she would find her way back to safety.'

'Of course she did. She's my horse. She's very well trained.' He paused. 'Although not as loyal as I thought. How did you even get her to leave with you?'

Feeling bold, Rose leaned up on her tiptoes and whispered into Shen's ear. '*Hush, hush, rush.*'

He stared at her. 'How on earth do you know about that?'

'You told me. On the beach.' She smiled, sheepishly. 'You were drunk.'

He shook his head. 'Princess, have you no shame? I should have never trusted you.' His tone belied his harsh words, and Rose swore she saw mischief dancing in his dark eyes.

'You don't really mean that.'

'It's true, Rose. I'm distraught. Can't you see my tears?'

'No.'

'Well, that's just because it's dark.'

Rose lifted a hand to his cheek to find it dry. Shen caught

it with his own, moving her hand until his lips met her palm. He gently pressed a kiss there.

'*Oh.*' A small gasp escaped Rose. She never knew her palm had so much feeling. Shen smiled against it, kissing it again before placing it against his chest. His heart thrummed beneath her fingers. She felt the riot of her own heartbeat in her chest, her head suddenly dizzy with desire.

'I don't think I could ever stay mad at you, Princess.' His smile was slow, revealing the imprint of his dimple. 'Honestly, I'm impressed you managed to pull it all off.'

Rose cleared her throat, her words breathier than she intended. 'Well, then it's your fault for underestimating me.'

'Trust me, I won't make that mistake again.' He dropped his gaze, taking her outfit in. 'Huh. I thought people wore fur to keep warm. You must be freezing in this . . . whatever it is you're wearing.' Rose didn't miss the way his throat bobbed. 'Don't get me wrong, I like it . . .'

She wrapped her arms around herself. 'I'll have you know this is a Gevran ceremonial gown.'

'Some ceremony,' muttered Shen. 'And here I thought your nightgown was my favourite of your outfits.'

'Tonight is the Gevran Feast.' Rose continued her attempt at conversation, even as she yearned to feel his lips on her skin again. 'It's all part of the festivities leading up to . . . the wedding day.'

Shen raised an eyebrow. 'You mean . . . *your* wedding day. How is your beloved fiancé, by the way?'

Rose sighed. 'If I admit that you were right about me not being in love with Ansel, will you lord it over me forever?'

'Of course.'

'Well. Then all I'll say is that for . . . various reasons, Wren and I are going to make sure the wedding does not happen. Ansel is no longer my betrothed.'

Shen didn't even try to hide his smile. 'Does *he* know that?'

Rose bit her lip, guiltily. 'Not yet.'

'You've met your delightful sister, then,' said Shen, flipping the subject before she could dwell on it. 'I wish I could have seen that reunion.'

'Fortunately, we both survived the encounter. How are things back in Ortha?'

'Banba is none too pleased that you ran off.'

Rose tried not to flinch. 'Well, I have more important things to worry about than my grandmother's volatile moods.'

'Like dressing up as a seductive wolf and drinking Gevran frostfizz?'

Rose flushed. 'I am not dressed as a seductive wolf!'

Shen eyed her outfit again. 'As I said, I like it.'

'Oh, do stop teasing me!'

He held up his hands in surrender. 'Princess, I'm not lying. You look beautiful. Truly.' He reached out and tucked a wayward curl behind her ear. Rose went very still. 'But then I thought you looked beautiful after two days travelling through the Restless Sands.'

Rose's mouth went dry. 'You did?' She shook her head. 'Then you must think my sister is beautiful, too.'

Shen's brow furrowed. 'It's different. *You're* different.'

'How?' she said, warily.

'Wren is my closest friend. I'll always look out for her and I know she'll do the same for me, but there's no spark between us. There never has been. But you, Rose . . .' He paused, tilting her chin up so she was looking directly into his eyes. 'You set me on fire.'

Shen's words sent such a searing rush of heat through Rose, she thought she might burn up right there in the alcove.

Be wise, she reminded herself. *Be wary.*

After all, a future queen could not fall for pretty words and flattery.

But *oh*, if only her future king could set her alight like this. Ansel certainly didn't.

Ansel. The feast. The key. The seer in the tower. It all came rushing back in. She couldn't stay here, hidden away in the rose garden with Shen. She stepped back, breaking their contact. 'Why have you come to Anadawn, Shen?'

'To scold you for stealing my horse.'

'The real reason.'

His face grew serious. 'Rose, do you know how worried I was when I realized what you'd done?'

'You should have had more faith in Storm. She was always going to be fine.'

'I wasn't worried about my horse. I was worried about

you.' He rubbed his forehead, clearly frustrated. 'I was afraid a blood beetle would attack you and you'd never make it back. That you'd get yourself killed a million other ways in the desert. Or that you'd somehow return in time to marry your Gevran prince and I'd never see you again.' He pulled her back to him. 'I came here to see you, Rose.'

'I'm still mad at you,' she reminded him, but her voice was soft, and in his arms, so was she. 'Forever.'

'How can I shorten such a cruel sentence?'

Be brave, she told herself. *Be bold*. After all, a future queen may never have a moment like this again.

She reached up and wrapped her arms around his neck. 'By being very, very nice to me.'

Shen's hands came to her waist and the feeling of his touch on her bare skin sent lightning bolts sizzling through Rose's veins.

'I don't know how to kiss,' she blurted out, then winced. Oh, that was not at all what she meant to say.

'I suspect you might be a natural.' Shen leaned down close, closer, until their lips were almost touching, and then he paused. Rose held her breath. 'I can't kiss you without your permission. You are the princess, remember?'

She smiled against his lips. 'Then I order you to kiss me, Shen.'

Shen's mouth curved. 'With pleasure, Princess Rose.' And then his lips were on hers and his arms were tight around her waist and *this* was kissing. Rose sighed into Shen's mouth and suddenly her lips were open, his tongue brushing softly against hers, and *oh*, she was wrong before because *this* was kissing. She felt as if she was melting, as if Shen's arms were the only thing holding her together.

Time slowed, and Rose basked in every delicious second of it.

After a perfect eternity, Shen grew very still. He pulled her against him. 'Someone's coming,' he whispered. He pressed a kiss beneath her ear. 'I was right, by the way. You are a natural.'

'Shh,' said Rose, her cheeks aflame.

Shen peered out through the bushes, his body coiled with tension. After a moment, Rose felt him relax. He let out a low whistle that sounded just like the call of an owl. A pause, and then the same whistle echoed back.

A minute later, Wren's head popped through the foliage. 'What in rotting hell is going on in here?'

Rose grabbed her sister. 'Get in here before someone sees you!'

'Why aren't you at the bloody feast, Rose? I've just returned the key to Celeste and *you're* supposed to help her return it!' Wren's eyes narrowed as she took in Rose's flushed cheeks and mussed hair. She turned on Shen, and said his name through her teeth. '*Shen*. I swear if you hurt my sister, I will gut you like a fish.' She reached for her dagger but Shen knocked it out of her hand before catching it by the blade tip.

He dangled it in front of her nose. 'You mean with this?'

Wren scowled as she snatched it back. 'What did I

explicitly tell you? Do not lose *or* seduce my sister.'

Shen cleared his throat, awkwardly. 'I hate to be the one to tell you this but she seduced me.'

Wren raised her eyebrows. 'I don't know if that makes it better or worse.'

'Nobody seduced anybody,' said Rose, quickly smoothing down her fur skirt. 'And of course he won't hurt me. Otherwise I'll throw him in the dungeons.'

'Great,' said Shen, sarcastically. 'Are you both done threatening me? I actually came back to make sure you two hadn't killed each other.' He looked between them. 'What exactly are you planning tonight?'

Wren told him quickly of the seer in the tower, and their plans for her escape. 'Wait for me down by the bridge,' she said. 'Once we make it out of Anadawn, I could use your help getting her through Eshlinn. When it's done, we can drink to my success.'

'Only if you're buying,' said Shen, by way of agreement.

'Let's go, sister.' Wren stepped out of the alcove, pulling Rose with her. 'They'll be missing you at the feast. You're the main event, after all.'

'Rose,' said Shen, grabbing her hand. 'Be careful.'

'You too, Shen.' Rose squeezed his hand and then followed her sister out of the bushes.

The Gevran drums thundered through the air as Wren slipped away into the darkness, winding her way towards the west tower. Back in the courtyard, the dancing had already begun, and Rose knew Ansel would be looking for her. With the shadow of Shen's kiss on her lips, she lifted her chin and returned to the feast.

Princess Anika was dancing alone in the middle of the courtyard, swinging her hips to the beat of the drums. Twelve white wolves pranced around her, howling in time with the music.

Rose hovered at the edge of the crowd, her mouth agape. She had never seen anything like it in her life, and she didn't know whether to be intimidated or impressed. Surely the Gevrans didn't expect her to do *that*, did they?

Never mind that now, she told herself. She would dance with twelve wolves if she needed to, but first, she had to find Celeste. Rathborne was standing at the edge of the dance floor by the half-devoured squid. He waved her over impatiently, and Rose obliged, scanning the crowds as she went.

'Where have you been?' he demanded through a mouthful of squid. 'Prince Ansel has been looking everywhere for you.'

Rose opened her mouth to respond just as Celeste glided out of the crowd and jostled straight into Rathborne. She dropped the golden key with a faint *clink* as he went stumbling into the table. He cursed as he righted himself, brushing bits of squid from his trousers.

'Oh, forgive me, Willem!' Celeste slurred, waving her empty goblet at him. 'My feet have developed a mind of their own this evening!' She giggled as she skipped away, weaving left and right, as though she couldn't quite remember how to walk.

Rathborne fumed at the back of her head. 'Irritating, *insolent* girl. If it wasn't for her father, I'd have kicked her out of Anadawn long ago.'

Rose bent down and picked up the golden key. 'Oh. I think you dropped this, Willem.'

Rathborne snatched it from her and curled it in his fist. 'Go and find your prince. I won't tell you again.'

Rose had barely taken two steps away from him when Chapman came scurrying towards her like a frightened, sweaty rat.

'You're here!' he said, taking her by the shoulders and shaking her. 'I knew it! I *knew* it.'

Rathborne yanked him off her. 'Chapman! What on earth do you think you're doing?'

'Sir, there's an *imposter*!' heaved Chapman. 'An imposter in the palace!'

Rose was flooded with alarm. '*What?*'

Rathborne grabbed him by the lapels. 'Keep your voice down,' he hissed. 'Are you trying to make a scene?'

Chapman shook his head, vigorously. 'The princess! She looked just like the princess, but she was running away.' His moustache twitched as he gasped for breath. 'Running to the west tower! I came here as soon as I saw her!'

Rathborne snapped his chin up, snaring Rose in his narrowed gaze.

She was careful to control her face. 'I think someone has had a touch too much frostfizz tonight,' she said, mildly. 'Perhaps Chapman should take a turn about the gardens and get some fresh air.'

But Rathborne had stopped listening to her. He was staring at the key in his hand. 'Rose, go and perform your dance with Ansel. Chapman, alert the guards and check the gates for a breach,' he said, without looking up. 'And for goodness' sake, *be discreet.*'

Without another word to either of them, the Kingsbreath spun on his heel and took off.

Chapman whirled in the opposite direction, taking small hurried steps so as not to arouse suspicion.

With panic guttering inside her, Rose threw caution to the wind and raced after Rathborne. It only occurred to her when she reached the winding stairwell of the west tower that she should have grabbed a weapon.

Wren
CHAPTER 41

Wren slipped into the west tower of Anadawn and crept up the stairwell. If everything went to plan, she'd be returning this way in a matter of moments with Rathborne's seer, and with her, his grip on the future. And she'd be freeing a witch from his clutches. She paused at the top and pressed her ear against the door, listening to the faint rustle of starcrests in their cages. She used the iron key again, the lock yielding with a faint *click*.

She gagged as a putrid smell swept over her – sawdust and moulting feathers soaked in piss and bird excrement. There were birdcages everywhere, stacked all the way to the ceiling and arranged along the stone walls. The starcrests peered at her from within, their beady eyes shining in the dimness. They were eerily still now and Wren couldn't shake the thought that they knew something she didn't.

She took a cautious step into the room. It was the twin to Rose's bedroom in the east tower but this chamber had fallen into reeking disrepair. It was freezing cold and hopelessly cluttered, dust motes as thick as her fist spiralling in the air. Battered furniture huddled between moth-eaten oil paintings and broken chairs. In the middle of the room, a rotting armoire had been turned on its side like a beached whale, old petticoats and tattered dresses spilling out. A narrow bed was nestled between two of the largest aviaries. Wren stared at it.

A floorboard creaked.

She spun on her heel, searching the shadows. 'I'm not here to hurt you . . .'

A bird flapped in its cage, startling her.

Wren turned again, slower this time.

With a blood-curdling shriek, a white shape lunged from the darkness. Wren was thrown backwards, her head hitting the floor with a painful thud. A pair of hands closed around her neck and a face appeared in the darkness, barely an inch from her own.

The seer's face was gaunt and creviced, a purplish hue lingering around her lips and in the shadows underneath her eyes. Her teeth – which were bared like a wolf's – were sparse, and her long white hair was matted and wild. Her bony fingers were surprisingly strong as they constricted around Wren's windpipe.

Wren managed to squeeze out a single word. '*Please.*'

The seer snapped her fingers away. She blinked, rapidly, as if only just seeing Wren for the first time. 'Lillith's girl,' she rasped. 'Not the princess. Not the flower. *The bird.* The bird that flew away.' She scrabbled back from Wren. 'I've been calling you. Sending my starcrests to find you.' Her lips began to tremble. 'You have brought the shadow of death to Anadawn.'

'You know who I am?' Wren thought of the starcrests who had been following her since she arrived at Anadawn. 'Who are you? How long have you been locked up here?'

'Too many years to count. Too many to remember.' The seer staggered to her feet, her white nightgown pooling around her ankles so that in the moonlight, she looked more ghost than human. 'But I do remember who I am. My name is Glenna.'

Wren's blood ran cold. *Glenna.* She hadn't heard that name in many years, could never have imagined she would hear it here, at Anadawn. 'You're Banba's sister,' she breathed. 'You're *alive.*'

The seer shuddered. 'During Lillith's War, the Kingsbreath kidnapped me and brought me back to Anadawn. My birds flew after me but they could not protect me, could not save me from my fate. I thought he would kill me but he had something worse in store for me. He caged me like an animal, forced me to use my gifts against my own people.'

Wren's heart lurched. 'Oh, Glenna. You've been a prisoner here all this time?'

The old woman nodded. 'He uses my visions to guide his decisions. Some I have tried to hide from him but others . . .' She trailed off into a shudder. 'He has found ways of making me talk.'

Wren's fists tightened. She didn't think it was possible

to despise Rathborne any more than she already did and yet fresh hatred bloomed within her. 'I'm here now, Glenna.' She got up slowly so as not to startle the seer. 'And I'm going to set you free.'

Glenna's face darkened. 'There is no future for me beyond this tower.' She spread her arms, the blue veins catching in the moonlight. 'Round and round the starcrests fly, painting your destiny in my sky. I have called you here to warn you of the curse I have seen in your stars.' She padded towards Wren. 'The world is tilting. Can't you feel it, little bird?'

Wren took a step away from her.

'*Look*,' said Glenna, her gaze not on Wren's face but at her feet. Wren looked down to find herself staring at a broken portrait. It was covered in dust and Glenna's bare foot was obscuring half of it but Wren glimpsed what it beheld. A girl who looked just like her – the same emerald-green eyes and heart-shaped face. She was wearing the gilded crown of Eana on her head.

'That is Ortha Starcrest,' said Glenna, confirming her suspicion. 'The last witch queen of Eana.'

'She looks just like me,' whispered Wren. Ortha, the last-known true descendant of Eana, the first witch, wore the same face as Wren. She looked at Glenna, her voice trembling. 'I don't understand. Is this part of my destiny somehow?'

'Look again.' Glenna lifted her foot and revealed the other half of the painting. Wren's breath caught in her throat. There was a girl seated beside Ortha. Only her face was thinner and her lips were pursed, as if in disapproval. She was wearing a crown, too.

'Twin queens,' rasped the seer. Queens who looked just like Wren and Rose. 'The twin's curse.'

A terrible coldness trickled down Wren's spine. 'What are you talking about?'

'The witches are rising in the west, Wren Greenrock. The rivers of Anadawn will run red with blood and an old curse will bloom, deep and ugly as a wound in the heart of the world.' Her gaze turned milky and her voice suddenly sounded far away. 'Beware the curse of Oonagh Starcrest, the lost witch queen. The curse runs in new blood. It lives in new bones.'

Wren tensed. 'I don't understand, Glenna. Tell me what happened to Oonagh.'

'Listen well,' said the seer. 'And I will tell you of the curse that haunts you.'

So, Glenna spoke and Wren listened to every single word.

When it was done and the story of Oonagh Starcrest had been told in all its truth, Wren was silent. She let the tale sink into her blood and her bones, knowing somehow a part of it was already inside her. Then she pushed aside her horror and took the old woman's hand. 'We'll worry about the curse later. I'm getting you out of here.' She tugged her towards the door. 'There's a secret tunnel that will lead us straight to the river. There's someone waiting for us by the mill.'

But Glenna shook her off. Her pale lips curled and in the quiet of her smile, Wren saw hints of Banba. Before Wren could stop her, she began flinging the birdcages open, one by one.

'Stop!' Wren rushed to close them but the starcrests screeched as they soared over her head, higher and higher, shriller and shriller. 'Rathborne can't know I'm up here!'

Glenna flung open another cage. 'The Kingsbreath already knows you're here, Wren Greenrock. He is coming to find you.' Another cage, another flurry of wings flapping around Wren. 'You have brought death to this tower tonight.'

For every cage Wren slammed shut, Glenna ripped three more open. Within minutes, the starcrests were all free and screeching.

'Fly free at last! Go and find your way home!' Glenna raced to the window and threw it open. The birds flew over her head, launching themselves towards the moon. When the last starcrest had soared out into the night, the seer turned her face to the stars. Her eyes glazed and she fell perfectly still.

'Come away from the window,' hissed Wren. 'We have to hide.'

Glenna kept her gaze on the sky. 'I have been hiding for far too long.'

Outside, Wren heard the echo of footsteps in the stairwell. Her heart thundered. He couldn't be here already. The feast was still in full swing. It was too soon . . .

Glenna stared at her over her shoulder. '*Run.*'

The door to the tower swung open and Willem Rathborne stepped through it. Rose whimpered in his grasp. He dragged her into the room with him, one hand twined roughly in her hair, the other pressing a silver dagger to her throat.

Wren froze.

'It appears the old witch was right,' he said, in a low voice. 'The enemy does indeed wear two faces. But they are much closer to me than she had me believe.'

Rose's eyes filled with tears. 'Chapman saw you,' she sobbed. 'I wanted to warn you but Willem caught me in the stairwell.'

'That's enough out of you,' growled Rathborne, twisting her hair until she flinched.

Wren palmed her dagger. 'I swear on Ortha Starcrest's grave, if you hurt her one more time, I will tear you limb from limb, you snivelling son of a—'

'So, *you* are a witch,' interrupted Rathborne. 'I had suspected this one was Rose, but thank you for making it so abundantly clear.' He levelled Wren with a dark look. 'The question is, where did you come from?'

'Your nightmares,' said Wren, as she rounded on him. 'It looks as if you weren't as thorough as you thought you were the night you murdered our parents.'

Rathborne's nostrils flared as he made sense of the twins. Of his mistake. 'I should have chased that conniving midwife down and killed her.'

'Your time is up, Rathborne,' said Wren. 'You've long

outstayed your welcome at Anadawn.'

'And yet I am the only one guaranteed to leave this tower alive.' He glared at Glenna, who had turned from the window to watch him. 'Prophecies are ever-changing, are they not, witch? I think I will quite enjoy turning this one on its head.'

Wren's mind reeled as she searched for an escape plan. A way to save all three of them. But the sight of Rose in pain – and that bead of blood already sliding down her neck – filled her with a pulsing panic that made it impossible to think straight.

'You can't kill Rose. She's your only way into Alarik's good graces,' she said, quickly. 'And by the sound of things you're already hanging on by your grimy little fingernails.'

Rathborne's lip curled. 'You forget I only need one of you to play nice.'

'And you want it to be *me*?' Now it was Wren's turn to smile. 'Oh, you pathetic, hapless idiot.'

Rose's eyes flared in warning.

A vein bulged in Rathborne's forehead. 'You can't manipulate me, witch.' He moved the dagger underneath Rose's chin, tilting her head back with its point.

'NO!' Wren's panic erupted inside her, white-hot and blinding. At that same moment, Rose gasped.

'*Ah!*' Rathborne cursed as he snapped his hands away from her. 'You burned me! How did you—'

Rose slammed her elbow into his stomach and leaped out of his reach.

The seer crossed the room, flinging her finger back and forth. 'Ortha and Oonagh! Oonagh and Ortha! The Starcrest sisters haunt this tower!'

'Glenna, get back.' Wren tried to yank the woman out of harm's way but Rathborne was quicker. He flung her into a birdcage, her bones cracking as she crumpled to the floor. 'I've had quite enough of your babble, *witch*.' In one fell swoop, he brought his dagger down across the old woman's throat.

Rose screamed as she reached for Glenna but the seer was dying, blood gushing from the wound in her neck. Rose pressed her hands against it, trying desperately to staunch the flow. 'I don't think I can save her! There's too much blood!'

Rathborne raised his knife again but Wren was on him in a heartbeat, knocking the dagger from his grip as she wrestled him to the ground. He opened his mouth to shout but she slammed her fist into his jaw. He smashed his forehead into hers and Wren reeled backwards, seeing stars. Rathborne grabbed her wrists and crushed them against his chest. '*Enough*,' he snarled, holding her still. 'Stop fighting.'

Wren spat in his face.

Glenna's dying words spilled out in ribbons of blood. 'Break the ice to free the curse. Kill one twin to save another.'

She collapsed with a final gurgle, her milky eyes staring unseeing at the faraway moon.

Rose crawled towards Rathborne in her tattered dress, through blood and grime and dust and her own streaming tears. 'You *monster*.'

'Careful now, Rose, darling,' he threatened, but his hands were full restraining Wren. 'I'd hate to see you get yourself in any more trouble tonight.'

Rose grabbed the dagger from where it had fallen. She staggered to her feet, rage and violence flashing in her eyes, just as the door swung open and two palace guards burst in.

They looked between Wren and Rose, their eyes growing wide. 'Er, Princess?'

'Guards! Arrest this imposter at once!' Rathborne shoved Wren towards them. 'This witch has stolen the princess's likeness and used it to commit a heinous murder. It's only by the grace of the Protector that Rose and I have survived at all.'

Rose tried to battle her way towards Wren but Rathborne swept her into his arms and crushed her head against his chest.

The guards converged on Wren, binding her hands roughly behind her back. When she protested, they stuffed her mouth with rags, holding her between them as she thrashed and struggled.

'Oi, Gilly, she's a lively witch, this one.'

'I always heard they were slippery. Like eels.'

'Wait! Listen to me!' cried Rose.

'Hush now, Rose, darling. It's over. You're safe.' He dragged his hand through her bloody hair, petting her like a dog. 'This *witch* will be brought swiftly to the dungeons where she will await judgment. *Of course* we could kill her right this instant if I decreed it.' He looked meaningfully at the guards and they reached for their swords. Rose cried out, struggling violently in his arms.

'*However*,' Rathborne went on, drowning her out, 'I think it would be best if we kept her alive until after your wedding.' He paused to let the meaning of his words sink in. 'If all goes smoothly tomorrow, as I'm *sure* it will, then perhaps we may be feeling charitable in regards to the fate of this . . . miscreant. There might even be room for clemency.'

He released Rose but kept a hand heavy on her shoulder. 'After the wedding, perhaps you can take her with you to Gevra as your maidservant. King Alarik is, after all, more . . . *accepting* of her kind.'

Wren seethed in silence. The bargain was plain – her life in exchange for a Gevran alliance and all the carnage that would mean for Ortha. Protest further and Rathborne would have them cut Wren's throat right there in the tower. And no one in Eana would ever know the truth.

Rose's gaze met Wren's, and in that fleeting glance – fraught with frustration and regret – an unspoken decision passed between them.

Rose blew out a breath. Then she rolled her shoulders back. 'She is not to be harmed in the dungeon. Bring her food and fresh water and a blanket to keep warm.'

'But nothing from outside,' warned Rathborne. 'And nothing that has grown pure from the earth. I suspect this witch is a sordid enchanter.'

The guards shifted, uncomfortably. 'What if she enchants *us*?'

Wren rolled her eyes.

'Search her before you cage her,' said Rathborne, impatiently. 'And muzzle her if she tries to bite.'

'Don't you dare hurt her.' Wren could tell her sister was battling to keep her voice calm but tears slipped freely down Rose's cheeks and her blood stained hands were trembling. 'I will deal with this matter *privately* after my wedding to Prince Ansel. Is that understood?'

The guards exchanged a dubious glance. 'Very well, Princess.'

Rathborne shooed the soldiers away. 'Go and lock this abomination in the dungeons.' He glanced at the dead seer, his nose wrinkling in disgust. 'And then dispose of this body. Feed it to the Gevran beasts if you like but I want it gone by first light. The smell of blood makes me sick.'

Wren was hauled into the dark stairwell. She left her sister standing in a pool of blood, with a look of such violence in her eyes, she hardly recognized her.

Rose
CHAPTER 42

On the morning of her wedding day, Rose woke at dawn. She was certain she'd only slept an hour, after spending most of the night sobbing into her pillow. Wren was trapped in the dungeons and Rose had no choice now but to marry Prince Ansel. If she put even a toe out of line, Rathborne wouldn't hesitate to kill her sister. This new, terrifying destiny was galloping towards her and there seemed to be no way to stop it.

Rose went to the window, cupped her hands around her mouth and whistled. Nothing. She tried again, this time tucking her thumb between her fingers. She managed a ragged noise, but it still didn't sound remotely like an owl. She kicked her bed table in frustration, and then immediately regretted it. What was she thinking? Even if Shen did hear her, what could he do now? He might be a powerful warrior witch, but even he couldn't take on all of the guards in her tower, not to mention the extra ones Rathborne had stationed in the courtyard last night.

Rose dropped her hand, as another terrible thought

occurred to her. What if Shen had been caught, too? No. She couldn't let herself think such a thing. Today was bad enough already.

She turned from the window and sat at her mirror with a sigh. Dark circles pooled underneath her eyes and her skin was hopelessly wan. If she had to be a bride today, she at least wanted to look her best. Rose knew her beauty was another kind of power, and she would need it later for bargaining. So, she washed her face in cold water to brighten her eyes and brushed her hair until it shone. She lathered her face in cream and applied some rouge to give the appearance of a blushing bride. She darkened her lashes and painted her lips until they glistened in the dawn light.

There was a knock at the door, and Agnes bustled in.

'Happy wedding day, Princess!' She beamed at Rose. 'Well, by the Great Protector! Don't you look beautiful.'

'Thank you, Agnes.' Rose craned her neck as the door drifted shut. 'Have you seen Celeste this morning?'

As if summoned by the mention of her name, the bedroom door swung open again and Celeste burst in, clad in a purple satin nightgown, her hair still in a silk sleeping wrap. 'What happened to you last night? Chapman said you'd retired early but when I came to check on you, the guards turned me away.'

'I had a headache from all the drumming,' said Rose. With Agnes standing between them – and beaming from ear to ear – she couldn't offer her friend the truth, just the strained look in her eyes. 'The evening . . . got away from me.'

Celeste nodded, in understanding. 'I see.'

Agnes clapped her hands briskly. 'Right, then. Let's get you in your wedding dress. There are more than enough laces and buttons to keep us busy.' She looked at Rose and her cheerful countenance cracked. Her eyes filled with tears. 'I wish your dear mother was here to see you wed. I remember her wedding day as if it were yesterday. She was so happy, filled with the light of the world. It was practically shining out of her face.'

Rose blinked. 'You were at my mother's wedding?'

'Of course I was! Who do you think got her ready?' Agnes sniffed as she scrubbed the tears from her cheeks. 'And now here we are, all these years later. I hope today is as happy a day for you.'

'Lillith got to live in her own country after she got married,' Celeste reminded Agnes as she wandered about the bedroom. It was quite obvious to Rose that she was idly searching all its nooks and crannies for Wren. 'Rose won't be so lucky.'

Agnes sighed. 'I know you two will miss each other frightfully but you'll be able to visit. And I'm sure in time, you'll find your way in Gevra, love. We both will.'

Oh, you don't know a thing at all, thought Rose, sadly. But she grasped Agnes's hand all the same and squeezed tightly. 'I'm so very grateful for you, Agnes.'

'You know I'll go anywhere with you, Princess. Even the icy mountains of Gevra. I'll just have to pack myself a couple of warm shawls and some hot buns for the journey. *Oh!*' She threw her hands up. 'Goodness gracious, I've forgotten the breakfast pastries Cam made special for you! Let me fetch those right away,' she said, as she hurried across the room. 'Then we'll get you in your lovely dress!'

As soon as Agnes left, Celeste abandoned her search. 'What on earth happened? Where's Wren?'

Quickly and quietly, Rose filled her best friend in on how everything had gone so terribly wrong. By the time she was finished, she was almost in tears again.

'What a mess,' muttered Celeste, as she pulled her into a hug. 'Don't cry. There's still time to put this right. You just concentrate on keeping Rathborne happy and I'll see if I can find Wren. At least I'm not being kept under lock and key.'

Rose's gaze flitted to the door. 'Yet,' she said, nervously.

Celeste slipped away when Agnes returned with a tray of heart-shaped jam pastries, announcing to the maid and all the guards in the tower that she was off to get ready, too. Rose forced herself to eat a pastry while Agnes spread her wedding gown out on the bed. It was one of three that the dressmaker had sent over, each more elaborate and intricate than the last.

The dress was beautiful, made of the softest ivory satin, trimmed in fine lace and embroidered with delicate gold beading. The top of the bodice sloped gently off Rose's shoulders, the breast-line lavished in gold filigree, before winnowing to a point at her waist. Ruffles cascaded over the underskirts in layers of ivory and pale gold lace that flowed magnificently with even the smallest movement. At the back, along the ridge of Rose's spine, the bodice was lined with hundreds of pearl buttons, which gave way to a billowing train.

'You are a vision, my love,' said Agnes, standing back at last. 'I reckon the Kingsbreath will tear up when he comes by to collect you.'

Rose felt like tearing up, too. When she looked at herself in the mirror, all she could see was a frightened puppet in a decadent gown.

Agnes departed soon after, the door closing with a resounding thud, leaving the princess all alone in her wedding dress.

Rose drifted to the window and gazed out on to the courtyard. Just beyond the golden gates of Anadawn, high on a humpback hill and shining like a jewel in the sunlight, lay the Protector's Vault. It played host to all important Eanan ceremonies, including, as of this morning, her own wedding. Inside, the Protector's Eternal Flame would be burning on its ceremonial plinth, looked after by the esteemed keeper – a stern-faced old man called Percival Reeve, who guarded it with his life.

It was all so absurd, now that Rose thought about it, but tradition in Eana meant everything. People held it to them as a comfort – a promise that the Protector would keep them from harm so long as they kept his flame alight. That way, he could always find them in the dark. Rose knew now that he *was* the darkness. That he had been all along.

A sharp knock at the door announced the Kingsbreath's arrival. He wore a burgundy suit trimmed in black, the polished hilt of his sword glinting at his hip.

'I'm pleased to see you're holding up your side of the bargain,' he said, approvingly.

Rose glared at him. 'Is my sister alive?'

'For now,' he said, darkly. 'I suggest you do as you're told if you want to keep it that way.' He held out his arm. 'Now come. It wouldn't do to be late to your own wedding.'

Wren
CHAPTER 43

Wren sat in the dungeons of Anadawn Palace, trying to rub the crick from her neck. After a night of tossing and turning on the damp stone ground – without the blanket she had been promised and with only the palace rats for company – morning had finally come. She was surprised to see it but she wasn't fool enough to think her luck would last much longer.

Overhead, she could hear the servants rushing about, preparing for the princess's wedding. The honour guard were being assembled in the courtyard while the Gevran guests were leaving the palace in their droves, making the short journey up the hill to the Protector's Vault. Any minute now, Rose would be getting married and soon after that, she would be on the first ship to Grinstad.

Stars. How had it all unravelled so quickly? Wren had to get out of here. And *fast*.

A slant of sunlight reached Wren through the window in her cell. It was high off the ground and guarded by thick iron bars that made escape impossible. Even so, she had been fantasizing about it all night.

She lingered at the door of her cell now and watched a rat skitter past. At the end of the damp stone passageway, the dungeon master was napping at his post. *Finally.* She crept back to the window and released a low whistle. It floated through the bars of her cage, soft and soaring as an owl's call.

Wren paced her cell as she waited.

And waited. And waited.

And then—

Shen's face appeared at the window. 'So, last night went well, then.'

'Shh.' Wren jabbed her finger over her shoulder. 'We have company.'

'You promised me a victory drink, Greenrock,' he whispered. 'I waited at that bloody mill until dawn.'

Wren tapped her foot, impatiently. 'Can I get a little help in here, please?'

Shen passed a red rose through the bars. 'Just make sure you tell your sister what a gallant hero I am. I've only just got on her good side and I want to stay there.'

'How you managed that after kidnapping her I will never know.' Wren ripped the head off the rose and crushed the petals in her fist. She tipped her chin to the bars, an incantation already gathering on her tongue. 'My magic hasn't exactly been behaving itself lately so I would advise you to stand back. This could go horribly wrong.'

Shen disappeared in a breath of cool wind.

Wren flung the petals at the window, watching in satisfaction as the bars began to tremble. The iron slackened and when Shen crept back into view, he bent them easily apart until there was a medium-sized hole between them. 'I was hoping for something a bit more showy.'

'Then watch this.' Wren took a running jump at the wall. Her feet scrabbled against the stone as she flung her arms out, Shen catching her by the wrists. He pulled her up towards him, Wren wincing and cursing as she squeezed herself through the bars.

She got stuck halfway through.

Shen frowned. 'What's happened?'

'Cam's almond cookies happened!' The morning breeze frittered about her face as though it were taunting her. 'My hips are stuck.'

Shen did a poor job of holding in his laughter.

Wren glared at him. 'Come on, warrior. Put your back into it.'

Wren shifted on to her side as Shen grabbed her upper arms, his face straining and *straining* until a voice rang out behind him.

'Oi, you there! What do you think you're doing?' A heavy hand landed on his shoulder, and then another, as twelve palace guards quickly converged on Shen. He'd been so focused on helping Wren, he hadn't sensed them and now it was too late. He released her with a curse and she fell with a thud. When she looked up, he was already being hauled away, his hands bound behind his back.

Hissing seaweed.

Moments later, Shen was sitting in the cell opposite hers.

'That went well,' said Wren, dryly. 'Now what?'

He laid his forehead against the bars. 'Now we wait for a miracle. Or our untimely death. Whichever comes first.'

Rose

CHAPTER 44

Rose had always hated the Protector's Vault. It reminded her of a gilded cage with its curved metal beams and dangling chandeliers. Today, the marble floor was so polished she could see her reflection in it. Beams of coloured light streamed in from the stained-glass windows, each one depicting the Great Protector riding gallantly on his horse. Rose frowned up at his stern face as she fixed her veil over her own.

The harpist began to play, and a gentle melody filled the Vault.

Up on the altar, the Eternal Flame flickered majestically. Beside it, Percival Reeve, the keeper of the Eternal Flame and officiant of the ceremony, stood next to a stoically weeping Ansel.

Oh, Ansel.

'Neck straight, chin up,' hissed Chapman's voice in her ear. He prodded her in the back. 'Aaaaaand *walk*.'

With a stiff spine, Rose began her journey down the aisle, arm in arm with Willem Rathborne. She focused on her breathing, calmed by the gentle strumming of the harp and the morning sunlight warming her bare shoulders.

She had promised herself she would not marry Ansel for anything, but now she knew there was little she would not do for her sister. She would save Wren, and then, somehow, together they would find a way to save the witches. Rose couldn't give up hope, not yet. Otherwise she would fall to the floor and never get up again. She eyed a snow tiger dozing at the edge of a pew. Perhaps one of the Gevran beasts would even finish her off.

The Protector's Vault was full of chancellors and courtiers, the noblemen and noblewomen of Eana all gathered together in one place. Names Rose only knew through the Kingsbreath, and faces she hardly recognized. Willem Rathborne had controlled every single element of her life since the moment she'd been born. She had so few people truly on her side and had never even known it. She'd been such a fool.

King Alarik and Princess Anika were sitting in the front row. Alarik was dressed all in black, while Anika wore a dress as red as her hair, her fox curled up in her lap. Tor stood to the right of Ansel, his jaw so tight, it looked as if he was in physical pain.

That makes two of us.

Rose searched for her best friend in the crowd, but there was no sign of Celeste anywhere. Had she been caught on her way to find Wren? Celeste's father, Hector Pegasi, sat in the middle of the Vault, smiling at Rose as she passed. She couldn't return it, fear creeping up her throat until she thought she might get sick. One step, and then another.

Inch by inch, Rose moved towards her future, feeling more adrift than ever.

When they reached the altar, Rathborne placed her hands in Ansel's, which were even clammier than her own. The prince's gaze roamed along her veil. 'I might burst from anticipation, my flower,' he whispered. 'Even without a face, you are too lovely for words.'

Rathborne leaned towards Rose, and to all the guests it must have appeared as if he was giving her a fatherly kiss on the cheek.

'Behave yourself,' he hissed in her ear. Then he strode all the way back to the Vault's entrance, where he stood like a sentinel, blocking the only way out.

The harpist lifted her fingers from the strings and the music melted away.

The keeper cleared his throat in a pointed squeak. 'Today is a special day. We join not only two people, but country and country. And we do so by the grace of the Great Protector.' He bowed his head, along with all the Eanan guests. The Gevrans did not bow. Nor did Rose. Instead she looked up. And as she did, she noticed a strange shadow flitting in the uppermost window.

The keeper moved behind the ceremonial plinth. 'And so, we begin with the chant of the Eternal Flame. For no true marriage can be blessed until—'

He was interrupted by the sound of shattering glass. And then the cry of Wren's voice, clear and ringing as a bell. 'I OBJECT!'

Wren
CHAPTER 45

Wren leaped from the uppermost window of the Protector's Vault and sailed through the air, grabbing hold of the chandelier with a bellowing cry.

Below her, the wedding guests tipped their heads back in alarm. Someone screamed. Chapman fainted. The guards – both Gevran and Eanan – grasped the pommels of their swords, while King Alarik blinked rapidly as though he was imagining this second princess bride dangling from the ceiling like a white ribbon. Perhaps wearing the wedding dress had been a tad indulgent but it certainly added a dramatic flair to Wren's objection.

She swung her body back and forth, using the force of her momentum to propel her towards the altar. She released the chandelier, the folds of her dress rippling around her as she landed in a crouch, right in the centre aisle.

There was a collective gasp, followed by a ripple of shocked silence as Wren rolled to her feet and smoothed her skirts. The wedding dress was nowhere near as fine as Rose's beaded gown but then it was a backup dress. Wren only had seconds to wriggle into it after Celeste had shown up at the eleventh hour, having used her father's good name to gain entrance to the dungeons where she'd promptly knocked the dungeon master out with a sconce and sprung both of them from the dungeons.

Under the gaze of five hundred stunned wedding guests and far too many soldiers, Wren picked up her skirts and marched purposefully towards the altar.

'I hereby declare this wedding cancelled!' she announced, just in case anyone had missed her stirring objection the first time.

The Gevrans stiffened in their seats. Rose was the only person in the entire Vault who looked happy to see Wren, with the exception of Tor, who was gaping at her with a mixture of horror and relief.

Ansel's mouth bobbed open and closed as he struggled for words. 'Who is . . . Where did she . . . How did . . . I don't understand.' He looked between the girls, back and forth, back and forth. 'Rose?' he said, uncertainly.

Wren clucked her tongue. 'If you can't tell the difference between your bride and her enigmatic sister, then I'm afraid you don't deserve to marry either of us, Ansel.'

'ENOUGH!' Rathborne drew his sword as he marched up the aisle. 'Get away from the princess at once!'

Wren lunged for Ansel's sword, pulling it from its scabbard before the prince could even register what was happening. She spun as she hoisted it in front of her, staggering a little under its weight. 'Or what? You blathering, troll-faced weasel.'

Rathborne snorted. 'If you wish to intimidate me with your poor swordsmanship, you have already failed.'

Wren heard the whisper of steel behind her as Tor stepped forward. His sword appeared in the next heartbeat, a flash of silver in the corner of her eye. He angled it at Rathborne.

The Kingsbreath skidded to a stop. 'Drop your weapon, Gevran. I am not the enemy here.'

Tor didn't move.

Rathborne turned to Alarik. 'Your Majesty, tell your soldier to stand down at once.'

Alarik cocked his head, watching the scene with glimmering fascination. 'No.' He gestured between the brides. 'Not until you explain *this*.'

Rathborne's eyes went wide. 'What is there to explain? This girl is quite plainly a *witch*! Look at her!' He whirled to face the rest of the guests. 'She has stolen the face of the princess. She has come here today to do us harm!'

The guests shifted uncomfortably. Some courtiers cried out in alarm. The Gevran soldiers drew their swords, waiting for instruction, while their beasts growled at their feet. Rose stepped forward to speak but Wren threw her arm out, holding her back. She had minutes – perhaps seconds – to seize control of the situation. She swished the sword back and forth. 'Actually, Rathborne, I've only come to do *you* harm. Everyone else is free to leave. Or watch, if you like. But one way or another, I'm ending this charade.'

Anika clapped her hands together. 'What theatre,' she

purred. 'And I was just beginning to get bored.'

Beside her, Alarik's hands were steepled in front of his mouth, his gaze unblinking.

'Guards!' shouted Rathborne. 'Kill this imposter at once!'

At the back of the Vault, six palace guards jolted into action. They drew their swords as they marched up the aisle, while four more inched around the side passages.

Tor didn't even blink.

'Make sure to take her head from her shoulders!' snarled Rathborne. 'This witch is nothing but an evil enchanter sent to twist our thoughts and—'

'Liar!' Rose ripped the veil off her face and marched to Wren's side. 'You have been lying to me my entire life! You have been lying to Eana for eighteen years and you have the nerve to stand here today, under the eyes of your precious Protector, and lie again!'

The crowd had fallen stone-silent, every pair of eyes now trained on the twins. The palace guards stalled, uncertain of what to do. Wren grabbed her sister's hand, anchoring Rose as she came down on Willem Rathborne with the fury of a blazing inferno. '*You* killed our parents eighteen years ago. *You* poisoned my father in his bed and cut my mother's throat! *You* blamed the witches and sent us all to war! I am sick of playing along in your twisted games. Sick of letting you control my every move, my every thought! My sister might be a witch but she is not a liar. She is as real as I am and her very existence is *proof* that *you* lied! The only imposter here is you!'

Murmurs erupted throughout the Vault. Fear curdled into confusion as the truth was laid bare before them.

King Alarik's smile was slow and menacing. 'Perhaps we should have the witch instead of the princess.'

'Perhaps we should have both, brother,' said Anika.

'You foolish, addled child!' Rathborne slashed his sword through the air as if to fell the truth of Rose's words. He spoke not to her but to the entire congregation, grasping desperately for their trust. 'That girl is nothing but a plotting, scheming witch! She has clearly wormed into your head and distorted your thoughts.'

'*No!*' hissed Rose, taking a step towards him. Slowly, imperceptibly, Tor inched forward, too. If they weren't in the middle of a reckless stand-off, Wren might have dropped her sword and kissed him right there in front of everyone.

The palace guards hovered awkwardly, no longer sure of where to point their weapons.

'Seize her, you doddering idiots!' cried Rathborne. 'You answer to the Kingsbreath!'

'*I* am your princess and first you will let me speak!' Rose turned her face to the crowd, her voice arcing as she addressed all the courtiers and nobles of Eana. 'Although my coronation has yet to fall, I hope you will permit me this first act as Queen of Eana, in light of the truth that has been exposed today. Willem Rathborne has failed in his role as Kingsbreath in the worst way. Not only has he betrayed me by killing my parents and hiding the truth from me for all these years but he has betrayed this country, too. As such we must, as a people, relieve him of his duties at once.'

The congregation stiffened in their seats, cautious eyes darting back and forth between the twins, and Wren got the sense that the tide was finally turning against Rathborne.

Rose looked down on him with withering disdain. 'Willem Rathborne, I command your arrest for the murder of King Keir and Queen Lillith of Eana.' She squeezed Wren's hand but no one else in the Vault could tell she was trembling. Her face was placid and her voice was strong – it was, Wren realized with sudden surprise, the voice of a queen. 'I command your arrest for the murder of thousands of witches in a senseless war of your own making.'

Rose raised her finger, and though she wielded no weapon but her anger, a deadly silence fell inside the Vault. 'I command your arrest for plotting, even now, the destruction of the Ortha witches as well as the bartering of your *own* sovereign to a bloodthirsty nation against her will.' Rose's eyes flashed, green and furious. 'Your time in power is over.'

With a deep, shuddering breath, she summoned one final truth from within her. 'These last few weeks have taught me more about myself than you ever have. I know now that I am a healer witch and I vow to heal this country from the wounds and division *you* have inflicted upon it.'

Silence, then. Row after row of shocked faces peered up at Rose as if they were only truly seeing her for the first time. Even Wren was lost for words. Her sister had found her courage and, though there had been no coronation here today and she wore no such crown on her head, she had become a queen before their eyes.

Slowly and without fanfare, Rathborne lowered his sword. 'Are you quite done, Rose, darling?'

Rose glared at him. 'Drop. It.'

The sword fell with a clatter.

Wren kept her sword raised, her smile all malice. 'I can't wait to watch you hang from this Vault. Our justice will be your swift and bitter execution.'

Rathborne surprised her by laughing. It was a wild, manic sound that hiccoughed out of him. He flicked his wrist and a dagger slid into his palm.

'After you, witch.'

He flung it straight at Wren.

Wren froze as the blade hurtled towards her. Time seemed to slow, Rose's terrified scream ringing in her ears. Then she felt the weight of something hard and fast barrelling into her as Tor grabbed her by the waist and knocked her sideways. They crashed to the floor, the blade sailing cleanly over their heads.

There was a beat of silence.

Then a blood-curdling shriek split the air in two as the dagger landed in Prince Ansel's heart.

The Gevran prince fell to his knees, hands grasping at nothing as crimson blood bloomed along his ivory doublet.

He fell sideways with a resounding *thud*.

And then, all at once, he was dead.

Rose
CHAPTER 46

Rose stared in horror at Prince Ansel's body. Her hands were trembling violently, her wedding dress splattered with his blood. Chaos erupted around her, but she felt removed from it all. There was only Ansel lying at her feet, and her magic tingling to life inside her. She came to her knees and laid a hand against his cheek. 'I'm here, Ansel. I'm going to help you.'

Ansel stared past her with lifeless eyes.

'It's going to be all right.' Rose's panic joined the buzz of her magic. She pressed her palms against his chest, her fingers connecting around the knife as she felt for a pulse. Her hair fell around them like a curtain, as Ansel's blood seeped out through her fingers.

'Come back to us,' Rose murmured, over and over, like a chant. Her fingers thrummed with the heat of her magic. She was pouring every bit of her energy into the prince's body, trying to rouse his sleeping heart, but she couldn't tell if it was working. '*Please*, Ansel. Please come back.'

She squeezed her eyes shut, trying to focus, but the

shouting was getting louder. There came a sudden thunder of stomping boots as the Gevran soldiers stormed the altar. In the quiet of her mind, Rose reached for the thread of Ansel's life. She found it in the darkness – a thin gold line quickly fraying away. If she could just remove the knife from his chest and stem the blood flow—

A hand closed around her arm. 'Get off my brother,' came a snarling voice from above. King Alarik stood over her, with bright, violent eyes.

Rose tried to shake him off. 'Let me go. I can help him! I can heal him!'

Alarik dragged her away from the dead prince, his soldiers swarming at his back.

Tor pushed his way through. 'Let her go to him, Alarik! Let her try.'

The king turned on his soldier with the icy rage of a blizzard. '*You* have done enough, Tor.' He bared his teeth menacingly, but his voice cracked with the fissure of his grief. 'Ansel is *dead* because of you.'

'Move, all of you! GET OUT OF MY WAY!' Princess Anika jostled her way through the gathering soldiers, wailing as she beheld her brother's body. She yanked the knife from his chest, blood spurting on the marble floor as she raised it above her head.

'Where is the imposter princess?' she screeched. 'I want blood. And I want it *now*.' She pushed her way towards Tor. 'Where is she? The one *you* saved over your own prince?' She was brandishing the knife, wildly. 'I'm going to drive the dagger meant for her into her heart!'

'No!' cried Rose. 'It's not Wren's fault! We never wanted this!'

Anika pointed the knife at her throat. 'By killing our brother, Eana has declared war on the great nation of Gevra. Mark my words, Princess, we will bring you to your knees!'

'It was Rathborne! Where has he gone? We need to find—'

'*Silence*, you snake!' Alarik shoved Rose at one of his soldiers. 'Take this one to my ship and bind her arms. I've had enough of mind games and poisoned magic.' He pulled Tor back. '*You* can bear my brother's body. Make sure to protect it better than you did when he was alive.' Alarik turned from the altar and glared out at the remaining guests, his voice solemn. 'The wedding is off.' He heaved a dramatic breath. 'Now we are at war.'

The last of the guests scattered in a panic as the soldiers advanced towards each other. Several Gevrans swarmed Rose, grabbing her roughly by the arms and carting her away from the altar. 'Guards! Help me! Do something!' She kicked and screamed but it was no use – their grip was like iron, and her own soldiers were hopelessly outnumbered, the snow tigers growling and snapping at their legs.

Where was Wren? And what had become of Rathborne in the chaos?

She could hear Celeste yelling her name, but Rose was lost in a sea of Gevran shoulders. She couldn't see a thing over her towering captors. They moved as one, creating a living cage around her. A prison through which she couldn't possibly hope to escape.

There came a faint breeze, followed by the whistle of steel as Shen dropped from the rafters of the Protector's Vault and stole a Gevran's sword right from under his nose. He drew his elbow back and smashed the hilt into the soldier's jaw, while kicking another's legs out from under him. They both fell with a clatter, Shen grabbing a second sword mid-spin. He flattened the blade and drove it into the back of another's knees, Shen smashing his forehead against the soldier's nose as he crumpled to the floor.

Another soldier ran at Shen, but he spun in the air, swiftly kicking him in the face, before skewering the foot of another with the point of his blade. He removed it in the same beat, the soldier whimpering as she staggered backwards.

Shen gripped a weapon in each hand and brandished them at Rose's two remaining captors.

'Hands off the princess.' He sharpened the blades against each other. 'Or I'll be forced to remove them myself.'

The Gevrans exchanged a panicked look as King Alarik came striding purposefully down the aisle. 'And who are *you* supposed to be?' he demanded.

'Someone you wouldn't want to meet alone on a dark night.' Shen spun again, kicking the soldier holding Rose's right elbow squarely in the chin. He crumpled at the king's feet. 'Or right here and now, as it turns out.'

The other soldier released Rose and took a careful step back. Rose collapsed against Shen's chest as her own guards finally broke through.

'Gevrans! Do not yield!' roared Alarik. 'He's only one man!'

Shen smiled, blandly. 'Actually, I'm a witch.' Then he threw one of the swords directly at Alarik's head. It skewered a branch on his crown, ripping it from his hair and carrying it across the altar, where the blade embedded itself in the ceremonial plinth.

Alarik went deathly pale. He backed away, gingerly patting the top of his head. 'Tor! TOR!'

'Please stop showing off,' said Rose, in alarm. 'You're going to start a war.'

'I think it's a bit late to worry about that.' Shen curled an arm around her waist. 'You look beautiful, by the way. Is it bad luck to kiss the bride?' Without breaking her gaze he used his free hand to punch another advancing Gevran. 'On second thoughts, I don't care.' Then he dipped Rose and kissed her.

It felt for a moment as if time stopped. Then the world crashed back in as a Gevran soldier barrelled into them. Shen spun Rose out of harm's way, and kicked the soldier's ankles out from under him. The clash and clamour of steel echoed throughout the Vault as the soldiers fought each other across the pews and in the aisles.

Celeste, who had managed to burst in through the front door while Shen had made his entrance from above, finally broke through the fray. She elbowed a dazed-looking Chapman, who had only just staggered to his feet. 'Thank goodness you're all right!' She grabbed Rose and pulled her close, glancing briefly in Shen's direction. 'He's very handsome but you should know that for all his warrior skills, *I'm* the one who had to break him and Wren out of the dungeon.' Celeste pulled back, scanning the tide of green and blue. 'Wait. Where *is* Wren?'

'In trouble,' said Shen, who had hopped up on to a pew to scan the crowd. 'Come on!'

With Shen leading the way, Rose and Celeste picked up their skirts and hurried towards the back of the Vault, where despite everything, the Eternal Flame was still burning on its plinth. Shen fought off three more Gevran soldiers while Celeste grabbed a sword and swung it wildly at a silver-fanged wolf, clearing the way for Rose to duck around the altar.

She skidded to a stop. '*Oh!*'

Wren was facing off with Percival Reeve. The keeper was jabbing a flaming iron poker at her. 'Be gone, you wretched witch!' he cried, as he lunged. 'Our Protector will keep us safe!'

'I know Rathborne's back there!' Wren was struggling to keep Ansel's unwieldy Gevran sword aloft. 'Let me at him! He has to pay for what he's done!'

Rose didn't notice the small room at the back of the Vault until the keeper leaped in front of it, his mouth foaming like a rabid beast. He swung again, nicking Wren in the shoulder. 'Your curses will not work here, witch!'

Rose took off her shoe and flung it at the keeper. 'Take that, you wrinkled old buffoon!'

When Wren spotted her sister, she blew a stray curl from her eye. 'I need a weapon, Rose. Something I can actually use!'

With a mighty roar, a Gevran soldier came thundering around the back of the altar.

He gasped once, then collapsed like a felled tree.

Shen appeared behind him, dusting his hands. He pulled his dagger from the soldier's back and cleaned it on his cloak before tossing it to Wren. 'How about this?'

Wren beamed as she caught it. 'This is why you're my best friend.'

Shen was already gone; he was halfway across the altar now, embroiled in a fight with four burly Gevrans.

The keeper slashed his poker, sending a shower of sparks raining down on Wren. 'Back! Back! Back!'

Wren arced around him. 'Cover me, Rose!'

'*How?*' cried Rose. Oh, *goodness*. She whirled around, searching for a weapon of her own, only to find herself face to face with King Alarik.

'*You* are supposed to be on my ship,' he growled.

Rose screamed as he seized her arms. Across the altar, Shen spun around at the sound of her distress. 'Rose!'

The Gevrans seized his distraction and lunged, tackling him at the waist and knocking him to the floor.

Alarik dragged Rose away, kicking and shouting, just as Willem Rathborne emerged from the room at the back of the Vault, where he had retrieved Sanguis Bellum, the Protector's ancient sword, from its safe. Rose glimpsed him hoist it up, his savage expression reflected in its shining steel. The Kingsbreath and the keeper closed in on her sister, until Wren was pressed up against the blazing ceremonial plinth, with nowhere to run and no one to help her.

Rose shouted for her sister, but she was already halfway

down the aisle, her cries muffled by Alarik's hand.

There was a flash of lightning, followed by a thundering roar as the doors to the Vault burst open and a howling storm swept in.

The altar was blown apart, Rose pinwheeling backwards until she crashed head first into Celeste. She sat up in a daze just in time to see Banba lead the witches of Ortha into the Protector's Vault.

The wind, fierce and rising, came with them.

'The witches have returned to Anadawn and this time, we are not leaving!' bellowed Banba, and all the winds of Eana bellowed with her. 'Drop your weapons and stand aside or prepare to meet your precious Protector in the next life.' The old witch's cackle soared, the wind carrying it to every corner of the Vault.

'What an entrance,' said Celeste, dizzily. 'Who *is* that?'

'That is my grandmother,' said Rose, with no small amount of dread. Banba had come to Anadawn with fire in her eyes and revenge between her teeth. If they didn't do something fast, she would lay waste to everyone around her, including the people of Anadawn, and the Silvertongue River would run red with their blood.

King Alarik emerged from behind an upturned pew and staggered down the aisle. 'At long last. A witch truly worthy of my attention.'

Banba didn't even glance in his direction.

'Show yourself, Willem Rathborne!' She conjured another fork of lightning, splitting a pew down the middle with an almighty crack. Rowena and Grady stood behind her, adding their own howling gales, while Rose spied Bryony and Thea lingering at the back, nervously surveying the carnage. 'If you want to fight us, then draw your sword and fight us here and now. We will not wait for your ambush. We have come ready for war!'

'And that goes for you Gevrans, too!' shouted Rowena. 'We don't fear your king or your beasts!'

Alarik's glittering gaze was still fixed on Banba. If he was intimidated by her display, he didn't show it. Rather, he looked positively thrilled. 'Why would power like this fear anything but itself?' He whirled around, searching for his soldiers in the fray. 'Forget the others! SEIZE HER!'

Without even glancing in his direction, Banba flicked her wrist and sent the Gevran king careening into a wall. 'Where are my granddaughters?' A wooden rafter cracked in two, the chandelier dangling precariously above her head. And still, the storm thrashed. At the back of the keep, Chapman struggled to his feet, only to be swiftly knocked out again by a soldier. 'If any harm has come to either one of them, all of Anadawn will pay!'

While the last of the palace soldiers fled in a panic at the sight of the witches, the Gevrans fought their way towards them, straining against their storm. The witches pushed them back, casting the Gevran beasts aside as they advanced further into the Vault.

'WREN! ROSE!'

The wind rallied against Rose as she crawled across

the altar looking for Wren. She passed Shen's unconscious body, tears streaming down her face as she inched onwards. Finally, she spotted her sister pinned beneath the ceremonial plinth. It had fallen over in the storm, flattening the keeper's skull and trapping her legs. Wren's eyes were shut, and she wasn't moving. The toppled Eternal Flame burned around her in a circle.

Rathborne had lost Sanguis Bellum in the blast, but he was already back on his feet, stalking towards Wren. Rose scrabbled for her sister. 'Wren!'

Rathborne grabbed the sword Shen had stuck in the plinth. 'See how the Protector favours me!' He laughed madly as he pulled it free. 'He wills your death, just as he wills the death of all witches!'

'NO!' The fire licked at Rose as she threw her body between Wren and Rathborne, bracing herself for the blow.

As the blade whistled through the air, something jolted deep inside Rose. For a terrifying heartbeat, she thought it was the sword embedding in her back. But the spark became a burning blaze, and suddenly, she felt her magic bursting like a star within her.

Below her, Wren gasped awake, a twin fire shining in her emerald eyes.

There was a beat of nothing, where time warped and darkness curled them in its mighty fist.

Then the world exploded around them, and the Vault came down in a hail of fire and glass.

Wren
CHAPTER 47

Through a haze of smoke, Wren saw Rathborne lying dead, singed from his hair to his boots.

The plinth had been shattered into smithereens and she was relieved to find she could move her legs again.

Rose rolled off her. 'What just happened?'

'I think . . . *we* happened.' Wren surveyed the smoking ruin that had been the Protector's Vault only moments ago. Everything was bright and burning, and there were bodies strewn across the altar. The ceiling had been blown off entirely and glass was still coming down like raindrops. One of the walls had been ripped away and in the distance, at the bottom of the hill, Wren spied the rushing waters of the Silvertongue and the grey sails of the Gevran ships.

Alarik led the Gevrans' panicked retreat, soldiers and nobles hobbling down the hill, shouting about magic and poison and curses.

In the aisles and among the pews, the witches groaned as they returned to consciousness. While Rose went to help Shen and Celeste, Wren staggered to her feet and searched for Banba. She spotted her lying on her side at the edge of the Vault.

'Banba!' She limped towards her grandmother. 'Wake up, Banba!'

The old witch groaned. 'My little bird . . .' she wheezed. 'My little . . .' She trailed off, dropping her head once more.

'I'm here, Banba! I'm coming!' Wren's legs were leaden beneath her, her chest aching with each stride. Ahead of her, a Gevran soldier emerged from a mass of groaning bodies and plodded towards Banba. He reached her before Wren, scooping the unconscious witch easily into his arms.

'NO!' Wren lunged but her foot caught on a broken step. She crashed to her knees. When she dragged herself to her feet, the soldier was already marching down the hill.

'Stop!' Wren stumbled out on to the grass. Her head was still spinning madly and she couldn't see straight. 'You can't take her! She's ours!'

The soldier kept marching, leaving the burning Vault far behind him.

'Please!' Wren screamed her voice ragged as she threw herself down the hill, momentum propelling her fast and hard towards the river.

She couldn't let them leave with Banba. She was the only family Wren had ever known, the only one who had a plan for the future, for the throne they had fought so hard for. She would be lost without her grandmother. Banba would be lost without the witches.

She couldn't let them take her.

She *wouldn't*.

By the time Wren reached the bottom of the hill, her legs were trembling and her lungs were stinging. She had lost sight of Banba – the soldier must have taken her on to one of the ships and the last of the Gevrans were climbing up the ladders, preparing to set sail.

And then Wren spotted Tor – stiff-backed and solemn – as he carried the body of the dead prince on to the king's ship. Elske padded wearily at his side. Her tail was singed and her fur was stained with soot.

'Tor! Wait, please!'

Tor came to a halt. He looked at Wren over his shoulder with such anguish in his eyes, it sent a fissure through her heart.

'*Please*. They took my grandmother.' Her eyes filled with tears as she stumbled towards the ship. 'Please don't let them take her from me.'

Tor's face crumpled. He opened his mouth to say something just as Princess Anika appeared on deck, still drenched in her brother's blood. His jaw hardened and his demeanour changed in an instant. 'Get away from here, witch,' he said, as though he didn't know Wren. 'You have no business on this ship.'

His eyes flashed but Wren ignored his warning. She didn't want his protection, she wanted her grandmother back. She staggered on. 'Please! Take me instead.'

'And what would we do with you?' said Anika, her voice cruel and mocking.

'I've got magic, too!' said Wren, desperately. 'That's what your king wants, isn't it? A witch of his own?'

Anika's lip curled. 'You have caused enough carnage already.' She glanced at Tor. 'Don't you think it's time for her to reap what she's sowed, soldier?'

'I think it's time we stopped wasting our time and resources on these shores.' Tor continued across the ladder, without looking back. 'Clearly, they're cursed.'

Anika leaned over the ship's railings. 'Well, I say we leave them with a parting gift.'

Tor stiffened. 'I don't think—'

Anika clicked her fingers. 'Voldsom, *attack*.'

Wren screamed as a mighty snow leopard leaped from the ship and landed on the riverbank. It took one look at her, then pounced.

Wren barely made it two steps before the leopard's claws pierced her shoulder and pulled her down on to the grass. It rolled her over with its paw, its mouth frothing as it roared. Anika roared with it, the sound turning to manic laughter as the beast sank its teeth into Wren's side.

A blood-curdling shriek ripped out of her. The sky blurred as her skin tore open, the leopard's teeth sinking through muscle and bone. The beast released her just as quickly, and Wren felt the heat of her blood as it gushed out. The leopard rounded on her, sniffing at her neck. It opened its mighty jaws . . . then whimpered, as a white blur appeared from nowhere and barrelled into it.

Elske growled menacingly at the snow leopard before

ripping its throat open. The leopard let out a keening cry as it took its last breath and Wren felt the same weakness as she lay back on the grass. The king's ship was pulling away with Banba and there was only one person standing on deck now.

Wren watched Tor sail away from her and found she couldn't bear it. They couldn't leave. Not like this. With a hand pressed against the wound in her side, she dragged herself through the grass, screaming for her grandmother. The world dimmed at its edges but she pushed and *pushed*, ignoring the pain as it lanced through her.

For a long time, there was only the Gevran sails fluttering in the distance, the world getting darker and quieter. Then a familiar pair of arms closed around Wren, tugging her back. Elske came to sit beside her, and when the last ship disappeared into the mist, the wolf threw her head back and howled.

Rose

CHAPTER 48

Rose held a sobbing Wren in her arms as the last Gevran ship sailed out of sight.

'Let me go.' Her sister struggled feebly against her but Wren's' arms were getting weaker and weaker. 'I can't . . . let them . . . take her . . . Please . . . I can't . . .'

Rose only held her tighter, her gaze on the wound in Wren's side. She didn't need her magic to know the severity of it. Even now blood seeped through the torn wedding dress, soaking the grass around them. 'Be still, Wren. You're hurt.'

Wren fought, even as the last drop of energy left her. 'Please,' she said, going limp in Rose's arms.

'We will save Banba,' said Rose, softly. 'I promise we will.' She laid her sister down on the grass. Her hands trembled but there wasn't time to take her to Thea who was still back at the Vault; no time to second-guess herself either. It was up to Rose to save her sister, to do for Wren what she could not do for Ansel. She couldn't lose her, not after everything they had gone through to find each other again.

She pressed her hands against the wound in Wren's side, her magic fluttering in her fingers. It felt stronger somehow, surer. She reached for the thread of Wren's life and found it, glowing dimly in the darkness. She kept her thoughts on it as she willed the wound to close, knitting the splintered bone and ravaged muscle back together. 'You will be well,' she murmured. 'I will make you well again.'

Sweat dripped down Rose's spine as she worked, anxiety churning in her stomach as her magic bound itself to Wren. For a while, she couldn't tell where she ended and her sister began. Only that there was a current passing between them and the healing was working, slowly, slowly. It was draining her, too. Soon, Rose's breathing grew laboured and her eyelids began to droop. When the colour returned to Wren's cheeks, she gave in to her exhaustion.

On the banks of the Silvertongue, Rose curled up beside her sister. 'We will rise from this,' she murmured, as she fell asleep.

Wren
CHAPTER 49

Wren stood in the doorway of the west tower, staring at the blood on the stones. Glenna's body was gone. There was nothing left but a rusted stain and a stray wisp of white hair. The birds were gone, too, their cages all toppled and broken.

'We should have buried her. She deserved that, at least.'

Rose placed a hand on Wren's shoulder as she stepped into the room. 'All these years at Anadawn, and I never even knew she was here. He *kept* her from me. He kept her from the world.' Her voice wobbled as she drifted to the window, where the sun was melting into the evening sky. 'Oh, Glenna, I'm so sorry,' she whispered. 'We will make this right. I promise.'

Wren lingered on the threshold, a hand pressed to the phantom wound in her side. Only this morning, she had lain dying on the riverbank and now she was here. And Banba was not. They had changed out of their ruined wedding dresses, spent hours scrubbing the blood from their hair, and yet Wren still felt unclean. Guilty. She had failed her grandmother. She had cursed Banba to a fate worse than death and now the witches were left without a leader.

Rose shoved a birdcage out of the way to retrieve the painting underneath. It was the portrait Glenna had shown Wren last night. She held it up to the light.

'That's Ortha Starcrest,' she said, in barely more than a whisper. 'I've seen her once before. In a vision at the Mother Tree.' She frowned as she beheld the girl sitting next to her. 'But who on earth is that?'

Wren joined her sister by the window. Her gaze lingered on the other sister. A part of her didn't want to say her name aloud, as though it held an ancient, wicked power. 'That's Ortha's twin sister, Oonagh.'

Rose gasped. '*Twins*,' she said. 'It's just like Banba said.'

Wren glanced sidelong at her sister, feeling a strange twisting in her gut. In all her life, Banba had never uttered a word to her about the existence of Oonagh Starcrest. Until this very moment, Wren had believed that Glenna was the only living witch who even knew of the lost twin.

'What did Banba tell you?' she asked her sister.

'Nothing. It's as if she was afraid to say anything at all.' Rose frowned at the portrait. 'I don't understand. Why are there two crowns?'

Wren recalled the seer's words to her in this very tower last night, the story she had unravelled in the darkness as she told her of Oonagh Starcrest. Wren had squirmed hearing it but she knew it was a truth she owed to her sister. After all, the Starcrest sisters were their legacy.

'Because they were both queens,' said Wren. 'At least before it all went to hell.'

Rose clutched the painting to her chest, her eyes growing wide. 'Tell me what happened.'

So, Wren did.

'A thousand years ago, the witch queen Moira gave birth to twin girls. Ortha and Oonagh. They were born holding hands, so close they were said to be of one mind. One soul. The twins were powerful, too. And their power was at its strongest when they were together.'

Rose's brow furrowed and Wren knew she was thinking of that strange explosion in the Vault, the blinding power that had burst from them when they'd held each other. Wren didn't know if what had happened was a good thing or a bad thing, only that it had unsettled her.

She could tell it had unsettled Rose, too.

'Ortha was mild-mannered and fiercely clever. She had a soft heart and an enquiring mind,' she went on. 'Oonagh was rebellious and prone to outbursts. She had a sharp tongue and a sharper temper.' Wren tried not to linger on their similarities, especially knowing what came after. 'But the girls loved each other and they believed they could rule together.'

Rose grimaced. 'So, they just . . . *both* became Queen?'

'It was Moira's Law,' said Wren, with a shrug. 'She didn't want to separate them so she rewrote the rules of the kingdom.' A pause, then she added, 'That was a mistake.'

'But Ortha was a good queen. Wasn't she?'

'The best we ever had.'

The silence stretched.

Rose shifted uncomfortably. 'And . . . Oonagh?'

'Oonagh ruined everything.' Wren turned to the window. The Vault was a blackened shell upon the hill. Guards were still milling back and forth, retrieving the bodies. 'As the kingdom's love for her sister grew, Oonagh got jealous. And obsessive.' Wren rested her elbows on the windowsill and looked to the trees. 'One day, when she was riding her horse through the woods, she trampled a fawn. It was an accident. But when the animal's blood seeped into Oonagh's fingers, everything changed. She found a new way to be powerful. To be better than her sister.' She glanced at Rose, over her shoulder. 'She turned to blood magic.'

Rose clutched at her sleeves. '*Blood* magic? I've never heard of such a thing.'

'The witches like to pretend it doesn't exist. It keeps the young ones from getting ideas . . .' Wren offered her a half-smile. 'And the older ones, I suppose.'

Rose wrinkled her nose. 'So, Oonagh killed animals for power?'

Wren nodded, still trying to navigate the difficult truth of it. 'At first. But blood magic is twisted and difficult and when you take something that doesn't belong to you, you lose a part of yourself. The more Oonagh took from living things, the less human she became. Her magic twisted. And so did her soul.' A shudder passed through Wren at the memory of the seer's words, at how haunted she had looked when she'd offered them to her.

'And that's when Oonagh turned to human sacrifice.'

Rose gulped. '*Stars*. What happened to her?'

'Ortha killed her.'

Rose lowered herself on to the rumpled bed, hanging on Wren's every word. 'She *killed* her own sister?'

Wren's voice hardened. 'Not on purpose. But Oonagh was a monster, Rose. What else could she have done? The Protector and his men were closing in, exploiting the growing unrest in Eana for their own gain. And it was Oonagh who started the fight with her sister on the banks of the Silvertongue. It was only by sheer luck that Ortha was able to protect herself. She struck her sister in self-defence and Oonagh fell in and drowned. Who knows what this country would look like if she hadn't?'

'I doubt Oonagh would have fared any better against the Protector,' said Rose. 'Banba said the Valharts cursed Ortha and destroyed her power.'

'I thought so, too. But Glenna said the truth is darker. Closer.' Wren picked up the portrait of the twins and traced the frown on Oonagh's face. 'It was Oonagh who cursed her sister. As they fought, she used a blood spell so powerful we can't even guess at it. When she drowned that day in the Silvertongue, their magic – and the magic of all the witches in Eana – splintered into five different strands. After that, it was easy for the Protector to take the throne for himself. Ortha was just an enchanter and what could a single enchanter do against the might of a stirring rebellion?' Wren flung the painting away. 'And we know the rest. After Oonagh and Ortha, nothing in Eana was ever the same again.'

'*Beware the curse of Oonagh Starcrest, the lost witch queen,*' the seer's words echoed in Wren's head. '*The curse runs in new blood. It lives in new bones.*'

She kept that to herself for now. There was no sense in worrying Rose after everything that had happened. But even as she swallowed the warning, she knew it was fear that made her do it, the terrifying possibility that the curse was rooted in a new twin of a new generation. That the darkness might one day bloom in her, too.

Rose rolled to her feet. 'I could have sworn Glenna said something about a curse when she died. Something about breaking the ice.' She shook her head. 'I can't remember.'

'Never mind,' said Wren. 'You should turn your thoughts to your coronation tomorrow.'

Rose blinked at her in surprise. 'Aren't you going to fight me for it?'

'I don't want it any more. Not without Banba.' Not for the first time that day, Wren thought about what lay beyond the Sunless Sea. How long would it take the Gevrans to reach Grinstad and what would their wicked king do with her grandmother once he got home?

Banba was a fighter. She had survived Lillith's War and the howling isolation that came afterwards, living on the edge of a country determined to forget her, but for all the faith Wren had in her grandmother, she didn't know if she would survive Alarik Felsing. If any witch possibly could.

She sank on to the bed, the springs creaking as she scrubbed her hands through her hair. She was weary and angry and heartbroken, and the idea of ruling anything right now, even her own emotions, suddenly seemed like far too much work. 'You can have your crown, Rose. Your throne. All of it. It's meaningless to me now.'

Rose was silent for a long time. And then in a voice so quiet Wren barely heard her, she said, 'We could be different, Wren.'

Wren looked up her. 'What?'

Rose was wearing a smile she had never seen before – never learned – and behind it, she sensed the ghost of a plan. 'What if we ruled this land together? You and me. Side by side.'

Wren frowned. 'Didn't you hear a word I just said? About what happened the last time two sisters tried to rule together?'

Rose stamped down on the portrait, cracking the frame. 'We are not them, Wren. We are *not* cursed.' She sounded surer by the moment, her eyes as bright and green as the Errinwilde. 'I should have realized it before. That we could do it together. We've been apart our whole lives but now we can make that sacrifice mean something. Look at where we come from, look at everything we've learned along the way. We are both Valharts and witches, and together we can mark the beginning of a new era in—'

'Rose, we can't just—'

'Yes, we can, Wren! We have the same vision now.'

'Which is why we only need one of us to carry it out.'

Rose shook her head. 'I always thought I would rule this land with a husband by my side. A king who was clever and strong and fearless. Why can't it be a sister instead? Why can't it be you? If it has been done before, it can be done again. Only this time it will be different. It will be better.'

Wren stood up, slowly. 'What makes you so sure of that?'

'You felt what happened in the Vault today. Together we are more. Together we have true power.' She took Wren by the shoulders. 'War is coming. The Gevrans will return and when they do, you and I will face them together. I say we stand side by side and meet their ice with fire.'

Rose stood in the shadow of Glenna's blood, looking stronger than Wren had ever seen her before. She realized that her sister was right. Banba was gone. The world was tilting and if Wren was going to rule this land with anyone, she wanted it to be Rose.

Suddenly, it seemed as if that was the answer all along.

'We will not be a curse,' she said, more to herself than to her sister. 'We will be a blessing.'

Rose held out her hand and Wren stepped over the portrait of Ortha and Oonagh to take it. Somewhere deep in her bones, she felt the flare of her magic.

She smiled at Rose, and Rose smiled back.

Wren knew she could feel it, too.

Rose
CHAPTER 50

In all the ways Rose had imagined her coronation day, she had never pictured it like this.

High up in the east tower of Anadawn, she stood side by side with her sister as they gazed at their reflections in the mirror. Rose's hair was piled in decadent curls that had been pinned away from her face with bejewelled hairpins. She wore a magnificent pale gold ballgown, trimmed in delicate filigree and finished with a generous train. Wren had left her hair long and loose, and had chosen a slender satin gown of emerald green.

Together, they shone green and gold – the colours of Eana.

'I still don't see why I couldn't just wear my trousers,' said Wren, as she rubbed blush on her cheeks. 'They're far more comfortable than any dress.'

Rose wrinkled her nose as she adjusted her skirts. 'Because this is our *coronation*, Wren. It's our chance to show the people of Eana that we're going to take our duties seriously, that they can trust us to lead them. And since your trousers are practically moulding, they present a thoroughly unsuitable impression.'

Wren pouted. 'Can't I at least have a ceremonial sword?'

'We've already given the goldsmith a headache making your crown,' Rose reminded her. 'The poor man was up all night. I'm afraid your new weapon will have to wait.'

Wren stuck out her tongue.

Rose sighed as she shook her head. How had Wren ever fooled *anybody* into thinking she was Rose? Her sister had the worst manners and she told the *bawdiest* jokes, which were enough to make even the sternest palace guard blush. Even now, in her anger and grief, Wren was smiling at Rose in the mirror. Setting her at ease, as though she could sense her nerves.

Elske whined as she pushed her face between them, staring at herself in the mirror.

Wren scratched behind the wolf's ears. 'Maybe you aren't the vainest one in this tower after all, Rose.'

Rose eyed the wolf warily. 'I still don't understand why you have to take her *everywhere* with you.'

'Because she's a princess, too,' said Wren, fondly. 'And I have to take good care of her until . . .' She trailed off but Rose knew she was picturing those grey-sailed ships in her mind, the lone soldier standing out on deck. Without his wolf. Without her. Wren was already thinking about what lay beyond tomorrow, beyond the Sunless Sea.

There was a knock at the door.

Shen stepped inside, limping a little on his left foot. Rose had offered to heal his ankle twice since the explosion but the warrior had refused her both times, insisting a natural recovery was better for his pride. Rose suspected he was rather more concerned about her energy after how much she had used on Wren's wounds, but she hadn't pressed the matter.

His gaze found hers in the mirror. She looked away. She couldn't allow her pesky feelings to get in the way of duty today. With the witches of Ortha attending the same ceremony as the highest-ranking members of the Anadawn court, she couldn't afford a lapse in her attention. Even if the bandit *did* look particularly handsome in a billowing white shirt, clean boots and dark trousers.

'Nice outfit, Shen,' said Wren, reading her sister's thoughts. 'Do you want to swap?'

'I'm not sure green is my colour,' said Shen, but he was still looking at Rose. 'You look beautiful.'

'Thank you,' said Wren.

'I was talking to your sister.'

'We have the same face.'

'And yet you couldn't be more different.'

Rose adjusted a curl in the mirror to find something to do with her hands. Her thoughts.

Wren snorted. 'Stop staring at her like that, Shen. If she goes any redder she'll burst into flames.'

He cleared his throat. 'Are you two almost ready? I can't say I ever thought I'd be escorting two queens to their coronation.' A pause, then he continued, 'Or any queens at all, come to think of it.'

'Hopefully now you'll treat me with some proper respect,' said Rose, primly.

Shen flashed his dimple. 'As much as you like, Your Highness.'

Her lips twitched into a smile, and she let herself enjoy it.

A moment later the door opened again and Celeste swished in, looking resplendent in a periwinkle gown with a high neckline and a generous skirt. 'All of the Anadawn nobility are here,' she said, breathlessly. 'And it looks as if every town has sent a representative. Even the Errinwilde!'

'Not every town,' said Shen, quietly, and Rose didn't miss how he gazed out of the window towards the Restless Sands.

'Frankly, I'd be insulted if the throne room wasn't filled to bursting,' said Wren. 'Don't they know how momentous today is? We're making history.' She paused. 'Again.' Another pause. 'But better.'

'Are there guards posted at every entrance?' said Rose, anxiously. 'I've asked Chapman to double them but he's not quite his usual bossy self. He's still in a daze over everything that happened in the Vault.'

'Well, he'd better snap out of it soon,' muttered Wren. 'Unless he wants his precious quill swiftly shoved up his—'

'Wren!' scolded Rose. Her sister might be taking this whole thing calmly but Rose feared some of the guests may have come today with ill intentions. After all, the Kingsbreath had been respected across Eana and news of his deception – and death – was still spreading. She knew there would be concerns about their worsening relations with Gevra as well as questions about Wren – the long-lost princess of Eana.

And now this – twin queens.

Witch queens.

There was still much to explain.

Much to prove.

Rose hoped they would be given a fair chance.

'Don't worry about your safety today,' said Shen, who had moved soundlessly to her side. 'I have eight different weapons on my person as we speak.'

Rose gaped at him. *'Where?'*

He tapped the side of his nose. 'Warrior's secret.'

'And you have your witches,' added Celeste. 'Quite a few have shown up. And so far they seem to be behaving themselves. Though you could certainly call the atmosphere . . . *strained.*'

'I suspect after the Gevran tigers the people of Eshlinn aren't so easily spooked,' said Wren.

Rose wrung her hands as she stepped away from the mirror. 'Well, let's just hope today will be peaceful.'

'Oh, cheer up. It's our birthday,' said Wren, and Rose was surprised to find she had almost forgotten. 'No one should be unhappy on their birthday.'

Outside, the bells in the clock tower began to chime.

Shen's smile was wide and gleaming. 'I believe that's your cue.'

Rose threaded her arm through Wren's. Despite

everything that had turned her world upside down these past few weeks, with her sister by her side and the future ahead of them, she *was* happy. Perhaps more than she'd ever been before.

With Celeste and Shen beside them, Rose and Wren left the east tower and set off for the throne room of Anadawn. They paused for a moment outside the heavy oak-wood doors, the palace guards standing to attention as the coronation party gathered their breath.

Rose felt her sister hesitate, and glimpsed a shadow flitting behind Wren's eyes. She knew she was thinking of Banba, itching to go after her. Even if she wanted to, Rose knew she'd never be able to stop Wren. But they could have this moment, first.

The moment that would change everything.

'Are you ready?' she said, taking her sister's hand.

Wren hardened her jaw. 'I'm ready, Rose.' She was steely-eyed now, her gaze focused. 'For this. And all that comes after.'

'Then so am I,' said Rose.

'Your Majesties,' the guards announced as they pushed the doors open. 'Your throne awaits.'

And together, the twins stepped in to claim it.

Acknowledgements

We loved writing *Twin Crowns* and are so happy that readers are going to discover the world of Eana. Bringing the book to life was a true team effort, not only between the two of us, but with incredible support on both sides of the Atlantic.

First we'd like to thank our agent, Claire Wilson at RCW, AKA Princess Claire, for being the best champion and agent that any author could ask for. We're so lucky to have you in our corner. We'd also like to thank Sam Coates at RCW for taking *Twin Crowns* global – cheers to you Sir Sam!

Thank you to Pete Knapp at Park&Fine Literary Agency for leading the way in the US for *Twin Crowns*. We are so happy to have you on our team, and you'll always be Prince Pete to us.

We are also very grateful to our film agents working to bring *Twin Crowns* to the screen – thank you Berni Barta and Michelle Kroes at CAA and Emily Hayward-Whitlock at the Artist Partnership.

We couldn't have asked for more enthusiastic and amazing editors. Huge thank you to Lindsey Heaven and Liz Bankes at Farshore in the UK, as well as Kristin Daly Rens at Balzer&Bray in the US. Knowing that you all love the book as much as we do is the best feeling and we are so glad we have you to help us make the book the best it can be.

The whole team at Farshore deserve crowns for their incredible work on the book – and we'd especially like to thank Olivia Carson, Jasveen Bansal, and Bethan Chaplin Dewey on the marketing team, as well as Hannah Penny and Pippa Poole on the PR team. We'd also like to thank Catherine Coe for her excellent copy-editing skills, as well as Susila Baybars for her proofread.

Ryan Hammond at Farshore is the King of Design. We are so lucky to have you working on our book and making it so beautiful! Thank you as well to Charlie Bowater for your beautiful cover illustration.

Thank you to all of the booksellers, librarians, teachers, and book bloggers who have already started to support the series.

Thank you to Stephanie Garber, Roshani Chokshi, Louise O'Neill, Kiran Millwood Hargrave, Kendare Blake, and Sarah J Maas for your gorgeous and generous quotes – it means so much to us to have the support of author friends who we greatly admire. And thank you as well to Alwyn Hamilton, Kate Rundell, and Anna James.

We would like to thank our friends and families for their ongoing support and belief in us. Thank you to Cat's parents, Grace and Ciaran Doyle, and her brothers, Colm and Conor Doyle. And thank you to the Webber side, Katie's parents, Rob and Virginia Webber, and Jane, to whom the book is dedicated. Katie would also like to thank the Tsang side of her family, with a special thank you to her mother-in-law Louisa Tsang who was one of the very first readers.

Thank you to Jack Webber and Kevin Tsang, both of whom have been hugely supportive throughout the entire publication process, from puppy and toddler wrangling and talking through plot points, to keeping us alive by feeding us, and being there whenever we needed support. And thank you to Evie, who didn't help at all with the writing but brings so much joy and never fails to boost morale!

We would like to thank each other. *Twin Crowns* is, above all, about the magic of sisterhood. We are so fortunate to have found that magic in knowing and working with each other, and are so excited to share it with everyone.

And finally, thank you to you, reader, for coming along on the adventure with us. We hope you love it.

COMING SOON . . .

TWIN CROWNS 2

CATHERINE DOYLE & KATHERINE WEBBER are both bestselling and award-winning writers of YA and children's books. In addition to co-writing *Twin Crowns*, they are soon to be sisters-in-law.

Catherine grew up beside the Atlantic Ocean, where her love of reading began with great Irish myths and legends. She is the author of the YA *Blood for Blood* trilogy and several magical middle grade books, including the award-winning *Storm Keeper* trilogy. She lives in the west of Ireland with her fiancé Jack and their dog Cali.

Katherine is from Southern California and spent much of her childhood in the Palm Springs desert. She is the author of *Only Love Can Break Your Heart* and *The Revelry*. For younger readers, she also co-writes the *Sam Wu is Not Afraid*, *Space Blasters*, and *Dragon Realm* series with her husband, Kevin Tsang. She is currently based in London with her husband and young daughters.